BLUES JAM

a novel

Best wishes,
Stephen Rice

STEPHEN RICE

email: stephen.rice@highbridgeventures.net

Published by:

Manhattan Book Group
447 Broadway 2nd Floor, #354, New York, NY 10013
(212) 634-7677
www.manhattanbookgroup.com

Printed in the United States of America
ISBN-13: 978-1-962987-37-0

Library of Congress Control Number: 2023915073

To my wife, Trish, for her love and support, which were essential to me realizing my dream of writing a novel. And also for joining me in living out our dreams daily.

CONTENTS

CHAPTER 1

YOU CAN'T PICK YOUR FAMILY

"You have a beautiful baby girl!" the doctor called out. Art Zonnen smiled, although he would have to admit thoughts of a boy had been in his head. Those thoughts quickly vanished as he laid eyes on his little girl.

Kerstin was exhausted. Her baby came quickly, too quickly. There hadn't been time for an epidural. It was a quick, painful delivery.

Art and Kerstin had been married for only a few months. They had met at Paul's Place, a bar in Roseville. Their attraction had been immediate, resulting in them spending the night together, but their relationship had been a struggle. Both were hampered by various addictions. His was primarily alcohol, hers had drifted to opioids after a head injury and broken arm from a teenage accident.

Regardless, this moment was miraculous. They had created another human being. It was remarkable that two such imperfect people could create something so beautiful. Throughout the pregnancy, Kerstin had stayed mostly clean. She drank wine a couple of times and smoked a little pot. In the beginning, Art tried to join her in sobriety but quickly failed, succumbing to long nights of whiskey drinking.

"Do you have a name picked out?" asked the nurse as she wrapped up the baby and handed her to Kerstin.

"Yes! We do!" replied Kerstin, locking eyes with Art.

"Yes! It's Sarah," Art declared.

"That's wonderful! Hello little Sarah," responded the nurse, taking in the tiny baby.

They had struggled with names. If the baby had been a boy, they had settled on Julian. The girl's name was between Elizabeth, Kerstin's mom's name, or Sarah. Although Sarah wasn't a family name, they loved that it meant princess. If they had a girl, they decided she would be their little princess.

Sarah was an active baby, always on the move. When she heard music playing, she would bop in what her parents soon noticed was perfect time. Soon she would begin banging toys to the beat. Art and Kerstin enjoyed different styles of music—everything from rock and country to jazz, classical, and blues.

Their marriage had sometimes been a challenge. This wasn't due to Sarah, as she was loved by both. But opioids had tightened their grip on Kerstin. She had become addicted years earlier, hiding it from everyone, including Art and her sister Melissa. Art had continued to drink, sometimes to excess, often staying until closing time.

Even so, steady employment wasn't a problem for Art and Kerstin. Art was working as a driver for a company transporting elderly people to and from their appointments. It was flexible and easy enough that he could wake up after another bender and complete his day's work.

Kerstin was working as a salesclerk at a local drugstore. Although there was irony in this, she was good at helping customers since she knew a lot about the various medications. She had learned how to "obtain" drugs she wanted or needed from the pharmacy. Sometimes, she would miss a few days when she was either incapacitated or just uninterested.

They managed to raise Sarah together. They loved her and wanted the best for her. Raising a child was already a difficult task, and their separate habits made it even harder.

CHAPTER 2
GOODBYE MOM

Suddenly Kerstin was gone. Sarah had just turned three. Kerstin had taken her over to her mother's house in the Midway area of Saint Paul. She had then gone back home, and called into work saying she was unable to make it in that day. At home was newly purchased heroin. She hadn't used heroin for some time. With Sarah off at Grandma's and Art working, Kerstin planned to spend the day "channel swimming" as she liked to say to herself.

Laurie, an acquaintance and drug supplier, had run into Kerstin at Walgreens. Laurie told Kerstin she had amazing stuff, calling it heroin joy flakes, that had to be tried. Kerstin was torn, feeling on the precipice of a turning point in her life. Sarah was a joy. Even her feelings for Art were coming back. She appreciated their life together and loved their acceptance of each other as they were. Maybe, just one more time, she thought. In the end, her addiction was strong, still potent enough to overpower her with the need of another high.

At home, Kerstin prepared the heroin. Even though she hadn't shot up for a while, old habits returned easily. She found a spoon from the drawer and a clean syringe, along with some saved paraphernalia. She started her favorite playlist, heated the heroin with water, pulled it into the syringe, tied off her left arm, then plunged the needle into a welcoming vein.

Immediately, Kerstin could tell this time was different from the over-the-moon rush as she drifted off. Unless someone intervened, she was never coming back from this trip. At first, she thought to fight it, but then she let the building euphoria take her away.

The medical examiner later found that the heroin had been laced with fentanyl. A cruel end had begun with unimaginable pleasure.

Art found her after his driving shift. Overcome with sadness, he managed to call 911. He took the next couple of weeks off from work while Sarah stayed at Kerstin's mom's house for the next month.

CHAPTER 3
KERSTIN

Kerstin was of Irish descent. Her grandparents on her mother's side had traveled to America for a better life. Elizabeth, her mom, was the youngest of three girls. Kerstin's dad, Eric Foley, was born and raised in Saint Paul. Elizabeth stayed home to raise her kids until they all were in school. Then she worked as a receptionist in a dentist's office. Eric was a furniture salesman working downtown.

The oldest sister, Olivia, was six years older than Kerstin. Olivia was intelligent and knew it. She often would scold her sisters for doing something she thought was stupid, like slipping on the snow. Maybe she resented her sisters, thinking they were prettier than her. Olivia was thin and statuesque. She had stringy hair and, as a teenager, a complexion dominated by acne. She studied hard at school and hoped to become a teacher.

Melissa was two years older than Kerstin. The two of them developed a close relationship. Melissa had dark flowing hair, high cheekbones, bright-blue eyes, and a warm smile. As she grew into a teenager, her body developed into that of a full-figured woman.

Unlike Olivia, Melissa wasn't all that interested in school, even though she excelled at it when she tried. Maybe it was a lifetime of being told how stupid she was that made her believe it, at least to some extent. Melissa may not have been book-smart, but she did have a street-smart way about her. Boys were always hanging around. By middle school, she was swapping out boyfriends like other girls were swapping nail polish.

Melissa and Kerstin were best friends as well as sisters. They often stayed up late listening to records and laughing. Sometimes Olivia would join them, but usually she was too busy with schoolwork or, once she started working, her job. Kerstin looked up to both her sisters but was closest to Melissa.

Kerstin grew to be tall and thin. She had wavy, sandy hair. Like Melissa, she had high cheekbones and a warm smile, but Kerstin had what everyone thought were the coolest hazel eyes. She was thin and athletic rather than full-figured. And like her older sister Olivia, as a teenager she had acne. She also followed in her older sister's footsteps academically. Kerstin was smart and successful at school, also acquiring some street smarts from Melissa.

Life changed for Kerstin one night while partying with Melissa and her friends in the Wabasha Street Caves. Melissa's friends enjoyed drinking beer, doing shots of tequila, and smoking joints. Kerstin often came along at first as some sort of mascot and then later as an almost full-fledged member of the group.

On this night, Jimmy Dotty had too much of everything. He was stumbling around the top of a rough-cut stairwell when he bumped into Kerstin and sent her flying down the stone stairs. Melissa was in another room when she heard a loud scream. She and several of her friends went running.

"Oh no! It's Kerstin!" someone yelled.

It wasn't easy to get to the bottom of this rocky stairwell. Joe Knight was the first to reach Kerstin. Blood was everywhere. Kerstin's left arm was obviously broken, as one of her forearm bones was clearly visible through her skin. But it was her head that was bleeding. She had a huge gash above her left ear. Joe took off his shirt to wrap it around Kerstin's head, hoping to stop the bleeding while being as careful as he could with her neck.

"Call an ambulance!" Joe hollered.

"Is she okay?" Melissa asked, sobbing as she reached the top of the stairs. Joe didn't immediately answer. He could tell Kerstin was breathing but unconscious. He didn't see any additional injuries, though the two he saw were horrific.

Kerstin was in a coma for a week at Regions Hospital in downtown Saint Paul. Her parents had switched off nights staying with her. Melissa had stayed there whenever she wasn't at school. Olivia was also there most days.

Tragedy had come so suddenly to Kerstin. Everyone's life had been changed. Even Jimmy had fallen into a deep depression, fearing that he had killed poor Kerstin. Eric was angry with Jimmy for his carelessness, but he also blamed Melissa for her negligence in bringing her younger sister to the cave party. Olivia laid into Melissa on several occasions. Melissa was beaten down by her sister's and father's reprimands. She wept every night as she tried to fall asleep next to her dear, broken sister.

Kerstin stirred one morning after her mom and Olivia had left her room. Melissa was there gazing out the window. Kerstin's eyes opened slowly to see Melissa sitting there.

"Melly?" said Kerstin weakly. Melly was the nickname she gave Melissa when she first learned to speak.

"Kerstin!" Melissa jumped up to greet her sister. Kerstin's lips slowly formed a smile.

That evening the whole family was together in Kerstin's room. Although conscious, she was in a great deal of pain. She was now taking oxycodone intravenously. This left her in a groggy state with her drifting off to sleep every so often. It also marked the beginning of what would become an addiction to opioids for the rest of her life.

Years later, Sarah would learn about Kerstin's fall in the cave from Melissa and Grandma Elizabeth. Grandma Elizabeth never fully recovered from the grief she felt those days following the accident. Melissa, who also never truly recovered, told Sarah the truth as she remembered it. She shared the fun they used to have together. Even after the accident, once Kerstin had recovered, the two sisters continued their close relationship. Melissa would become emotional whenever she spoke of that night. It would take her back to how she was gripped with fear when she learned it was Kerstin who had fallen, and how shocking it was to see her in such a state.

The pain Kerstin felt would eventually subside, but her love for the high she got from opioids never did. She would hide it from everyone. Melissa began to suspect Kerstin had a problem and regretted that she never stepped in to help her. She felt this responsibility the same as she had when she brought Kerstin along on that fateful night.

Kerstin wasn't interested in school, sports or careers after her accident. She graduated high school and worked as a salesclerk, first at the Northern Lights record store on University Avenue. Music became her passion. She loved listening to it and being a part of the local scene at bars and nightclubs. While she worked at the record store, she was able to explore many different styles of music. One of her favorite genres was blues. It spoke to her. She was fascinated by Howlin' Wolf and his unique, booming singing style.

When Northern Lights closed, Kerstin moved on to clerking at drug stores. Like music, she had developed a thorough knowledge and passion for drugs.

Sarah barely remembered her mom as she grew older, being only three when Kerstin died. Keeping her mom's memory alive were Melissa and Grandma Elizabeth, who were both instrumental in raising Sarah. Melissa often babysat and would meet Art and Sarah at Wilebski's, a Saint Paul bar. Art and Melissa would have happy hour drinks while Sarah played video games. Sometimes Sarah would bring a friend along. And there were times Art or Melissa would have their latest partner with them. Although Art and Melissa weren't involved with each other romantically in those days, their relationship was close.

Many times, as their food was served, and Sarah was pulled away from her video games, Art and Melissa would tell her Kerstin stories. Those, along with Grandma Elizabeth's recollections and photos, were how Sarah grew to know and love her mom. Grandma Elizabeth would proudly reflect on Kerstin's accomplishments and potential. Still, mention of "the accident" quickly ended any conversation with Grandma. The thoughts of sadness and what might have been hung in the air, not to be traversed.

Oddly, unlike the accident, Kerstin's addiction wouldn't stop conversations; instead, it led to long discussions. Sarah wondered how and why someone would be attracted to something that they knew could kill them. She questioned Art and Melissa over and over about how they didn't know and couldn't stop Kerstin. They explained their suspicions about something going on. Art had come to accept that maybe anyone could love something, even if it could kill them. Melissa remarked how people could die in many ways, how some were cut down quickly by some quirk of nature, while others take their last breath anonymously, long past their prime in a nursing home. Still others had their lives snuffed out by another. Kerstin went quickly and kind of on her own terms.

"Left a pretty corpse," Melissa would declare in a way that only she could feel Kerstin might appreciate.

Sarah never understood loving drugs so much that they came for you. She pledged she would never use opioids. She hated them and what they did to her mom.

But time can sometimes blur heartfelt promises.

CHAPTER 4
ART

Art was born and raised in Saint Paul. His parents, Gene and Kim Zonnen, were schoolteachers. Gene taught physical education and Kim was an elementary teacher. Gene's father, Clarke, had moved to Minnesota from northern New York. Clarke apparently wanted to attend college in the Twin Cities, although he had dropped out of Augsburg College after one year. He stayed and worked odd jobs until he started working as a car salesman. He began selling used cars before moving on to new Buicks.

Kim had hoped to go to law school but never followed through on that dream. Instead, she enjoyed teaching kids before developing an interest in writing. Even though she didn't have any formal training, she was able to publish a few short stories after years of rejection letters.

Gene and Kim had four children. First was Cindy. She was five years older than Art. Three years older was brother Karl. Art was the third followed by his sister, Kelly, six years later. A family joke went that Kelly was an unplanned addition to the family. Whether there was any truth to this or not, it left an eleven-year difference between the oldest and youngest of Art's siblings.

Cindy was like Kerstin's oldest sister Olivia. She helped with her younger siblings but was quick to scold them when they misbehaved, or at least when she felt they misbehaved. Cindy and Karl were the scholars of the family. Art and Kelly were the clowns.

Disaster didn't strike Art's family the way it had Kerstin's. Gene and Kim were able to make a middle-class living teaching. Kim was good at saving money by cooking, cleaning, and sewing clothes for everyone in the family. Gene and Kim didn't have expensive tastes besides always having a new or nearly new Buick from Clarke's dealership.

Cindy went off first to junior college at the local Hennepin Community College, followed by two years at Winona State University. She went into teaching science. When she graduated there was a need for teachers in Alaska, so she took one of those jobs and moved to Juno. There she would meet her husband, George. They settled in Alaska, only rarely making the trip back to Saint Paul.

Karl was the athlete of the family. Gene had coached him in various sports growing up. Karl was tall at 6'2". He played quarterback on the high school football team and shooting guard on the basketball team. The sport he loved best was golf. Even though he was right-handed, he played golf left-handed. He had this feeling that he was really left-handed and that no one else understood. Golf was the only sport he played left-handed, although he did practice throwing footballs and baseballs left-handed. Whatever the case, Karl had a natural left-handed golf swing and always hit it further and better than his competitors. However, putting didn't come easily to him. It was the one thing that held him back from possibly making a career of playing professionally.

Karl may not have been a pro golfer, but he was still impressive and good enough to earn a scholarship to the University of Minnesota. He studied business in college and, when he graduated, got a job with a local bank. He moved around a few times, finally settling at US Bank. He married his college sweetheart, Stella, and started a family.

Kelly didn't have any interest in college. After all her clowning around, she had developed a fascination with acting. This led her to perform in various traveling productions as soon as she graduated high school. The family would sometimes not know where Kelly was for weeks at a time. Then she might suddenly show up at the door to spend a few nights in her own bed.

After Kerstin was gone, Kelly would stay with Art when visiting. Sarah was close with Kelly. They shared a love of adventure and performing. Kelly was Art's closest sibling. Kelly and Melissa both helped Art raise his daughter. Sarah saw Melissa as an aunt who was always there. Kelly was like her sister and intimate confidante. They had an eternal bond, no matter how many miles separated them.

Art wasn't the athlete his brother Karl was, but he did participate in football and basketball. He didn't play in games much but was always there for the post-game parties. After a few drinks, Art would entertain whoever was around with humorous stories about the coach's speeches.

One memorable speech was made as the team was ready to get off the bus that had driven them the forty minutes to the opposing school. The head coach and assistant coach had a strained relationship. The year before, the roles of the two coaches had been reversed. Due to school district politics, the former assistant coach had been given the head coaching job. This didn't make up for the fact that the prior head coach, now assistant, was the better coach. Not only was he better at coaching, but he was also very effective with pre-game and halftime speeches, helping to motivate the team.

On this occasion, after the bus parked, the new assistant coach rose and gave an impassioned speech about beating that week's opponent. When he was done, Art and the other players exploded out of their bus seats to take down their unsuspecting opponents!

Just then, the head coach said, "Wait, wait, everybody have a seat." What could he possibly add to the super-charged speech from his colleague? The head coach stated matter-of-factly, "Now make sure you take your cleats off after the game before getting back on the bus."

Art and the other players looked at each other in disbelief. Moments before, they were all ready to storm the gates of their opponents; now they were sitting quietly, reviewing how to take care of their shoes after the game. Predictably, their team lost the game. Thereafter Art was goaded into repeating the story whenever he ran into any of his old teammates.

Art's high school career ended with average grades. He had no desire to attend college so started bouncing around various jobs.

His focus was finding the next party. He would visit his friends at their different colleges, enjoying the merriment without the worry of studying or grades.

One job Art held for a while was as a security guard. He worked various shifts guarding something or other. A regular assignment he enjoyed was working concerts. He couldn't enjoy the concerts as the fans did, but it still exposed him to various types of music.

He always liked the blues in a Rolling Stones way. Now he began to gain a greater enjoyment of it. Of course, there was Eric Clapton. Somehow, Art didn't connect with him. He liked his guitar playing but didn't care for his singing voice. He saw Luther Allison as an opening act for Clapton once and was amazed. The way Allison played, sang, and captured the audience moved him. Another blues man who played at that concert was Chum Fella. His presence while performing was something Art had never experienced.

As Art's friends graduated college, he still hadn't found a career that suited him. He tired of the security work, so he quit and moved from one job to another. While searching online one day, he saw a posting for a driving job. It was for a company called Kare Kabs. The job would be driving elderly and disabled people to and from their various doctor and other appointments. He applied and was hired. This would turn out to be exactly what he was hoping for in a long-term job.

Though it didn't pay well, what it lacked in monetary compensation it made up for by offering daily interaction with unique people needing rides, as well as health care workers at the various care facilities. And it suited him not having to work in an office. Drivers would meet up while on break or at happy hours, leading to Art developing several close friendships with the other drivers and dispatchers.

CHAPTER 5

ART AND KERSTIN

Paul's Place was a hotel with an adjacent bar in Roseville not far from Kare Kabs. Art would go there after a daytime driving shift for drinks with co-workers. There were video games like *Pac-Man* and *Galaxian*. Art's co-workers would play while Art drank beer at the bar, talking to the bartender or watching *SportsCenter* on TV.

One afternoon, Art noticed a woman playing *Galaxian*. It was Kerstin. She was there with her sister Melissa before going to a pre-wedding night out for one of Melissa's friends. They were both part of the wedding party.

Melissa had grown to be even more striking than she had been in high school. Kerstin still felt she wasn't as attractive as her sister. She wasn't voluptuous like her and didn't dress as stylishly. Despite how she saw herself, she had grown into a natural beauty with a fresh face and radiant eyes.

One of Art's friends, Ron Salver, was watching the women play. They were all in a good mood, being a couple of drinks into happy hour. Art was soft-spoken but could be charming when he tried. He noticed Melissa first, as most men did. She looked good dressed in a halter-top and short shorts. Kerstin was wearing an oversized, old Northern Lights t-shirt with shorts. She looked cute in sort of a grunge way.

Art made his way over to join Ron with the video gaming women. Ron had been talking up Melissa as they watched Kerstin try to take out the army of spaceships in *Galaxian*. Art said, "You're killing it!" to Kerstin. She smiled but didn't lose her focus on the game. Melissa and Ron weren't paying attention. They'd moved away from the game and were talking about how they both came to be at Paul's Place this early evening. Art watched Kerstin play until the enemy spaceships finally ended her game.

"Ugh! I thought this time I was going to beat that level," said Kerstin in frustration.

"Ha! You made it pretty far," Art said with a laugh.

"Yeah, I guess so."

"How did you get so good at that game?"

"Practice and a lot of quarters."

"Makes sense."

Melissa interrupted, "Hey cutie, Ron said you guys are going to beat us at pool. And I'm Melissa."

"Hi, Melissa, I'm Art," he replied, surprised to be called cutie. He then shifted his gaze to Kerstin who introduced herself.

"Okay, let's play!" Melissa said, Ron already racking up the balls on the barroom pool table.

The four of them played a few games of pool. It was obvious none of them were very good, but they enjoyed playing in between flirting. Kerstin found Art funny and attractive in an average-guy kind of way. Although Art might have thought of himself as almost six foot tall, as he would say, he wasn't quite 5'10". He had thick black hair that fell over his ears and touched his collar in back. He had never been much of a lady's man like his friend Ron, but he had a couple of serious girlfriends in his past—even though they both left him. He thought it was because he didn't have a well-paying job. He had become content with the occasional hookup, thinking that marriage might not be in his future.

Kerstin was between relationships. She had several boyfriends since her accident, but none were serious. They were comforting for a while, plus she enjoyed having sex. Even so, she hadn't had a one-night stand. She had become friends with the men she dated before sleeping with them.

This evening, Art and Kerstin were drawn together. They both found it easy to talk. From the beginning, Art fell in love with her extraordinary hazel eyes. He would be sure to look her directly in the eyes so he could admire them. Kerstin could tell he fancied them. She would look sideways to mess with him. Art didn't mind and enjoyed their flirting.

When the pool playing ended, Melissa said they should get going and meet up with their friends. Neither Melissa nor Kerstin was the maid of honor, but they felt it was important to attend even though their presence wasn't essential to the proceedings. Ron suggested they meet them back at the bar after the rehearsal.

"Ha! Maybe Ron, maybe," Melissa said. She then turned toward Art and winked at him. Art and Kerstin said goodbye, thinking they might never see each other again.

Ron and Art ordered dinner from the bar, temporarily forsaking alcohol for water, hoping the women would come back. Ron was six foot with shaggy blond hair. Even though he was a little overweight, he carried it well. He had the gift of gab, which Art didn't usually possess. This made Ron a great guy to hang out with if Art hoped to meet women. Although normally it was only Ron who would achieve a hookup. Art liked to believe he was pickier than Ron, rather than lacking any womanizing skills.

That night, Art was hopeful Kerstin would come back, and if not that he might run into her in the future. He thought they had connected and that he might even have a chance with her.

While waiting and hoping the women would return, Ron talked about his future. He was going to be leaving Kare Kabs soon to pursue a career in the restaurant business. He hoped to have his own place in a few years. But first, he was going to get a job, any job, in a restaurant so he could learn how to run the business from the inside.

Art shared that he didn't have any plans to quit driving. He enjoyed not working in an office and being out on the road all day. Ron mentioned that even though it was a decent job, he didn't think it was a *career*. Art found himself thinking that even if Kare Kabs wasn't a career, driving could well be. Art didn't want to get into it with Ron, so he told him, "Yeah, I know," and left it at that.

Art noticed Kerstin poking her head around the corner of the barroom door. She could tell he saw her, so she walked in. Art was thrilled to see her. Ron noticed Art's smile and turned to see Kerstin approaching them.

"Hi guys. I wasn't sure you'd still be here."

"Hey, where's Melissa?" asked Ron.

"She's still with the wedding party. I'm not sure if she's going to make it."

"What? I thought she had a thing for me," said a disappointed Ron.

"Ha! Maybe so, Ron, but I don't think she's coming back," said Kerstin.

"Oh well. I'm glad to see you're back," Ron said, changing his focus to Kerstin.

Art was annoyed Ron didn't leave Kerstin and him alone. The three of them had another couple of drinks before the bartender announced last call. Ron finally got the message that Kerstin was interested in Art and not him. He said good night and left Art and Kerstin with their last call drinks.

Their flirting was interrupted by the bartender saying it was closing time. Kerstin looked deeply into Art's eyes before slowly gliding in and kissing him. Art gazed into her hazel eyes before standing up and saying, "Let's go." He took her hand and led her over to the Paul's Place hotel reception desk, getting them a room. Kerstin was laughing and holding Art's arm tightly. Neither one of them had done anything quite like this before. They went up to their room with no luggage and fell into bed, becoming lovers mere hours after they met.

Over the next few weeks, Art and Kerstin began a relationship. At first, Art would call and talk to Kerstin. He asked if she would be free this night or that, but Kerstin would always say she was busy. They continued talking over the phone and Art kept asking her out until one day she said yes.

Art thought maybe Kerstin was reluctant to get into a serious relationship. This was true, although the reason wasn't because she was interested in someone else or that she didn't like Art. It was because of Kerstin's opioid addiction. She was reluctant to bring Art into her world. Still, she felt an attraction to Art that was different from the other men she had dated.

Art and Kerstin were closer than most newbie daters. Kerstin brought Art home to meet her family. Of course, he already knew Melissa, who liked him and thought he was good for Kerstin. Olivia was cordial, even though she was always critical of the boyfriends Kerstin or Melissa brought home. Elizabeth was also reluctant to approve of any boyfriends, while her dad Eric was just glad to have someone to watch sports with. Over the course of their first year of dating, all of Kerstin's family accepted Art.

Art also brought Kerstin over to meet his family. Kelly was immediately enamored with Kerstin. Cindy was only around one time, but she accepted her since she was glad to see Art happy. Karl was also glad for Art, yet he wondered how they had formed such a strong attraction so quickly. Kim and Gene welcomed Kerstin with open arms, although it would irritate her when they would constantly go on about college. She didn't know why they talked about it so much, especially since Art hadn't even gone. Kerstin came to the conclusion that Karl was the golden child of the family, having gone to college and now with a successful business career.

Art came to suspect Kerstin was hiding something from him. She was. Her addiction continued throughout their relationship. Sometimes she would call in sick to work and "medicate" herself for the day. If she were injecting heroin, she would be careful to use new veins in her body so as not to be caught. She would also snort or smoke it depending on how she felt. After an intense high, she would stop using for a few weeks. One reason she did this was to prevent going through withdrawals; another, more practical reason, was that she couldn't afford it. She was seriously addicted but determined not to get caught. She had concealed it from her family, even Melissa, and now she was confident she could keep it from Art.

One day, Melissa told Art about the serious accident Kerstin suffered. She didn't think Kerstin had ever fully recovered. Kerstin never talked about it to anyone, not even Melissa. Once, when Art asked Kerstin about what looked like needle marks on her arms, Kerstin became agitated and told him that she gave blood and plasma regularly.

Theirs may not have been a classic love story, but they had developed a real bond. They enjoyed each other's company along with their budding sexual partnership. For the first time in her life, Kerstin had started using birth control pills. Neither was particularly risqué in the past, but their intense connection resulted in some racy hookups. Art had picked up Kerstin one night with his Kare Kabs van after his shift. He drove her to the High Bridge in Saint Paul. Kerstin was aware of the High Bridge since it was close to the Wabasha Caves that had changed her life.

Somehow, they conceived of having sex while driving down the bridge. And this wasn't just any bridge; it was an old, rickety bridge that was one hundred feet higher from the West Saint Paul side. Driving to downtown Saint Paul from that side of the bridge felt like landing in an airplane. Their erotic idea was to begin in the parking lot to the side of the bridge entrance.

They both took their pants and underwear off in between kissing and giggling. They should have been worried about getting caught, but they weren't. In their favor, it was a quiet night with light traffic and no other vehicles in the parking lot. Aroused, Kerstin climbed onto Art's lap and with her hand guided him inside her. They were now in the throes of passion.

"Babe...let's drive," Kerstin whispered into Art's ear. Art had momentarily lost himself with desire. Now he looked to see her hazel eyes gazing back at him. He kissed her passionately, then held her tight, positioning her so he could drive. They were both excited as she moved slowly on him. He shifted to reverse and began backing out of the parking spot. Her lips moved behind his right ear.

"Don't you dare drive me off this bridge!" she sensually whispered.

"Never, darling," Art replied as he shifted into drive and began their journey.

She held him tight and snuggled in behind his ear. He had a firm grip on the steering wheel. As the van moved out of the parking lot to the top of the bridge, he could see the beautiful night view of downtown Saint Paul with the cathedral all lit up. The bridge itself probably should have been condemned years ago. It had been built in the late 1800s and had only been repaired a few times since. Besides giving the impression of landing an airplane, the sides were so close to the bridge deck that it felt like there were no sides at all, especially when riding high in vehicles like the Kare Kabs van. The river below ominously visible.

Art wasn't sure if he was excited or terrified. He feared losing himself in the moment and driving off the side of the bridge.

Kerstin was committed to the dangerous intimacy of their adventure, while choosing to ignore the possibility of falling to their death off the side of a bridge. The night sky out of the back of the van was her view when she peered past Art's headrest. The van felt like it was tilted straight down. He was trying to remain focused as Kerstin began riding him harder. He held on tight as he thrusted into her. About halfway down, he momentarily closed his eyes while experiencing unreal ecstasy.

The van swerved to the right, and his eyes flew open. He quickly straightened the van. Kerstin buried her head further into Art's neck. With his now enhanced concentration, he managed to keep his eyes open the rest of the way. They pulled off the bridge and turned left onto Goodrich Avenue. Art stopped the van, struggling to put it in park. It was in the middle of the road. Kerstin lifted herself and straightened her hands on his shoulders, feeling the steering wheel on her back. She ground herself on him until the two climaxed together.

This, while not their only racy sexual encounter, was the most memorable. Their sex life was otherwise normal, with all the familiar intimacy that implies. Maybe Kerstin needed the added adventure of the occasional dangerous hookup to pique her sexual experience, since her sex drive was also dulled by her addiction.

After the bridge episode, she stayed clean for a while. She confided in Melissa about that night. She couldn't believe they had done it but was delighted they were sexually compatible and enjoying themselves, and especially happy they didn't fall off that bridge.

About six months later, the morning after a particularly long night of lovemaking, Art looked at Kerstin sleeping beside him. He was in love. More in love than he had ever been. Just then she awakened. Her eyes slowly opened to see Art gazing at her.

"Hey, you're up," she said with a smile, her brilliant hazel eyes shining back at him.

"You're beautiful. Will you marry me?" asked Art.

"Yes!" she answered immediately as they hugged each other's warm naked bodies close.

And just like that, they were engaged. This was two years after they met at Paul's Place. They had been living together for almost a year in the house Art was sharing with a friend. After getting up and showering, they talked about making plans for their wedding. By this time, Kerstin's dad Eric had died of a heart attack. Her mom was living by herself in the Midway area. Melissa had a house with some high school friends near the state fairgrounds, while Art's parents were still living in the Highland Park area.

The first person they told was Melissa. She was thrilled. "I knew it!" she screamed. They laughed and talked about the night Art and Kerstin met.

Kelly was next. Like Melissa, she was thrilled, shouting, "Oh my God! That's so great! Love you guys!"

Next, they drove to Elizabeth's house. She was happy, although not overjoyed like Melissa and Kelly. Kerstin's accident still weighed heavily on her. She was glad Kerstin was able to find a partner but concerned her daughter had never truly recovered. This would turn out to be prophetic.

Art's parents welcomed the news. Of course, they had to add something about them finally settling down and having time to pursue their education. Art and Kerstin just nodded, keeping their feelings to themselves. Neither were interested in going back to school. They were happy doing what they were doing. They may not have been making much money but were happy with their jobs and, more importantly, their lives.

The wedding was small but celebratory. All of Kerstin and Art's siblings and their partners were able to attend. Melissa was dating a lawyer, and Kelly may or may not have been seeing a school friend she brought along. Fittingly, they held their wedding reception at Paul's Place. They were gifted the bridal suite after Melissa told the Paul's Place manager that was where Art and Kerstin met. Kerstin ducked out of the dancing to play a few games of *Galaxian*. Melissa, who was maid of honor, added a reference to the High Bridge to her speech. She was careful not to tell the full story, just an inside joke that gave Art and Kerstin the intended scare.

Just before their wedding, the pair moved to an apartment in Roseville just off Snelling Avenue near the Rosedale Mall. Art continued driving for Kare Kabs, while Kerstin took a job at a nearby Walgreens. Kerstin had mostly stopped shooting up, instead snorting heroin or ingesting oxycodone. She had discovered a method of sneaking oxycodone pills from the pharmacy. Amazing herself, she was able to pocket ten or more at a time without being caught. She learned one of her co-workers, George, was stealing pharmaceutical cocaine. Eventually the two of them worked together to support their respective addictions.

A few months after their wedding, Kerstin missed her period. They had talked about possibly having children, and although they weren't trying to start a family, they weren't not trying either. Kerstin had run out of birth control pills for a time before renewing them. She took a pregnancy test, and it was positive.

Over the next few days, Art and Kerstin had earnest conversations about whether they were ready to be parents. Kerstin somehow had managed to control her opioid addiction, or at least so she thought. Working at drug stores meant she was sure to always have access to methadone. She would "prescribe" it to herself to come down from her oxycodone or heroin binges.

But Kerstin knew that her addiction was a problem when choosing to have a baby. She had thoughts of finally beating it and living a clean life. They both knew the financial and emotional strains of raising a child might overwhelm them. Art wanted to have the baby but would respect Kerstin's choice. Kerstin was curious about bringing another human being into the world. She wasn't sure she could be a good mother or that Art would be a good father. Even though Kerstin was the one with the opioid addiction, Art had been drinking more regularly. Recently, he had changed from drinking mostly beer to whiskey. There was always a bottle of Jameson or Bushmill in their apartment. Art would often make himself a large glass of whiskey on ice and drink it before going to bed. Kerstin was astonished he could still get up and work all day after his late nights.

Even though they were anxious, they decided to have their baby. The two of them secretly hoped this choice would improve their sometimes imperfect marriage as well as their individual lives.

CHAPTER 6

BABY SARAH

In the days since Art and Kerstin decided to have their baby, they tried to temper their addictions. Kerstin was more successful staying clean. She only had a few glasses of wine and puffs from a joint the entire pregnancy. Art tried not to drink as much, and though he was successful at first, after three months, he fell back into his regular whiskey-drinking routine.

Kerstin became increasingly tired as the months dragged on. If her shift ended at 6 PM, she would eat and go to bed less than two hours later. Art began going out after she was asleep. His favorite spot became Wilebski's Blues Saloon. He enjoyed listening to the music and hanging out at the bar. He would have a few drinks then come home for his regular "nightcap" of a large whiskey on the rocks.

They finally settled on names for the baby. It would be Sarah if it was a girl and Julian if it was a boy. They decided not to be told by the doctors and nurses from the ultrasounds. Kerstin was openly rooting for it to be a girl, while Art secretly hoped for a boy.

Sarah was delivered into the world quickly. Art and Kerstin immediately fell in love with the little baby girl. Art felt he had been foolish for wanting a boy. He cut the thick umbilical cord while the nurse put ointment on Sarah's eyes. Kerstin was relieved to be done with the delivery. She was exhausted, though welcomed little Sarah with open arms, cuddling her with fascination. In that moment, she had a powerful sense it would be her first and only pregnancy.

Soon members of both Kerstin's and Art's families made the pilgrimage to the hospital to greet Sarah. Kelly had joined a local theater group and, as Gene would say, was "acting" somewhere. Melissa stopped in with Elizabeth. They were both sure Sarah looked exactly like Kerstin when she was born, thrilled to see the way Kerstin's hazel eyes were shining when she held her newborn daughter.

After a couple of days in the hospital, Sarah was ready to come home. Art and Kerstin were surprised that after a few days of constant nurse supervision they were now suddenly in charge of this tiny person. Kerstin was wheeled down to Art's car, now with its hand-me-down infant car seat in place. They carefully put Sarah into the thing, making sure to fasten all the straps as they had practiced.

Their apartment was furnished with a crib that, like the car seat, they had gotten from Karl who was married with two older kids by this time. His youngest had just turned three and moved to a twin bed. Fortunately, Art and Kerstin benefited from their older siblings handing down their baby things—everything from the crib to toys, clothes, and books. Although it was a hassle, they had recently moved across the hall to a two bedroom apartment, meaning little

Sarah had her own room. Another hand-me-down item was a baby monitor that allowed them to see and hear Sarah when she was supposed to be sleeping.

The first year went quickly. Sarah had a good temperament. She quickly slept through the night. Once she could do more than lie down and look at things, she was holding toys and sucking on anything she could get her hands on.

Art and Kerstin always had music playing when they were home. Neither watched a lot of TV. Instead, they would play albums, tapes, or CDs. Since Kerstin's days working at Northern Lights, she always had a large collection of music, including some local bands that were her favorites like The Replacements, The Suburbs, Crash Street Kids, and Lamont Cranston. Of course, Prince was played along with his colleagues, The Time. Kerstin and Art both loved the blues, playing artists including BB King, Robert Johnson, Muddy Waters, Jeff Healey, Chum Fella, and Howlin' Wolf. Country and even classical music would also feature.

Sarah seemed to love hearing any and all music, which reinforced Art and Kerstin always playing something. As Sarah approached her first birthday, she began bouncing up and down to the beat. Soon after she turned one, she started banging her toys along with the beat, like a kind of baby drummer.

CHAPTER 7

TODDLER SARAH

Sarah started walking soon after she reached fourteen months. Once she started, she couldn't be stopped. She wandered around the entire apartment. Art and Kerstin had to "baby proof" the place as best they could. They might hear a bang from the other room as the alarm clock was pulled off the table by its cord again.

Music continued to be a fascination for Sarah. She had a natural rhythm as she seemed to bop in time to whatever music was playing. Their pediatrician said some people were born with more of a creative knack than others. Sarah certainly had a gift for music, but that wasn't the only one she possessed. She was also interested in reading, as well as endlessly playing both catch and fetch.

Art and Kerstin were amazed by their young child. This brought them closer for a time, and it was a happy time as both stayed relatively clean from their addictions.

Still, they couldn't afford daycare. Luckily, Elizabeth had volunteered to watch Sarah as needed. Art would usually start his driving shift sometime between 7 and 9 AM. Kerstin normally started at ten. Between them, they would arrange to have Grandma Elizabeth come to their apartment or drive Sarah over to her house.

Grandma Elizabeth found this to be a great deal of work and exhausting, but she was overjoyed to be bonding with Sarah. She also felt it brought her closer to Kerstin and even Art. Before Sarah, she felt her relationship with Kerstin had never fully recovered after the accident.

As Sarah turned two, she began to talk. Art and Kerstin were trying their best to raise their daughter, their lives consumed with Sarah's schedule. They had moved her into a twin bed, another hand-me-down from Karl.

But their sex life had suffered. They grew reluctant to engage with each other, afraid that Sarah would hear them. Their concerns were realized when Sarah stuck her head in their room as they were about to make love. Occasionally, they would have Melissa stay over with Sarah, and they would go to downtown Minneapolis for the night. They would splurge and stay at the W, the fancy hotel in the Foshay Tower. They would try to recapture some of their former passion, with varying degrees of success.

Art began drinking more, while Kerstin began taking days off from work to get high at home. She started smoking more pot, hoping that it would help her opioid urges. It didn't. Sarah would spend most of her days at Grandma Elizabeth's house. She had transformed her basement into a play area for Sarah. It was a large, carpeted space with room for various toys and books. Grandma Elizabeth had even gotten a small plastic drum with a plastic stick that Sarah could use. She was surprised how Sarah could make something close to music on that toy. So much so that she bought a second plastic stick. Again, she was amazed how naturally Sarah began playing with those two sticks.

Soon Grandma Elizabeth noticed when she had the radio on while they were in the basement playroom that Sarah would sometimes stop what she was doing, go over to the toy drum, pick up the two drumsticks and start playing along in perfect time with the music.

"My goodness, Sarah, you're playing drums!" an excited Grandma Elizabeth declared. Sarah stopped, looked up at her and smiled the most beautiful smile her grandma had ever seen. Grandma Elizabeth smiled back at her, leapt to her feet, and picked Sarah up, giving her a big bear hug, as big a bear hug as the aging Grandma Elizabeth could muster. Sarah laughed and hugged back as hard as a two-and-a-half-year-old could.

That evening when Art picked up Sarah, Grandma Elizabeth gushed about how Sarah was playing drums. Art smiled and said, "That's great! Maybe we have ourselves a little Keith Moon."

Grandma Elizabeth felt the sarcasm in Art's voice that wiped away her smile. She also wasn't happy with the reference to Keith Moon, the crazed—albeit wonderfully talented—drummer for The Who that had died an unfortunate death at a young age.

"I'd say more like Ringo Starr," Grandma Elizabeth replied coldly.

Art had forgotten the conversation by the time he got home, so he didn't mention it to Kerstin. Neither of them were working that weekend so they stayed home, only going out to Como Park for a time on Sunday.

On Monday, Grandma Elizabeth had purchased a cassette player for the playroom. She had a few cassettes, mostly ones that

Kerstin had acquired for her while she worked at Northern Lights. There was *Revolver* by the Beatles, the Rolling Stones' *Let It Bleed*, and *Led Zeppelin IV*. As with the songs on the radio, Sarah would listen and play along with Ringo Starr, Charlie Watts, and the great John Bonham.

Sarah seemed to enjoy all the songs, although one was her favorite: "Love in Vain" from *Let It Bleed*. It was an old blues cover song written by Robert Johnson. Johnson, known as the King of the Delta Blues, was a legendary songwriter and performer who tragically only lived to twenty-seven.

One day when Art was picking up Sarah, she and Elizabeth were down in the basement. Sarah was playing her toy drums along with Charlie Watts and the Stones. It was common for them to be in the basement, but this was the first time he paid attention to Sarah's drumming. Grandma Elizabeth heard him coming down the stairs and got up to greet him.

"Hi Art. I hope you had a good day."

Art smiled. He turned to watch Sarah banging in rhythm to "You Can't Always Get What You Want" and for a moment was speechless.

"See! I told you she's quite the little drummer!" declared Grandma Elizabeth.

"Oh, yeah. That's right," replied Art.

"She's been playing like this for a few weeks now. It can be tough to get her to stop!"

Art listened some more. Sarah looked up at him and grinned, not breaking her beat. That night, Art remembered to tell Kerstin how he witnessed Sarah playing drums along to the Stones. Kerstin was happy her little girl had such a gift.

"Who knows? Maybe she'll be in a band someday," Kerstin wondered.

"I don't know about that, but she was good at it for being almost three years old," said Art.

While preparing for Sarah's birthday which was only a week away, they weren't sure about getting toy drums at home, given the unappealing thought of constant banging in the apartment. Instead, they bought her a little Sony cassette tape player. They thought she could listen to her music and bang around with the toys she already had.

Sarah's third birthday party was held at Grandma Elizabeth's house. Karl and his wife Stella, along with his six-year-old daughter Anna and nine-year-old son Jason arrived first. They were followed by Olivia and her latest boyfriend, David (who insisted on being called David, not Dave). Gene and Kim showed up too, followed by Melissa. Kelly was in "parts unknown" as her father had become accustomed to saying.

There were ham and cheese sandwiches followed by Sarah's favorite vanilla iced chocolate cupcakes. Sarah played games with Anna and Jason while the adults forced awkward conversations. Melissa had just started as an assistant at a software consulting company. Although she didn't have any college or training, the work made sense to her, leading to a fast promotion. Olivia was working on her doctoral thesis in history. David (not Dave) was also in the program. Karl was doing well at US Bank, even if he was starting to think about moving on. Stella, who had a loud, cackling laugh, also worked at US Bank. She was happy there and claimed she was going to stay, even if Karl left.

Karl joined Olivia in questioning Art and Kerstin about their future. The couple had suspected this conversation might arise. They were prepared with a few quips but otherwise didn't get into it with the others. In truth, they had talked together about how to improve their lives, but those discussions always ended with a promise to think about it and talk more later. Both were complacent; they were getting by, even if they weren't making a lot of money.

Unknown, although suspected by the others, they were also both content with their addictions. Kerstin was in a job where she could occasionally lose herself for a day or so. Art had grown accustomed to drinking too. Though he was a drunk, he wasn't an angry drunk. They both had happily become both physically and emotionally addicted. Kerstin knew Art was drinking too much, while Art suspected something was going on with Kerstin. Still, both were satisfied to let the other have their vice, as long as they could have their own.

Sarah and the older kids had fun playing tag and then went down to the basement and played Trouble and Uno. The adults were delighted the kids played so well together. Even though Sarah was the youngest by far, she was able to understand and play the games as well as her older cousins. Soon, the party was over, and it was time to go.

Unfortunately, the next family gathering would be very different indeed.

CHAPTER 8

GRIEF

Just a few weeks after Sarah's third birthday, Kerstin was gone. She had taken a chance with what she thought was heroin, even though she felt the urge to be clean. Plans swirled in her head about finally telling Art and Melissa of her struggles with opioids. She had started considering doing something more with her life and becoming the mother that Sarah deserved. Just this one last time, she thought. Instead, she slipped away from this world in the throes of euphoric regret.

"Kerstin, NO! Kerstin! Don't go!" Art cried when he found her on the couch. She was already gone when he had gotten home, although he didn't know it yet. Frantically, he called 911. An ambulance was there in a few minutes, followed by the police. Art was sobbing, still holding Kerstin. The paramedics noted the syringe and what looked like heroin next to her. Despite trying their best, they couldn't revive her. One paramedic tried to calm Art down while the other called the mortuary to come for Kerstin.

The two police officers, one man and one woman, carefully looked over the scene. They huddled and radioed their office. To them, it was a clear-cut accidental overdose. Unfortunately, they had witnessed far too many of them in their careers. A few minutes later, two men from the coroner's office arrived with a stretcher on wheels. Art was mumbling in a daze, holding Kerstin's hand.

"No, no, this can't be… How? Why? She can't leave us, not now…"

One man from the coroner's office talked briefly with the paramedics and the police then turned to Art.

"We're deeply sorry for your loss. My name is Jules, and this is my partner, Vincent."

Art looked up at Jules and then over at Vincent as he nodded. "Mr. Zonnen, you can have as much time as you like with your wife. Please let us know when you're comfortable with us taking her," stated Jules.

Looking back at Kerstin through tear-soaked eyes, memories of her raced through his head. The wonderful night they met, lying in bed when he proposed, when their beautiful Sarah was born, and that crazy time on the high bridge. He sobbed as these flash-backs rattled around his head. How could he let them take her? She was there next to him, looking every bit as lovely as she did the morning he proposed. He struggled to believe that this time she wouldn't be waking up to see him staring at her. She would never, ever wake up next to him again. He closed his eyes and sobbed.

"I love you. I love you. I love you. I'll love you forever," Art bent down and whispered to Kerstin, holding her hand. Then he gently kissed her mouth. After a moment, he stood up, still looking at her closed eyelids hiding those sweet hazel eyes.

"Alight, do what you must," he said as he walked away, crying louder the further away he moved. The police bid farewell, leaving a card in case Art needed to speak with them. The paramedics also packed up their things and left.

Jules and Vincent performed their gruesome duty as sympathetically as possible. It was trying for Art to see them pull out the drab body bag and roll Kerstin onto her side and position the bag next to her. They then rolled her lifeless body back into the awful thing, and the sound of the zip was deafening to him.

Art couldn't stand it. He turned away and continued to cry for Kerstin.

"We're sorry, Mr. Zonnen. Very sorry," Jules said.

They lifted Kerstin gently, positioned her on the stretcher, then fastened straps to hold her in place, before carefully extending the stretcher to full height.

"Mr. Zonnen, we are leaving now," Jules said. He waited for Art's acknowledgment. Art looked at Jules, then at his wife, bagged on the stretcher, then back at Vincent.

Art couldn't say anything, instead just grimaced and nodded. Jules and Vincent quietly rolled Kerstin out to the waiting hearse.

CHAPTER 9
SINGLE PARENTING

The days following Kerstin's passing were a blur to Art. He had called Grandma Elizabeth first, sobbing. She offered to keep Sarah as long as needed. Art appreciated her offer and agreed it was best if Sarah stayed, at least for a few weeks. Next, he called Kelly, his closest sibling. No one answered at the number she'd left for him, so he left a message for her to call him back as soon as possible.

Then he called Melissa. She sobbed uncontrollably with Art as he told her the terrible news. Years earlier, she had thought Kerstin might die from her fall in that cave. But not now. Like Art, she was unaware of Kerstin's opioid addiction, even though she suspected something was happening with her sister. But now it was too late to do anything.

Art called other family members that night. Gene and Kim offered to help in any way they could, as did Karl. Cindy said she would come home in a few days. Kerstin's sister Olivia said she would do anything she could. Art tearfully thanked them all.

Preparing for the funeral was more like some sort of somber business deal than preparing to say goodbye to a loved one. There were many small details that needed to be handled, including picking Kerstin's burial site near her dad, and her simple gravestone.

Art tried to do as much as he could, relying on Melissa to help. Karl had offered to cover the expenses. Art accepted, although he and the rest of the family also contributed.

The day after Kerstin's death, Art had gone over to Grandma Elizabeth's house and spoke alone with Sarah in the basement. She had just turned three, could talk and possessed a burgeoning realization of the world. Sarah was sad and didn't understand that Kerstin was gone, gone forever. Art held her and told her how much Kerstin loved her. He explained she would be staying with Grandma Elizabeth for a few weeks but that he would stop by as often as he could to visit.

In those days after Kerstin's death, Art decided that he and Sarah would move. He couldn't stand living in the same space where his wife had died. The Roseville apartment building let him break their lease. There was an opening at an apartment complex on the east side of town called Maple Manor. He liked the location as it was just off Highway 35E and close to Highways 36 and 94. There was a basement apartment available, and while he would have preferred one with a balcony, this was less expensive. Another factor for Art was that this apartment was only a mile from Wilebski's Blues Saloon, which had become his favorite bar.

Days passed slowly at first, even after the move to Maple Manor. There were a few other kids about Sarah's age that she would play with around the apartment complex and the playground just behind it. Grandma Elizabeth continued watching Sarah during the day, though now she came to Art's apartment.

This put a damper on Sarah's play-drumming. Art thought it was too loud to have in his apartment, what with the neighbors in close proximity. Sarah found other things to play with, as well as spending more time with her apartment friends. Grandma Elizabeth would continue to mourn the loss of Kerstin for the rest of her life. She read to and taught Sarah, but she was no longer able to listen to music. Grandma Elizabeth found most songs were about lost love, leaving her reflecting on Kerstin.

Art's social life may have been limited with Kerstin, but now it was practically nonexistent. Occasionally, he would let Grandma Elizabeth know he would be a little late coming home and stop at Wilebski's for happy hour. A few of the other drivers who lived nearby would join him and sometimes stop by to watch some game on TV. After Sarah went to bed, he continued his habit of drinking a large glass of whiskey on ice before going to sleep.

Melissa became even closer to Art and Sarah. The three of them would go to Wilebski's after work. Sarah would play video games, and sometimes they would bring one of her apartment friends along. She was affable and had a way of making friends with the other kids there, even if they were a little older. She didn't care if they were boys or girls. If they were shy toward her, she was able to smile and get them to play with her.

This gave Art and Melissa time to talk. Melissa had moved up from being an assistant to a business analyst at the consulting firm. Art loved to hear how she, who was once so uninterested in school or business, was now in the middle of the always-growing computer industry. Melissa delighted hearing stories from Art's driving. He still enjoyed his job, but was more worried every day about how he was going to provide for Sarah. Dreams about living in a house seemed far away.

Some days, either Art or Melissa or both would be joined by a date. Melissa was content being single. Some of her dates would want to get serious, and this would be about the time that she would move on. Art wasn't interested in a serious relationship either. There were some women who were friends and occasional sexual partners, but that was it.

Melissa once told Art the night she and Kerstin first met him that she was more interested in Art than his friend. Even so, Melissa was happy for Kerstin that she was able to find and experience love with him. Art smiled, glad he was able to find and experience love too.

When Kelly found herself back in the Twin Cities, she would often stay on Art's couch. She and Sarah had always been close. This bond became stronger as Sarah grew older. They would stay up and talk late into the night. Sarah couldn't get enough of Kelly's stories from different parts of the world. One story made Sarah laugh so loud that she woke Art up on a workday at 3 AM.

"Come on Kelly. I want to hear another one," demanded Sarah.

"I have one more story but then we really need to go to sleep."

"Okay. One more. Then I'll go to sleep. Promise."

"Alright. Well, this happened one summer when I was supposedly an actor but more of a camp counselor. They would have us keep the kids busy during the day with different activities. Arts and crafts things like finger-painting, or sports like soccer and swimming."

"Sounds fun! I want to go!"

"Ha! You could go, but I won't be doing that job anymore. I'm a real actor now!"

"Really? What's that mean?"

"Come on Sarah. If you don't let me finish this story, we'll never get to bed."

"Okay, okay, I'm listening."

"It was sort of a poor man's *Dirty Dancing* place, if you know what I mean."

"Ah, no. What's that?"

"Never mind. It was just a summer camp. It was a six-week job for us counselors, um, I mean actors. Most campers would be there for two weeks and then a new group would come in. At the end of the summer, there was one final show."

"Wow! A show? That sounds fun!"

"Yeah, it was about the only time we would act. We would plan and rehearse various skits. When the big night came the entire camp, all the campers, counselors, and other staff would cram into the small auditorium."

"Auditorium? What's that?"

"It's a place with a stage and some seats. The actors perform on the stage for the people in the seats."

"Oh."

"Anyway, there wasn't anything memorable about the show. The memorable part was afterward!"

"Really? What happened?"

"At the end of the show the lead counselor, who I just happened to be dating at the time, was chased out of the auditorium by me and a couple of the other actors. It was supposed to be a sort of joke. And then the show ended."

"That's the story?"

"Well, we ran out of the auditorium and back to our cabin."

"Kelly, you were staying with the guy?"

"Yes, Sarah. I'm an adult, you know. Adults sometimes, if they like each other, stay together."

"Yeah, I get it. I know Melissa has had boys stay over."

"Anyway, we thought the show was over. We started changing out of our goofy clothes. Just then, there was a loud knocking at the door. There was a window in the door. We saw about ten of the campers, kids, at the door. We were both in our underwear!"

"WHAT?" Sarah shrieked.

"Shhh, quiet. You'll wake your dad."

"Sorry. Sorry. What did you do?" whispered Sarah.

"I jumped under the bed, and my boyfriend ran into the bathroom. The kids kept pounding on the door until finally he came out with a towel on and told them they had to leave."

"Oh no! I can't believe it. Kelly, you're so naughty!"

"Ha! Well, maybe. Though I don't know what those kids were thinking, chasing us to our cabin after the show."

"They loved you guys!"

In between laughing, Kelly said, "Maybe. Now we better go to bed."

Sarah laughed with her. She couldn't get the thought of Kelly standing there in her underwear out of her head.

"You two need to go to sleep! Right now!" yelled Art from his bedroom.

Kelly and Sarah giggled, finally falling asleep on the couch together. Art was irritated to be awakened on a work night but at the same time was filled with joy that his sister and daughter were so close.

CHAPTER 10
TRAVERSE CITY

The summer after Sarah's fifth birthday, Art and Melissa decided to rent and share a cottage for a week near Traverse City in Michigan. Melissa had just started dating a software engineer named Brooks Loughty. He was a large, broad shouldered man with curly brown hair. Art likewise was bringing a date, Lydia Alquist, a fellow Kare Kabs driver. She was almost as tall as Art and rail thin with short black hair. They pooled their resources to rent the cottage and a van, so they could all make the ten-and-a-half-hour drive together.

Art packed up Sarah's and his things for the trip and then collected Lydia before swinging by Melissa's. Brooks was already there. Maybe he was staying with her? Art didn't think so because Melissa hadn't said anything about it. In any case, they were ready to hit the road.

Sarah had an old Nintendo Game Boy to keep her busy, while the adults played music and talked. Brooks told Sarah over and over that they were going to "Drive, drive, drive" until they got there. Sarah didn't know why he thought that was either funny or a good thing to keep saying. At first, she would just smile at him and say, "Yep." But after a while she just half smiled wishing he'd stop.

The van only had a CD player which limited Art's music choices. By then, his collection was mostly on MP3, or else cassettes and vinyl records. Brooks had a bunch of CDs but would always pick Boston's first album when it was his turn to choose the music. Sarah liked some of the songs but was tired of it being played over and over. When Brooks picked it for the fourth time, at about the six-hour mark, Sarah had enough.

"NO! Please, something else!" she yelled.

Everyone perked up, surprised at the little girl's reaction, even though they all felt the same.

"Yeah, come on man. Let's hear something else," implored Art.

"Alright, alright," Brooks said as he looked through his CD case. "Here's one for ya," He popped out the Boston CD and slid in the one he picked. The car filled with the sound of Howlin' Wolf singing "Smokestack Lightning."

Sarah's mood was immediately lifted. As the CD played on, she sat back, closed her eyes, and reveled in what she was hearing. It had been a few years since Grandma Elizabeth had played blues music for her. Art didn't play music as much as he did when Kerstin was alive. Sarah's memory of her mom and her life with her was fading. But this music awoke something in her.

"Can we hear that one again?" asked Sarah when the CD was over.

Everyone laughed. Brooks, who was sitting in the passenger seat, turned back and greeted her with a big smirk. Sarah smiled her biggest, best smile back at him. He laughed and played the CD again.

They stopped for gas when they reached Traverse City. The cottage was just a short distance north on Southwest Bay Shore Drive. Everyone was tired, but knowing they were almost there filled them with renewed energy. They even let Brooks play his Boston CD the rest of the way.

Just before the cottage, Art noticed the West End Tavern Grill. He thought it looked like a good spot to have a few drinks, while Sarah was more interested in the ice cream place on the other side of the road. Driving on Bay Shore Drive, they had seen a lot of water and boats, as there was a marina by the tavern. They were all ready for this vacation.

The cottage itself had a wooden porch with blue painted wood clapboards and a shingled roof. It was old, small, and looked like it had seen better days. There were cottages on both sides—one brown and rustic looking, the other gray and newer. They unpacked the car and piled into the cottage. Next door, it looked like there was a family in the brown cottage with an adult couple sitting on the porch, and two teenage boys throwing a football around.

Inside the cottage, there was a sink, oven and refrigerator in a small, narrow kitchen that opened to a larger living area. There were three bedrooms and one bathroom with a door that, even when shut, left a small opening. The most surprising feature was a shower in the middle of the upstairs hallway with a flimsy shower curtain. They would later learn there was barely any water pressure in that shower, making it nearly useless. For this week, they would wash by swimming in the lake.

Sarah hurried through unpacking. She had a room facing away from the lake. Art was with Lydia in the middle room and Melissa was with Brooks in the lakeside room. As Sarah finished putting her things away, she noticed there were three kids next door in the brown cottage. One girl and two boys, who all looked to be teenagers about the same age. The adults were still putting their things away as Sarah left to go outside to meet the neighbors.

"Hi!" Sarah said, approaching the three kids. They were setting up some sort of lawn game. Well, one of the boys was doing all the setting up. The other boy and girl were standing by the side, offering suggestions on how to best set up whatever it was the boy was doing.

"Hi! I'm Jessica. Want to play?" asked the girl as she came over to Sarah.

"I'm Sarah. I'd love to, but I don't know the game."

"Oh, it's easy. We'll teach you. Oh, and these are my brothers, Sam and Scott."

"Hi Sam and Scott," said Sarah.

The boys nodded at her. Sam was the one setting up the game, while Scott continued to harass his brother rather than help.

"The game's called croquet, and you play it with those mallets," said Jessica. She pointed to some large sticks with a piece of wood on the end. Each mallet had a different colored stripe that matched a ball.

"It's easy. You'll learn in no time," Jessica assured her.

The boys didn't say much as the game began. Sarah picked the yellow mallet and ball and followed their instructions, trying to learn the game. She was used to playing a lot of different games with her friends back at Maple Manor. For a young girl, she had grown strong and ran faster than most kids her age. This ability didn't come from her dad; it was Kerstin who had a natural way with athletics.

Soon all four kids were laughing. Sam and Scott liked to goof around with each other. Sarah found them hilarious. Jessica was a little more serious but also enjoyed her brothers and their hijinks. After the game, Sarah joined the boys playing catch with their football. Jessica didn't care much for catching footballs since spraining her finger trying to catch one of the boys' throws.

That night, Art and Brooks grilled hotdogs for their group. After dinner, they met the neighbors, Alex and Lynn Davies, who were professors at Michigan State University in East Lansing only about three hours away. Beer and wine flowed among the adults, while the kids went down by the lake. Art trusted the older kids to take care of his Sarah.

Two other girls joined the group. Like Sarah, they had just arrived with their family. Tessa was eight and Tori six. Jessica was glad to have some more girls around. She was even happier when she learned they had an eleven-year-old sister, Mae, and a little two-year-old sister, Helen. Mae quickly connected with Jessica when she brought little Helen down to the shore. Sarah liked that Tori was about her age and that now Helen was the youngest. When the kids came back up to the cottage, Joe and Peggy Campbell—Mae and her sisters' parents—were talking and drinking with the other adults. They were staying in the large cottage on the other side of Art's. The boys went about setting up the croquet course again for what turned out to be a long, seemingly never ending game. It had to be called off when it was too dark to play. Since mosquitoes were hijacking the party, everyone retreated inside their respective cottages for the evening.

In the morning, Sarah could hear someone quietly playing a guitar. She got up, dressed, and went downstairs. Art and Melissa were having coffee. Brooks and Lydia were sleeping in. Most of them drank heavily the previous night, so it wasn't surprising some would still be in bed. Art too had several drinks, although he was accustomed to drinking before bed and still being able to get up early for work. Melissa was the one adult who drank only a couple of beers. The two of them were making plans for the day. Sarah quickly ate a bowl of cereal and then went outside.

She found Jessica sitting on their porch, strumming an acoustic guitar.

"Cool!" Sarah said.

"Oh, thanks. I'm just having fun and trying not to wake anyone up."

"How long have you been playing?"

"Um, gee, good question! I think it's been about three years. Do you play an instrument?"

"No. Not really. I used to play with a toy drum set my grandma gave me."

"Drums! That's great! Sam has a starter drum kit. He plays okay for a beginner."

"Really? I'd love to hear him play."

"Sarah, my new friend, you're in luck! Me and my brothers are trying to learn how to play as a band. We're going to put on a show for anyone that wants to hear it at the end of the week."

"Wow! I can't wait!"

Jessica smiled and then softly played the Beatles' song, "Michelle." Sarah leaned back, enjoying the sound of Jessica's guitar.

The rest of the day was spent on a sightseeing boat tour for Sarah's group. It was a little rough out on the lake which affected the adults more than Sarah, their late-night revelry catching up with them. After returning to the cottage, Sarah met up with the other kids to go swimming. The adults gathered on the shore with a cooler of beer. Brooks had stopped by a local store and after asking what the best beer in Michigan was bought a case of Bell's Two Hearted along with some White Claws for Lydia.

"Hey Brooksy! Okay if I call you that?" Art yelled over to Brooks. "No. Not at all. My mom always called me Brooksy. Okay to call you Arty?"

"Ha! Ya, go for it."

It was Brooksy and Arty for those two for the rest of the trip.

Before dinner, the girls met at the big cottage. Mae had asked Jessica and Sarah if they would want to come with them as she, Tessa, and Tori strolled Helen. They were going to go about a half-mile down the road to a small bridge over a creek.

"You girls be careful on that road," warned Peggy.

"We will, Mom," Mae assured her, and off they went.

Helen was a happy toddler, especially when she was being strolled.

"Your mom is nice," Jessica said when they started down the road.

"Yeah, I guess. She just worries a lot," answered Mae.

"Mainly about Helen," Tessa added. Tori and Mae both giggled.

"I like your mom too," Tori said to Jessica.

"Thanks. She always said that she had three kids at once since I'm only a year older than my brothers."

"I told you they were twins!" Tessa said, looking at Tori. Tori smiled and shrugged.

"What's it like having brothers?" asked Mae.

"Oh, it's okay. They do play together a lot. When they were little, they had their own language." Everyone laughed. Jessica added, "We mostly get along though."

"I wish I had a brother or sister," Sarah said softly.

"Don't your parents want another kid?" asked Tessa.

"My mom's dead," stated Sarah matter-of-factly.

Mae stopped pushing Helen's stroller, and the group came to a halt.

"I'm so sorry. I thought Lydia was your mom," said Tessa.

"Oh, don't be. How would you know? My mom died when I was little. Now, I don't remember her too good."

"That's sad," Tessa blurted out before adding, "Oh, sorry."

"Tessa!" scolded Mae. Sarah nodded at Tessa, trying to let her know it was all right, as they all start walking again in silence.

The girls were all smiling and laughing as they came back to the cottages. When they made the turnaround at the bridge, Sarah told a knock-knock joke she had heard from Kelly. From that point on, they took turns telling jokes and funny stories.

The adults were relaxing on the patio next to the beach. The little cottage they were staying in may have been close to collapsing, but the patio was new, solid, and beautiful. There were a few trees giving shade to the area. The shoreline was in front, so either swimming or just watching the boats go by and waves roll in was perfect.

"Hey Arty," called out Brooks.

"Yeah," replied Art, just about to reach a seat and relax.

"Why don't you get some of those Two Hearteds? I'd say it's time we start hitting it again," Brooks said.

"You would ask just as I get back down here. But sure Brooksy, I'll get some. Anyone else?"

"Sure, I'll take one," said Melissa.

"You can get me a White Claw," Lydia stated before adding, "Arty, dear."

"Ha. Okay, Lydiay! Hmm, guess that doesn't sound right," Art said as he turned around and headed back to the cottage. He returned with a small cooler filled with everyone's drinks.

"Thanks, sweet pea," Melissa said with a wink as she took a beer.

Melissa would sometimes call Art affectionate names ever since they first met. Over time, their relationship continued to morph into something more than in-laws.

"Tell me Arty, are you going to be driving old people around your whole life?" asked Brooks after a mouthful of beer.

"Come on Brooks. That's none of your business," said Melissa, shocked at her companion's rude question.

"I'm just making conversation. I know it's not my business. Just wondering how long Arty is going to drive."

"What about me? Want to know how long I'm going to drive?" asked Lydia.

"Well, yes. I do. How long you driving for, Lydiay?" Brooks tried to lighten the mood after being surprised his line of questioning drawing the ire of his cottage pals.

"Thanks for asking, Brooksy. I'll tell ya," Lydia teased, adding, "I love the job but don't see myself doing it very much longer."

"How long have you been there?"

"Oh, about two years. I met Arty about a year ago and he finally asked me out on a date last month."

Art, who had a difficult time even thinking about dating while he mourned Kerstin, only recently even noticed Lydia. When he did, she was open to his advances.

"I'm planning to leave driving and go into dispatching full-time," she said.

Lydia had already worked part-time as dispatcher when the one and only full-time dispatcher was off. Lydia was hoping that either he would leave, opening the regular job for her, or that she could land a job dispatching at another company. Art knew all of this. Lydia thought she'd said enough to satisfy Brooks' curiosity, so she just smiled and drank her White Claw.

Melissa, still annoyed with Brooks for beginning this conversation, said, "What about you, Brooks? I mean Brooksy. How long are you going to do… What is it you do again?"

"Very funny, Melly," Brooks responded. Melissa smiled, thinking of how Kerstin used to call her Melly.

"You know I design computer systems for our clients. It's okay and it pays very well, but someday I'd like to own my own consulting company," Brooks said.

Melissa did indeed know what Brooks did. He was a quiet guy around work but was very good at his job. She didn't know how much he was making, although she thought it was well over six figures. A six-figure income was a milestone for most working people. Brooks had higher ambitions, though, than just making a lot of money.

Like Brooks, Melissa was making a good income. But, unlike him, she was crippled by imposter syndrome. She hadn't gone to college, and once she found her way into the consulting business, she moved up the company ladder by delivering solid results. She was a natural at bringing teams together and leading them. Even though she was making a very good salary, she would have made even more if she were a man. A sad commentary, still true for many working women.

"Satisfied, Melly?" Brooks interrupted Melissa's thoughts. "Your turn. How long are you going to do whatever it is you do?"

"Now you're the one being funny," Melissa said, glancing at Brooks. "My job is making sure the grand plans of people like our Brooksy here succeed. I need to coordinate with everyone involved and keep track of their progress, so that Brooksy can say he delivered a great system."

"Ha, ha! You know she's right about that!" Brooks affirmed.

"I don't know how long I'll do what I do now, but I'm happy where I'm at right now," stated Melissa.

"Thanks Melly. Arty, you know I'm sorry for starting this awkward conversation. Just trying to get to know you better, man. I know you and Melly are good friends—she's your ex-wife's sister, right? Are you still friends with your ex-wife too?" Brooks asked, again stirring the pot.

"Come on Brooks," Melissa said firmly.

"What did I say?" protested Brooks.

"Nothing. You're fine," Art said, speaking up.

"Let's move on," Lydia chimed in, hoping to redirect the conversation from where she knew it would go if she didn't. Lydia knew all about Kerstin and how her death had shattered Art. Now, she felt Art was just about ready to move on. She liked him and wanted to enjoy their time together, even if it might not be for the long term.

"I know, Lydia," said Art as he reached for another beer. "Maybe it's the company, but I'm alright talking about…well, things."

Brooks has a squeamish look on his face, unaware what he had uncorked.

"My wife, Melissa's sister, Kerstin, is dead," Art said.

"Oh, I'm so sorry. I didn't know," Brooks said.

"Thank you. Yes, Kerstin died about two years ago," continued Art. Lydia and Melissa both bowed their heads.

"Kerstin struggled with drugs. Opioids. I didn't even know," Art said, tearing up. "How could I not know?"

"I didn't know either. And I should have…I should have known," Melissa added, now misty-eyed herself.

Brooks looked down, slowly shaking his head. He didn't mean to bring up such painful, raw memories. Now Art was struggling to continue. Lydia brought his hand to hers. They shared a comforting look.

The four of them sat silently, hearing only the splooosh, sploosh of the waves gently rolling into the beach. Birds chirping. A motorboat on the lake. And silence. Then in the distance, children laughing. On hearing this, the adults all looked at each other and smiled.

Before long, there was only one more day of vacation left. The families had bonded in their short time at the three cottages. Even the boys had loosened up and joined the strollering of little Helen to the bridge and back.

That evening Jessica, Sam, and Scott set up for their "rock and roll show" the next day. Alex had found a plywood board Sam used as a platform for his drum kit. Sam's kit was a three-piece with a cymbal and snare, base, and tom drums. Scott had an old Fender electric bass guitar. He was the least interested in music but would humor his siblings by trying to play along. Jessica had two Fender guitars, one acoustic and one electric. She was the one who was most serious about music. The boys enjoyed playing in their "band" but didn't care much for practicing. For now, Jessica was okay with them and their limited interest and abilities, as at least it gave her an outlet for her passion.

Adults were barred from the practice session. This wasn't a problem, since by this point in the vacation they had all grown comfortable with their kids spending time together. They trusted that Helen would be cared for and everyone would stay out of trouble.

After making salad and sandwiches for the kids' dinner, the adults all crowded in Art's rental van, bid the children farewell, and drove down to the West End Tavern Grill. There they found a patio overlooking the marina on Lake Michigan. The evening was beautiful—sunny with low humidity, a warm breeze, and a few wispy clouds roving in the sky.

Brooks pulled Art aside on the way to their table.

"Hey Art. I wanted to tell you how much we've enjoyed our vacation with you. And, you know, I'm really sorry about the other day."

"Don't worry about it. You couldn't have known. Besides, it is what it is, like they say," Art said reassuringly. "And what's with calling me Art? Come on, Brooksy."

They both laughed and joined the others at the table.

The lobster-stuffed mushrooms the group ordered were incredible, followed by tasty pizza to share. Drinks flowed as the group enjoyed their time together.

It was Jessica's job to lead her "band." Sam was bashing away at the drums while Scott, who was barely interested, plucked his bass. Mae was charged with keeping track of Helen, while Tessa, Tori, and Sarah sat together watching the practice.

"Alright guys," Jessica said, stopping the random sounds coming from the boys. "Let's decide on songs to play."

"I want to play 'My Generation' and then smash my guitar," said Scott with a big smile. It was hard to know if he was serious or not.

"We can play it, but you aren't smashing that guitar," stated Jessica firmly.

"Okay, okay, I was just kidding," said Scott with a wink.

"We'll play 'My Generation' first and 'Michelle' last. I think we only need two more songs," said Jessica, trying to come to an agreement quickly so they could start practicing.

"I want to do 'More Than a Feeling'!" declared Sam.

"Ugh!" Sarah blurted out before asking, "That's Boston, isn't it?"

"Yeah, it's Boston. So what?" Sam questioned.

"Ah, nothing really. Only that we had to hear it a bunch on the drive up here because Brooks loves them," Sarah clarified.

"Someone with taste! I love them too!" Sam said. Sarah frowned, realizing they're going to play it after all.

"I want to do 'Love in Vain'," said Scott. That was the only song he knew how to sing.

"Hey, I know that one!" Sarah said, remembering Grandma Elizabeth playing it while she practiced on her toy drum set.

"Oh, great. Now Sarah's putting together our setlist!" Sam said, smiling at her.

"Alright. We have the songs. We'll play 'My Generation' then 'More than a Feeling' followed by 'Love in Vain' and ending with 'Michelle.' Now let's practice!" declared Jessica, ready to get started.

She had a tape player and tapes with their songs on them. She started by finding The Who's "My Generation" and queuing it up. She planned to have them play along with the tape a few times and then play on their own.

Jessica used her electric guitar to blast out the opening chords of the classic song. Sarah was impressed with how well she played. Sam was trying to keep up on drums while Scott looked like he didn't know how to play at all. Sam stopped and got up to show Scott how to play the song. Sam had started playing bass before losing interest and moving to drums. Even so, he was a much better bass player than Scott. While the boys kidded each other, everyone could clearly see Sam was unhappy with Scott. Jessica stayed out of it, although she also knew how to play bass better than Scott.

After playing along with the tape they tried a couple on their own. They were much better with the tape or maybe it was just the tape itself that made them sound better. In any case, they thought they had it down well enough for the show and moved on to the Boston song.

Jessica played her electric guitar again with this one, but giving it a softer sound than the famous band's version. Her singing was also more subdued than the tape. Sam played along with the drums, still seeming a bit slow but passable. Scott again struggled with bass, although this time Sam offered a few words of encouragement—he knew there wasn't anything that could make Scott a better bass player before tomorrow night.

Jessica played her acoustic guitar with "Love in Vain." This one really let her skills shine through. Scott's somewhat exaggerated singing worked well as some sort of junior Mick Jagger. Sam kept time a little better but didn't really add anything to the song. Scott struggled more with the bass guitar than the earlier songs since he was now singing and playing an instrument he didn't know how to play.

"Michelle" highlighted Jessica's guitar playing even more than "Love in Vain." Sam, seeming to get into a rhythm as the practice continued, did his best playing on the drums. Scott, having sung already, was now almost completely checked out. Sam and Jessica knowingly looked at each other with thoughts about whether they would sound better without anyone playing bass.

They finished by playing without the tapes through the four songs. All the girls watching thought they did well. Sarah worked up the nerve to ask Sam if he would mind her playing his drums. He said okay before adding, "Just don't break anything, little one."

Sarah sat on the stool and picked up the drumsticks. Sam showed her how to hold them and then how to play the bass drum with her foot. At first, she just practiced hitting all the drums and cymbals to hear their sounds. Then she played a bit of a shuffle she remembered hearing in Grandma Elizabeth's basement. Both Sam and Jessica immediately took notice.

"Hey, you've played before," stated Sam.

"Well, not really," replied Sarah, adding, "I did use to play around with a plastic drum set when I was a kid."

Now laughing, Sam said, "Ha! When you were a kid! You're still a kid!"

"Yeah, I guess so. I mean when I was a younger kid than I am now."

"Sarah, you said you knew 'Love in Vain,' right?" asked Jessica.

"Yes. I know that one. My grandma used to play it for me. But it's been a long time."

"Oh, don't worry. We're just having fun. You want to give it a try?" Jessica asked.

"Sure, I guess, if it won't bother you guys," replied Sarah.

"I'll play bass. Scott, you just worry about singing," said Sam as he grabbed Scott's bass guitar. Scott looked relieved.

"Fine with me. I can't play anyway," Scott said, stating what everyone else already knew.

Jessica loaded up the tape and hit play. She started the guitar part while Scott offered his best Jagger impression. Sam played bass like they hadn't heard it played this evening. Sarah perfectly duplicated Charlie Watts' entrance to the song. Her timing was flawless. This improvement along with Sam's adequate bass playing, drove the song to heights it had not achieved earlier. Sam and Sarah started watching each other and playing together, something that Sam and Scott never did successfully. Jessica felt and understood this connection which accentuated her guitar playing.

"Wow!" exclaimed Jessica, adding, "Let's do that again! This time without the tape."

Sarah smiled. Mae, Tessa, and Tori all smiled back at her. "You go Sarah!" Tessa shouted.

"I'll have to admit that sounded good. How old are you, kid?" asked Sam.

"Five," Sarah answered with a smile.

"GD. You can play," Sam said, careful not to swear in front of the children.

"Okay. Let's do it again," Jessica commanded as she started the guitar part.

Scott, now energized by not having to play bass, gave his best singing performance yet. Jessica let her fingers go, freely gliding across the guitar, no longer worried about how the band was destroying the song. Now she was enjoying the sounds they were making. Unbelievable, she thought. This was the first time they had played without a tape helping them that sounded like a real song!

"Wow, wow, wow!" exclaimed Jessica when they finished; all the girls watching were loudly clapping and shouting.

"Scott, do you mind if Sarah plays drums with us?" Jessica asked.

"No. Not at all," answered Scott quickly. He didn't have any interest in playing bass and only did so because his siblings needed him to.

"Maybe I could sing 'My Generation'?" Scott asked, since he thought he knew the words to that one well enough.

"Okay, Scott. Let's try it," said Jessica putting in The Who tape. Sarah had never played along with that song. Grandma Elizabeth wasn't a fan of Keith Moon, so she didn't play The Who's music. Jessica hit play and off they went.

Playing along, Sarah felt the chaotic energy of Moon's style. She kept the beat, but with this song she let herself go with the music instead of playing along exactly with the tape. Sam picked up on this and played what he knew was the best bass of his life. Sarah's drums drove the song.

After only one time playing with the tape, they tried it on their own. As they were playing, everyone was looking at one another in amazement. Could this be the same "band" that was playing earlier? No way, they thought. This was a real band! Sarah, now into the music like she had never experienced before, was playing naturally in sync with Sam's bass playing. The song finished with a flourish with Sarah doing her own take on Keith Moon's powerful ending.

Jessica looked around. The energy from the girls watching was amazing. Scott sang well, buoyed along by the sound of the band backing him. Jessica knew she was playing better than ever before.

"Oh my! That was fantastic!" Jessica finally said to more whoops and hollers from the girls.

"Okay, let's try 'More Than a Feeling' now," she declared. This one rocked like the previous songs, so they moved on to "Michelle." Sarah handled the subtle drum parts as well as the rollicking ones from the earlier songs. Then they played the set through twice. Everyone agreed they were ready.

It was a long drive back to the Twin Cities. They had left early so Art could return the van by seven that evening. Most of the adults were hungover after celebrating long into the night with their new cottage friends. They all promised to get together again (a promise often broken when random people connect). The kids had also stayed up late, energized by their successful rock and roll show.

Sarah drifted in and out of sleep. The memories of performing with Jessica, Sam, and Scott filled her head. She felt a joy that she hadn't experienced since banging the plastic drum with Grandma Elizabeth. It energized her to see the kids and adults moving with the music. Even little Helen was bopping along to the beats. The adults stood and clapped at the end, yelling "Encore! Encore!"

Sarah didn't know what it meant until Jessica said, "Let's play one more." They played "My Generation" for the now raucous fans. She and the other kids laughed and told stories about the experience. Sarah couldn't get over how Brooks had jumped up at hearing "More Than a Feeling" and pointed at her and shouted, "I knew you loved that song!"

Somewhere around Eau Claire, they stopped for some fast food. Back on the road, Brooks turned around and asked Sarah, "Did you play 'More Than a Feeling' for me?"

"That's funny. You know I told everyone you had overplayed Boston on the drive up."

"Yeah, I suppose I did. By the way, I know I told you last night, but you can really play the drums."

"Oh yeah, you were great sweetie," added Lydia.

"I loved it!" Melissa said.

"You even surprised me Sarah," Art said.

"Thanks everybody. It was fun," said Sarah, blushing.

"Where did you learn to play like that?" asked Brooks.

"Well, I guess it was from playing a plastic drum set Grandma got for me," replied Sarah.

"Arty, did you know your daughter was a gifted drummer?"

"You know Brooksy," Art replied, "I heard her play that plastic drum set a few times at her grandma's house. She was good. But it's too loud to play at the apartment, so I haven't heard her play for a while. Until last night."

"Wow. She's a natural then. Sarah, you should keep playing," encouraged Brooks.

"Maybe. It sure was fun."

CHAPTER 11
PEOPLE TO PEOPLE

On entering the fifth grade, Sarah was now playing drums in her elementary school band. She still loved it, even while developing other interests—one of which was playing basketball. She was a good shooter along with being able to handle the ball better than most kids her age. There was a hoop behind Maple Manor, and she would practice there by herself for hours at a time.

Grandma Elizabeth continued coming over after school to keep Sarah company. Art was still driving and stopping at Wilebski's for happy hour. He and Lydia had stopped seeing each other, although they remained friendly. Lydia had realized her hope of becoming the full-time dispatcher since the previous dispatcher finally moved on to another job.

Melissa was promoted again in her company. She had broken off her relationship with Brooks and was enjoying being single. She was also now earning a salary of more than six figures. She was proud of herself but found it difficult to share with others, even her mom. She ended up telling Art at Wilebski's. He was thrilled for her and not at all jealous. He didn't share her financial goals, though he wouldn't complain when he would get a raise. A recent increase had lifted him over fifty thousand a year, more than he ever thought he'd make.

Kelly was still traveling here and there, performing as an actor for local theater companies. Art said there was a chance she would be performing at the Chanhassen Dinner Theater in a few months. Sarah was hoping this would come true. She really missed seeing Kelly, but at least she could spend long hours talking with her on the phone.

Sarah had been dominant, or at least as dominant as a ten-year-old could be, at fourth-grade basketball. Her coach at the time called her the "Michael Jordan of the team." Tartan High School had a camp in the summer and LaVonda Chatman, the girls' basketball coach, had talked to Art about having Sarah try out for traveling basketball in fifth grade.

Traveling basketball was a way for kids to play against better competition. There was a cost of several hundred dollars to participate, since traveling sports were run by the local athletic association rather than the area school. Art was concerned about the expense, but he understood the competition was better, and if Sarah wanted to stick with basketball, he wanted to help her.

Around this time, an organization called People to People sent a brochure to Sarah. They must have gotten her name from a list of basketball camp attendees. Sarah was immediately interested in it, since it would mean traveling to Europe or South America with a bunch of kids to play basketball. They represented themselves as sort of a junior Olympics, except with a three-thousand dollar price tag. That was money Art simply didn't have.

Art wasn't sure whether to take Sarah's interest seriously. He thought maybe she would just forget about it. Instead, over the course of the next few weeks, Sarah continued to ask if she could go. She was so persistent that Art eventually gave in and took her to an introductory meeting down in Apple Valley one Saturday morning.

The People to People program was explained. They would travel with several hundred kids aged nine to twelve. This summer's destination was Haarlem in the Netherlands. Once the group arrived in Haarlem, they would meet up with two other groups traveling from the United States. There would be many more groups from various other countries. United States teams would be formed during a two-day camp. The goal was to have equal teams instead of a best-to-worst ranking.

On the drive back to their apartment, Art quizzed Sarah about why she wanted to go.

"Tell me, why is it you want to go play basketball in a foreign country with kids you don't even know?"

"I'll know them once I go."

"Yeah, you know what I mean."

"It sounds like fun. I like playing basketball. It sounds like an adventure."

"Yeah, an expensive adventure."

"They said there was some sort of way to raise money for the trip."

"You're right. Did you hear what you would need to do? You'd need to sell magazine subscriptions to people."

"What's that mean?"

"You would go around and knock on people's doors and ask them to buy these magazine subscriptions. A subscription means that every week or month, whenever the particular magazine comes out, it would be either mailed or made available on the internet to whoever buys the subscription."

"I can do that."

"Oh yeah?" Art said as he considered the seriousness of Sarah's interest. Finally, he said, "Okay, we can give it a try. If you can sell enough to go, then we can talk about it some more."

"Really! I can go!" Sarah said excitedly.

"Well, maybe. I'll learn some more about it. If it checks out and you sell enough, yeah, I guess you can go, if you still want to by then."

"Thank you, Dad! Thank you! Thank you!"

Art was surprised how well Sarah sold those magazine subscriptions. She had knocked on all the doors at the Maple Manor and sold to about half the residents. Many of them would ask, "Are you the girl who's shooting hoops all the time?" She replied, "Yes! That's me!" which was usually followed by a sale. Art had dropped off some forms at the Kare Kabs dispatch office with Lydia. A few of his co-workers bought subscriptions, but he did much better with the forms he dropped off at Wilebski's.

The bartender, Cullen Samuels, an affable, stocky man, made sure to promote Art's daughter's basketball dream. Although Cullen didn't look like a basketball player, he had played through high school and loved it. Art had grown more interested in basketball since Sarah started playing. He had spent some happy hours quizzing Cullen about whichever game was playing on the bar TV.

Others at the bar also took an interest in promoting Sarah's magazine subscriptions. Waitresses Roxanne Thate and Spring Bushorn pushed them on their regular customers. Both were athletes—Roxanne played soccer for Saint Paul Central, and Spring was a runner, even participating in the Twin Cities Marathon.

Another supporter at the bar was the bouncer, Aamir Calder. He was tall with broad shoulders and a thin waist. He had played football at Hamline University, a college in Saint Paul, and now he was taking graduate classes in the hope of achieving his dream of becoming a business leader.

The support of the Wilebski's staff, along with Sarah's own selling, soon pushed her to earn the money she needed for the trip. Art had to decide if he was really going to let his little girl go off to a foreign country without her knowing anyone. He hadn't found any information about People to People to discourage him, and they seemed like a legitimate organization. He asked Melissa to meet him for happy hour at Wilebski's one Friday. He needed some help to decide whether to allow Sarah to go.

Melissa showed up around 5:30, and Art was already there. He was drinking Bell's Two Hearted which had become his favorite beer since the summer trip to Traverse City. Just about every Twin Cities bar was stocked with Two Hearted. Art had taken to drinking beer at happy hour rather than his beloved Irish whiskey. Melissa's drink of choice varied with her moods; today she was drinking chardonnay, which indicated that she was happy.

"Thanks Cullen," Melissa said as Cullen filled a glass of Decoy chardonnay, one of Melissa's favorite less expensive wines. Art signaled that he was ready for another beer.

"So, I've got to decide whether to send Sarah on that basketball trip."

"What's the decision? She earned enough money for it, didn't she? I thought you told me she did."

"Yeah. She did. It's just tough for me to send her on that trip. It's so far away. And without her knowing anyone."

"You know she might be young, but she's mature for her age," Melissa reassured him, adding, "She's way more mature than I was at twice her age. Maybe more mature than I am now!"

Art smiled, just as Cullen arrived with his Two Hearted in a frosty pint glass.

"Sorry for intruding, but I couldn't help hearing your conversation about Sarah's basketball trip," Cullen said, hoping he wasn't meddling.

"Oh, go ahead. What's your opinion? As if I don't know," Art said with a smile. He knew what Cullen thought. If it weren't for Cullen helping sell Sarah's magazine subscriptions, she might not even have had the opportunity to go.

"Okay, I know you know what I think. But since you've brought Melissa here to talk about it, I want her to know too."

"Yes, Cullen! I want to hear what you think," stated Melissa.

"Well, you know I played a little basketball in my day..." said Cullen.

"Oh, you did?" Art said sarcastically, having spent several hours listening to Cullen's stories about his glory days.

"Yes, I did," Cullen said, adding, "and you know playing basketball is one of my best memories of growing up."

"That's interesting to hear. Our parents didn't let me or Kerstin play sports," said Melissa, which was only half true. Her parents didn't *encourage* them to play sports, but they didn't prevent them either. Both she and Kerstin had taken swimming lessons and even competed on the middle school swimming team. They might have continued with it or other sports if they had been interested. Instead, Melissa became interested in boys and parties, while Kerstin focused on her schoolwork. Playing sports was left to others.

"If she wants to go this bad, I think she would enjoy it. It's really a once-in-a-lifetime experience. You never know, it could be the beginning of her playing maybe all the way to college..." Cullen paused, before adding, "Or it could be the end."

Art took a sip of his beer, considering Cullen's words. He was worried about sending his daughter so far away by herself.

"I know. Let's go watch her play in Amsterdam! You and me, Art. Let's go over there!" declared Melissa.

Art laughed. They all knew he couldn't afford to go on a trip like that.

Melissa looked at him. "Don't worry Art. This one's on me. I've always wanted to go to Amsterdam. We'll travel as cheaply as we can. And we get to see Sarah play!"

"Wow. Nice. If he doesn't go, I will!" Cullen said with a laugh, leaving them alone.

"Melissa, that's a wonderful offer. You know I can't take you up on it though," said Art.

"Why not, Art? I can do this for you, and Sarah..." she paused before adding, "and Kerstin."

The mention of her name momentarily rattled Art.

"You know what I mean. I mean, I have all this money now. Money I never expected to have. I might as well spend it on something. I *want* to do this."

Art took a longer sip of his beer, before sitting in silence for a few moments.

"She…she would be proud of Sarah," said Art, looking ahead.

"Yes! Oh my God, yes! She would be *so* proud of her. And you know what? She'd be proud of you too. You've raised her baby, and Sarah has become a wonderful young lady."

Art looked at Melissa and said, "Thanks. I'll give your generous offer serious consideration."

Arriving home, Art could see Sarah outside shooting hoops. Inside, he thanked Grandma Elizabeth for being there for Sarah after school. He then sat down and reviewed the People to People information for what seemed like the hundredth time. Melissa had recently given them her old laptop computer. Art hadn't used it much yet but decided to turn it on and surf the web. This time, instead of researching People to People, he looked into staying in Amsterdam.

A couple of days later, it was decision time. Melissa told him that her offer was still good. Sarah was just as willing to go as she had always been. Art felt bad that he couldn't afford to pay his own way, only having limited savings to contribute. To clear his head before deciding, he turned on the TV. There was George Clooney, Brad Pitt, and Matt Damon walking down a crowded street in Europe, in *Ocean's Twelve*. It was unmistakably Amsterdam. The bikes, the shops, the trams, the people. He found it entertaining, mostly due to the setting. When the movie finished, he thought, *What the hell? Let's go.*

Sarah was thrilled with her dad's decision, while Melissa was surprised and happy. They had several weeks before Sarah was leaving. She would be gone twelve days, while Melissa and Art would follow three days after Sarah left and planned to stay through her last game.

There were four meetings before departure, as a way for the kids to get to know each other. At one of the meetings, Sarah met Tina Wilson. She was about Sarah's height with the same sandy hair color and blue eyes. Tina was from Eagan, a suburb just south of Saint Paul. The two of them bonded quickly and became inseparable.

Melissa's offer to fund her trip with Art turned out better than she hoped. There were discounts available from her consulting firm for various hotels, rental cars, and airlines. They would stay in the Hard Rock American Hotel in the Leidseplein area of Amsterdam. Art knew from his research that this was a lively area. It was within walking distance of several museums, restaurants, and even the famous Amsterdam coffee shop, The Bulldog. Another attraction within walking distance was the Paradiso, an old church that had been converted into a concert venue. Although Sarah would be playing games all around the Netherlands, the deal Melissa got at this hotel was too good to pass up. Art and Melissa, having rented a small Volkswagen Golf, would drive to wherever Sarah was playing.

The weekend before Sarah was leaving, Tina asked her to sleep over. Art thought it was a good idea for Sarah to have a friend ahead of the trip, so he drove her down Saturday morning and planned to pick her up midday Sunday.

Sarah only knew city life, and the drive down Interstate 35E seemed like a long way. She noticed how wide open it was south of Saint Paul. They pulled into a cul-de-sac and into Tina's big driveway in front of a three-car garage. Art was driving a used Nissan Maxima, which had over one hundred thousand miles on it, but still worked and looked decent enough. Tina and her parents were sitting on the big wrap-around porch. There were other homes in the large cul-de-sac with plenty of room between them.

"Sarah!" Tina greeted her new friend. "We are going to have so much fun!"

"Hi Tina! Thanks for inviting me," replied Sarah as they hugged.

"Hi, I'm Mark and this is my wife, Brix," said Tina's dad as he reached his hand out to shake Art's.

Art shook Mark and Brix's hands in response. "I'm glad the girls are getting along so well before their big adventure."

"I heard from Tina that you're going over for a few days to watch them play," said Brix.

"Yes, I am. My sister-in-law and I are going," replied Art.

"That's great! What's your wife think of that?" Mark blurted out.

"Oh, well, my wife passed away when Sarah was three," explained Art.

"I'm sorry," said Mark, who now looked crestfallen.

"Thank you. You couldn't have known. Melissa, my wife's sister, has always been close with us. She really wanted to go, so we decided to go together," Art said.

"How wonderful. Mark and I are going for a few days too," Brix said.

"Really? Maybe we can meet up for a night out over there," suggested Art.

"Yes, we have to!" Mark agreed enthusiastically.

Sarah and Tina had begun moving toward the porch.

"Bye Sarah!" Art called after her.

Sarah turned around and quickly said, "Bye Dad!"

"I'll pick you up about noon tomorrow, okay?"

Sarah grinned and slipped into the doorway with Tina, and they disappeared.

"Well, I guess they're all set," Mark said.

"Yes, it looks like it. See you tomorrow," Art said before getting into his Maxima and driving away.

Sarah and Tina found their way to the backyard where Tina's trampoline was waiting. They both jumped on it and happily bounced around. Sarah had only been on a trampoline in gym class. She found it incredible that Tina could go out and jump on it anytime she wanted. After tiring themselves, they both lied down, looking up at the evening sky.

"Sarah, I'm so glad I met you. I wanted to go but was worried I wouldn't make any friends."

"Me too! We're so lucky to have found each other before we even left."

"You know, I love playing basketball, but I mostly wanted to see the world," Tina explained.

"I did too, although I don't know why. I've barely seen any of Minnesota!" stated Sarah.

"Really? My parents have dragged us to every part of the state," Tina said.

"Us? You have a sister?" asked Sarah, who'd always wanted a sibling.

"Well, a brother. He's two years older than me. We get along pretty good. I sometimes wish he was a sister though."

"I'd take either. Really, I would," Sarah declared.

"Okay, you can have him!" Tina said, and the two friends shared a hearty laugh.

Inside, Tina's brother Kyle was headed to the basement. He was thin with dark, curly hair. When he saw Sarah, he stopped with only a dazed look on his face. Apparently, no one had told him his sister had a friend over.

"Come on, Kyle. Is that any way to welcome Tina's friend?" scolded Brix.

"Ah, hi," Kyle managed.

"Hi, I'm Sarah," she replied softly, before whispering to Tina, "He's cute!"

With that, Kyle opened the basement door and vanished.

"Kyle can be a little shy," Brix said, adding, "You'll see more of him though. He's coming with Mark and me to watch Tina's games. I really hope you two end up on the same team."

"I do too! We really *need* to be on the same team!" yelled Tina.

The two of them stayed up late watching movies and talking. Then they fell asleep on Tina's floor in sleeping bags with the windows open.

When Art came by at noon the next day, he could tell Sarah was exhausted from staying up with her new friend, and he couldn't have been happier.

CHAPTER 12

INHOLLAND

Art took Sarah down to MSP airport. The People to People group had gathered on the lower level, and they were glad when they saw Tina, Mark, and Brix. The girls hugged and started talking about their upcoming trip. This would be the first time Sarah had flown on an airplane. She felt both excited and nervous. Tina, on the other hand, had flown many times before. She enjoyed it, which was comforting to Sarah.

The young women athletes were all wearing their People to People supplied white t-shirts and blue jackets and carrying their blue duffel bags. The coaches and other support staff were wearing white polo shirts and orange jackets and certainly stood out. There was one adult for every ten kids, and it was the parents' task to get their kid to the proper group. Luckily, Tina and Sarah were part of the same group.

"Are you ready to see your little girl off to Europe?" Mark asked Art.

"No," Art said emphatically then grinned, adding, "I'll send her, but I'm not ready for it."

"I feel the same way," agreed Brix.

"I hope we can meet up one of the days we're all over there," Mark said.

"We will, Mark. I gave you Melissa's phone number, didn't I?" Brix reminded her husband.

"Yes, I have it. I sent her a text, so she has mine too," acknowledged Mark.

Just then, the leader of the People to People group asked everyone to be quiet. All eyes focused on the young woman leader named Paige. They had seen her at some of the preparatory meetings but didn't realize she was the leader of the entire group. She rallied the young athletes and then told the parents to say goodbye to their kids. Paige said they would be back in twelve days with a lifetime of memories.

Sarah was in a window seat near the back of the plane. Tina was a few rows up on the aisle. She was able to convince the girl next to Sarah to switch seats with her so the friends could sit together. After watching the ground fade from sight taking off, they both slept until the landing in Boston woke them up. They had a three-hour layover before meeting with an even larger group of People to People kids, ready to fly to Amsterdam. Again, Sarah and Tina were able to get seats together. After an awesome takeoff over the Atlantic Ocean, again they slept until arriving at Schiphol Airport in Amsterdam.

Buses were waiting for the large group of young athletes and their adult supervisors. Sarah and Tina's supervisor was Paige

Horowitz. They recognized her as the leader of the Minneapolis group. Paige gathered her ten athletes together and led them to their bus. She explained that they were going to the Inholland University dorms in Haarlem. They would practice for two days, then pick the teams, practice with their teams, and finally play some games.

Tina leaned into Sarah and said, "I really want to be on your team."

"Me too! I hope we get to play together!" agreed Sarah.

Paige heard them. She didn't say anything, just smiled and helped her group get on the bus.

Everyone was tired, even though most had slept while flying. The landscape was beautiful, and they got to see some of the famous Dutch windmills. Arriving at the dorms, Paige told her group to check the room assignments at a desk in the lobby. Sarah and Tina were disappointed to see they weren't in the same room. Sarah was in 204 with Emilia Caldwell, and Tina in 208 with Sabrina Jones. At least they were on the same floor, with only a few rooms between them.

There was a knock on the door at 7 AM. Sarah was already up.

"Emilia? Emilia? It's time to get up," Sarah said to her new roommate. They had barely introduced themselves before quickly falling asleep the night before.

"Ugh! I want to keep sleeping," Emilia replied in a groggy voice before adding, "I'm not much of a morning person."

Sarah smiled, already getting ready. She never seemed to need much sleep. Emilia forced herself up and began to get ready too.

"I'm going to check on my friend Tina. She's in 208," Sarah said as they left the room. Emilia, still drowsy, offered a half-smile and a nod.

"Tina? Are you up?" Sarah asked, quietly knocking on the door. Sabrina answered, groggily.

"Alright, alright, we're getting up," she said, thinking it was the wake-up call again.

"Oh, sorry, I'm Sarah, Tina's friend."

"Well, hi there. I'm Sabrina. Tina mentioned she had a friend here with her. Lucky."

"Yeah, I guess we are."

Tina came out of her bathroom, dressed and ready to go.

"Sarah! Good morning!" Tina greeted her friend. Like Sarah, Tina didn't need to sleep much. "It's all yours, Sabrina."

"Thank God!" Sabrina said, walking into the bathroom and shutting the door. The friends hugged.

"Tina, this is my roommate, Emilia."

"Hi Emilia! So good to meet you."

"Hi Tina. Good to meet you too. Sorry, but I'm just barely awake."

"That's okay. It was a long day yesterday."

"Sure was. Doesn't look like it affected you two."

Tina and Sarah shared a laugh.

"No, well, it did, I think. The two of us don't sleep much. Maybe that's why we're such good friends," said Tina.

The four of them went down together. At breakfast, the girls got to know more about each other. None of the others had needed to sell magazine subscriptions for the trip. Sarah told them her dad didn't have a lot of money so if she wanted to go, she knew she had to sell those subscriptions. They finished eating and were directed to the gymnasium.

At the gym, players were grouped by position: guards, forwards, and posts. Sarah, Tina, and Emilia were with the guards, Sabrina with the forwards. They were put through various drills by some of the coaches, while the other coaches took notes. After a short break for lunch, they continued until 3 PM when they were led back to the dorms. There would be a sightseeing trip after dinner at 6 PM.

The four new friends walked together on the tour. They found Haarlem to be amazing. It was different than any city they had ever seen. The canals, trams, shops—and bikes, lots of bikes. There was a comfortable vibe to the city that even these youngsters picked up on.

"I *love* this place!" Sarah said after a few blocks.

"Wow, girl! We just got here!" said Sabrina.

"I know. There's something, I don't know…something in the air," Sarah said.

"I won't go as far as loving it yet, but it is lovely," said Emilia.

"You too, Em?" Sabrina joked.

"Come on, roomie. You have to admit it's, well, like Em said, lovely," said Tina, joining the conversation.

"Maybe. There sure is a lot going on. The Dutch are all fit riding around on those bikes," Sabrina said. The other girls nodded in agreement, noticing this too.

"I think I can pick out the tourists," Tina said, adding, "They all look like Coach Finch." The new friends shared a hearty laugh. Coach Finch was one of the coaches putting them through drills.

He was short and pudgy with a round face, thinning hair, and glasses, and looked much older than his forty years.

The next day after the morning practice, the players were sent back to the dorms for lunch and rest. The coaches stayed in the gym and had sandwiches delivered while assigning the players to teams. Their objective was to put together ten evenly matched teams. The goal of the competition was to use sport to relate with kids from other parts of the world. They purposely didn't want to create a team with all the best players on it, and consideration was given to keeping roommates together on the same team, since they already knew each other.

Some player-ranking decisions were easy for the coaches. There was a point guard from Sacramento, Alexis January, who was clearly the best, most aggressive player at the camp. A post player from Atlanta, Georgia, Brittney Jones was considered the best in her field. The coaches decided to group those two together, with eight other average-ranked players to form the Yellowjackets team.

Tina was rated above average and a little higher than Sarah, who was rated just above Emilia. Sabrina was in the top half of the forwards. This helped them be able to stay together on the Cardinals team, with the rest of the team filled with below-average players. Their coach would be the familiar Kevin Finch. Assisting would be Paige Horowitz, the supervisor of the Minnesota contingent. Paige had never played basketball, and only helped coach on previous People to People trips but was enthusiastic and would assist Coach Finch and the girls as best she could.

With the players all assigned to teams, word was sent back to the dorms that the girls should come back to the gym to learn their fate.

The four new friends walked together to the gym. They were nervously silent, knowing they wanted to be playing on the same team together. As the athletes entered the gym, they were told to check the posters on the far wall for team assignments. Once they found their team, they were to stay by that poster. Sarah, Tina, Emilia, and Sabrina gave each other a hopeful look and headed toward the poster wall. The team names, clearly visible, were:

BLUE JAYS, BUMBLEBEES, YELLOWJACKETS,
PANDAS, DALMATIANS, CARDINALS,
GOLDFISH, BUTTERFILES, SUNFISH, PARAKEETS

Some girls were already cheering and hugging after finding their names together on a team.

"None of us are Blue Jays," Sarah said, moving to look at the next list as the others followed along. Nope, they weren't Bumblebees either. She looked at the next poster and frowned. "Ah, we're not Yellowjackets either. I was hoping that would be our team."

Before she could look at the next one, Emilia cried out, "Here I am! And Tina, you're here too. Hey, we're all here. We're the Cardinals!"

The four of them crowded around the poster. Sure enough, all four friends' names were printed in red permanent marker on the Cardinals poster. A group hug followed.

"Who's our coach? I hope it's Coach Brown!" Sabrina said.

Coach Flip Brown was popular with all the players. He was in his thirties, about six feet tall with bushy brown hair and athletic build—basically the opposite of short, pudgy, Coach Finch. Coach Brown had an easygoing manner, and it seemed he was always either giving directions or making wisecracks. The friends took another look at the poster to see who their coach was, and all groaned in unison.

"No! I can't believe it! We get Coach Finch," said Sabrina, obviously disappointed. Just then, they realized Coach Finch was standing right behind them.

"Hello girls."

The girls, now embarrassed, slowly turned around.

"Hi Coach," said Sarah, adding, "looks like we're all Cardinals."

"Yes, that's right. I think we have a good group," stated Coach Finch, ignoring the girls' initial reaction to him.

The girls nodded, and soon all the players were gathered by their team posters. Right next to them were the Yellowjackets. Sabrina nudged Tina when she saw Coach Brown was the Yellowjackets' coach. Tina frowned back at Sabrina.

After a short speech about competing and having fun, the coaches were left to run their individual practices. Coach Finch took his team down to the far end of the court, where they had a half-court area to themselves. He introduced himself and Coach Horowitz, who corrected him and said the team could call her Coach Paige or just Paige. Coach Finch told the team he was Junior Varsity Head Coach and Assistant Head Coach at Monona Grove High School in Madison, Wisconsin. Paige, meanwhile, introduced herself as being from Savage, Minnesota. She apologized that she didn't know basketball very well, but that she would do anything she could to help.

The four friends may have been disappointed not to be on Coach Brown's team, but they were thrilled to have Paige. Tina and Sarah had known of Paige since the preparatory sessions back in Apple Valley, seeing her as the leader of their Minnesota contingent, so having her as a coach on their team was awesome.

Coach Finch may not have had the personality of Coach Brown, but he knew his basketball. He had a gift of being able to work with the young athletes so they would understand what he wanted, without making them feel inept. Paige was great at encouraging the kids, lining them up as Coach Finch wanted, and also excelled at chasing loose basketballs around the gym.

The four friends enjoyed practicing together. They had gone through the camp sessions earlier, but those didn't have a feeling of being on a team. Now, they were openly rooting for each other.

Soon, the first practice was over. They would go back for dinner and another sightseeing walk around Haarlem, while the next day there would be another practice session in the morning, followed by scrimmages with the other teams in the afternoon.

"Girls, we the best team here!" Sabrina confidently stated to her friends the next day. They were sitting in the cafeteria for lunch before the afternoon scrimmages.

"Yeah, we the best!" echoed Emilia.

Sarah and Tina broadly smile and say, "Yeah we are!"

They knew their other teammates weren't as good as the four of them, but they had practiced together as if they had been teammates for years.

Over at another table, Alexis and Brittney were confident their Yellowjackets were the best team. Even knowing the limitations of their teammates, they believed they were the best two players on any team. And they were right.

Coach Finch gathered his team together. They were going to play the Goldfish in their first game. He knew from running drills with everyone that the Goldfish had a couple of good guards along with a decent forward. Finch listed his starting lineup as:

Tina – point guard
Sarah – "2" guard (shooting guard)
Emilia – forward
Sabrina – forward
Carla Henderson – post

Carla was a tall, heavyset girl from Spooner, Wisconsin. She had short blonde hair and a strong personality. The girls had taken note of her preferring to shoot 3-pointers rather than rebound, even though she was by far the best rebounder on the team. She was a good, strong player and, being twelve years old, was a year older than most of the girls.

Bench players included forward Rae Davis who was also from Minnesota. She was almost as tall as Carla but thin with intense, bright blonde hair that showed her Norwegian roots. Rae hadn't played much basketball but had some natural abilities for rebounding and scoring when she was close to the basket. She also had a sharp sense of humor, often asking joke questions to Coach Finch. He eventually caught on and knew to expect her wacky questions.

Another one was guard/forward Sharon Beckers from Las Vegas. She was the granddaughter of an American man and a Japanese woman and like Rae possessed a quick wit but was utterly serious when practicing or playing.

Celica McCabe was a short, overweight guard from Seattle, and while she loved basketball she hadn't played much. She was the class clown of the team, able to imitate all the players and coaches (notably Coach Finch), not only how they talked but also how they dribbled, shot, and played basketball. This quickly endeared her to her teammates and coaches.

The Cardinals started slowly against the Goldfish that first scrimmage. Soon though, the four friends found their rhythm. Coach Finch subbed out Carla for Rae. This turned out to be key to getting the best out of the team. Rae played post as she was coached, rather than drifting out to the 3-point line like Carla. On the bench, Coach Finch explained the importance of rebounding the ball to Carla. He said once she rebounded it, she could put it back up. It was like receiving a pass. Carla would argue that she was a good 3-point shooter, so Coach Finch did his best not to hurt her confidence.

Everyone got to play for about the same amount of time, even Celica. Coach Finch would tell Paige his thoughts on the different players and how they performed together with various teammates. They both could see that, even with the best efforts to keep the teams equal, their Cardinals team might well be the best of the bunch.

The coaches were told to keep the focus on players giving their best effort, and not keep score. Even so, all the players knew the score. After about ten minutes, the teams rotated so that all of them would play each other that afternoon. The Cardinals only got better as the session progressed. After flushing the Goldfish, they easily routed the rest of the teams, leaving only the Yellowjackets left to play. The Cardinals heard the Yellowjackets with Alexis and Brittney had also easily defeated the other teams. For a competition that wasn't supposed to be keeping score, everyone in the gym knew exactly what was happening.

After a short break, the Yellowjackets and Cardinals gathered on the designated court. Coach Brown came over to say hello to the Cardinals players, his natural charm on full display as it had been in the group practice sessions. Likewise, Coach Finch acknowledged the Yellowjackets, albeit lacking Coach Brown's charisma. The coaches met at mid-court to talk privately away from their players.

"Looks like you ended up with a good group, Kevin."

"Flip," Coach Finch said with nod. "Yeah. Same for you."

"Well, at least I have two exceptional players. It's all about building skills and having fun, right?" said Flip with a smile.

They both knew that was the goal of the program, even if neither minded having one of the better teams.

"You know, Coach, maybe we should make a little wager on this scrimmage," suggested Flip with a wink. "How about if the Yellowjackets win, you run a killer? I'll do the same if the Cardinals win."

Coach Finch looked surprised. Apparently, Flip wasn't kidding. Killers were an exhausting drill for conditioned athletes, and even more so for out-of-shape coaches.

"I don't know, Flip. How would that look to the girls?" asked Coach Finch.

"Oh, come on Kevin. The girls all know who's winning anyway," stated Flip, winking. Coach Finch was confident in his team, but he was reluctant to flaunt the goals of the program, especially so obviously on the first day of scrimmages.

"How about this—we rotate all our players so everyone has some playing time. Then we'll finish with our best group for the last five minutes. The contest will be just those five minutes," suggested Coach Finch.

"Um, I like that, Kevin. Yeah, I like that. You're on!" acknowledged Flip.

The two coaches shook hands and walked toward their respective teams. The players had been watching the coaches interact, and rumors in both groups began to fly. The coaches didn't say anything, but just had their teams begin warmups like usual.

As the Cardinals were doing a layup drill, Paige leaned into Coach Finch and asked, "What's happening?"

"Well, the Yellowjackets want to have a friendly competition. Although if we lose, I'm the one who has to pay." He then explained the bet and how they'd play.

"I don't know, Kevin. We're supposed to be building camaraderie," said a concerned Paige.

"I know, I could excuse it by saying it was his idea, which it was by the way, but these are all basketball players. They might be young, but they want to compete. We're fortunate enough to have one of the better teams. You've seen the other teams—the Yellowjackets are the only one who could play a competitive scrimmage with us."

While Paige was listening, she looked over at the Cardinals warming up. They were all chattering and encouraging each other.

Then she glanced toward the Yellowjackets who were doing the same. Both these teams looked like they had played together for much longer than an afternoon scrimmage session.

Somehow, through the luck of trying to pick even teams, they had instead put together two superior teams. Sure, they had good players, but the difference looked to be the chemistry of the personalities.

"Okay, Coach Finch, I think I understand," said Paige, leaving to run the next warm-up drill for her team.

The Cardinals started the same group as they had all afternoon. Rae, recognizing she had outplayed Carla but still was starting the game on the bench said, "Hey Coach. Sorry I'm such a slouch." Coach Finch just smiled at her, having adjusted to her witty banter. As everyone suspected, Alexis and Brittney both started with the Yellowjackets.

Both teams were a little ragged those first few minutes. Although the other players on the Yellowjackets weren't of the caliber of their two stars, they complemented them well. They ran an offense that basically had Alexis handle the ball and either drive to shoot or drive and pass to Brittney. Defensively, they played a zone, where the goal is to prevent close-range baskets by forcing your opponent to shoot further from the basket. The Cardinals only played man-to-man defense, which meant they would match up to an opposing player and guard that player. It took more skill and effort to play man-to-man, but it can be tough, especially when there were exceptional players on the other side.

The Cardinals quickly found that Alexis and Brittney were tough to match up against. Tina started out guarding Alexis and Carla took on Brittney. As Coach Finch substituted others in, he pulled Sarah, Tina, and Emilia over to talk about how to guard Alexis. His plan was to try to make the other players score rather than the two Yellowjackets stars. He always wanted a double team on Alexis. Whichever girl wasn't part of the double team would be ready to help if Alexis were to escape.

He then talked to Sabrina. He wanted her to match up with Brittney. Sabrina was more athletic than Carla, which gave her a better chance. The same double team idea would be used if she got the ball. Either Carla, Rae, or Sharon, whoever was in the game and positioned the best, would leave their player and help defend Brittney.

As the teams substituted, it was clear the starting fives for each team were superior to the rest of the rosters. The Cardinals were better whenever the Yellowjackets had either Alexis or Brittney on the bench. But, when those two were playing, no matter the combination for the Cardinals, it looked like the Yellowjackets were better. Coach Brown blew his whistle.

"Okay teams! That was fantastic! We have a lot of great players here!" he shouted then looked to Coach Finch with a slight nod, who returned the signal.

"We'll take a short break and then play a final five minutes," added Coach Brown. The teams then gathered at their respective benches.

"What we doin' now, Kevin?" Rae quipped, sensing something was happening.

"Well Rae, we're going to play us some basketball!" replied Coach Finch with a smile.

Something about the way he said it caught the attention of the rest of the girls.

"Coach, come on, what's up?" Sarah echoed Rae's question.

"Well, Sarah, Rae, and Cardinals…" The team all leaned in to listen, Coach Paige included, as Coach Finch continued, "We are going to play a five-minute game against those Yellowjackets."

The Cardinals erupted with whoops and hollers, jumping up and down excitedly and hugging one another. Coach Finch and Paige were surprised by the team's reaction to a competitive game against an opponent that looked to be very strong.

On the other bench, Coach Brown hadn't told his team in those terms about the upcoming five-minute "game." His team, seeing the reaction from the Cardinals bench, turned back to their coach.

"What was that? What's going on, Flip?" Alexis questioned.

"Looks like those Cardinals want a game!" was all Flip said. His team knew exactly what he meant and began their own whooping and hollering and hugging.

Several coaches had been on previous People to People trips but had never seen anything like this at the scrimmage. Some teams were done for the session and were about to leave. Instead, they circled the court where the upcoming game was about to start. Coach Brown and Coach Finch asked a couple of the other coaches to referee so they could be on the bench with their teams.

Although this sort of game wasn't supposed to be part of the People to People experience, this year they happened to have selected two teams that were far superior to the rest. Since they had never re-picked teams after the initial selection, these teams were going to stay as they were.

The rules were that 2-point baskets counted as 1 and 3-pointers as 2. There would be no free throws. If a player was fouled, their team would keep possession. After three fouls, a player would need to sit out the rest of the game. Each coach had one timeout. It was a five-minute running time except for timeouts. The coaches gave their last bits of wisdom to their teams and the starters took the floor. Both benches cheered loudly.

"You know, I'm not sure if I'll be able to get everyone in," Coach Finch said in a low voice, leaning into Paige.

"Oh, come on Coach. You can get them all in. Do it early then finish with your best group," replied Paige.

"Why Coach Paige! I thought you didn't know basketball!" a surprised Coach Finch replied, looking straight at her. They shared a laugh before focusing on the game that had just started with a jump ball.

Brittney won the jump as she tapped it to Alexis. Alexis drove in toward the basket right by Tina. Sarah was a half-step slow going over to help, leading to an easy basket for the Yellowjackets. The Cardinals didn't fare as well with their first possession. Tina missed a jump shot and since Carla had been outside by the 3-point line Brittney got the uncontested rebound. A quick pass to Alexis, who drove in for an easy bucket. This unfortunate start for the Cardinals continued until it was 5-0 for the Yellowjackets. Coach Finch called his only timeout. He decided to rotate Sarah, Tina, and Emilia in two spots and Carla, Rae, and Sharon in one spot. The other two spots would be filled with reserves until everyone played for at least thirty seconds. This included Celica, who was a great cheerleader but their weakest player.

This strategy worked partly because Coach Brown also subbed in his other players. He always kept either Alexis or Brittney on the court while briefly resting the other. The few moments one of them was on the bench helped the Cardinals get closer. Leading into the last minute, Coach Brown called his timeout. The score was 9-6 in favor of the Yellowjackets. Coach Finch sent in four of his starters, Sarah, Tina, Emilia, and Sabrina but chose to send in Rae instead of Carla. Not playing with the other starters upset Carla, but she kept it to herself as best she could.

The Yellowjackets had the ball. Alexis drove in again but this time passed to Brittney for an easy basket. 10-6. Time was running low. Sarah brought the ball down and saw Tina cut open to the right corner. Sarah passed the ball right on target to Tina's hands. Tina faced the basket and shot.

SWISH! A 3-pointer, well, in this game a 2-pointer.

It was 10-8 now with about thirty seconds left. Alexis took a big step toward the basket. Both Sarah and Tina went with her, hoping to cut her off from an easy bucket. This time though, it was a fake. Alexis stepped back behind the 3-point line and shot. All Sarah and Tina could do was watch and hope they would get a chance for a rebound. They knew if this shot went in, the game was all but over.

The court was now surrounded by players from other teams and fans (mostly the players' families) whose games had finished. What had started as a quiet scrimmage between the two teams was now a spirited happening. Various teams had sided with either the Cardinals or Yellowjackets—maybe because they knew one of the players or liked one of the coaches better, or maybe just because they liked one team name better than the other.

As Alexis shot flew toward the basket, the gym grew quiet. The shot looked perfect…instead, it was almost perfect. As it approached the hoop, it hit the back rim bouncing high in the air. It hung there for what seemed like an eternity before coming straight down. Watching, Sarah and Tina both thought it was going to drop right through the basket. Somehow though, it grazed the back rim, but instead of flying up in the air like before, it bounced in ping-pong fashion forward hard off the front rim then again hard off the backboard and finally over the front rim.

Rae had positioned herself perfectly to jump and try to grab the rebound. Brittney wasn't far away and moved to jump for it too. Rae grabbed the ball and held on tight. She kept it in her two hands in front of her face like Coach Finch had taught her. Brittney was behind her and tried to grab the ball as best she could. It was a foul known as an "over the back." A rebounder can't reach over the back of an opposing player to get a rebound. In this game though, there was no foul called. The nervous referees didn't want to be the cause of the outcome.

Rae turned and used a pivot move she learned from Coach Finch to free herself and the ball from Brittney. She noticed Emilia a few feet away, her hands ready for a pass. Rae passed the ball to Emilia who passed to Sarah. Sarah drove toward the top of the key, ready to shoot as she saw Tina break open on the right side of the court just like before. Sarah again passed perfectly to Tina's ready hands. Tina faced the basket and shot.

10-10! The game was tied!

There were only fifteen seconds left. No timeouts, and the clock was running. Brittney gathered the ball and passed it over to Alexis. They could still win if Alexis could drive in for another layup. Sarah had noticed Alexis often dribbled only with her right hand when driving hard to the basket. Sarah decided to lunge at the ball as Alexis was dribbling, rather than position herself to stop her drive. It was a risky move. If she failed, Alexis would have a clear lane to the basket. Sarah quickly swiped at the ball, moving her feet as fast as she could. The ball came loose from Alexis' strong hands. Sarah was able to gather it in with her left hand and start dribbling toward the basket. As she moved past the top of the key, she could see Brittney there in the lane moving toward her. Instinctively, Sarah stopped just short of the free throw line and took a jump shot. BUZZ! The timer went off with everyone's eyes focused on the ball as it seemed to hang in the air, then... SWISH! She made it! The Cardinals won 11-10! The team rushed and swarmed Sarah.

"I can't believe it! I can't believe it!" Sarah yelled as the Cardinals piled on each other.

That night the Cardinals and the Yellowjackets gathered in Tina and Sabrina's room. They had a good time laughing and playing music. The game they played that afternoon would be the only time these two teams played against each other. The rest of the trip, they would be playing teams from other countries. Alexis joked that Sarah had fouled her. Rae, for once, wasn't joking when she claimed Brittney did foul her. Celica imitated Coach Brown running the killers. Then she pretended to be Coach Finch if it would have been him running the killers, making everyone laugh uncontrollably.

As it grew late, they took turns playing their favorite music. Tina played Taylor Swift's *1989*. They all danced and sang to "Shake It Off." Emilia followed with Lady Gaga's hits including "Poker Face." They all mugged their best poker faces for that one. Sabrina played her Jay-Z best of with "Empire State of Mind." Brittney played Rihanna's "Umbrella."

After those two, Paige came to the door. She was going to have them quiet down and turn down the music. Instead, when she saw how much fun they were having, she joined the party! She even played Madonna's "Vogue." Alexis chose Carly Rae Jepsen's "Call Me Maybe." That brought Coach Finch to the door. He was glad everyone was having fun and even surprised to see Paige with them. Even so, he asked them to try to ramp it down (they didn't).

That was just in time for Sarah's turn. She played her Howlin' Wolf tape. The other kids had never heard anything like it and couldn't believe she liked that type of music. Sarah didn't care. She'd sing along, getting Tina, then Sabrina and Emilia to join in, and finally even Alexis and Brittney. Celica was the best at mimicking Howlin' Wolf's unique singing style. She sang "Wang Dang Doodle" as loud as she could using the TV remote as a mic while prancing around the room.

They rolled around laughing, laughing as hard as any of them could ever remember.

CHAPTER 13
ART AND MELISSA

Sarah had been in the Netherlands for a few days when Art and Melissa began their trip. The two would fly to Newark and then a few hours later fly to Amsterdam's Schiphol Airport. They were traveling light after hearing some horror stories of people losing their checked bags. Each would be taking a large duffle bag with a smaller backpack. They were thrilled to see an airport bar right next to their departing gate.

"Two Heinekens!" Melissa said, excitedly ordering for them both.

"Yes, let's get in the spirit!" Art said, adding, "I never drank much Heineken. Too expensive. Plus, I swear it's skunky sometimes."

"Green bottles," stated Melissa shaking her head.

"What?"

"Yeah, it's the green bottles that make it skunky."

"Sure, Melissa. Green bottles. Right."

"I'm serious! Paul, a beer nerd at the office, was trying to impress me with his knowledge."

"You have a lot of winners at that place."

"Yeah a few," conceded Melissa with a chuckle. The bartender delivered two green 12 oz bottles of Heineken. Fortunately, these weren't skunky, adding to the good feeling about their trip.

"Cheers!" Art said, tipping his bottle toward Melissa's.

"Cheers! Can't wait!" replied Melissa. They both took healthy drinks from their green bottles.

"Melissa?" Art said, looking seriously at his travel companion.

"Yes?"

"Are you sure you're okay staying in the same room?"

They had booked one room with two double beds to save costs. They were something like brother and sister, yet not brother and sister at all. Even so, Art didn't want Melissa to feel uncomfortable sharing a room with him.

"Yes, I'm sure. Come on, Art. We already went over this."

"Alright. I just wanted to be sure." The bartender was cleaning just to his right. Since they had both nearly finished their beers, Art waived his green bottle and said, "We'll have two more of these."

The landing in Newark was a little bumpy. Apparently, there was a storm moving in. After deplaning, they again found themselves at an airport bar. It was a few hours before their flight left for Amsterdam. They hoped the storm wouldn't slow them down. Arriving at the bar, this time Art ordered the Heinekens.

"You know, Art?"

"What's that?"

"This one does taste a little skunky," Melissa said, making a yucky face.

"Let me try it," Art said then took a sip from Melissa's green bottle.

"Um. Maybe. I can't really tell."

"Okay then, let's switch bottles," Melissa offered.

"Sure thing," he replied, and they swapped bottles.

"Have you heard from Sarah?" asked Melissa.

"No. With the time difference it's late over there by the time I'm home from work. I hope she's doing all right."

"I'm sure she's okay. I was just wondering. She's so mature, that girl, you know?"

"Yeah, I know." Art looked down suddenly deep in thought about how Kerstin would have loved how grown-up her little girl was now. Sensing this, Melissa put her hand on Art's shoulder. After a short time, Art looked up.

"To Sarah!" he said, raising his green bottle toward Melissa. She clinked his bottle.

"Yes, to Sarah!" she toasted. "Did you have a chance to look into what else is happening when we're over there?" Melissa asked.

"Some. There's a concert place called the Paradiso close to the hotel. Sounds cool. It was an old church that's been converted to a concert venue," replied Art.

"Cool. Who's playing while we're there?"

"That I don't know. I'll see if I can find out when we get there. We are close to a few museums and nightlife. There's a Hard Rock Café on a canal. Even a casino."

"Maybe you could win enough playing poker to finance another trip," Melissa joked, knowing Art wasn't a gambler.

"Not me! You could try it, but not me."

"I know. Just kidding," Melissa said with a grin. She then asked a question she hoped he would think was funny…

"Any high bridges over there?"

Art, having just taken a drink of beer, spit some out.

"Whoa, man, sorry. I wasn't expecting that question!" said Art.

"Oh sorry, just kidding," said a now sheepish Melissa.

They sat in silence for a few moments before she turned the conversation in a different direction, asking, "So, Art, are you seeing anyone now?"

Art, wiping his face, turned and smiled smugly at Melissa. "No. No I'm not," adding, "Right now."

"I didn't think so," said Melissa, who wasn't seeing anyone either. Although she still would hook up with Brooks, her date from the Traverse City trip years ago. Neither had yet to find a long-term partner. She decided to keep her relationship, if that's what it was, with Brooks to herself since she wasn't emotionally attached to him, or at least that's what she told herself. Art wasn't continuing the conversation. She wondered whether he knew of her situation or if maybe he didn't care. Or maybe he was taken aback by her high bridge question.

"Of course, I'm still on my own, but you probably knew that. I don't think I'm meant to be hitched," said Melissa.

"Ha! Yeah, I don't think I am anymore either," said Art not having observed Melissa's struggles with her half of the conversation. The gate attendant came on the intercom to let everyone know the storm was circling around the airport. They planned to have everyone board the plane and then decide if they could take off.

"Oh, great. Now we have to outrun a storm!" Art said, throwing back the rest of his Heineken. Melissa nodded and downed her beer.

Melissa sat in the window seat and Art the aisle. They were about halfway back on the Airbus 330, glad to be by themselves in the two seats on the side rather than stuffed in a middle row. After the plane was boarded, the pilot came on to say the storm was still coming in, but they were going to try to depart before it stopped them.

"Did he say 'try'?" Art whispered to Melissa.

"Yes," she replied with a hint of nervousness.

The doors were closed and as it pulled away from the gate, the flight attendants gave their preflight talk along with the usual pointing out the exits and demonstration of how to use the oxygen masks. After which, they took their seats and fastened their seat belts. There was some quiet talking along with the sounds of children. There was a baby behind them who wasn't too happy about the prospect of flying through a severe storm.

"I know how that baby feels," Art said.

"I'm sure they know what they're doing," Melissa said, trying to reassure her companion.

The airplane turned and started down the long runway. It was now pitch black outside. The airplane lifted off, then immediately banked hard to Art's side. He suddenly looked straight down at the ground.

"Oh boy," he muttered, thoughts running through his head about whether it was such a good idea to go watch Sarah play. Melissa grabbed his hand to try to calm him, or maybe it was to calm herself.

The plane then turned and felt like it was headed almost straight up. They were high in the sky, surrounded by dark clouds, and couldn't see anything. Even so, it was smooth for the time being. A few minutes later the smooth flight came to an abrupt halt. It felt like a giant toddler was shaking the plane. There were some gasps from other passengers. Art put his arm around Melissa, and they held on to each other as the violent jolts pummeled the plane. The pilot comes on the intercom.

"Hello from the flight deck. I know this is uncomfortable for you. We should be out of the worst of this turbulence in about a half hour."

Art and Melissa both exchanged unimpressed glances with one another.

The pilot continued, "We were lucky to get out of Newark when we did."

Lucky, really? Art and Melissa didn't need to talk. They knew what each other was thinking.

"All air traffic has been halted. No more takeoffs or landings, probably for a couple of hours."

Yeah, lucky to be in this flying maraca than be back at that airport bar!

"We are hoping for a smooth flight after this initial disturbance."

With that, the pilot went silent. He wasn't the only one hoping for a smooth flight. Art could see the flight attendants looked concerned. They were all in this together. The flight path was on almost all the screens of the in-seat monitors. There were a few people watching movies or TV shows. It looked like an *Avengers* movie on one and a *Manifest* TV episode on another. The plane continued to tremble.

Forty minutes went by without the storm letting up. They were now north of Boston along the coast of Maine. Art and Melissa had loosened their hold on each other. Unbelievably, they had somehow gotten used to the enormous plane shaking like a toy.

The pilot came back on the intercom.

"Well folks, as you know we haven't outrun the storm yet."

Yes, everyone was well aware of that.

"We should be out of it in a few more minutes."

There was a long pause and a few more bumps.

"We will be flying up the coast of Cana—"

He abruptly stopped as, just then, the plane began a terrifying free fall. Some items passengers had with them flew to the ceiling of the plane. It felt like a rollercoaster ride falling from the highest point. An awful enough feeling made worse being on an airplane thirty-thousand feet in the air. Melissa once again held tightly onto Art, as he did her. Were they going down? Just as suddenly as they fell, there was a loud BOOM! It felt like the plane hit some sort of floor. Then quiet. What was happening? Were they crashing? A few of the longest minutes went by, giving everyone a chance to see their lives pass in front of their eyes.

The pilot finally returned.

"Well folks I hope everyone is okay back there. The flight attendants will be around to check on you as soon as it is safe for them to do so. We just flew out of the storm. It should be smooth sailing the rest of the trip."

After a momentary pause, there was loud applause in the cabin. The pilot returned.

"We feel the same up here," acknowledging he had heard the noise from the passengers before adding, "I must tell you that we are assessing any damage that may have occurred on that bumpy ride."

Everyone again fell silent. Confused looks passed between the passengers. What did that mean? The flight attendants looked baffled too. The pilot came back.

"I don't mean to alarm you. Everything appears to be fine at this point. If we do find a problem, we may need to land in Goose Bay, Labrador. I will let you know as soon as we know more."

What? Goose Bay? Where is that? Art and Melissa looked at each other, both puzzled by what was happening.

"Melissa, I'm not sure what that means. If we get stuck in Canada somewhere, maybe we won't even get to Amsterdam in time to see Sarah."

"I know, I know. Let's not worry too much. We'll make it. That's what I'm going to think. We're going to make it. Positive energy, you know?"

Art smiled as they loosened their grip on each other. The plane was now flying smoothly through the clear night sky. Nearly twenty minutes later, the pilot returned.

"Okay folks. We have the go-ahead to continue to Amsterdam."

Another loud outburst of applause came from the passengers. The pilot didn't add anything more. Soon the seatbelt sign was turned off and the flight attendants were checking on the passengers. Melissa lay her head on Art's shoulder and just before falling asleep she whispered, "See ya, Goose Bay."

It was a smooth landing, leaving the rough start to the flight as a terrifying memory. It was nine in the morning and they had flown overnight, sleeping most of the way, and now feeling as refreshed as had been possible. After deplaning, they followed the signs to the rental cars, having rented from some European company called SIXT because Melissa got a big discount through her work. Before going to the counter, they bought coffee from a nearby Starbucks, appreciating the familiar brand in a faraway place.

After a short wait, they were off in their Volkswagen Golf. It was a small car, but since they didn't bring many bags and didn't anticipate driving anyone else around, it suited their needs. Art asked if Melissa wanted to drive some.

"Sure, Art. You're the professional driver and think I want to drive?" she replied.

"That's fair. Just thought I'd let you know you're welcome to drive."

Leaving the airport, it seemed like they would have an easy time driving around the Netherlands. But as soon as they approached Amsterdam and began navigating to their hotel, this sense of comfort disappeared. Suddenly there were narrow one-way roads and bikes everywhere. And trams, lots of them. Melissa could see even her professional driver was tense. She had the navigation on her phone, while Art tried to avoid the varied obstacles.

The directions to the hotel felt like they were being led in circles. Finally, the phone said they had arrived. Art pulled in, deciding to valet-park even though it would add to the cost of the trip. There was no way they wanted to hunt around for a parking spot when they were barely able to find the hotel. Gathering their few bags, Art gave the keys to the valet and went to check-in.

Armond Uherek was the hotel clerk who also functioned as the concierge. He was about six feet tall, thin with short brown hair and a wispy brown mustache. He had a quick wit while trying to keep all the guest check-ins and check-outs straight.

"*Hallo, hoe kan ik u helpen*?" he said to Art and Melissa while appearing to be doing two or three other things at the same time.

"Oh. Sorry, we don't speak Dutch," replied Melissa.

"No problem, young lady!" Armond said, immediately switching to perfect English.

"Oh, okay, glad you speak English," Melissa said.

"Of course! How could I not with such lovely English-speaking guests staying at our *fantastisch* hotel!" He effortlessly sprinkled a Dutch word in the middle of his English sentence. Melissa couldn't tell if he was legitimately charming or just sort of smarmy.

"We're here checking in under Melissa Foley," she replied.

"Hmm, under Miss Foley. Yes, yes, I'll check. Under Miss Foley, you say. Sounds wonderful," he said with a smug look. "Here you are Miss Foley. Unfortunately, your room won't be ready until 3 PM this afternoon." It was just about 11 AM. He continued, "You and your guest," Armond acknowledged Art for the first time, "are welcome to leave your luggage with us. We'll keep it safe for you until you can check-in."

Walking out of the hotel, Art looked at Melissa and said, "What was that? I think that dude likes you."

"Oh Art. He's gay."

"What? How do you know that?"

"Oh, I just know," she said. In fact, she wasn't sure but had her suspicions.

They walked out to the overcast day. There was a beautiful fountain in front of the hotel, along with an outdoor patio with table service. There was a large area with rows of tables and chairs just across the street. The individual restaurants had seating extended across the area parallel to one another.

"I'm hungry. Let's eat," stated Melissa.

They took a seat at what they soon learned was the Café in the City. They hadn't eaten much on the flight over, since the meal served on the plane was some disgusting matter masquerading as a breakfast sandwich. Now, they could either have breakfast or lunch.

A waitress stopped by their table, saying, "*Goede dag*," and handed them menus. Again, the Americans apologized.

"That's okay. My name is Nadine. Would you like anything to drink?"

Art looked at Melissa, wondering if it was too early for alcohol.

"Hello Nadine, we'll have two Heinekens," Melissa answered, adding, "in bottles."

"Very well. Thank you." And with that, Nadine headed off to fetch their drinks.

"Beer already, Melissa?"

"Yes. We're on vacation! Besides, we have to see if the Heinekens are skunky over here."

Nadine brought over two charming little 7 oz bottles of Heineken.

"Are you ready to order some food?" asked Nadine.

"Yes, we are. I'll have the Dutch breakfast with scrambled eggs and bacon," Melissa said, while Art ordered a cheeseburger with fries, deciding to play it safe.

"Very well. Thank you," said Nadine, taking the menus with her.

The two sat there and looked around at their new surroundings. There were bikes whizzing around everywhere among the many people walking. Chiming trams went by every few minutes, sometimes two at a time.

"Cute little bottle. And it tastes fresh," Melissa said.

"Makes sense since they brew it here."

"You know, they don't actually brew it in Amsterdam," said Melissa.

"What?"

"No really. Beer nerd Paul told me that," replied Melissa.

"But there's a brewery nearby here. I saw online there are tours. I was hoping we could go," said Art.

"Yeah, there's a brewery. They just don't brew beer there anymore. I guess. Or maybe Paul's full of shit. I don't know," joked Melissa.

"Interesting. Either way, it was the right order. The only problem is I need another one now," said Art, having quickly enjoyed the tiny Heineken.

Before long, Nadine arrived with their food.

"Thank you, Nadine. We'll take two more Heinekens, although we'll have draft this time," Melissa said.

"Very well. Thank you," Nadine said, taking their small bottles with her.

After she left, Melissa turned to Art and said, "Very well. Thank you," in her best impression of their waitress. Art laughed.

"Oh, come on. Maybe she doesn't know much English."

"Maybe. I'm just kidding. I'm glad everyone speaks such good English here. I was thinking we should have learned a little Dutch, but it doesn't look like we need to."

After their meal, the pair started exploring the area. Art quickly discovered the Bulldog Palace. It had a bar upstairs and a coffee shop downstairs. Coffee shops in Amsterdam didn't just sell coffee, also offering marijuana in various forms.

"See that, Melissa?"

"What?"

"That's The Bulldog coffee shop."

"Oh, yeah. Looks cool."

"Are you thinking of smoking any pot while we're here?"

"Um, well, it's legal. So why not?"

Art had smoked a little dope but had mostly stuck to alcohol with his beer and whiskey, along with an occasional cigarette. He didn't know if Melissa had smoked pot. In fact, she had started back in high school and continued as she grew older. Despite not being a regular smoker, she would occasionally spend a weekend getting high.

"I guess so. When in Rome. Although we're not in Rome," replied Art with a chuckle.

They continued walking, getting used to dodging bicycles and trams.

"See there?" Art said, pointing out the Paradiso, "That's the concert venue I mentioned. It was converted from a church."

"Cool. Look at you with your local knowledge. You did do some research, didn't you? Glad you're putting that laptop to good use."

"Thanks again for it."

"No problem. Let's look at the posters. Maybe there's a concert while we're here."

There were a variety of posters on the side of the charming building, and while they didn't recognize most of the bands, the one they did was for Chum Fella. They both knew Chum was a famous blues guitarist who'd played with Howlin' Wolf for a short time.

"How about that?" Art said. "I saw him open for Clapton once. He was good. Maybe we should go."

They continued their walk, first noticing a large casino and then the Aran Irish Pub. As they got closer, they noticed a large street chess set with two people drifting around the board playing as spectators watched.

"Look at that. Let's check it out," said Art.

They walked over and watched the players first study the board and then lift the large chess piece they wanted to move with two hands, carrying it over to its new square. The two of them had never seen anything like it.

"Think they're any good?" asked Melissa.

"Beats me. They're better than me, I'm sure," replied Art.

Next, they noticed the Hard Rock Café a short distance away.

"Let's check that place out," Melissa said.

"Hoping to see your friend from the hotel, are you?" joked Art.

"Very funny. Let's go."

They both had been to the short-lived Hard Rock Hotel in the Mall of America. The atmosphere was cool with rock music always playing. Melissa's dad had brought back Hard Rock t-shirts for everyone when he had traveled to London once. Melissa and her sisters always loved those t-shirts.

This café was like the Mall of America one, except this one was right on the Singelgracht Canal. It was now 1:30 PM, and they had another hour and a half to go before they could check into the hotel.

"Let's have a drink outside on the canal!" declared Melissa.

"Okay, why not?" replied Art, feeling more tired by the minute.

They sat down and ordered drinks.

"You must be planning on crashing out if we ever get our room," Melissa said, after noticing Art went for whiskey this time.

"You got that right, Melissa. I'm going right to sleep if your boyfriend Armond lets us into that place."

"Um, okay, maybe I'll sneak off with Armond…" she said with a smile.

The pair thoroughly enjoyed watching the long canal boats with their tourists passing by, mingling with smaller boats—everyone having the time of their lives. It was a magnificent place to be in the world at that moment. They sat there quietly, sipping their drinks, feeling like they were in some sort of trance. Finally, 3 PM arrived. They paid their bill and walked back to the hotel.

"Miss Melissa! Are you," Armond greeted them, "and your guest ready to check-in?"

"Yes, my dear Armond. We are," Melissa answered Armond sardonically.

Their room was on the second floor with a view facing the same Singelgracht Canal they had just been watching a little further down at the Hard Rock Café. The room was small by American standards but nice enough.

Art changed into some sweats and lied down, falling asleep immediately. Melissa put some of her things away, then booted up her laptop. She didn't intend to work much on vacation, but she hadn't risen in her company by not paying attention to what was going on. After scanning her email and surfing a few websites, including the expected weather for the next few days, she shut the computer off and fell asleep quickly.

The two of them slept through until 6 AM the next day. After showering and getting dressed for the day, they took out a map and planned their rendezvous with Sarah. They hoped to find her at the Hotel NH Noordwijk. In between games, Art and Melissa planned to take a trip to the ocean since it wasn't far from Leiden. They went downstairs to have breakfast.

"Are you ready to drive around today?" asked Melissa after filling her plate from the cafeteria-style setup. Being a Hard Rock Hotel, omnipresent rock music was playing.

"Yes, I think so," Art said, a hearty plate of eggs and sausage in front of him, adding, "Just need to avoid those bikes."

Just then, their now-familiar hotel connoisseur walked by.

"Why hello there! It's my favorite guest…" Armond greeted them, adding an intentionally awkward, "…sss."

This time, before Melissa could say anything, Art replied, "Hello there Armond. I'm Melissa's…" Art let his words hang in the air before adding, "very good friend, Art."

Caught off guard, Armond pivoted and said, "Hello Art. Melissa must like men who have names beginning with A." This brought a smile to both Art and Melissa. Armond added, "Now Melissa and Art, you'll let me know if I can do anything for you? Either of you." Then he took his leave, moving around the room.

"I think he was hitting on both of us," Melissa observed.

"Who knows? Let's finish up and get out of here," said Art.

Once the two Americans left the Amsterdam city limits, it was an easy drive to Noordwijk. They found the hotel and parked in the loading area near a couple of large buses.

"Those must be for the players," Art observed, parking the car.

"I hope so. That means they haven't left yet. I'm not sure how we're going to find Sarah here," replied a concerned Melissa.

They went through the revolving doors and, to their surprise, Sarah was sitting against the wall directly across from them! All three of them froze in a moment of disbelief. Then Sarah got up and ran to Art's waiting arms. Melissa joined for a tight group hug.

"Dad! Melissa! It's so good to see you!" Sarah said in between her tears of happiness.

"We weren't sure we'd find you here," replied Art. "Let me look at you." Holding her at arm's length, he said, "You look great!"

"Sarah, you do look great! Are you having fun?" Melissa asked.

"You guys look great too. Yes, I'm having a blast. Although last night was tough."

"Why? What happened last night?" Art asked, concern in his voice.

"Well, I'm good. It's Tina," Sarah said, turning back to the wall where Art and Melissa noticed Tina sitting on the floor, being held by her mother Brix. Tina was ghostly pale. Her father Mark and brother Kyle were also on the floor with them.

"Oh no! What's wrong with Tina?" asked Art.

"She was really sick last night. Throwing up all over. Coach Paige thought it was food poisoning. They called a doctor. By the time she got there, Tina was sleeping." Sarah paused, looking back at Tina who lifted her head and smiled at the three of them, mustering a wave. "I think she's okay now."

"Oh my God! That poor girl! Should we go say hi?" Melissa asked.

The three of them walked over to where Tina and her family were sitting on the floor. Tina wiped the tears away from her eyes and managed to stand up. Her family followed suit and stood up to greet their Minnesota friends.

"Tina, I sure hope you are feeling better," Art said.

"Thanks Mr. Zonnen. I do feel better," Tina said unconvincingly, still looking quite unwell.

"Thank you for your concern," Brix said, gliding over to Melissa, hugging her, then moving over to Art and hugging him. Mark then hugged Melissa and extended his hand to Art for a handshake. Kyle stood there uneasily, looking at Sarah. When their eyes met, they both quickly looked away. Sarah smiled.

"I'm glad to hear you feel better. I can't believe we found you girls right inside the hotel," said Art.

"I know. They were right here. I'm not sure I'm going to let Tina out of my sight now," remarked Brix.

"Oh Mom! I'm fine," said ghostly Tina, still not convincing anyone.

Just then, Coach Paige announced that it was time for the players to get on the bus for the short ride over to the gym in Leiden. Tina and Sarah started to gather their things.

"Tina, there's no way you're going to play! You're coming with us!" declared Brix.

"No, Mom! I can play. I'm alright. Tell her, Sarah," Tina pleaded.

"Mrs. Wilson, I think Tina's okay. I'm sure Coach Finch will take it easy on her today," Sarah said in support of her friend.

Brix looked at Mark with a panicked look, saying, "I can't believe our daughter would play in this condition. Mark? Can you?"

Mark looked flustered. By this point, Tina had gathered her things and was ready to leave for the bus with Sarah. He stammered, "Well, I…I…I mean if she feels up to it. I guess she could try."

Brix's mood turned from panicked to angry. At that moment, Coach Paige appeared.

"Hello, Mr. and Mrs. Wilson. My name is Paige Horowitz, one of Tina's coaches. I'm glad you found Tina. She had a rough one last night."

The Wilsons recognized Paige from leading the People to People Minnesota contingent. They were glad to hear she was one of their daughter's coaches.

With the formalities out of the way, Brix pressed Paige about Tina going with the team and playing today.

"Paige, do you think it's a good idea for Tina to travel with the team and maybe even play today?"

"If she feels up to it, she's welcome to travel with the team. It will be up to her and Coach Finch if she plays, though. We have the best interests for the girls in mind," said Paige before adding, "You know, Brix, if there's one thing I've learned from these young athletes, is if there's a way for them to play, they will."

"Mom, I'm going with the team. I'll see you at the gym," Tina said emphatically. Even with her ghost-like appearance, she was strong-willed.

"Okay Tina. We'll see you there," said Mark as he side-eyed his wife, thinking she would overrule him.

Instead, Brix backed down and hugged Tina, softly whispering, "Love you."

Tina and Sarah ran toward the door, joined by Sabrina and Emilia, before disappearing onto the bus. Mark and Brix smiled at each other and then at Art and Melissa. Tina might have looked like a ghost, but at that moment, at least she was a happy ghost.

The gym in Leiden was a long way from home but it was just like the gyms Sarah had played in back in Minnesota. Art and Melissa sat up in the stands close to the Wilsons. The United States teams playing there that day were the Cardinals, Yellowjackets, and Sunfish. The European teams came from the Netherlands, England, and Germany. The format was round-robin games, and like the scrimmages the point wasn't to have a champion. One difference was they did keep score with 3-pointers along with shooting free throws. They played thirty-minute games with running time (no time stoppages except timeouts) then rested for twenty minutes before rotating and playing another team. The US teams only played the European teams. They would play each team once in the morning, have lunch, then rotate through the opponents again in the afternoon.

To the American fans, the games were surprisingly competitive. The Yellowjackets and Cardinals both won all three of their morning games, although Germany and the Netherlands teams played them close. The Sunfish lost to those two teams, only beating the team from England.

Tina didn't play much in the morning games; Coach Finch only played her for about five minutes in each. Sarah played well, and Art was proud of his daughter—even though it didn't surprise him, since she'd spent so much time shooting at that Maple Manor playground hoop. The overall talent of the teams amazed him, making watching the games genuinely enjoyable.

The afternoon session again ended with the Yellowjackets and Cardinals being undefeated. This time though, they won each game easily. The Sunfish were able to beat both the English team and then, at the buzzer, the Netherlands team. The lunch break had served Tina well. In the afternoon she had shed her ghostly appearance and merely appeared her normal pale. She played more minutes contributing several 3-pointers, helping the Cardinals to their comfortable wins.

The adults met up with the girls before they were to ride the buses back to Inholland. Some of Sarah and Tina's friends came over to say hi.

"Hi, I'm Celica, and we just *love* Tina and Sarah!" Celica said, announcing herself in style, as Emilia, Sabrina, Alexis, and Brittany joined her.

"Hi Celica, I'm Brix, Tina's mom. And this is Mark, her dad. And over here…" She looked around before spotting Kyle a few feet to her right, "is Kyle, Tina's brother."

"Hi Kyle," Celica said with a wave and a big smile.

"Oh, cut it out, Celica!" Tina said.

"What? He's cute!" declared Celica.

The rest of the girls introduced themselves, and though there was some confusion about Melissa not being Sarah's mom, they moved past it.

"You guys are good," stated Mark, adding, "Now, you're not all on the Cardinals, are you?"

"No way. Me and Brittney are Yellowjackets. We're better than the Cardinals!" Alexis stated proudly.

"What! We beat you guys!" Celica declared.

"Oh, you mean that scrimmage where Sarah fouled me?" Alexis said with a smile.

"There was no foul, Alexis!" Sarah said jokingly, pushing Alexis.

"Yeah, well, it wasn't called," Alexis replied, laughing.

"I guess you started something, Mark," Melissa said.

"I guess so!" Mark said, adding, "Anyway, it was fun watching your teams play."

The girls said their goodbyes and left for their bus, giggling and shoving each other.

Mark turned to Art and said, "Hey, maybe tomorrow night we should meet up for dinner or something?"

"Yeah, I think that should work. We might go to a concert at the Paradiso close to our hotel. Where are you guys staying?" asked Art.

"We're in Haarlem, but we could come into Amsterdam for dinner."

"Great. Let's do it," Art confirmed.

Art and Melissa returned to their hotel and, still feeling the effects of jet lag, they decided to order room service and call it a night.

The next morning, Art and Melissa somehow avoided seeing Armond at breakfast. Unbeknownst to them, he had the day off.

The games that day were all at the Inholland gym in Haarlem. The three teams that had stayed at Noordwijk were now back at Inholland for the remainder of the trip. The other teams switched places with them, and would finish their stay at Noordwijk. The three European opponents lined up today were from Italy, Sweden, and Greece. Art and Melissa met up with Mark, Brix, and Kyle to watch the morning games. By now, they all knew the Cardinals and Yellowjackets were the strongest United States teams, but it didn't take long to recognize Italy as the best of the day's opponents. Both the Cardinals and Yellowjackets narrowly defeated Italy, while dispatching the other two easily. The Sunfish were even able to beat the others, but Italy defeated them handily. At lunch, Sarah sat facing Art and next to Melissa away from the others.

"Dad, did you know about Anne Frank?" asked Sarah.

"Yes. Well, I know a little about her. I read her diary as homework back in high school."

"Really? I didn't know anything about her or her diary, but I heard some kids at school were upset when they banned it from the library," said Sarah.

"They banned it. What? Why?" questioned a stunned Melissa.

"I don't know. I just know some kids were upset about it being banned. And now, after learning about her, I can see why," stated Sarah. "Everyone should know her."

"How did you learn about Anne Frank?" asked Art.

"They took us on a field trip after dinner yesterday to where she was hidden and wrote her diary. It was just us from People to People. That apartment Anne and her family hid in was so small."

"I didn't know they were bringing you there. We were thinking of going too if we can find the time," said Art.

"She was a young girl, just like me," said Sarah.

"I know. Very sad," acknowledged Art.

"I don't understand. Why would anyone want to kill Anne or her family?" Sarah asked.

"There were...are some bad people in the world. And bad governments. It doesn't make any sense," Art said, trying his best to explain.

"It seems so unfair. She was such a smart person. It makes me so sad that she died so young," Sarah said, tears in her eyes.

Art and Melissa looked at each other, not knowing exactly what to say. Melissa leaned into her and held her tightly. "I know, dear. It's sad. Sometimes bad things happen to good people. That's why we need to celebrate the good people," Melissa said, trying not to burst into tears herself.

Art tried to reassure her, "Unfortunately, we all die sometime. Poor Anne, though, died way too soon. And for no good reason. Like Melissa said, we need to celebrate her, and others like her...In a way, her memory can live forever through her book."

Sarah forced a smile through her watery eyes. None of it made sense, except the love she felt there with Art and Melissa in that moment.

"Thanks Dad. And Melissa," she managed, as Melissa hugged her even tighter. "I'm glad they found her diary. What if it hadn't been found? No one would ever know her story."

This left Art and Melissa speechless. After a moment, Sarah noticed her teammates gathering for the afternoon games. Seeing Tina doing some stretches, her eyes widened, and a slight smile came to her face.

"You know there was something funny, well, maybe not funny but weird when we were visiting Anne Frank's place."

"Really? What happened?" Melissa asked.

"Well, you remember Tina had food poisoning—"

"Yes, she looked awful when we first saw her," Melissa interrupted.

"Yeah, well, Anne's place was really small. Tina started feeling crowded in and uncomfortable. She thought she was going to get sick again."

"Oh no! That's awful," Melissa said.

"She was afraid she was going to throw up right there in Anne's apartment!" Sarah paused. "Luckily, she was able to leave and wait for us on the sidewalk. We were worried we'd lose track of her. We found out that Coach Paige left to be with her and kept her safe."

"Oh my! Poor girl," said Melissa.

"She felt better on the ride back to the dorm though. We all kinda laughed thinking how bad it would have been if she had gotten sick inside."

"Yes! That would not have been good!" agreed Melissa with a chuckle.

Sarah said Tina was back to normal today. Art and Melissa grinned and shared a look over at Tina, who indeed looked upbeat. In fact, Tina had thrown up outside Anne Frank's house in a garbage can. It was fortunate Paige was there to comfort her. Tina and Paige kept this mishap to themselves.

Following the afternoon games, the girls said their goodbyes to the adults and went back to their dorms. Mark and Brix made plans to meet with Art and Melissa at the Hard Rock American Hotel café. They planned to have dinner before Art and Melissa's concert at the Paradiso. Mark said they were going to let Kyle stay in the hotel for the night. He was fine with that, since there was a PlayStation in the room and he loved gaming.

Returning to the hotel, Art noticed Armond wasn't on the reception desk.

"Are you disappointed your boyfriend isn't working today?" Art teased Melissa.

"Oh no! I was going to hook up with him tonight!" she quipped.

They rested for a while, trying to find something to watch on TV. They ended up watching a darts match, something they had never seen televised in the United States.

"So, Art, are you sure we'll be able to get tickets for Chum Fella?" Melissa asked.

"Yes. Well, pretty sure anyway," Art responded.

Melissa wore the best outfit she brought with her. It was a red two-piece sleeveless jumpsuit, only slightly exposing her midriff with a short blue denim jacket. Art wore a Wilebski's Blues Saloon sweatshirt with cargo shorts.

"Melissa! Wow! I never realized…" Art paused.

"Okay, Art, never realized what?"

"You're *hot*!"

"Oh, come on. Don't embarrass me."

"No, I'm serious. You look great!"

"Well, thank you. Now let's get going. And you look great too."

"Ha, good one!"

They found a table on the patio, perfect to watch the bikes and trams whizzing by. They took in the scenery before a young waitress interrupted them.

"*Hallo, ik ben je serveerster Avian.*"

Art and Melissa looked up at a young woman with wavy shoulder length dark hair and a freckled bronze complexion. They both wondered whether everyone in Amsterdam is good-looking.

"Sorry, we don't speak Dutch," Melissa said.

"Oh, no problem. Hello, I'll be your server. My name is Avian. Would you like something to drink?"

"Thank you, Avian. We're waiting for another couple. We'll take two Heineken bottles. The 12 oz ones." said Art.

"I'll be right back," said Avian as she seemed to glide away effortlessly.

Art turned to Melissa and said, "Is everyone here in good shape? It makes me feel so fat."

"Yes, I think everyone here is fit. Americans are easy to spot. They all look like us," replied Melissa. Art made a face, since he thought Melissa looked every bit like she could live in Amsterdam.

Just then, Mark and Brix approached them. He was wearing a light-brown thin leather jacket over a polo shirt with golf shorts and sneakers. Like Melissa, Brix was dressed in a lovely outfit consisting of a long-sleeved white sheer shirt that partly showed off her black bra underneath, and a pair of jean shorts that highlighted her statuesque legs.

The group exchanged hugs and greetings. Melissa and Brix complimented each other's outfits before sitting down. Just then, Avian returned with two green bottles of Heineken.

"I'll have a Heineken like them," replied Mark.

Brix said, "I'll have a glass of Chardonnay."

"It's amazing how well everyone here speaks English," said Brix as Avian left them.

"Yes, I know. It makes me feel like I should at least learn one other language," joked Melissa. Avian returned with their drinks, and the four of them ordered dinner.

"Tina told us about the Anne Frank house visit the other day," Mark said.

"Yes. Sarah mentioned it," added Art.

"I'm glad they went. We were able to go the other night on our tour. It was too bad Tina wasn't herself," said Mark.

"Yes, too bad," Melissa said, not letting on that they had heard all about Tina's queasiness. "Sarah told us they banned Anne's diary for some reason at their school. I just can't believe that."

"Really? Wow! I had heard there were some groups trying to ban books. That's the same thing the awful people who killed Anne and her family did," Brix stated as they all shook their heads at how bad politics had become even back home.

"They say history repeats itself. I sure hope that's not true," Mark finally said.

"Yes, let's hope not," Art agreed.

Avian returned with their food. Everyone was quiet for some time, not knowing how to pick up the conversation after it had taken such a cheerless turn.

"So, your concert is close by?" asked Mark.

"Yes. It's just over there," Art replied, pointing across the street along the canal.

"Who are you seeing there?" asked Brix.

"Chum Fella. He's a blues guitarist," replied Art.

"I've heard of him. Do you have good tickets?" asked Mark.

"Good one, Mark," Melissa said, as Mark looked confused.

"Oh, Melissa doesn't think we'll be able to get tickets outside,"

Art explained, continuing, "I almost always buy tickets from scalpers outside."

"Really? I'd be worried about being ripped off," Mark said.

"Me too," Melissa said, frowning at Art.

"It's never happened to me yet," Art stated confidently, now having to defend his concert ticket strategy.

"Well, hope it works out for you," Mark said as he held out his beer to offer a cheers. Art clinked his bottle with Mark's.

They finished up, paid, and thanked Avian for her service, before walking across the street to take in the sights.

"So, have you been to a coffee shop yet?" asked Mark.

Art and Melissa chuckled. She answered, "No, we haven't. We talked about it though. Have you?"

"Yes, we went to one in Haarlem the other night. Kyle was happy playing his PlayStation in the hotel, so we left him for a couple hours."

"Good for you. Was the dope strong?" wondered Melissa.

"Oh yes. We don't smoke much pot anymore," replied Brix, although the way she looked at Mark, it left Art and Melissa wondering if this was true.

"Well, maybe we should smoke some now?" Melissa asked.

"Fine by me," Art added.

"You know, Art told me about a famous coffee shop right over there," Melissa said pointing just across the lively street.

"It's The Bulldog! I've heard of that one too. Let's go!" said Mark, now leading the way.

When they got there, they saw there were steps in front leading upstairs and downstairs. The upstairs looked like a bar, while downstairs was the coffee shop.

"Since you're experienced at this, you can take the lead," Art said to Mark.

"Sure, follow me," Mark said, confidently heading downstairs.

There was a short line in front of a door that had its top half open, with a man explaining the various strains of marijuana to the couple at the front of the line. Mark was given the go-ahead to buy whatever he wanted as the other three bunched up a few feet away. After a short time, he got to the front of the line and made his purchase. He turned and waved for everyone to follow him toward the upstairs bar, rather than staying in the smoky coffee shop.

"The guy said we can smoke upstairs," explained Mark, as they walked up the winding steps. The upper floor looked like any other large bar, except there were people lighting up at the various tables and even along the bars on both sides. There was a long bar top to the right that wrapped around the side near the front. The left side had a smaller semi-circular bar top. There were spiral stairs in the front leading to what looked like private seating areas on the second floor. Loud electronic dance music was playing. There was an open high-top table about halfway toward the front. Mark signaled the others to follow him there.

A server approached them. She looked very much like Avian from earlier, but as she got closer they could see that, unlike Avian, she had a nose piercing and tattoos on her hands. Though it was so loud they could barely hear her, they ordered four Heinekens.

Mark had bought several pre-rolled joints. He prepared one by tapping it on the table and lit up, taking a big drag.

"Babe, take it easy!" yelled Brix over the music, before taking an equally big drag herself and passing the joint to Melissa. Melissa and Art cautiously took smaller hits. After a couple of hits apiece, they put the simmering joint in the ashtray. The music was so loud, they couldn't hold any sort of conversation, and the four of them became glassy-eyed quickly. Melissa encouraged everyone to leave. The group was careful not to bump into anyone as they made their way out into the park-like area in front of The Bulldog.

"Wow. Good shit, man!" Melissa said with a smile.

"Yes, maybe it was the atmosphere, but I feel more buzzed than the other night," Brix said.

"I agree," was all Mark could say.

"Let's get a drink over at the Hard Rock Café next to the canal and watch the boats go by," suggested Art.

"Lead the way," replied Mark.

They were able to get four seats together outside on the canal, and all ordered Heinekens.

"Have you heard that green bottles can leave beer smelling skunky?" asked Art.

"I didn't know it was the green bottles, but I have had skunky beer before," replied Mark.

"Well, Melissa here is a beer expert, and she said it's the green bottles," Art said, teasing Melissa.

"Oh Art! It's not me. Paul the beer nerd from work said that," said Melissa.

"Funny, I haven't really noticed. Is that why you order the bottles rather than drafts?" asked Mark.

"Yes, I guess it is. I thought we could do a taste test," replied Art.

"I see they have drafts, and they look bigger for the same price as the bottles," said Mark.

"Really? Okay, we've tested enough green bottles. Next time, let's get drafts!" Art declared.

"Go ahead. I'm moving to wine," Melissa said.

"Me too," agreed Brix.

They had a few more drinks watching the canal boats go by, while some of the tourists waved at them. One thing they couldn't do at the Hard Rock Café was smoke pot, so they would take turns going out by twos in the courtyard area by the large chessboard. Brix and Melissa went together, then Mark and Art. More drinks and conversation followed.

The four of them sat in silence, watching the canal. They had hit some sort of Amsterdam wall without realizing it. Brix was the first to speak.

"Honey. I think we should get back and check on Kyle."

The two of them had been lost enjoying the night with their new friends.

"Kyle's fine. He texted me a few minutes ago saying he was still playing his games," assured Mark.

"That's good, but we should still go," said Brix.

They split the bill and then Mark and Brix decided to get an Uber back to Haarlem rather than trying to take the train. Art and Melissa agreed that was a good choice considering how stoned and drunk they all were.

As Mark and Brix were leaving, they hugged Art and Melissa goodbye.

"You guys! What fun!" Brix said in between hugs.

"You two are such a cute couple!" declared Brix.

Art and Melissa shared a smile with each other.

Leaving the Hard Rock Café, they walked toward the Paradiso. As they approached, they hear Chum Fella's band playing the blues.

"Do you think we can get in?" asked Melissa.

"I don't know. But let's try!" Art said, grabbing Melissa's hand and running up to the door, where they were greeted by two security guards.

"*De deuren zijn gesloten*," said one of the guards.

"Sorry, English?" asked Melissa with a smile.

"The doors are closed, ma'am," the guard replied, switching to perfect English.

"Oh please? It must be almost over. We just want to watch a few songs. Please?" pleaded Melissa, trying her best to get in.

The two security guards looked at each other. Melissa was half pouting and half smiling, while Art stood there awkwardly.

"Oh. Okay. Go on in. But don't tell anyone we let you in!" the guard said, opening the door.

"We won't! Thank you! Thank you! Thank you!" said Melissa. This time, she was the one grabbing Art's hand, pulling him into the Paradiso.

"Good job, Melissa. I didn't think they were going to let us in," Art said as they came into the sounds of Chum's famous song, "Washing the Killing Floor." The two of them stop to get more beers and then find an area on the second-floor deck, where they inconspicuously slipped into a couple of seats to watch the show.

Chum was playing inspired blues for the crowd, and in between songs he would tell stories about how he came to write them. One was about a girlfriend's obsession with her hometown baseball team that led him to write, "My Baby's White Sox Lost Again." He finished that one with a long guitar solo. His last song, or at least the last one before his encore, was his most famous song, "Janitor Blues." Art and Melissa, knowing the words, sang along with the crowd. They decided to leave before the encore so they wouldn't have to fight the crowd down the stairs and out the door. On their way out, Melissa smiled broadly at the security guards.

"Thank you! Thank you!" she said to them again. Reaching the sidewalk, she grabbed Art's arm and proudly told him, "Looks like it's me that can get us into any show!"

"Let's have a nightcap over there!" Melissa exclaimed, pointing at the Aran Irish Pub not far from the Hard Rock Café. Art agreed and they found themselves on the outdoor patio. The view of the canal was still spectacular, but not quite as intimate as the Hard Rock's. This time, both ordered Guinness.

They laughed about getting to see some of the Chum Fella show without even buying tickets. After the beer, the two of them decided to stop in their hotel's bar for one last drink. Walking into the bar, they saw Chum Fella and his bandmates.

"It's him!" Melissa said.

The band was by themselves. A few other customers were scattered around the bar. It was hard to tell if anyone else even knew that the band that had just played the Paradiso was right there, sharing the space with them.

"We'll have two 12 oz Heineken bottles," Art ordered what was now his Amsterdam drink of choice. Melissa, meanwhile, had started a conversation with one of Chum's bandmates. They waved Art over when he got the beers. Chum apparently was spent and said his goodbyes to the band without acknowledging Art or Melissa. They whispered to each other that they understood him being tired but wondered if they should say hello to him. After all, when would they get this opportunity again? Regardless, before they could say anything, Chum disappeared. The drummer explained how spent Chum was after shows. Unlike Chum, he was much more engaging and even took a selfie with them.

Materializing as if from thin air, a drunk Armond came over and put his arm around Melissa.

"There you are, my dear!" he announced. Melissa pulled away from him.

Art, now tired of Armond's suggestive advances toward Melissa, stepped in between the two of them saying, "Come on, man. Leave her alone."

"What?" protested Armond, adding, "I can't help it. You're my favorite guest!"

"Unbelievable," muttered Art.

Melissa, taking control, grabbed Art tightly and said, "Let's go to bed!" She led him out of the bar and up the stairs as they laughed and held each other tight.

Upon opening the door, they entered the dark room, finding themselves both overcome by the moment. Melissa threw her jacket on the floor as Art pulled off his sweatshirt. They fell into a passionate kiss and slumped into Melissa's bed. Stoned and drunk, they were now on some sort of sensual cruise control.

Melissa maneuvered herself on top of Art, grinding against him, and she could tell even through their clothes that he was fully aroused.

She pulled her top off and then her strapless bra. Art struggled to take his t-shirt off, needing Melissa's help.

They embraced once more and rolled around, taking pleasure from each other's warm bodies.

Lost in the ecstasy of the moment, Art whispered, "Oh, Ker…"

Wait! What? He felt he was with Kerstin. He never thought he would feel her against his body again. They kissed passionately.

Art slowly opened his eyes. Melissa was looking at him. Even through the drunken fog, he understood he was in bed with Melissa and not Kerstin. He wasn't sure if she'd heard him start to say Kerstin's name. Their passion paused, Melissa closed her eyes and held Art tightly, not saying a word. Then they passed out, holding each other.

Art's eyes slowly opened. It was morning, or at least he thought it was. He was spooning Melissa. They were both completely naked. What happened? He remembered them falling into bed together but nothing else. Did they have sex last night? He couldn't remember. At that moment, Melissa stirred.

"Good morning, darling," she whispered, apparently not concerned that they were lying naked next to each other. "What time is it?"

Art managed to sit up in bed then looked at his phone.

"Oh no! It's almost ten! We'll miss the morning games."

"I need a shower. Are you taking one?" she asked.

"Yes, I'll take a quick one now."

"Okay," replied Melissa, still lying in bed.

The two of them got ready and left without breakfast. Armond was working, but neither he nor they acknowledge one another.

CHAPTER 14
TOT ZIENS BASKETBAL

Sarah and Emilia were both and awake staring at the ceiling until their alarms went off. They had one more day of games before leaving for home the following day. Sarah rolled toward Emilia, seeing she was awake.

"Emilia?" she asked quietly. Emilia faced her and smiled.

"Good morning, Sarah."

"Good morning. You're awake," said Sarah, stating the obvious.

"Yes, and so are you," replied Emilia, then asked, "What were you thinking about?"

"Not much really. Just remembering the fun we've had and how I don't want it to end."

Emilia smiled. "Yeah, me too. I'm glad we were roommates."

They had become good friends and with Tina and Sabrina then Alexis and Brittney, all six of them had grown close.

"Do you think we'll ever see each other again?" asked Sarah.

"I hope so! I really hope so!" replied Emilia.

"Me too!"

The two roommates lay in silence for a few minutes as both imagined how they could visit each other.

"Do you think you'll keep playing basketball?" asked Emilia.

"Yes," replied Sarah immediately, adding, "How about you?"

"I think so, but I don't know for sure. I mean, this has been a lot of fun. But I've started getting interested in singing and maybe acting."

"That's cool! I bet you'd be good at it," stated Sarah.

"Thanks, maybe. Well, I hope so anyway. I've been singing in church and the choir at school. I like it a lot and my parents think I'm good."

"That's so cool," Sarah said again.

"How about you? What else do you want to do?"

"Um, well, I like music," then after a short pause, she added, "I play drums in the school band."

"You do? Now *that's* cool!"

"I guess so. I think I could play in a band someday, but I don't know. It's expensive and my dad doesn't make a lot of money. Plus, it's so loud. I don't even have my own drum kit, and even if I did, I couldn't play at our apartment. But I do like it, and it's fun to play with the school band."

"Well, I bet you're good at it. I'd love to hear you play," said Emilia, thinking for a moment before asking, "What was that weird music you played after we beat the Yellowjackets?"

"Oh that. That was blues. I love the blues. My grandmother used to play it while I banged on a plastic drum. It was so natural. I feel it. It's always been inside me, always. You know?"

Emilia smiled. "No, not really. I like to listen to music and even sing, but I don't play an instrument."

They fall silent again until Sarah's alarm went off seconds before Emilia's. They both laughed.

"Ha! We don't need those stupid alarms today!" declared Emilia.

Sarah and Emilia met up with their other friends at breakfast. They all promised that they would keep in touch with each other when they returned home. At the gym, they see their opponents on this final day were Italy, Germany, and a team they hadn't played yet—Spain.

Alexis said, "Spain must be good. Italy and Germany were the two best from the other days. I think the Europeans want to beat the best American teams before we go."

"You really think so?" said Tina.

"Who cares! We're the best! They won't beat us!" declared Sabrina.

The six friends came together in a huddle, bent over with hands draped over each other's shoulders. Sabrina yelled a cheer she heard at her high school.

"Genie, genie, grant my wish! Let me hear that ball go swish!"

The others all laughed and started repeating it with her, getting louder each time. Everyone else in the gym stopped and looked at this huddle of young women chanting their goofy cheer. Finally, the six friends ended with a loud, "LET'S GO!"

Sarah looked around for Art and Melissa but couldn't find them. As her team gathered with Coach Finch, she said to Tina, "Funny, I don't see my dad or Melissa here yet."

"My mom said they met them for dinner last night. Sounds like they had fun. She said your dad and Melissa went to a concert. Maybe they stayed up late?" replied Tina, then seeing Sarah's concern added, "I'm sure they'll be here soon." Sarah gave her a nervous smile as Coach Finch started his pregame talk.

Coach Finch told them that they would be playing three games today—all forty-five minutes with a halftime. They would begin playing Italy, then Germany, followed by lunch and finishing with Spain. The Cardinals were confident they would beat the other teams. Even though the competition wasn't supposed to be concerned with "winning," everyone in the program realized that both the Cardinals and Yellowjackets were the best from the United States. Spain had been playing the other groups of United States teams and had handily beat them all. They were considered the best European team, so the organizers rescheduled them to end the competition in the same group as the best US teams.

Spain would start with the Sunfish followed by the Yellowjackets. Even though the Cardinals and Yellowjackets were thought of as equally good, word of the Cardinals' narrow victory over the Yellowjackets (leaving aside Alexis' foul claim) left the Cardinals as Spain's final opponent.

Sarah's team played well against Italy and won by ten points. Sarah turned the ball over a few times, preoccupied by not seeing her dad in the gym. The Sunfish were destroyed by Spain, whose talented Gigi Perez was perhaps the best player in the entire program. Alexis was thought to be the best US player, and she was exceptional, but Gigi was fast, tall, and could shoot from anywhere. Her Spanish teammates were also solid players.

After a short break, Sarah's Cardinals faced Germany. They won easily, even with a distracted Sarah not at her best, while the Sunfish lost badly to Italy. Surprisingly, at least to the Americans, Spain defeated the Yellowjackets in a thrilling game. Alexis had made a driving layup to break a tie with ten seconds left. Gigi then dribbled past the Yellowjacket defenders and shot a long 3-pointer. SWISH! She made it as the buzzer sounded to lead Spain to its narrow victory. The crowd stood and cheered the efforts of both teams.

Everyone broke for lunch. Sarah, Emilia, Tina, and Sabrina joined Alexis and Brittney to console them on their loss. Although they wished they had won, both were still flying high from the excitement of such a tough, competitive game. They were amazed at how gifted Gigi was. Alexis told the Cardinals that they should double team Gigi the whole game and leave someone else open. As they were talking, Sarah could see that Art and Melissa were over talking to Tina's parents.

"Glad to see you could make it," said Mark.

"I was worried," added Brix.

"Yes, sorry we're late. Our alarm didn't go off," Art said, which was true even if he didn't fill in the rest of the details. Art and Melissa glanced at one another with a knowing look.

"It's good to be here now. What did we miss?" asked Melissa.

"Some good games…The Yellowjackets lost to Spain," stated Mark.

"Really? I thought they were the best team," Melissa said.

"Maybe, although our Cardinals beat them, or at least that's the story I was told. And we play Spain in the last game. We did win our games with Germany and Italy, so this one is for the championship. Well, it would be if they had such a thing," said Mark.

Sarah approached and leaped into Art's arms.

"Dad! I'm so glad you're here!"

"Sarah, I'm sorry we're late. We're okay, just a mix-up with the alarm," Art assured her, feeling guilty for letting down his daughter.

"I'm sorry too," said Melissa, making it a group hug.

"It's okay. I'm just glad you're here now," Sarah said before rejoining her team.

Brix nudged next to Melissa, leaned in, and whispered, "Soo…"

Melissa knowingly grinned and replied, "Yes, Brix?"

"How was last night?" asked Brix, trying to coax some information out of her new friend.

"It was fun. Thanks for meeting us for dinner," answered Melissa, not giving anything else away.

"Yes, yes, it was fun to meet up. It's been years since Mark and I have been out like that." Brix said, before asking a straightforward question. "But, you guys. You and Art. You must have had a wild night…to sleep in so late."

"Oh Brix!" said Melissa, then insisted in a faintly sarcastic tone, "Nothing like what you're implying happened."

"Okay, I see," Brix said as they both giggled. Not everything needed to be said out loud.

Mark was talking to Art too, even though he was talking about basketball rather than a late-night tryst between Art and Melissa.

"Spain are tough. They have a player who might be the best one here," Mark said.

"Oh yeah? So, they really beat the Yellowjackets?"

"Yes, they needed a last-second 3-pointer to do it, but they beat them. Our Cardinals will have their hands full."

"Sounds like it should be a good game," Art said, his thoughts still on being late and unsettling his daughter.

Coach Finch gave a short talk to his team before sending out the starting lineup of Sarah, Tina, Emilia, Sabrina, and Carla. He planned to play everyone throughout the game until the last five minutes when he would stick with his best five. Having seen the end of the Yellowjackets and Spain game, he was well aware how good a team Spain had. He also, like everyone else in the gym, saw the talent of young Gigi. Still, his focus was on giving all his players a chance to play. If that meant the Cardinals would lose their last game to what might be the best team in the program, so be it.

All his players had improved since his team was formed. He didn't feel he had any weak links. Even Celica had become better at handling the ball and playing aggressive defense. Carla wouldn't drift outside for 3-point shots nearly as often, instead staying closer to the basket and battling for rebounds. She was so strong that if she got her hands on the ball, it was hers. Rae had improved as a shooter and had natural instincts for getting in the right position for rebounds. Sharon had also improved as a shooter and her natural aggressiveness helped her as a defender. Coach Finch knew his team was good, but beyond that he had enjoyed being around them. They had a personality and an energy that was infectious. He and Coach Paige often would talk about how lucky they were to have this group.

The other games were the Yellowjackets versus Italy and the Sunfish versus Germany. Most of the spectators though had gathered at the Cardinals versus Spain game. The teams took the court, there was a jump ball, and the game was underway. Both teams looked to be a little nervous and turned the ball over a few times. Sarah, though, wasn't nervous. Having her dad and Melissa show up before the game settled her. She was playing well and started the scoring with a 3-pointer from the right corner. Gigi answered back with a driving layup. The lead went back and forth throughout the first half as both teams substituted freely. At halftime, the score was tied 25-25.

Both the Yellowjackets and Sunfish were already into the second half of their games. The Yellowjackets had a 15-point lead against Italy. Alexis and Brittney were aggressive, wanting to end their time playing together with a convincing victory. Germany led the Sunfish by 2 points in a game that looked like it might be decided in the last minute.

After allowing his team to get hydrated and catch their breath, Coach Finch brought them together.

"Cardinals," he said, looking each one of them in the eyes. "It has been my and Coach Paige's great pleasure getting to know you all." He glanced at Coach Paige who smiled and nodded back.

"However we did it, we were able to put you athletes together. You have bonded to form a fantastic basketball team," continued Coach Finch.

"Yay! Cardinals!" the girls yelled.

He smiled and then added, "This second half will be the last time we play as a team. I just want you to know that neither I, nor Coach Paige, will ever forget you."

The huddle of teammates grew closer, their arms over each other's shoulders, some heads bowed with water-colored eyes.

"Coach?"

"Yes, Sarah."

"We're so glad we had you and Coach Paige as our coaches," declared Sarah. The team erupted again with a loud cheer.

"We, all of us, will never forget our coaches!" added Sarah. Another loud cheer followed. Sarah then looked across the huddle at Tina and struggled to say, "Or, or…our teammates."

This time, instead of a cheer, the team all pulled each other together muttering how much they loved each other.

After a few moments, Coach Paige noticed Spain's starting group was on the court ready to begin the second half. At this point, the Cardinals resembled a pile of mush more than a basketball team. Paige moved to the center of the huddle, knelt, and looked up at the group of emotional players holding on tight to each other. She smiled and raised her right hand in a fist. First Sarah followed by Tina then the rest of the team put their hands on Paige's.

Paige said loudly, "WE ARE…"

Sarah softly replied, "The Cardinals…?"

Paige nodded and again shouted, "WE ARE!"

The girls now looked at each other, smiled and replied in unison, "THE CARDINALS!" Paige led them on two more booming cheers, before shouting, "LET'S GO!"

Coach Finch was near tears. He never imagined he would be so fortunate to coach this group of remarkable young women. Somehow, he pulled himself together and sent his starting five back on the court for the beginning of the second half.

Play continued much as it had been in the first half. Neither team led by more than a few points. With the game tied again at 40 and with only five minutes left, Coach Finch called a timeout then sent out Sarah, Tina, Emilia, Sabrina, and Rae. Carla usually would complain to either Coach Finch or Coach Paige if she were left out of the group near the end of a game. This time, though, Carla was the loudest one cheering her teammates on.

"Let's go! We can do this!" she yelled.

Emilia missed a driving layup. Rae slid over and gathered the rebound, passing it back to Sarah, who saw Tina open on the left side of the court. Sarah fired a pass right to Tina's hands who immediately let it fly. SWISH! A 3-pointer!

Gigi brought the ball down and drove hard to the basket. Sabrina left the player she was guarding and moved to block Gigi's path. Without hesitation, Gigi passed it to a teammate at the 3-point line. Even though Emilia was guarding her closely, the Spanish player shot a 3-pointer. It bounced high off the rim and then fell right through the hoop. The game was tied again.

Both teams missed their next shots. Rae again rebounded the Spanish miss, passing it to Sarah. Gigi almost stole the ball, but Sarah kept control, finding Tina open this time on the right side. SWISH! Another 3-pointer. Again, the Cardinals had a 3-point lead…and time was running out.

Only a minute was left in the game. Gigi handled the ball past half-court. Sarah guarded her as Coach Finch motioned Emilia to leave her player and double-team the talented Spanish player. Gigi recognized this and passed the ball to the player Emilia had been guarding. Emilia took a step back to guard her. Gigi, seeing this, cut hard to the basket. Her teammate passed her the ball and Gigi made a driving, left-handed layup.

Now only thirty seconds remained, with the Cardinals up by a single point. The other games had ended. The Yellowjackets had won by 30 points, while the Sunfish lost by just 2. All the teams and spectators from the other games moved over to watch the end of the Cardinals game.

Coach Finch had the Cardinals spread out and pass the ball when pressured. Emilia bounced a pass over to Tina. It looked like a good pass, until suddenly Gigi sprang forward to knock the ball away, gaining control. She sprinted while dribbling the ball toward the basket at the far end of the court. She pulled away from the Cardinals players and drove in for a layup. Spain was now up by a single point with barely ten seconds left.

"*Olé*! *Olé*! *Olé*! *Olé*! *Olé*!"

The famous cheer rang throughout the gymnasium from the European fans and players. Their best team was positioned to defeat both the best American teams.

Just then, Emilia retrieved the ball. She saw her teammates spread out on the court, each with a look of confidence on their faces. She quickly passed it over to Tina, who drove to mid-court. Tina then passed it to Sarah who was a few feet in front of her. Gigi again sprang to steal the ball. The crowd gasped. If she stole the ball, the game was over right there. This time she barely missed it, grabbing air instead of the ball that hung a fraction of an inch from her fingers.

Sarah gathered the pass and without hesitation drove toward the basket. Three Spanish players converged on her as she laid the ball up with her right hand.

KABOOM!

The three Spanish players crashed into Sarah and drove her to the floor. The ball softly bounced off the backboard, then kissed the front rim. Everyone in the gym was glued to the scene.

A piercing scream rang through the sound of the crowd that was erupting with cheers.

There it was again. The gym grew silent.

"It's Sarah! Oh, no, it's Sarah!" yelled Melissa, as she rose from her seat. Art jumped up and ran down to his daughter on the court.

Sarah was crumpled on the floor, sobbing uncontrollably while holding her left knee. When she saw Art, she reached for him. He bent down and wrapped his arms around her. "I'm here. Sarah, I'm here."

"It hurts, Dad! It hurts so bad!" Sarah cried.

"I know, Sarah, I know," was all Art could say as they held on to each other.

Coach Finch and Paige had come over along with the rest of the Cardinals. Alexis and Brittney joined them. An EMT was there, who up to this point had only dealt with a few blisters and mild sprains. Now she had to stabilize Sarah's leg and try to calm her down. An ambulance arrived with more EMTs wheeling a stretcher. Sarah was lifted onto the stretcher and fastened in position. Art was told they would take her to the Spaarne Gasthuis Haarlem Noord Hospital. Melissa couldn't, or didn't want to, drive, so she would ride with Sarah in the ambulance while Art followed in his car.

Sarah was in a great deal of pain. Even so, she reached toward her teammates who were gathered close to her. Tina was the first to lean down and say how sorry she was that Sarah got hurt. Sarah hugged her tightly. Emilia, Sabrina, Alexis, and Brittney followed.

The EMTs waved everyone else away as they wanted to get Sarah to the hospital.

One final player bent down to say a word before they wheeled her away. It was Gigi. She leaned in close and whispered in perfect English, "Sarah, I'm so sorry. You're a great player. Did you know? You made the shot. You won! Get better soon, okay."

Sarah forced a smile through her agonizing pain, having momentarily forgotten about her shot, and replied with one of the few Spanish words she knew, "*Gracias,* Gigi. *Gracias.*"

Art parked his car and ran to the hospital. He was directed to the emergency room where Sarah was being evaluated. She was sobbing as the physician held her leg carefully, trying various movements. Art could see immediately that every movement was excruciatingly painful for his daughter. Melissa was holding Sarah's hand, trying her best to offer some comfort. As Art approached, the young woman doctor removed her hands from Sarah's leg and told her assistants to take Sarah to her own hospital room for further examination.

Upon seeing Art, Sarah reached out for him. They embraced.

"Mr. Zonnen?" asked the doctor. "I'm Dr. Sari."

"Yes. That's me. How is she?" replied Art.

"Yes," Dr. Sari answered quickly, adding, "she has suffered a knee injury. Unfortunately, this is common with women athletes; ah, all athletes, really. I need to look closer to see exactly what is wrong."

"Yes, yes, of course. Do what you need to…" Art paused before continuing. "She is in a lot of pain. Is that normal?"

"Everyone is different when it comes to pain tolerance. However, a serious injury like an ACL or MCL tear would be very painful."

Dr. Sari then added something that shook Art.

"Since she's eleven years old, I'm going to prescribe oxycodone to help relieve her pain."

Art could feel all the blood stop moving in his body. It was as if he were entering a state of shock.

"Mr. Zonnen? Mr. Zonnen? Are you feeling alright?" Dr. Sari asked, now becoming concerned for Sarah's father.

Melissa was still trying to comfort a distressed Sarah when she noticed Art suddenly looking ghostly pale talking to the doctor. She whispered, "Sarah, I need to check on your dad. Okay?"

Sarah looked up, and she too could see something was wrong with Art. "Yes, sure, you go check on him. I'll be okay." Melissa gave Sarah's hand a squeeze and went to Art's side.

"Art, what's going on?" she asked him, but he didn't answer.

"I'm sorry, but I need to attend to your daughter now. You are in a good place if you need medical treatment," Dr. Sari said as she turned and went over to talk with her assistants.

"Melissa," Art said, "they want to give Sarah oxycodone."

Melissa's expression went blank. She now understood why Art was in such a state. That was the same drug that started her sister Kerstin's journey toward addiction. Art and Melissa both stood silent for a few moments. Sarah was doing her best not to yell out in pain. Dr. Sari directed her assistants as they started moving Sarah to her hospital room before returning to Art.

"Mr. Zonnen? Are you feeling better?"

"Yes. Well, I think so," he replied.

"Hello, I'm Melissa, Sarah's aunt," Melissa said introducing herself. "Art and I are both concerned about Sarah receiving oxycodone."

"I understand," Dr. Sari replied, having no idea of the root of Art and Melissa's concern.

"No. I'm not sure you do. Or that you could," Melissa said.

"No, perhaps not," conceded Dr. Sari, adding, "but we need to address Sarah's pain quickly."

As Sarah was wheeled by on the way to her room, they could see her whinging in pain. Art and Melissa knew she needed help. They weren't sure what to do. Sure, oxycodone would relieve her pain. But could she get addicted to it at an even younger age than her mother? This time, they both were aware of the dangers of that awful drug, and knew the signs to look for if Sarah were to fall prey to addiction. At that moment, they heard a loud scream from the end of the hallway, and knew it was her.

"Alright, Doc. Do what you think is best," Art consented.

Melissa put her arm around his shoulder and whispered, "You had to. What else can we do?"

Dr. Sari left down the hallway. One of her assistants directed Art and Melissa to the waiting area, where they sat together anxiously.

Sarah had been in an agonizing fog since suffering her knee injury. Her leg felt like it was being torn off her body. The ripping sensation she felt after being driven into the ground wouldn't subside. She had blurry memories of being hugged by her friends, and even

Gigi telling her she made the last-second shot to win the game. She blacked out on the ride in the ambulance, only remembering Melissa was with her. At the hospital, Dr. Sari had her try to stay calm as she tested her damaged knee.

Art was talking to Dr. Sari when Melissa had left her. Sarah could see something was upsetting her dad and aunt. Dr. Sari came back and told her they were moving her to her own hospital room. Art and Melissa tried to assure her all would be okay as she was wheeled away on a stretcher down the hall. Near the end of the hallway, one of the assistants wheeling the stretcher lost his focus, and his hand slipped off the side of the stretcher and landed directly on Sarah's bad knee.

"AAAAGGGGHHHHH!" screamed Sarah.

The assistant apologized as he kept wheeling her around the corner to her room. Her knee was throbbing again. As bad as her pain was before, it was now even worse. Dr. Sari arrived shortly afterward. She told Sarah they would be administering a drug for the pain via infusion. She explained it meant they would be putting a needle in her arm with a clear bag of medicine attached. This allowed them to control the amount of medicine given, as well as have it take effect quickly. Sarah nodded, even though she couldn't understand anything but the awful, constant pain she was feeling.

Dr. Sari's assistants wheeled in a tall, metal structure that looked like a coat rack. They hung a bag with some sort of clear liquid in it, then one of them had Sarah extend her arm and clench her fist. The nurse drove a needle into Sarah's arm. Instead of looking away as they suggested, Sarah watched it closely. She didn't find it painful or gross. Kelly was the one who told her about a year ago how Sarah's mom overdosed by injecting what she thought was heroin. Sarah couldn't help but think of this as the nurse plunged that needle into her arm.

Next an assistant injected something into the clear bag now attached by a tube all the way to that same needle in her arm. Immediately Sarah relaxed. A rush of calmness overwhelmed her. She leaned back on her pillow and closed her eyes. A smile formed on her face. She felt like she was in a dream.

Then she saw her mom's face. At first it was blurry, then it formed clearly. There she was, her breathtaking mom. She had a slight smile and her eyes, her hazel eyes, were glowing, a color Sarah could only remember seeing in pictures. It was as if she was there, right there with her. She noticed a small tear running down the side of her mom's face. She was crying. Why? Why was she crying?

"Mom? What's wrong?" mouthed Sarah as she drifted off to sleep.

Sarah felt comfortable as her eyes slowly opened. Art and Melissa were sitting in her room. Sarah saw Melissa first to her left.

"Melly…" uttered Sarah.

Melissa jumped up and said quietly, "Sarah. You're waking up honey." Art, on Sarah's right, jumped up too.

With a slight smile, Sarah muttered, "Dad."

"I'm here Sarah. I'm here," answered Art.

"Take it easy, Sarah," Melissa said while gently rubbing Sarah's forehead.

"What's happening? Where am I?"

"Sarah, you're waking up from an operation on your knee. You're in a hospital. They cleaned out your knee so it wouldn't be so painful," replied Art.

As Sarah gained consciousness, she started remembering playing basketball then hurting her knee. It was a little blurry for her after that, but she recalled the awful pain. Laying there, waking up in a hospital bed, she didn't feel any pain.

"What day is it?" Sarah asked.

"It's Friday," answered Art.

Friday? Sarah thought. She and her group were going home on Friday.

"Friday? Am I going home today?" asked Sarah.

"I don't know," Art said, although he suspected she wouldn't be going back with her People to People group.

"It's eight in the morning. I think their flight is at six this evening. I don't know how you could go back with them," Art stated.

"Dad, I have to go back with my friends!" Sarah said, now almost fully conscious.

At that moment, a nurse came in and said, "Sarah! You're up! How are you feeling?"

"Good, I think," replied Sarah.

"Well, that's good. Dr. Sari will be around shortly to check on you."

"Will I be able to go home today?" asked Sarah.

"I don't know dear. We'll see what Dr. Sari thinks," replied the nurse.

Art and Melissa were happy that Sarah was awake and feeling better. They hadn't thought she would be able to travel back with the People to People group, but seeing how much she wanted to, they started to consider it. Art turned to Melissa.

"I didn't think she would be ready to travel today."

"Me either," replied Melissa, adding, "but she actually looks good. As good as I could have ever imagined."

"Well, let's see what the doctor says," said Art.

Just then, Dr. Sari knocked on the door and came in. She greeted Sarah.

"Sarah. It's good to see you awake. How are you feeling?"

"I feel good. How did you fix me?"

"Well, Sarah, I didn't really fix you. I did what is called a scope to clean out your knee. I found a nerve was being pinched. That's what was causing most of your pain. I was able to 'unpinch' it, if you will."

"Thank you!" Sarah said excitedly, not understanding exactly what Dr. Sari was saying, but since she wasn't experiencing any pain, she knew it must have worked.

"You're welcome…" said Dr. Sari pausing before adding, "however, unfortunately, you do have a serious knee injury."

Sarah's smile faded. Art squeezed her hand and Melissa rubbed her shoulder.

"You have what is known as an ACL tear, and I'm sad to say, also a MCL tear," continued Dr. Sari.

They had heard these terms about professional athletes who suffered knee injuries but didn't know what they meant.

"Could you explain what that means?" asked Art.

"Yes, of course. It means Sarah has experienced a tear of the ligaments that hold her knee in place. I believe she will need surgery to correct it; however, I'll leave that up to your doctor when you return home."

"Oh no," Sarah murmured as a tear formed in her eye.

"Sarah, if you do have the operation, you should make a full recovery," Dr. Sari said, trying to reassure Sarah.

"It doesn't hurt much now," replied Sarah.

"That's good. That's really good," said Dr. Sari.

"Sarah was wondering if she would be able to travel home with her team today?" Art asked.

"If she's up for it, I think she can. Let me have a closer look," replied Dr. Sari, who then held Sarah's leg and gingerly moved it, checking Sarah's reaction as she did so. Sarah nodded that she was okay. She wasn't feeling the pain from the night before.

"Sarah, if you want to, I think you can travel with your team," Dr. Sari said. Sarah smiled as the doctor added, "I am going to give you a local anesthetic shot in your knee. This will numb it for your trip. I'm also going to give you some painkillers. You only need to take them if you experience severe pain."

"Thank you, Dr. Sari! Thank you!" shouted Sarah. Art, Melissa, and Sarah shared a hug. "I really do feel pretty good," added Sarah.

"That's great honey," Melissa said.

"Yes, it is, amazing really," Art agreed.

Paige contacted Art and learned that Sarah was ready to rejoin her team for the trip back to Minnesota. Art would go to the dorm and collect Sarah's things and bring them home with him. Melissa stayed with Sarah while Art was gone. The bus would be at the hospital about two that afternoon to pick her up. Sarah was scheduled to go to rehab before they came and learn how to use the crutches she would need for the foreseeable future.

Following her rehab session, Sarah was using her crutches to walk with Melissa.

"You are really good with those," noted Melissa.

"Thanks. I don't know. They seem easy to me," replied Sarah, "I just can't believe I have almost no pain. It was so awful yesterday."

"I know. It sure looked bad," Melissa said. She was very surprised Sarah was up and around like she was after seeing her suffer that injury.

"Your doctor said the pain was mostly due to a nerve being pinched or something like that," continued Melissa.

"Yeah. That's what she said. Whatever that stuff they put into my arm was, it really knocked me out," responded Sarah.

Melissa nodded, knowing exactly what it was. She thought it best not to say anything more about it.

"You know Melissa, I thought I saw Mom just before I fell asleep," stated Sarah.

Melissa, shocked, stopped walking and turned to face Sarah who then stopped and looked back at her with a sheepish grin.

"I mean. I don't know. It was after the pain stopped. Maybe I was already asleep. Maybe it was a dream."

Melissa was at a loss for words. Had Kerstin come back to communicate with Sarah? No, she thought, it must have been the influence of the powerful, dangerous opioid. She could tell Sarah was a little embarrassed having told her.

"I…I think your mom was watching over you, trying to comfort you," Melissa finally replied.

Just then a commotion developed down the hallway. A sign pointing that way that read "Mental Health Unit." A young man had gotten up from a wheelchair, and it looked like a nurse was trying to get him to sit down again. A woman who may have been his mother was crying. She was yelling through her tears.

"He doesn't remember! He didn't mean to do it! He's a good boy!"

Two large men who looked like hospital security staff came through the door at the end of that hallway and firmly grabbed the young man, quickly restraining him. They walked him through the door while the nurse consoled the woman.

"Wow! What was that?" Sarah asked.

"I have no idea," replied Melissa. The sudden ruckus down that hallway had distracted them from their conversation about opioids. Though Melissa wasn't particularly religious, she wondered if Sarah's experience had been spiritual. Melissa looked over at Sarah, who she found was looking back at her. Melissa forced a tight-lipped smile. Sarah smiled back, then kept walking with ease on her crutches down the hall.

"My lord, you are really good with those things," Melissa said.

Art came back to Sarah's room having put her belongings in his car. He found Melissa in the room resting while Sarah was going back and forth in the hallway on her crutches. Art was amazed that Sarah was feeling so good and how proficient she was with those crutches.

"Hey there Melissa. Time to wake up," Art said, greeting a napping Melissa.

"Umm. In a minute," replied Melissa.

"We don't have much time," Art insisted, adding, "I talked to your boyfriend Armond and he's letting us check out late."

"Very funny," Melissa said, as she sat up and wrinkled her face toward Art. Just then, Sarah galloped into the room on her crutches before stopping.

"Wait! Melissa, you have a boyfriend? In Amsterdam?"

Melissa glared at Art before turning with a smile to Sarah. "Oh dear, your *hilarious* father was trying to make a joke." With a quick glance back to Art, she added, "Believe me, I don't have a boyfriend."

"Yes, that's true Sarah. Like Melissa said, I was trying to make a joke. Although I do think Armond is quite fond of your aunt," clarified Art. Now Art turned the conversation back to getting ready to leave.

"Seriously though, Melissa and I need to get going. Paige and your teammates should be here soon to pick you up." As soon as he said this, Art suddenly felt that perhaps they should stay and make sure Sarah was all right leaving on the team bus. He walked over to Sarah and held her shoulders.

"Sarah?" he said.

"Yes, Dad?"

"Are you sure you'll be okay going back with the team? We can still make arrangements for you to come with us."

"Oh Dad. I'll be fine. Don't worry. You and Melissa should make sure you don't miss your flight."

Just then, Paige entered the room. Seeing Sarah standing with her crutches, she called out to her.

"Sarah!"

"Coach Paige!" Sarah yelled as Paige rushed over and hugged her.

Paige leaned back, straightened her arms, grasping Sarah's shoulders in her hands.

"Sarah, we were so worried for you. How are you?"

"I'm good. My knee doesn't hurt now. They say I need an operation to fix it after I get home."

"Oh my. Well, good that it doesn't hurt." Paige then turned to Art and said, "We'll take good care of her on the trip home. Although, we certainly would understand if you wanted Sarah to travel back with you."

"No way! I'm going back with my team!" declared Sarah.

"There you have it. Sarah wants to travel back with her team," Art said. He looked at his daughter then back to Paige. "And that's okay with me. She's had a great time here... Well that is, until her injury. Even so, I'm glad she made such good friends and wants to travel back with them."

Paige smiled, and said, "You are a very understanding father. You know, Sarah's team and really the entire group this year is special. I've been doing this for a few years, and this is the closest group I've ever seen. They just clicked."

Paige paused and looked back at Sarah adding, "We all clicked." Sarah smiled broadly at Paige, who again hugged her. Art and Melissa smiled at each other.

"Okay then. We'll be heading out," Art said, as he walked toward Sarah while Paige backed up to give them some space. Art hugged Sarah.

"I love you," he said, giving her a gentle hug.

"I love you too Dad, I'll be good," Sarah said. Art moved away, trying not to cry. Melissa then came over and hugged Sarah.

"Oh Sarah, love you," said Melissa.

"Love you too Melissa. Thanks for taking care of Dad for me," replied Sarah, sharing a heartfelt laugh with her aunt. Then Art and Melissa gathered their things and left for their car.

Dr. Sari stopped by just as Sarah and Paige were about to leave. She wished Sarah well and reminded her that if she experienced any pain on the trip home that she should take one or two of the oxycodone and Tylenol pills. Sarah thanked Dr. Sari then demonstrated how good she was on the crutches before leaving with Paige.

As the two of them left the hospital, the bus carrying her teammates was parked to the left. There were whoops and hollers as the girls on the bus saw Sarah. She greeted them with a wide smile. She then raced on her crutches down the sidewalk toward the bus.

The noise from the bus grew louder.

Emilia started shouting, "Sarah! Sarah!" Tina, Sabrina, Alexus, and Brittany joined in, followed by the whole bus shouting in unison, "SARAH! SARAH! SARAH!"

Sarah hobbled up the bus steps and couldn't stop smiling.

CHAPTER 15
RECOVERY

Weeks passed after returning home. Sarah's ACL/MCL surgery had gone well. She was still using her crutches and would start physiotherapy soon. Art was back driving for Kare Kabs. He had spent more than he planned while away, leaving his credit card nearly maxed out. Meanwhile, Melissa was back at her increasingly stressful job.

Sarah had remained in touch via social media with her friends from their overseas basketball adventure. But since her knee injury and subsequent surgery, Sarah wasn't sure if she wanted to continue playing. LaVonda Chatman had stopped by to see her and told her that even though Sarah would miss out on playing in sixth grade, Coach Chatman felt she should be back to normal the following year. Sarah really appreciated her support.

While recovering, Sarah spent a lot of time listening to music. She fondly remembered the days playing the toy drum in the basement at her grandma's house. Also, the fun she had playing drums in the "concert" with the neighbor kids that one summer in Traverse City. She drummed along using pencils, straws, chopsticks—anything like that she could get her hands on. She knew now, more than ever, music was within her soul.

As always, she loved the blues. Howlin' Wolf continued to be her favorite. This led to her listening to other Chicago Blues style artists like Luther Allison, Elmore James, and Chum Fella. She found various artists on YouTube, and marveled at all the great blues musicians that she found, including the Kings, B.B., Albert, and Freddie. Sister Rosetta Tharpe stood out; Sarah loved the way she sang and played guitar.

Sarah also liked to discover local musicians. She was fascinated by Prince. She had heard of him, like everyone else who was born and raised in Minnesota, but she was amazed to watch some of the videos of his performances. The Time, Prince's contemporaries, was also one of her favorites because of their awesome drummer, Jellybean Johnson. She hadn't known much about Bob Dylan until watching him, and then she learned about his huge influence on music. She enjoyed finding other lesser-known acts like The Replacements, Ber, The Shackletons, and The Gully Boys.

No matter the style though, she would "drum" along with whatever she was using for drumsticks—anything from Jimi Hendrix, Led Zeppelin, The Beatles, and The Rolling Stones to Kingfish Ingram, The Clash, Harry Styles, and Phoebe Bridgers. She loved pretending she had a complete drum kit while smashing the pretend cymbals. The love and commitment she had for basketball, practicing by herself for hours, had begun shifting to music.

If Sarah's connection with music was positive since her knee operation, her experimentation with pain relievers was not. The adrenaline from reuniting with her friends made the flight home from Europe euphoric on its own, and she almost forgot about her pain. However, since returning home and beginning to feel isolated, she had started taking the pills she'd been given and continued after her surgery. Art was horrified, and pleaded with her to only take them if she was in a great deal of pain—which was what Sarah told him she was doing.

True, Sarah was in pain, but she had promised herself that she wouldn't fall victim to opioids like her mom. Now, after experiencing the pleasurable high of the pills, she found it an unwieldy promise to keep. In an odd way, the pills made her feel closer to her mom; she often drifted off after taking them, thinking she was feeling her mom's spirit.

One day Art went to say goodnight to Sarah and found her unconscious with an open pill bottle next to her.

He froze for a moment in terrified panic, before trying to wake her without success. Somehow, he gained enough composure to call 911. The paramedics came and were able to revive Sarah with the help of a small dose of naloxone. Art rode with them as they admitted Sarah to the Children's Hospital in Saint Paul. She was kept for five days so they could manage her withdrawal. Art was reluctant to tell Melissa or anyone else of Sarah's sudden opioid dependency. It was too painful a conversation for him to have. His worst fears had come to pass.

Sarah's time in the hospital was spent between opioid treatment sessions to help her realize the nature of the dependency she had developed, as well as support for how she could live without opioids in the future. Even though she was about to start sixth grade, she wasn't the youngest attending the sessions—opioids were taking their toll on people of all ages.

Art was glad to pick Sarah up and bring her home. He had come straight from work, still driving his old Nissan Maxima. The hospital staff wheeled Sarah down to the car, even though she could get around fine on her crutches. She stood up, hobbled over to the car, and got into the passenger seat. Art put her crutches in the back, before starting the short drive up to Maple Manor.

"Sarah."

"Yes, Dad," Sarah answered, ready for the scolding or warning she was about to receive.

"You know I love you..." Art began in an unsteady voice. Sarah looked to see her dad with two hands firmly on the wheel, a grimace on his face.

"I...I don't know...I don't know what to do." He didn't look at his daughter, fearing that he would completely break down.

"I'm sorry, Dad."

They had reached a stoplight. Art finally looked at Sarah. She could see his eyes filled with tears.

"I know what's going on isn't your fault."

The light turned green. They drove in silence, exiting 35E and turning into the long driveway leading to Maple Manor, passing the Fox and Hounds restaurant on the way. Art parked, then turned to Sarah.

"You didn't get to know your mom. She loved you. And she loved me. You're experiencing exactly what she did. You both were injured and given these awful drugs."

Sarah listened intently. They would sometimes talk about her mom, but almost never discussed her problems with drugs.

Art continued, "These drugs were powerful; in her world, they were sublime. They affect your brain in a way that, even once you realize it, it can be difficult to stop."

Sarah turned away, having heard all this before at rehab.

"Yeah, I know Dad."

"No, Sarah, no you don't. You weren't there when I found your mom..." His voice trailed off, but he pressed on. "I found your mom dead. She was dead! These drugs that have this pull, this fascination over you both, they took her. They took her from me and from you and from herself..." He paused before saying what he felt he needed to in this moment. "I was there when they zipped her up in that goddamn awful body bag and took her away to the morgue."

He didn't share this with Sarah to frighten her but wanted her to know the truth of her death. He was met with silence.

"She didn't want to die. Those drugs killed her. And she couldn't stop them. Now, I'm afraid you think you can stop them from killing you."

Sarah looked down. She didn't know how she'd become so attracted to these drugs; only that when she took them, nothing else mattered. Her feelings, her dreams, her core were swaddled for a few hours. There were days she couldn't imagine living without them.

Sarah tried to picture the horrific scene of Art finding her mom's body. Since she was three years old, she had been sad about losing her mom. She'd always thought of her having just left, disappeared in a way, leaving behind only a humble gravestone.

Art was quiet, leaving Sarah to her thoughts. How could Sarah, an eleven-year-old, possibly overcome something her own mom wasn't able to? She glanced at Art who had bowed his head on the steering wheel, perhaps not knowing what else to say.

Then Sarah thought of her music. She loved music. She thought of her basketball friends. She loved them too. She thought of her dad, then Melissa, then Grandma Elizabeth, and her favorite aunt who was more like a big sister, Kelly. Sarah wanted to live, not just for herself but for all of them.

She recalled the vision of Kerstin the first time she fell under the spell of opioids. What her beautiful mom had been reduced to. Sarah now felt she understood why she'd had this dream—Kerstin would have been heartbroken having her own daughter succumb to the same euphoria that killed her.

Sarah felt demoralized. How would she overcome the awful, sensational pull of the drugs she was now infatuated with? In that moment, she had no idea.

"Sarah, I want you to know, I'm here. Whenever you need me…whenever you're ready. I love you and I'm here," said Art, breaking the silence.

"I know, Dad. Thank you. I know. I love you too!" replied Sarah as she unbuckled her seatbelt and sprang over to hug her father.

A few weeks passed. School was starting soon, and Sarah's knee had healed well enough that she no longer needed crutches. In that time, she had avoided taking any more opioids. She had thrown away all that she had. Even though she intended not to use them again, she felt if she wanted to, she would be able to get some more.

For now, her love for music was keeping her at peace. One night, about a week before school started, there was a knock on the door. Art was cleaning up after dinner, so Sarah answered the door.

"Kelly!" yelled Sarah, flinging herself into her arms.

"Sarah! It's so good to see you!"

"You too! I've missed you so much."

Sarah and Kelly talked long into the night about Kelly's recent acting gigs and Sarah's basketball adventures. Kelly would be staying with them several days before she left for her next theater job, which was in New Orleans.

Art had left for work long before Sarah and Kelly awoke. Since Kelly didn't have a car, they decided to go on a walk. Sarah had been walking every day as part of her knee therapy, it was also helping her with what she had accepted would be a lifetime of fighting her unanticipated opioid addiction.

The two walked down the long driveway then turned east on Larpenteur Avenue. It was a warm, late summer's day with only a few clouds in the sky. They both wore tank tops and shorts. Sarah had a Twins baseball cap while Kelly sported a short-brim white straw hat that looked like it could be worn by a sun-loving gangster. Kelly brought along a tote bag she wore over her shoulder with two bottles of water.

Sarah was now almost as tall as Kelly, and the two of them could easily pass as sisters. Both were fit with sandy hair and fair complexions. Kelly had recently cut her hair into sort of a bowl-like haircut, while Sarah had let her hair grow past her shoulders.

They weren't going anywhere in particular, just walking.

"Why'd you cut your hair?" asked Sarah.

"I'm not really sure," Kelly said with a laugh, adding, "I had just finished a six-week run of this play called *Burn This*. My hair was longer than yours. Sometimes, after a show finishes, I feel like it's time for a change."

"I love that you do what you want to."

"Ha! I don't know about that. I love performing so I'll go where it takes me."

Just then, a car full of young men drove by, hooting their horn. One of them was hanging out the passenger seat window, saying something neither Kelly nor Sarah could make out.

"Creeps," Kelly said, shaking her head. Sarah laughed. She felt more like a little girl than a woman boys would cat-call. Sarah saw Kelly as a beautiful young woman full of confidence, while in truth Kelly had her share of insecurities like many who made their living on the stage.

"I think they thought I was older," said Sarah, after the car full of rude boys was gone.

"Yep, I'm sure they did," replied Kelly.

They walked a block in silence. Sarah always had a lot of questions for Kelly. Now, besides wanting to ask her about boys, she was considering asking about drugs. She didn't think Kelly knew about her problems with opioid addiction, since her dad hadn't even told Melissa.

Kelly noticed her looking sheepishly at her.

"Sarah? What is it?" she asked.

"I want to talk to you about something, but I don't know how."

"You want to talk about boys? And S-E-X?"

"No. I mean I do, but not right now."

"Oh. Alright, go ahead. You know you can talk to me about anything."

"Okay, I'll just say it." Sarah then paused without saying anything. Kelly could tell it was something serious. She stopped then noticed Sarah's watery eyes. Kelly grabbed her and held her tight.

"It's okay, Sarah. I'm here. I'm here for you," Kelly said. After a moment Sarah looked directly into Kelly's eyes.

"Kelly, I'm a drug addict."

"What? No, you aren't. No way."

"Yes. Yes, I am."

"Sarah, I don't know what you're saying. Here, let's sit for a minute."

They sat on a little hill halfway to the next block.

"Alright, tell me what's going on."

"It started when I hurt my knee playing basketball. It hurt so bad. Really bad. The doctor gave me a drug for the pain."

"Oh no…" Kelly said, now sensing what happened.

"Yes. And that drug, it made the pain go away and, besides that, I never felt so good. So, I started taking it even when the pain was gone."

"Oh no," again was all Kelly could say. Just like her brother, Kelly only learned of Kerstin's addiction to opioids after her death. Now she was shocked to hear that Kerstin's daughter, her awesome niece, had fallen victim to the same dependency.

"Kelly?"

"Yes."

"I'm so sorry." Sarah leaned over to be held. Kelly knew she had to find the right words.

"Oh, Sarah. Don't be sorry. You know it happens to lots of people. Those drugs, I know they're very addictive."

"Did you ever use drugs?" asked Sarah.

Kelly decided to be truthful. "Yes, I've used drugs. You know, alcohol is a drug and I drink it. I've also used marijuana. And cocaine. And mushrooms." She paused. "But never heroin or opioids." Kelly wondered how bad her truth must sound.

"I don't understand. What's the difference? Are you addicted?" asked Sarah.

"To be honest, I like occasionally smoking marijuana and having a drink, but I don't think I'm addicted to either. Maybe I'm wrong, but I don't think so."

Kelly didn't feel qualified to talk about opioids, but right now she needed to.

"I think the difference is that opioids make you want them so bad you don't think about anything else. Although I can't say I really understand it. I know alcohol and even marijuana can be very addictive for lots of people. I think it has to do with how they affect your brain."

Kelly decided not to discuss cocaine. She did enjoy it on the occasions she'd had it, but fortunately for her, she never seemed to have enough money to get it.

"Yes, you're right, or at least they said something like that in treatment," Sarah said while letting out a sigh.

Again, Kelly was taken aback. "Treatment? You went to treatment?"

"Yes, Dad took me in when he found me asleep."

Kelly thought of how devastating this must have been for her brother. He was the one to find Kerstin dead, and now finding his daughter passed out…

"I know, I haven't taken them since I left treatment. I don't really want to." Sarah paused, looked down and added, "Except when I do."

"You've grown up fast. No kid your age should have to deal with something like that," said Kelly.

After a few moments in silence, Kelly grabbed Sarah's hand.

"Let's go. You know you can always call me," said Kelly, before realizing she wasn't the easiest to get a hold of when she was away. "Even if you can't get in touch with me, close your eyes, and think of me and know I'm there for you. Always," she added, lovingly squeezing Sarah's hand.

"So, you know, I do want to talk to you about boys," said Sarah after a few blocks of them walking in silence.

"Of course you do. I'm not sure I'm much of an expert though!" Kelly said with a laugh.

"Oh, come on Kelly!"

"Okay, whatever. I'm not sure it will be any easier than talking about drugs. What do you want to know?"

"What's it like?"

"Wow! Starting off strong!" Kelly had always talked freely with Sarah. Shocked to hear about Sarah's drug problem, now she was considering how real she should get talking about sex. Sarah was very young, yet without her mother Kelly was probably the only woman—other than maybe Melissa—she could talk to about such things. Sex was more open now than when Kelly grew up. TV shows, like the HBO hit *Euphoria*, if not fully glamorizing teen sex, had at least normalized it, not to mention what could be found on social media.

"Well, honestly, in my experience—not that I'm much of an expert—it can be good. Some men don't know what they're doing though," stated Kelly.

"Does it hurt?" asked Sarah.

"No, not usually. As long as you both are ready, it won't hurt."

"How old were you, you know, when you first did it?"

Kelly thought back to her first time. It was when she was fifteen, and she had a crush on a seventeen-year-old boy. She had her friend set up a group date with him. They went to a dance together. The boy was very shy, and barely said a word all night. The thing she remembered most was near the end of the dance, Three Dog Night's version of "Try a Little Tenderness" played.

Kelly dragged her date up to the dance floor. The song started slowly. She remembered holding him tight and realizing he was aroused. After the dance, they held hands in the car on the way back to Kelly's friend's house, whose parents were away. Kelly had her first sexual experience that night with this boy who barely said a word on her friend's couch. It didn't lead to a relationship—in fact, Kelly later dated one of his best friends. Now, Kelly wondered if it was the right thing to tell Sarah her story. She decided she would leave the details for some other time. Even now, though, she still truly loved that Three Dog Night song.

"Sarah, I was young. I didn't love the boy. You probably wonder, do I wish I didn't do it? I don't know. I can't go back so it doesn't really matter. It wasn't awful, anyway."

Kelly laughed to herself, thinking it wasn't the ringing endorsement Sarah might have hoped for. They walked the rest of the block.

"How do you know if you like girls?" Sarah asked.

This walk had already been a lot different than Kelly had been expecting when they left Maple Manor, so by this time the question didn't surprise her. They walked a little further before Kelly replied, "That's a good question. All I can say is, I think you'll know. At least for me, there's a feeling I have when I'm attracted to someone."

"Sorry Kelly, I don't want to upset you."

"Oh, you can't upset me, sweetheart. You know you can talk to me about anything."

"Well, I was wondering…just that we never see you with a man. And with your acting job, if maybe, you were interested in girls, I…I mean women."

Again, Kelly wondered how truthful she should be, given Sarah's age—still, this was already one of the frankest conversations she ever had with anyone. She had always been close to Sarah; they had a similar inclination for adventure. Already Sarah had amazed Kelly by traveling to the Netherlands to play basketball, and Kelly had a feeling that Sarah would travel the country, and even the world, like she did.

Kelly had a crush on a fellow actor, Jess Sentore, who was a woman a few years older than her. They both were performers in a play called *Stop Kiss*. Jess was a short and curvy Japanese-American woman with thick, dark hair. The play was about two women growing closer and becoming lovers. Life imitated art as Kelly and Jess grew closer while performing together. They had slept over together a few times and shared a bed, and that was as far as it went. After the play, they went their separate ways.

Kelly decided to tell the truth about it as best she could. She started with a joke.

"I guess I just haven't wanted to bring any of the losers I've dated around!" Then adding in a more serious tone, "Yes, I was attracted to a woman once. And she was attracted to me. Maybe it had to do with us performing in a play together where the characters we were playing became lovers. That might be just an excuse though. Nothing came of it. We're still friends. That's about it…" Kelly paused before continuing.

"All I can say is if you're attracted to someone, I think you'll know and, with any luck they will be attracted to you too."

After saying this, Kelly cringed. She thought it was a stereotypical thing to say and she hated being stereotypical.

They continued their walk to the end of Larpenteur Avenue, then crossed Arcade Street boarding Phalen Park Golf Course. The two of them found a spot overlooking the green on hole seven. They were both familiar with golf since Art's older brother Karl and his family were avid golfers. Both Kelly and Sarah had played although neither had caught "the golf bug." Watching the amateur golfers try to play on to the green was entertaining, and offered a welcome break from their serious conversation.

"Ha! Did you see that shot?" Sarah said, laughing. "I did!" replied Kelly with a chuckle.

They had seen a golfer who was in the center of the fairway hit what is known as a shank, where a golfer hits the ball with the hosel of the club near the shaft. The ball would fly to the right, usually at about a 45-degree angle, and certainly not where the golfer was aiming. The golfer who hit this shank smashed his club into the ground, making a large hole in the grass. He then slammed his club in his bag and angrily stalked toward his ball.

The pair were laughing hard by this point and continued to laugh at some of the shots they saw or how certain golfers were dressed.

"Do you know why Karl plays left-handed? It never made any sense to me," said Sarah.

"Wow, Sarah, you really are getting me into some serious conversations today!"

They both laughed.

"I always wondered about that. I mean, he's right-handed, right?" asked Sarah.

"Ha! Yeah, he's right-handed. He said he's always thought he was born left-handed. Still, he does everything else right-handed, but he plays golf left-handed."

"That's either incredible or sad," Sarah stated.

"Yeah, it is. You want to hear something else?" Kelly asked.

"What?"

"He taught both their kids, Jason and Anna, to play left-handed too, even though they're both right-handed."

"What! You're kidding!"

"No, I'm not. He did. Both kids play golf left-handed and do everything else right-handed."

"Do they think they were born left-handed too?" Sarah wondered.

"I don't think so. They just did it because their dad taught them that way. I guess they're both pretty good golfers, so who knows? Maybe we all should be playing left-handed."

They laughed some more. The earlier clear sky was now filled with menacing clouds.

"We better get going. It looks like those clouds are full of water," said Kelly.

The two of them got up and left golf to the golfers. After crossing Arcade Street and starting to walk back on Larpenteur Avenue, Sarah had another question for Kelly.

"How did you know you wanted to be an actor?"

"Um, now *that's* a good question. I enjoyed playing dress-up as a kid. Since I was the youngest, I could get away with trying to be funny. Then I got involved with the school theater department. I loved losing myself by becoming somebody else for a while. And I loved being on stage! When I was in high school, I started joining local theater groups. They were always in need of actors. After high school, I just kept auditioning for roles. I found there was a whole community of actors and theater people. Ever since, I've always been able to find another acting job, some that even pay me, as long as I'm willing to travel."

"I love that you're so gutsy. Do you ever think you'll be in movies?"

"Funny you should ask—I just filmed a part!"

"Really? That's so cool. What's the movie?"

"It's a Sherlock Holmes movie. I'm just an extra, but I'm in a couple of scenes and have one line. If they don't cut it out, that is."

"I can't believe it! Kelly, you're a movie star!" Sarah was thrilled for her aunt.

"Thanks Sarah. I really appreciate it. Maybe it will lead to something more, or maybe not. Either way, I'll keep acting."

They fell into a comfortable silence.

"I know what I want to do, but I don't know how to do it," said Sarah.

"Oh yeah, what's that?" asked Kelly.

"I want to be a real drummer," replied Sarah without hesitation.

"Great! Why not? You already play drums, don't you?"

"Yeah, I play with the school band. But I want to play with a *real* band. And I know you'll laugh, but I want to play with a blues band."

Kelly knew from Art that Kerstin had loved the blues. Besides, Kelly had run off to act all around the country, usually for little or no money, so who was she to say to her young niece that she couldn't play in a blues band?

"Blues? Well, like I said, why not?"

"I think I need my own drum kit to learn how to play—I mean, how to play really good. And you know, I can't have one at the apartment, or Dad always said I can't, anyway."

"You know, Sarah, you're still so young. As long as you can play at school, you'll keep learning. Who knows, you might decide you want to do something else."

"Maybe," said Sarah, thinking to herself there was no way she would want to do anything else.

"Are you going to keep playing basketball?" asked Kelly.

"I don't know. Maybe, maybe not. You know the pain I felt? Well, I never dreamed anything could be that bad. So, I just don't know if I want to play anymore."

"I get it. At least you had fun while you played, plus you were good!"

"Yes, it was fun. I made such good basketball friends. I don't know, I might play again."

"At least you don't need to decide right away, right?"

"Yeah, I can't play this year anyway. I could start again in the spring if my knee heals up."

They crossed over 35E and headed back down the long driveway to the apartment. Just as they passed in front of the Fox and Hounds restaurant, rain started to fall. Sarah wasn't supposed to run, so Kelly walked alongside her. The clouds let loose, soaking the two of them just before they reached the door. Inside, they burst out laughing.

All too soon, Kelly was off to New Orleans. Sarah came to realize that whenever Kelly left, it would always take her a few days to deal with missing her. At the same time, she felt she had made a breakthrough with her addiction. She no longer felt compelled to take the pills while understanding, from her weekly treatment sessions, that it would be an ongoing struggle. Now though, she felt like a kid again. She was enjoying her walks where she pretended Kelly was with her and they could talk about anything.

Every day Sarah woke up and listened to a couple of songs on her phone, always drumming along. She had even started shooting baskets again. Often while dribbling, she would turn the basketball into a drum by rhythmically bouncing it to beats in her head. Art would sometimes come along and help rebound.

To their shared relief, their life was as normal as it had been for some time.

CHAPTER 16
MAPLE MANOR

Sixth grade came and went. Sarah stayed clean. She played with the school band, often remaining after school to practice. She enjoyed watching the basketball team's games, still unsure if she wanted to play again. Now that she was older, Grandma Elizabeth would only stop by a few times a month, rather than every day. Sarah would listen to music and do homework, and though she didn't have much interest in TV, she'd watch some shows on Netflix.

Cooking had become a new hobby for Sarah. Since she was home for a few hours before Art returned from work, she started cooking dinner after doing her homework. She began with boxed macaroni and cheese before moving on to spaghetti and meatballs, always playing music as loud as she thought she could. She loved using strands of spaghetti as makeshift drumsticks until they broke. She started looking up recipes and making lists of ingredients they needed to buy on their next shopping trip. Art was thrilled with her interest in cooking. He had been able to keep them fed through the years but had never been much of a cook.

Friday nights were pizza nights. Sarah learned how to make a good homemade pizza, but when they wanted a treat, Art would get one from Hearthside Pizza. It was located across the street from Wilebski's. Art and Sarah didn't always agree on food, but they both loved that pizza. Sarah's homemade pizza was modeled after Hearthside's. She felt it was close, but still preferred theirs.

Art and Sarah's apartment was on the first floor, although it was halfway below ground level. The view from their windows offered an excellent vantage point for seeing what kind of shoes people wore.

The two of them had grown comfortable living at Maple Manor, even though there wasn't anything fancy about it, and many residents moved out as soon as they could. To Art and Sarah, it was home.

The Fox and Hounds next door could be lively in the evenings. Only patrons who were lost or drank too much would end up in the Maple Manor parking lot. Occasionally, a drunk would park and sleep in his car overnight. Sarah, upon discovering one in the morning, would shout out to her dad.

"There's another *rummy* in the parking lot!" She had learned that word somewhere and it always made her laugh even when she said it herself.

One night, Art had gone out with some friends and told Sarah he wouldn't be home until later. He didn't stay out late like this very often, but he did that night. Sarah had started binging *New Girl* on Netflix, watching a few episodes before falling asleep on the couch. Art came home just before eleven. He decided to let Sarah stay sleeping on the couch rather than wake her. As he was getting ready for bed, he heard a loud door slam in the apartment just above him followed by an intense argument.

"What was that?" Sarah said from the other room, now awake from the noise upstairs.

"I don't know," Art replied as he came out to join Sarah on the couch. It became obvious that it was a man and a woman arguing. They didn't know the upstairs neighbors. Most people living at Maple Manor kept to themselves. Now though, the argument continued, and it sounded more threatening by the minute.

CRASH! Art and Sarah both jumped. It sounded like a heavy dresser with something glass on it had been knocked over. Then it was quiet. Eerily quiet. What happened? Was someone hurt?

Then a man's voice angrily yelled, "I hate you!" followed by the sound of a woman sobbing. They started yelling and, from what Art and Sarah could tell, hitting each other.

"I'm calling the police," Art said as he dialed 911 on his phone. He told the emergency dispatcher what was happening. She took the information about the incident then told him not to get involved. A few minutes later, two police cars showed up with their lights flashing. As Art and Sarah watched from a small opening in their curtains, the police took a man away in handcuffs.

"No, don't take him away! Please, no! He just got out! Don't take him!" the crying woman was yelling. The police told her that they needed to bring the man in, because there was a restraining order against him being within a hundred yards of her. She tried to argue that she didn't care but to no avail, and the police took the man away in a squad car, leaving her standing outside.

"Who called the cops?" the woman shouted. She continued cursing the cops and the cop-callers, whoever they were, for getting involved in her argument. Art and Sarah sat motionless listening. They were the cop-callers. No matter how upset their neighbor was, they knew they did the right thing. Eventually, the woman grew tired of her ranting and went back inside. Art and Sarah thought there might be repercussions from their upstairs neighbors, since they could figure out it was the people living just below them who called for help. In any case, nothing more came of it.

Sarah's seventh grade year passed again without her returning to play basketball. Tartan's varsity coach LaVonda Chatman still kept in touch with Sarah. She had become a mentor to her, even without Sarah playing basketball. Coach Chatman was also interested in music, having been a singer in her church choir and briefly with a jazz band. She would join Sarah in the band room after school to encourage her drumming. She was also fascinated by Sarah's love of blues music. Like Sarah, whose grandmother had introduced her to it, LaVonda had grown up with the blues. For LaVonda it was her grandfather, Otis "The Oat Man" Chatman. Otis grew up in Chicago and played bass with several electric blues bands. LaVonda always enjoyed the blues though was more interested in gospel, jazz and later hip hop and electronic dance music.

Along with Coach Chatman's counseling, Sarah's friendship with Tina, her People to People teammate, kept her involved with basketball. Tina continued playing, not only for her middle school team but also for the Amateur Athletic Union teams in the spring and summer. The AAU had been around for some time as a path for serious basketball players to compete against each other. When Sarah could find a way, she would go watch Tina's games. Sometimes, she would stay over at Tina's house in the suburbs. Although she very much enjoyed staying at Tina's house, Sarah never minded living in the small apartment with her dad at Maple Manor. It was all she knew and she had grown comfortable with everything about it, including the occasional police visit.

Tina also stayed over a few times at Sarah's. Tina enjoyed her stays, even agreeing Hearthside Pizza was the best pizza. But it was very different than what she experienced in the suburbs. The pair of them giggled when sometimes they'd hear the couple upstairs making love on their waterbed. It was like the apartment building was alive. Tina woke up in the middle of the night once while sleeping over. The bedroom window was open and she lay awake listening to the sounds of crickets, barking dogs, trucks, sirens, and cars racing into the night.

Sarah and Tina had both recently begun their periods. The friends learned about it, experienced it, and hated it together. They did like growing older though. Talking about boys and favorite movie stars and athletes would keep them up. Sarah felt like she could talk about anything with Tina, but the one thing she never spoke of was what she hoped was her brief foray into drug addiction. She kept any talk of that between her dad and Kelly.

Art continued working at Kare Kabs. The company had started doing rides from the Veterans Administration Hospital in South Minneapolis. These rides would be all over the state rather than within the Twin Cities like other trips. Since Art had been there longer than most drivers, he had a choice whether to become a primary VA driver. He enjoyed driving and longer trips gave him more time to see the entire state.

Some rides required that he get up as early as 5 AM for a pickup in one corner of the state to get the passenger in to the VA for an appointment. Sarah was old enough now that she would get herself off to school and come home without needing supervision.

One November morning, Art had a VA pickup in Virginia in northeastern Minnesota. This would mean an even earlier start time than usual. Virginia was just short of a three-and-a-half-hour drive from the Twin Cities. Art would need to leave at about three in the morning, the earliest start he ever had, to get his passenger back to the VA for their 10 AM appointment. Since he was leaving so early, he brought his van home the night before. An overnight ice storm had left the roads slippery. Art had to drive slower than he had planned, but even so, he arrived at the Virginia home at 6:30 AM. With the sun rising and roads improving, he felt confident they would make it to the VA by 10 AM as scheduled.

The woman answering the door seemed shocked to see Art. With the icy conditions she and her husband, whose appointment it was, were up but hadn't expected his ride to be there and on time. Art told them it had been slippery, but he felt the conditions were safe. The man, although reluctant, agreed to go on the trip down to the VA.

Though it was slow-going and slippery, Art was able to keep the Kare Kabs van on the road by driving carefully and sticking around fifty miles per hour. Even so, he could tell his passenger was anxious. With the sun coming up and melting the ice, Art knew that by the time they reached Highway 35, the roads would be smooth the rest of the way.

About ten minutes before reaching the turn for Highway 35, the passenger had seen enough. He asked Art to turn around. The rule for VA drivers was to do what the passenger asked, even if it meant returning them home without making their appointment. Art didn't argue, instead saying he felt the conditions were about to improve significantly with the sun rising, but to no avail. The passenger insisted on turning around. Art turned around and drove the icy roads back to Virginia. About fifteen minutes before arriving back to his passenger's home, the roads had indeed improved significantly, just as Art said they would. The morning sun was shining brightly, melting the ice from the road. Art didn't say anything but sped up slightly, demonstrating to his passenger how much better the roads had become.

The nervous passenger and his equally nervous wife were reunited. Art called in to Lydia and explained the situation. She understood and was even surprised he had made it up there on time with the road conditions that morning. Art said he was going to rest and maybe even doze off for a while before heading back. Lydia replied that was fine and asked him to radio in when he approached the Twin Cities, in case there were a ride needed in the northern part of town.

Art didn't smoke very often and never at home or in his Kare Kabs van. Lately, he had begun smoking at breaks or when he was at a bar. His cigarette of choice was Camel Golds, for what he felt was their smooth flavor. This morning he pulled his van over on a barren street and stepped outside for a smoke. Looking around at the beautiful early winter morning, he reflected on his future.

He enjoyed his job but wondered how he could better provide for Sarah. And Sarah…well, he always worried about Sarah. She had already been through so much in her young life. He thought maybe they should move to a better place. It was fun to think about, but he had no idea how they could do it.

Thoughts of Kerstin came to him. He wondered what life would be like if she had beaten her addiction. Then Melissa crept into his mind. After returning from Amsterdam, they had resumed their prior friendship but nothing more. A smile came to him recalling the morning they awoke naked in bed together, still not sure if they had consummated their bond. She was much more than Kerstin's sister to him. He was unsure whether he should pursue a closer relationship. Would she even be interested? He had no idea, as he finished his cigarette and soaked in the wonder of this cool Minnesota morning. At times like this, he felt like he had the best job in the world.

That morning Sarah awoke, put some Eggo waffles in the toaster, and got ready for school. She listened to music with her wired earbuds. Most of the kids had wireless earbuds, but Sarah was happy with her wired ones. She would sway, moving the wire from side to side with the beat. She had recently downloaded Luther Allison's *Bad News Is Coming* album. She loved it, especially Andrew Smith's drumming. After breakfast, she cleaned up and went out to catch the bus for school.

It was 10:15 AM when Art woke up in his van. He found a gas station, filled up the van and got a Pepsi. The drive back to the Twin Cities was smooth with little traffic and dry roads. When he was coming up to North Branch, he radioed Lydia to see if she had a ride for him. There was one to the VA at 11:30 AM for someone in White Bear Lake. Since he would be a little early, Art planned to eat lunch at Key's Café. Eating at good local restaurants was a benefit to the longer VA rides, compared to fast-food lunches when driving within the Twin Cities.

Upon dropping off his passenger at the VA, Art again checked in with Lydia. She told him he didn't need to, but if he was willing there was someone needing a ride from the VA to Red Wing, about an hour south. Taking this ride would give him his single longest day of driving. He decided to do it. This time Lydia said he didn't need to radio in when he was done, although she asked him to return the van for a night shift drive that evening.

Sarah's school day ended at 2:30 PM. She stopped by the band room to practice playing drums. She queued up "It's Been a Long Time" from *Bad News Is Coming* and played along. LaVonda stopped in to talk and listen for a short time. Sarah finished up and left to catch the bus home.

As the bus pulled down the long driveway, past the Fox and Hounds, everyone could see a large fire truck outside the apartments. Sarah and a couple of other Maple Manor kids were dropped off at the entrance a little further away than usual with the fire truck blocking the way. Approaching her building, Sarah could see the firemen were pumping out water. Strange, she thought—wouldn't firemen be using water to put out a fire?

"Oh no!" Sarah yelled as she discovered the water being pumped out was from her apartment. "What happened?" she asked the nearest fireman.

"Some idiot flooded out the ground floor apartment while filling his waterbed," he answered.

"How could that happen?" Sarah asked in disbelief.

"Apparently, he forgot he was filling the waterbed and left for work. He flooded his apartment and the one below."

"No!" Sarah said, telling the fireman, "That's my apartment!"

Just then the apartment caretaker, Tom, appeared. He was an old, heavyset man who had emigrated from Wales years ago with his young family. His accent was still thick, making it hard for some to understand him. Sarah had gotten used to it, having lived at Maple Manor since she was three.

"Sarah, I'm so sorry," said Tom as he reached her.

"I can't believe it. Our apartment? It's ruined."

"I know, I know. Again, I'm so sorry. We shouldn't even allow those ridiculous waterbeds. And that joker was so dumb to leave the water running."

"Can I go in and try to save some things?"

"Not right now. You'll have to wait until we're done," the fireman answered.

"Dad's not going to believe it," said Sarah, as she looked down and sighed.

The fireman left to go about his business.

"Do you have somewhere to stay?" asked Tom.

Sarah hadn't thought about that, still reeling from the shock.

"I…I don't know. I should call my dad."

"Okay, if you need somewhere, let me know."

"I will, Mr. Morgan. Thank you."

Sarah retrieved her cell phone from her backpack and picked "Arty" from her list of favorite contacts.

Art answered, "Hi Sarah. What's up?"

"Hi Dad…" Sarah said then paused.

"Sarah, what's going on?"

"Dad, our apartment…it's flooded."

"Flooded? What?"

"Yes, Dad," Sarah said, her voice cracking.

"I don't understand. I'll be home in about a half an hour. Are you safe?"

"Yes, I'm good. Mr. Morgan said I can let him know if I need somewhere to stay until you get home."

"Oh, that's good. I'll hurry home. What happened?"

"You won't believe me, but the guy upstairs was filling his waterbed and forgot all about it. The fireman said he left for work, and it flooded."

Mr. Morgan had Sarah go to an empty apartment on the second floor of her building. It was across the hall from the one that was responsible for the flooding. There she waited, seated on the floor, looking out the window at the firetruck in the parking lot for what seemed like forever. Finally, she saw Art's old maroon Nissan Maxima pull in the parking lot. The firemen seemed to be nearly done with removing as much water as possible from their drenched apartment. Art came in the door and ran over to Sarah. They sobbed as they hugged each other tightly.

Maple Manor agreed to compensate Art $2,000 for the inconvenience the flooding caused, and allowed them to move to the vacant apartment Sarah had waited in. It was considered a better apartment than the ground floor one, so its rent was $100 more a month, which Maple Manor waived. Art and Sarah decided to take them up on it and moved in.

Immediately after the flooding, the two of them stayed at Grandma Elizabeth's house for a few days. Though appreciative of the compensation, they felt their loss was way beyond mere financial consideration. Art had lost several photo albums of his life from even before Kerstin, through their wedding and the early days after Sarah was born, to the years of Sarah growing up. They both lost keepsakes, books, and artwork along with some old vinyl records. And then there were the "official" papers such as their social security cards and passports. Most of their furniture was also damaged. Luckily, Grandma Elizabeth and Melissa gave them some couches and chairs. Art splurged, buying them each a new bed with the compensation. They were lucky that the TV survived.

Soon enough they were back to a new normal, albeit a floor higher. Even though they enjoyed the balcony, oddly they both missed seeing people's shoes as they walked in from their old halfway-below-ground unit.

Sarah's eighth-grade year came to an end. She took a job at the Taco Bell at the corner of Larpenteur Avenue and Rice Street about a mile away. She would either bike or walk to and from work. Wilebski's, where Art still frequented for happy hour, was only about a block away from the Taco Bell on Rice Street. Sometimes if Sarah's shift ended around five, she would go play video games at Wilebski's and wait for Art. He would usually hang out with other Kare Kabs employees, and sometimes with Melissa.

Even before the flooding, Art had been drinking his whiskey before bed less regularly, and at happy hours he would stick to beer. Sometimes if Sarah was already at home, he would stay later than usual and end up walking home, leaving his car to pick up in the morning.

CHAPTER 17

THE FOX AND HOUNDS

A long day of driving on a Friday in June led Art to linger at Wilebski's. Lydia and a few others from Kare Kabs were there. Sarah was staying overnight at Tina's house in Eagan, so Art didn't feel the need to rush home.

Most of the happy hour crowd stayed as the blues band that night started to play. Art recognized the guitar-playing singer as BB Alight. He was a Minnesotan who had led various blues bands. This one was called The Thrill, an homage to BB King's "The Thrill Is Gone" as well as an inside joke since Alight would surely replace The Thrill with a new band soon. Art knew that if a BB Alight band was going to be playing, he would enjoy it. They played mostly blues classics, along with a few rock and roll numbers, and sometimes BB Alight originals.

Art and Lydia remained friendly and had even spent a few nights together since they had stopped dating. They both enjoyed each other's company so would often end up at happy hours together. The two of them had left the table of co-workers to have a drink at the bar. Art ordered a Bell's Two Hearted and a White Claw for Lydia from Cullen the bartender, as BB's band played T-Bone Walker's "Call It Stormy Monday but Tuesday Is Just as Bad."

"Hey, are you seeing anyone these days?" asked Lydia.

Art shook his head signifying no, then asked, "You?"

"No. Well, not really," replied Lydia.

"Not really? That's probably what you said when you were dating me."

"Yeah! I guess it depended on who was asking," Lydia joked.

"Ha. Good one."

"Honestly, I enjoyed our time together and still do now," Lydia said in a more serious tone. "You know me. I just don't know that I can be in a relationship with, well, with anyone. At least not right now."

"I understand, Lydia. I am glad to have you as a friend. Maybe I'm not meant for another relationship either."

"What about Melissa? You two are cute together," said Lydia, who then looked around asking, "Where is she, anyway?"

"She said she couldn't make it tonight," replied Art, then added, "I think we are about the same as you and me. Good friends. And you know, same as with you, I'm happy we are. I just don't know if it could ever work… Well, you know why."

"Yes, I do, but you know, sometimes, I don't know, it's corny to say, but time changes things. People change. If things had been different, who knows? But they're not. You're alone and she's alone and you have…" Lydia paused before adding, "chemistry."

"Chemistry? Hum, I wondered what it was called!" Art said with a smile.

The bartender, Cullen, left the two drinks in front of them with a nod and then turned to fill his next order.

"Don't we have chemistry?" asked Art.

"Sure, yes, we do have chemistry. You know if I wasn't such a loner, I wouldn't let Melissa or anyone else near you."

"Ah, that's sweet, Lydia," Art said then picked up his glass and said, "Cheers! Cheers to chemistry!"

They shared a laugh, clinking their drinks.

Lydia and the others left after a few more songs. Art stayed a while longer since he had decided to walk home anyway. During a break, BB Alight came up to the bar to get drinks for the band. Art lifted his glass to BB, who smiled and nodded back. They didn't know each other well, but since BB often played there and Art frequented the bar they had shared a few short conversations, even once a few months ago at the urinals.

Soon Art finished his beer and left the bar. Before starting his walk, he reached for his hard pack Camel Blues and fished out the last cigarette. He couldn't find his lighter. A tall, skinny, goth-looking woman enjoying her smoke held out a lighter for him. He took the lighter and lit his cigarette.

"Thank you," Art said as he handed the lighter back.

"Sure thing," replied the woman.

BB Alight's band was now playing BB King's "How Blue Can You Get?" Alight loved playing BB King songs. Art thought it was a BB thing, as well as those songs allowing Alight to show off his prowess playing the guitar.

"Good tune," the woman said.

"Yeah, this guy's good," replied Art, then feeling like he should introduce himself added, "I'm Art."

"Well hello Art. Jane here.

"Nice to meet you, Jane, and thanks again for the light," Art said looking at her. She was wearing a black leather jacket with what looked to be black yoga pants. She had a lot of black makeup around her dark-brown eyes. Even with her choice of fashion—or maybe because of it—her face was alluring.

"Of course. Anything for a fellow blackstack," she said, flicking her cigarette butt to the ground.

"Blackstack? I haven't heard that one," Art said.

Jane began to walk away before turning and winking at Art as she slipped back into the bar.

Art grinned and finished his cigarette. The night was beautiful, even though it had been hot and humid during the day, as June days often were in Minnesota.

Art walked over to check on his car. There was the old maroon Maxima in the back of the parking lot where he often parked when, like tonight, he thought he might leave it and walk home. Before starting his journey, he leaned against the Maxima and looked up to the clear night sky. BB Alight's band had started playing Ruby Toombs' classic "One Bourbon, One Scotch, One Beer." For a moment, Art considered going back to the bar and having another drink. Perhaps he could hookup with Jane. *Yeah, right!* He scoffed to himself and began his walk home.

As he walked, a police car drove past with its siren blasting. A few more police cars without sirens followed, still determined to get somewhere fast. There were the now familiar dogs barking at him as he walked, while large trucks would thunder down Larpenteur Avenue on their way to the highway. And of course, there were always a few youngsters seeing which of them had the hottest hot-rod. Then it could be eerily quiet. Just crickets and more crickets.

Turning down the long driveway to Maple Manor, the last song he heard tonight was still playing in his head. Since Sarah was over at Tina's, he decided to stop in at the Fox and Hounds. He hadn't been there for some time, so he thought, why not?

The place was quiet, which wasn't unusual as it was more of a dinner place than a late-night hangout. Art sat at the bar, where the bartender was at the register with his back to Art. Art pulled out his phone to see if he might have missed a call or text.

"What'll it be?" the bartender asked, sliding a coaster over to Art.

Art looked up and caught the bartender's eye.

"Ron?"

"Art! It's great to see you!"

The bartender was Art's old Kare Kabs friend, Ron Salver, who had left some time ago to pursue his interest in the restaurant business. Ron was with Art the night he met Kerstin.

"Ron Salver. I can't believe it's you," Art said, greeting his old friend.

"Yes, it's been a long time," Ron replied. "First, let me get you a drink."

"I'll have a Two Hearted."

"Coming up!"

Ron went to pour a pint. The two old friends spent the next hour catching up on their lives. Ron had heard about Kerstin's death, but didn't know Art was raising their daughter alone.

"That must be tough. You know, I got married too, but I'm divorced now," stated Ron.

"That's too bad. I'm sorry to hear that," said Art.

"Oh, don't be. I mean, my wife and I had some good times. We just weren't meant to be together. She wanted to move down south and hated my working these late hours," said Ron, adding, "We're still friendlyish."

The place had cleared out and the staff had started their nightly clean.

"Looks like I need to get going soon," Art said.

"Oh, no. Not unless you want to."

"Really? You'll keep the place open for me?"

"Sure. You want to stay, I'll keep it open—or we can lock up and just have another couple drinks with it closed."

"Wow, you really are the man here, huh?" a grinning Art said.

"You know it! I run this damn place since the owners are never around," Ron said with a wink, before going to see the staff off and locking up. On coming back, he poured them both fresh glasses of Two Hearted.

"Looks like a good gig running this place," Art said.

"Yeah, the pay's lousy and the hours are long but other than that it's fine."

"Ha. Must be good to be in charge, though. What's up with the owners?"

"The main owner, Bob, he has houses all over… Well, all over the world."

"Wow. Nice."

"Yeah, he's a good guy, even though whenever he does show up it's as if he feels like he needs to chew me out."

"That's too bad."

"I guess he just needs to get it out of his system. When he's done, he buys me drinks until we both need to Uber home. I consider myself lucky he doesn't show up much."

"Where's he at now? Or don't you know?" asked Art.

"He's on some cruise around the Horn of Africa. He loves cruises, seems like he's always on one."

"I don't think I'll ever go on a cruise," said Art.

"Me either…again, that is. I was on a nasty cruise once to Jamaica. Everyone got sick. I was so sick I thought I was going to die—"

"Enough! That's all I need to know!" interrupted Art, adding, "Now I'm *sure* I'll never go on one!"

They both took a drink from their beers.

"How does the guy have houses all over and be able to go on cruises all the time? This place never seems all that busy," wondered Art aloud.

"He's an interesting dude. He grew up in a trailer park and somehow has a knack for business. He owns several in the US as well as a few in Mexico. He won't have anything to do with a business that he doesn't own at least a 51% stake in."

"Must be nice!" said Art, shaking his head again.

"I'm not sure why he owns this place, although he is in constant contact with me about everything, micro-managing everything—even down to who is our napkin vendor. He is generous, though. He gives out yearly bonuses to all the staff. Maybe it's some sort of tax write-off or something."

"Umm…or maybe he's laundering money through it," stated Art.

"Maybe! I hadn't thought of that!" Ron said with a laugh.

They finished the beers.

"Want another?" offered Ron.

"Thanks. But no. I think I've had enough for one night."

"Okay. It was great seeing you. Small world you know."

"It was great seeing you too," Art said as he got up from his barstool, adding, "I'll be sure to stop in more often now."

"Hey, Art, before you go, want a tour of the place?"

Art stretched, thinking more of going to bed than walking around the place. But since he had never seen more than the bar, he decided to take his old friend up on his offer.

"Okay, sure. Let's do it," replied Art.

Ron led Art through the dining room and then back into the kitchen, which was large and clean. The enticing smell of meat slowly roasting for the next day's meals filled the air. On the other side of the kitchen was the sports bar. Ron said that side continued to grow in popularity, adding that maybe someday the entire place would be just a big sports bar.

They went downstairs to the event center. It was a large space that held weddings and other private gatherings. Ron said they don't book many events, mainly because they didn't make much money on them, so Bob told him not to put any effort into booking more. There was a smaller kitchen downstairs to handle canapé-style food.

At the far end of the event center there was another room. Ron used a key to open the oddly thick door.

"Hey! What's this?" asked Art.

"This, my boy, is an old rehearsal space for bands playing weddings and such. There are even a few amps over there," replied Ron, pointing to the side of the room.

"What? A rehearsal space? Why?"

"Good question. No one has used it since I've been here. The idea was that the band hired for a wedding would bring all their things here and practice for a few days before the event."

"Unbelievable!" was all Art could say.

"Have a look around. This room is sound-proofed. Well, sound-proofed as good as they could whenever it was they built it. And it even has its own bathroom over there," said Ron, pointing to the far corner of the room.

"What's that for?" Art asked, pointing to a plywood board leaning up against the wall.

"It's covering a door," answered Ron. He then walked over and pushed the plywood out of the way, unlocked the door and opened it. They both walked out on to the back end of the Fox and Hounds, which was down a slight incline from the large parking lot. A short distance away on their left was the 35E highway, and a little further away in front of them was the Larpenteur Avenue bridge.

Art walked back into the room, his head spinning with possibilities. Then his face lit up with a smile.

"Ron?"

"Yes, what is it?"

"You said nobody uses this?"

"Yeah, that's right. Not since I've been here. When we do have events, bands just set up their stuff in the event space. I guess they have their own place to practice. It's always locked except when we clean it once a month. Sometimes Bob surprises me by wanting to see it, so we have to keep it clean."

Art continued to smile, a faraway look in his eyes.

"Sarah, you know my daughter. She's quite the drummer. She plays in the school band and practices almost every day before taking the bus home. And you know what?"

"What?"

"I bet if Sarah had a place to practice…a place like this…she would practice a lot."

"You think so?" asked Ron.

"Yeah, I do," replied Art.

"Umm. Well, you know old buddy, I'd love to help you out. But you know I'll need to charge you something, since I'll have to tell Bob about it."

"Fantastic! I mean, it sounds good. I could pay you maybe fifty bucks a month. Does that work?" asked Art.

"It would, except, I'll only charge you fifteen bucks. Bob might want me to charge more or maybe won't let us do it at all, but I'll start by telling him my buddy's daughter is the next Ringo Starr. I think he'll let us."

"Man, I can't believe it!" Art said, reaching over to hug Ron.

"No problem, Art. If Bob's all good, I'll get you a key."

"Thank you, Ron. Wow. Thank you!"

A few days later, Ron had given the key to Art. Bob laughed and approved of the $15 monthly fee when Ron mentioned letting the next Ringo Starr practice in the space. Art planned to pick up a Hearthside pizza for dinner and would then surprise Sarah with news of a place for her to practice.

However, a major problem was that Sarah didn't have a drum kit. The only drums she used were the ones at school. She was still air drumming constantly, like she was when Art arrived home with the pizza. Sarah had her earbuds in, moving around the small apartment hitting the invisible snare drum while working the imaginary cymbals. She nodded to Art but kept playing until her song ended with a two-handed cymbal smash.

"Hi Dad."

"Hi Sarah. Ready for some Hearthside pizza?"

"Always!"

Art put the pizza down in the middle of the dinner table while Sarah set out plates, silverware, and hot seeds. They sat down and each grabbed a square of their piping hot pepperoni extra cheese pizza, the cheese leaving a string trail to their plates.

"How was work today?" asked Art.

"Fine. Mandy quit," replied Sarah. Someone was always starting or quitting at Taco Bell.

"How was yours?" she asked.

"Fine," answered Art without providing any other details. They ate in silence for a while.

"You know what?" Art said, now ready to break the news about the Fox and Hounds.

"What?"

"Remember I told you about meeting an old friend that works at the Fox and Hounds now?"

"Sort of, yeah, I guess so," Sarah said, more interested in eating her pizza.

"Well, his name is Ron, and he runs the place."

"Oh. Okay."

"Well, there happens to be a room downstairs that's made for bands to practice in."

"Oh yeah?" said Sarah, suddenly more interested in her dad's conversation. She looked over at Art with her mouth half full of pizza.

"Yeah. And this room, nobody uses it," continued Art.

"Really?"

"Yeah, so I asked Ron if you could use it."

Sarah was now *very* interested.

"You did? What'd he say?"

"He said…" Art paused as Sarah leaned closer, "Yes! He said yes you can use it!"

"Really? Wow, I can't believe it! Thanks Dad! You're the best!"

Sarah stood up and hugged her sitting dad around his shoulders.

"You're welcome, Sarah. I couldn't believe it either."

Sarah, now wound up with excitement, started walking around the living room air drumming, before turning toward Art.

"Did you see what kind of drum kit they have?"

Art finished the pizza in his mouth, wiped his face with his napkin, then lent back in his chair, looking at Sarah.

"Well, now that's the catch."

"Uh? What do you mean?"

"There isn't a drum kit there," Art stated matter-of-factly.

"What? No drums?"

Sarah visibly shrank, like the wind had gone out of her.

"No. Sarah. No drums. But you know what?"

Sarah just looked at him, not sure what to expect anymore.

"I'm going to buy you a drum kit!"

"What? Dad! Really?" replied a reinflated Sarah.

"Yes, that's right," Art said as Sarah again came over and hugged him.

"How?" asked Sarah in a curious tone.

"You know Maple Manor gave us some money when we were flooded out."

"Yeah?"

"Well, I saved some of it. Hopefully enough for a drum kit. Do you know how much they cost?" asked Art. He had some idea, having searched on the internet, but he wasn't sure what Sarah had in mind.

"I don't know for sure; I think under $500," replied Sarah.

"Good deal. We should be fine. Let's get you one!" Art declared, leading to another hug from his daughter.

Sarah stayed up late dreaming of practicing drums. She texted Kelly, Tina, and Emilia to let them know. Tina replied immediately saying how happy she was for Sarah. Emilia followed with a heart emoji. Kelly didn't text back until past midnight, but she too was thrilled for Sarah.

Art went to the Guitar Center in Roseville after work. A tall, thin, balding redhaired salesman with a goatee approached.

"Hello. I'm Todd. Can I help you?"

"Hi. Yes, I hope so," replied Art.

"Those are some great drum kits," Todd said as he faced the Pearl, Ludwig, Tama, and Yamaha sets arranged on the showroom floor.

"Yes, I'm sure they are."

"Are they for you?" Todd asked in a slightly condescending manner.

"No. Not for me. My daughter plays and I'd like to buy her a good drum kit to practice with."

"Oh. Well, over here we have our beginner kits," Todd said waving his arms to the left toward several drum kits. He added, "Although, I might refer to them as beginner, we only carry the finest equipment. Some experienced drummers swear by these kits."

Art walked over and looked closer. He loved the way a Tama kit looked. It was listed at $699 on sale from $800, which was still a little more than he wanted to spend.

"I see the three-piece ones cost less. But Sarah told me she would like a five-piece kit. She's pretty serious. I was afraid to bring her along. She might have wanted one of the $10,000 sets."

"Has she played before?" Todd asked, adding, "A true beginner could definitely start with a three-piece."

"Yes. She's played drums in the school band as well as a jazz band they have had for a few years now. She's always had a knack for it."

Todd nodded, having heard stories of musical prodigies more times than he'd care to remember.

"In that case, the Tama set you're looking at would be a good choice. I've always played Tama myself and love them."

Art hadn't thought that his salesman was a drummer, but then realized he'd seen Todd before sometimes playing with BB Alight's bands at Wilebski's.

"I think I've seen you play, if you've played with BB Alight," said Art.

"Yeah, that's me. I love the blues. BB and I have known each other for a while."

"I thought I recognized you. Sarah, my daughter, loves the blues too. That's what she wants to play."

"Really? Good for her. I don't hear of many young women who want to play the blues. In fact, these days, I don't hear of many young men either. It seems most want to play some sort of electronic, hip hop or rock. Or country, which now is really just rock. Not many are interested in either jazz or blues."

"Sarah loves listening to all types of music, but someday she said she wants to play in a blues band," stated Art.

"Interesting, I'm glad to hear it," Todd said as the two of them stood by the Tama kit.

"I'd love to get this Tama kit, but it's more than I planned to spend," said Art.

"What's your budget?" asked Todd.

"$500," replied Art.

"Umm, I can't sell a new kit for $500." Todd paused. "But I can make $650 work."

Art walked around the kit, which he thought was beautiful. Since it was going to be Sarah's kit, he wanted her approval before buying it.

"Thanks. I'll be back with Sarah soon," Art said.

"Here's my card. If you want to put $50 down, I could hold it for you at that price for a few days," Todd said, handing Art the card.

Art walked around the kit again. The extra $150 would hurt, but now he wanted to get this kit for Sarah.

"Alright, fifty bucks to hold it. I get it back if we decide not to buy it, right?"

"Yes sir, that's right," replied Todd.

Art gave Todd his credit card information to hold the set.

The next day, Art talked to Lydia about picking up a few weekend trips to make some extra cash. Weekend routes were highly sought-after, being about the only way to earn extra money driving. Lydia was happy to accommodate Art, especially after he told her he needed the extra money for Sarah's drums. She scheduled Art as one of the drivers for the next three weekends.

When Art came home, Sarah was ready to go look at drums. She had worked the lunch shift at Taco Bell then raced home on her bike. At the Guitar Center, Art asked for Todd, who wasn't working that day, so a young woman with her hair dyed a very bright pink greeted them.

"Hi there. I'm Zadie. What was Todd helping you with?"

"Well, he was helping me pick out a drum kit for Sarah here," replied Art, nodding toward Sarah, who smiled.

Art took out Todd's card with the Tama drum kit listed and the price of $650. Zadie took the card, staring at it for a moment, and then directed them to the Tama drum kit.

"Here's the Tama kit Todd showed you."

"Wow!" exclaimed Sarah. She had seen Tama kits before but this one was a five-piece in hairline black. Sarah circled the drum kit, admiring the components. There was a 10" and 12" tom, 14" floor tom, 20" kick drum, and 14" snare.

"It's a wonderful kit. What do you play on now?" asked Zadie.

"Just about anything the school has. They have an old Yamaha three-piece in the band room, but I've played tenor drums and bass drum with the marching band. Never one like this though," replied Sarah.

"Well, Sarah, today is your lucky day," Zadie said, as she extended her open right hand toward the drum throne.

"Huh?" asked a confused Sarah.

"Go ahead. Play!" Zadie said with a smile as she handed Sarah a pair of drumsticks. "I want to hear you. Besides no one is here and you know, this is a music store, so let's hear you play some music!"

"Come on Sarah. I want to hear you play too," urged Art.

Sarah was reluctant. She had never played a drum kit like this, except in her dreams.

"Okay, I'll try," she said, taking the drumsticks from Zadie.

Sitting on the drum throne, Sarah felt a rush of energy and excitement. She knew then that this was what she was meant to do. Suddenly her apprehension disappeared. She hit each drum to get a sense of its pitch. Like most drum kits on a showroom floor, the kit wasn't tuned. Sarah didn't go about tuning it but listened closely so that when she did start to play, she would know how it sounded.

Zadie and Art retreated off to the side. There were a few other sales reps over at the counter and a customer looking at guitars. Sarah figured she would play something she knew well. Since she had listened to the Luther Allison *Bad News Is Coming* album numerous times while practicing the drum parts, she decided to play one of those songs. She chose "The Stumble," a rollicking instrumental tune with a fun drum part.

She looked around, felt the anticipation of her father, and grinned at him. She hit the drumsticks together for a one, two, three and then started the tune. Everyone in the showroom stopped what they were doing and watched. Sarah could hear the rest of the band in her head as she played along to the song; everyone else could just hear her. Her joy shone through her playing.

As she finished with a cymbal crash, Zadie yelled her approval.

"Yeah! That was awesome! Whoa!"

Art was smiling broadly.

"That was fun, thanks," Sarah said.

"The pleasure is all mine. You, my dear, are a fantastic drummer," Zadie stated.

"Thank you. I really appreciate that."

"So, I don't know much about buying a drum kit. Do we carry it out from here?" Art asked.

"Oh no. There's a new one in the back. I see Todd is selling it for $650."

"Yeah, that's what he said," Art confirmed.

"You know, he isn't supposed to do that with this drum kit, but Todd sort of does things his own way sometimes."

"You mean you can't sell it for that?" asked a disappointed Art.

"No, I will. The company won't make any money on it though.

I know that's not your problem," Zadie said, before continuing, "You know what? If you like the showroom model, I could sell you that one for $550. There's nothing wrong with it. It's just been played a little bit."

Art looked at Sarah who was still sitting on the throne, tinkering with the drum kit.

"Hey Sarah," said Art, getting his daughter's attention before asking, "are you okay if we buy that drum kit? Or do you want a new one?"

"I thought we were buying this one. I love it!" replied Sarah.

Art and Zadie smiled at each other.

"Alright, we'll go with the showroom model," said Art.

Sarah's life would never be the same.

Sarah and Art set up the Tama drum kit in the Fox and Hounds practice room, both still in a state of disbelief that Sarah now had such a wonderful place to practice only a short walk from their apartment. Sarah tuned the kit and played the rest of the night. Art went upstairs, which he had to do by going outside and up around the hill to the front door.

Art had a beer at the bar while Ron went about his business. They both walked around upstairs to see if they could hear Sarah's drums. In the far corner of the main dining room, if you listened closely, you could hear the faint sound of drumming. During Ron's break, they went downstairs, since Ron hadn't met Sarah yet.

When he opened the door for an instant, he thought it was Kerstin sitting behind the drums—Sarah's face had grown to resemble Kerstin so much. She also had the slim, athletic build of her mother. Sarah stopped playing when she saw the two of them.

"Sarah, this is my friend Ron. Ron, this is my daughter Sarah."

"Hi Sarah, it's nice to meet you."

"Hi Ron," replied Sarah, adding, "Thank you so much for letting me use this room."

"Oh no problem. I'm happy we could do it. No one's used it in years."

"You know Sarah, Ron was with me when I met your mother," said Art.

"Really?" Sarah replied, faking surprise even though she had heard the story of her parents meeting many times before.

"Yes, that's right. Your mother was beautiful. I can see her resemblance in you."

"Er, thanks Ron," an embarrassed Sarah replied.

"To tell you the truth, I was surprised she chose your dad over me," joked Ron.

"Come on Ron, settle down," Art said.

"I'm just kidding. Don't stop for us. I want to hear you play," urged Ron.

"Okay. Sure," said Sarah.

"I wouldn't have any idea how to drum or where to even start," stated Ron, then asked, "How do you know what to do?"

"It probably sounds funny, but it's in my head—I hear it and just know, like sense, what to do," answered Sarah.

"Incredible. Art was right. You are the next Ringo Starr," Ron said, even though Art never told him that.

"Ha! I don't know about that. Since you like Ringo Starr, here's a Beatles song—'She Said, She Said.'"

Sarah then put in a tape that had the Beatles song on it with Ringo's drums muted so she could play the drum part. She got ready then pressed play.

The odd, wonderful song played with Sarah performing the drum parts. When the song finished, Ron and Art applauded loudly.

"That was great. You really are the next Ringo Starr!" declared Ron.

"Thanks Ron," replied Sarah.

"Well, we'll leave you to your practice. I'll be home. Call or text if you need anything," said Art.

"Thanks Dad. I'll be home in a little while."

"Bye Sarah," Ron said, flashing a thumbs up as he left.

Sarah would spend much of her free time practicing at the Fox and Hounds. This reminded Art of how she used to endlessly practice basketball. Sarah was fulfilling the gift she had for playing drums. Much of it came naturally to her, although she knew she needed to keep learning advanced techniques to become as accomplished as she dreamed of being. YouTube was a great resource. She particularly liked the lessons from Tony Coleman, who had played with BB King among others.

That fall, Sarah started high school. Coach LaVonda Chatman had all but given up on Sarah joining the basketball team. Even so, they still met in the band room before Sarah's bus came. LaVonda said she'd love to come listen to Sarah practice some time at her Fox and Hounds studio. This led to them arranging a time for LaVonda to stop by the next Saturday afternoon.

It was a cool fall day, perfect football weather. Sarah had already worked the lunch shift at Taco Bell before starting her practice. She was excited for LaVonda to watch her, so she ran through the songs she was going to play. A knock came at the door as Sarah was having a snack. When she opened the door, she was surprised to not only see LaVonda but also her grandfather, Otis, known as "The Oat Man" in blues circles.

"Hi Sarah," said LaVonda, "I hope you don't mind I brought my papa with me."

"Oh, no, of course not," Sarah managed to say, feeling starstruck. After LaVonda had told her about "The Oat Man," Sarah listened to some of his songs that were available on iTunes. She loved his bass playing style and how he interacted with his drummers.

"Hello Sarah, I've heard a lot about you," Otis said.

"Thank you. I've heard a lot about you too. I can't believe you're here!" said Sarah, still nervous.

"Enough of that, let's hear you Play!" Otis said.

As LaVonda and Otis came in, Sarah noticed that Otis had a guitar case embroidered with "The Oat Man" and his own small amp. Was he going to play?

And play he did. Sarah started playing some of her favorites as she planned. She had the audio without the drum parts so she could play along. Otis soon hooked up his bass using one of the amps in the room rather than the one he brought, and joined in. The two of them radiated joy while playing together. Soon, Otis had her stop the music and the two of them jammed. LaVonda beamed with happiness, seeing her grandfather and young friend play together.

Otis stopped playing and said, "Here's one for you." He then launched into a funky bass groove. Sarah listened for a moment before accompanying him. The two played looking at each other, then hammed it up for a while facing LaVonda, and then sometimes just by themselves, getting the feel of what the other was doing.

After a few hours of playing, the three of them sat together.

"You know Sarah, Vonny told me you were a fine drummer, but you know what, kid? You're better than fine," Otis said, using his nickname for LaVonda. "I can hear that you are starting to form your own style. Go with that. Be yourself. The best drummers are very much who they are. It's in them. And I can see it's in you too."

"Thank you, Otis. I'll try to be me," a blushing Sarah said, then added, "That was so fun. I never thought I'd get to play with you. Or even get to meet you."

LaVonda and Otis collected their things and prepared to leave.

"Thank you, Coach LaVonda," Sarah said, hugging her friend and mentor.

"Of course, dear. I'm glad you like my Oat Man. He's always been special to me."

Walking home, Sarah imagined herself and Otis playing along to the car noises, sirens, and crickets of the Saint Paul night. The high she felt was much greater than anything like the pills had offered, or basketball either.

She was more certain than ever—this was what she was born to do.

CHAPTER 18
WILEBSKI'S BLUES SALOON

Every Tuesday, Wilebski's had what they called a Blues Jam. Musicians would sign up and then wait for their names to be called. When they were, they would join whoever was called with them and play as a band. It was a fun way for musicians to get to know one another. Customers could enjoy the music without the usual cover charge. Friends and family of the musicians who came to play would often make up most of the audience.

Art had been to several Blues Jams but this Tuesday he went thinking Sarah might be interested in signing up and playing. He had gone home after work and ate dinner with Sarah before she left to go practice at the Fox and Hounds. Art had arranged to meet Melissa at Wilebski's. Arriving first, Art sat at the oblong bar on the side facing the stage. There was a small group of what looked to be musicians milling about.

"Hey Art," greeted Sunny Bushorn, one of the regular bartenders. She was thin with wiry, light red-hair and glasses.

"Hi Sunny. I'll have a Heineken tap," replied Art.

"Sure thing. You came in for the jam tonight?" asked Sunny.

"You know I did," Art said. The taps were across on the other side of the bar. Sunny nodded over her shoulder as she filled a glass.

"Here you go," Sunny said, turning around with his beer then asking, "Do you play?"

"Oh, no. I'd empty the place out if I did," Art replied with a chuckle. "My daughter though, she's a pretty good drummer."

"I knew Sarah liked music, but I didn't know she played," said Sunny.

"Yeah, she played drums in the school band, but now she has a real drum kit she's practicing with. How did you know she likes music?"

"Well, because I talk to her sometimes when she's playing video games or pool. And I see her groove to it," replied Sunny. "Of course, you're always too busy with the ladies," she teased.

Just as Sunny said this, Melissa sat down next to him. Sunny and Art's eyes met, and they shared a laugh.

"What? Did I do something?" asked Melissa.

"No, just Art being funny. What'll you have?"

"Looks like Art has a Heineken. I'll have one too."

"You got it," Sunny said, grabbing a glass and turning back to the tap.

"What's up, Art?" Melissa asked.

"Not much, just thought I'd check out the Blues Jam tonight. Glad you could join me," replied Art.

"Sure. Just another nothing night for me," said Melissa with a shrug.

"You're working too hard," Art said.

Even though it wasn't that unusual for them to get together in the evening, they hadn't for some time. The last time they saw each other was at happy hour weeks ago.

"Anyway, I wanted to see you and get your take on something," Art said in a serious tone.

"Umm, okay," Melissa said, taking a sip of her freshly poured beer.

"We're here to see if we think it's a good idea to have Sarah play at the Blues Jam."

"That's it?" said a relieved Melissa.

"Yes, that's it," Art said turning back to his beer. The musicians were still milling around with a few of them going up to the stage with guitar cases. Cullen, the other regular bartender, took the microphone and announced that anyone wanting to play should sign up, pointing to the sign-up sheet.

As Art and Melissa watched Cullen make his announcement, at the same time they both noticed something behind him.

"Who's Sarah Papenheim?" Melissa asked.

"I don't know," Art replied while studying the stage.

There on the bass drum was the name Sarah Papenheim surrounded by "All That Matters Is The Music" and two dates, twenty-one years apart. Sunny was pouring a beer across from them.

"Hey, Sunny," called Art. "Who's Sarah Papenheim?"

"Sarah played drums here. I heard she was really good too. It was way before I started working here."

"She died?" asked Melissa.

"Yeah, but I don't know any more than that. Maybe some of the old-timers know more."

"Thanks Sunny," Melissa said as Sunny left to attend to other customers since business was picking up.

"She must have been special for them to have her honored like that," Melissa noted.

They sat reflecting on what happened to Sarah Papenheim. Melissa searched for information on her phone and learned she had been senselessly murdered by a mentally unstable man in the Netherlands. Their hearts sank as they read the news reports, feeling a terrific loss for Sarah Papenheim.

The Blues Jam continued as Art and Melissa sat and listened while a variety of musicians played. To their ears, they all sounded decent. There were two different drummers most of the night.

"Todd Landry? Where's Todd? You're up on drums," Cullen said from the mic.

From behind them, Todd made his way to the stage.

"Hey, I know that guy," said Art, explaining the story of how Sarah got her drum kit.

Melissa looked at him and smiled, trying not to show the sadness she felt about being left out of Art and Sarah's lives during such a formative time.

The band started playing, and Todd looked like a good drummer. There was a short black man playing bass. Two guitar players and a singer made up this jam. They started playing the Chum Fella song "Janitor Blues." Art and Melissa perked up and looked into each other's eyes. For a moment, they were back at the Paradiso in Amsterdam.

"Let's get out of here," stated Melissa, standing up and touching Art's shoulder. He stood up, put two twenty-dollar bills on the bar, and they left together. This was the beginning of an encounter that, unlike Amsterdam, Art would clearly recall.

Sunny came over shaking her head as she cleaned the bar and mumbled, *"Fucking ladies' man."*

Several days later, when Sarah came home from school, she started doing her homework with her headphones on as usual. Art had done an early morning VA ride to Moorhead. It had been nearly four hours there and another four back. He could have done some more rides but instead called it a day and went home. By the time he got there, Sarah had started cooking their spaghetti dinner with Lil' Ed & the Blues Imperials' "Full Tilt" jamming on her headphones.

Art grabbed a Two Hearted from the fridge and set the table as Sarah drained the spaghetti and then took off her headphones.

"Hey Dad, how was your day?"

"Good, one long drive up to Moorhead and back. Just the way I like it. How about yours?"

"Good," Sarah replied as she loaded up the plates with pasta, butter, and sauce. "Coach Chatman asked if I could help her with the basketball team. She said I could run drills and rebound and stuff like that."

"Sounds good. Are you going to do it?" asked Art.

"I guess so. She said I wouldn't need to come every day. A couple of times a week would be fine with her."

"I bet you'll have fun," Art said. Sarah smiled as she twirled her spaghetti.

Art was going to ask Sarah if she would be interested in playing at the Wilebski's Blues Jam, but now he wasn't sure. Would she be too busy? After a few bites, he decided to see what Sarah thought of his idea. Maybe she wouldn't even be interested.

"Sarah, I was over at Wilebski's the other night with Melissa—"

Before he could continue, Sarah cut him off. "Whoa! You've been spending a lot of time with Melissa lately!" she said with a grin. "What's up with that?"

"Oh. Yeah, we've been hanging out some," Art answered. He blushed and hoped Sarah didn't notice.

"Oh, is *that* what they call it now?" a now laughing Sarah said.

"Umm, yeah, I guess—" Art stammered.

"It's okay, Dad. You guys are cute together."

"Anyway, I had an idea," Art said, trying to focus. "Would you have any interest in playing drums on Tuesday nights at the Wilebski's Blues Jam night?" he asked.

Upon hearing this, Sarah's ears pricked up.

"Me? Play at Wilebski's?"

She had dreamed of playing there but didn't know if she was either old enough or good enough to actually do it.

"Sure. Why not? You're good. Really good," replied Art.

"Am I old enough?" she asked.

"I don't see why not. There are young people there sometimes. Why couldn't a teenager play?"

"That's true," replied Sarah, now imagining herself playing on the drums in the bar she had practically grown up in.

Art could tell she was taking his idea seriously. He had another question for her. "Do you know who Sarah Papenheim is?"

Sarah took another bite of pasta before she answered simply, "I love her."

Art was surprised that Sarah knew of Sarah.

"You know of her?" asked Art.

"Yes, of course. She's on the drums. It's sadly beautiful."

From this comment, Art realized his Sarah knew of Sarah's fate. They sat in silence for a few moments, finishing their spaghetti dinner.

"Well, any Tuesday you want to go play at Wilebski's just let me know and I'll take you," offered Art.

"Will do, Dad!"

Sarah had been dreaming about playing in a band for some time, and her father's suggestion made it seem real. Was she really good enough to play in front of a bar crowd? With "real" musicians? Sure, she had jammed (once) with "The Oat Man." That was fun, but it was a private, casual jam session rather than a performance. Of course, she had played "concerts" for parents as part of school bands too, but both seemed very different than playing in a bar like Wilebski's.

In her head, seeing herself play behind the Sarah Papenheim honorary drum kit became clearer and clearer. Now when she practiced, she was practicing to play the Blues Jam at Wilebski's.

She was sure to practice as many classics like "Little Red Rooster" and "Got My Mojo Working" as possible, since she thought they would be the type of songs played. Finally, she told Art one weekend that she would like to play the next Tuesday night if he was alright with it. He was, so it was set. She would play on Tuesday night.

Since Sarah was practicing even more now, she decided not to help out at basketball practice. Coach Chatman was disappointed that Sarah wouldn't be a basketball team manager, but at the same time was excited for her to pursue her musical dreams. Sarah promised to help on game days by keeping score if she could.

Soon enough it was Tuesday and time for Sarah's first Blues Jam. Art had picked up a pizza on his way home from work. Sarah came home from school and then went to the Fox and Hounds for a short practice session before dinner. Melissa had joined them, wanting to give her support to Sarah who was excited and nervous. It was quiet as the three of them ate without saying much, like a baseball dugout when a pitcher is throwing a no-hitter. After cleaning up, Sarah put on her Tartan basketball sweatshirt Coach Chatman had given her and grabbed her drumsticks.

"Let's go!" declared Sarah. Art and Melissa smiled at each other.

"Rock and roll!" yelled Melissa, raising her hand in the classic devil horns sign.

The three of them rode in Melissa's new blue BMW 3 series car. Her career had continued to grow, and she was able to pay cash for the new car—something she had never dreamed of doing. She cranked up the Bose stereo system, playing George Thorogood's version of "One Bourbon, One Scotch, One Beer." Pumped up, the three of them leapt out of the car after the short drive to Wilebski's.

Cullen was over by where the sign-up sheet was on the bar closest to the stage, while Sunny was bartending. Both Spring and Roxanne were waiting on tables, with Aamir working the door.

"Looks more crowded than the last time we were here," said Melissa.

"Yeah. Yeah, it does. I wonder why," questioned Art.

"Hey there," Sunny said to Art and Melissa. She hadn't noticed Sarah following along with them. "Sarah!" she exclaimed upon seeing her.

"Hi Sunny," Sarah replied, trying to hide her nerves.

Sunny's face lit up as she put it together that Sarah was there to play in the Blues Jam.

"You're playing, aren't you?" she asked excitedly.

"Well, yes, I am," replied Sarah, again trying her best not to show she was getting more nervous by the minute.

"I can't wait!" an excited Sunny said.

"Thanks Sunny," replied Sarah with a smile. "Here you go. It's on me," Sunny said, opening a Pepsi for Sarah. She knew Sarah preferred Pepsi to Coke when she played video games.

"We'll have two Heinekens," Melissa said.

"Coming up," replied Sunny who turned to pour the beers.

"Hey guys," Cullen said as he came up behind the three now sitting at the bar. "What's up Sarah? Are you playing video games tonight?"

Sarah, in a small voice, said, "I'm going to play in the jam tonight, or at least try to."

"Oh yeah? That's great. What do you play?"

"Drums."

"Drums. Great. We sometimes only have one drummer. It'll be good to have another one," stated Cullen as he noticed Sarah's nervous smile. "You know, this is just for fun. You'll do great," assured Cullen sensing her jitters.

"Thanks Cullen."

"Are you two playing anything?" Cullen said with a smirk to Art and Melissa.

"Oh yeah, sure. I'll play guitar," Melissa replied with a smile.

"Great! I'd love to hear that!" Cullen said as he noticed BB Alight arrive.

"I'll see you guys later," he said leaving to greet BB with a handshake.

"That's why there's a bigger-than-normal crowd tonight," Art said nodding toward BB.

"Who's that?" asked Sarah.

"That's BB Alight. He's one of the better-known local bluesmen. His current band is The Thrill," replied Art.

"Oh, I've heard of them. They're good. Geez," said Sarah.

"Don't worry, dear," Melissa said, gently touching Sarah's arm.

Art hadn't said much since arriving. With the focus on Sarah, no one noticed that Art was nervously sipping his beer. He felt similar to how he did before one of Sarah's basketball games. Not knowing anything about performing in front of a crowd, all he knew was anxiety.

"Screw it. I'm signing up," Sarah said, standing up and walking toward the front of the bar. Melissa smiled and, for the first time, noticed Art's tension. She decided to tease him a little to loosen him up.

"Oh, come on Art. You're not the one playing," she said.

"Good one. You know I'll be a basket case watching Sarah."

The bar continued to fill up, the local music scene obviously aware that BB Alight was playing tonight. Art noticed Todd and

Zadie, the other salesperson who sold him Sarah's drums. He wondered if every Guitar Center employee played at the Blues Jam.

"Hello everyone and welcome! Thank you for coming out tonight. Those of you interested in playing, please sign up on the sheet over there by the bar. We'll get going in a few minutes," bellowed Cullen in his best MC voice from the stage.

A few musicians were milling about behind Cullen. Todd was settling in on drums. A short, black man was tuning his bass, who Art remembered seeing at the earlier Blues Jam. BB Alight was doing the same with his guitar. There was another sturdier, older black man tuning his guitar. Art walked around, looking for Sarah. He found her downstairs in the pool room. She was sitting there watching a pool game between a young couple.

"How are you doing?" Art said, sitting on the stool beside his daughter.

"Good. I think I'm ready," she replied. Art could tell she was less nervous than earlier.

The young woman playing pool suddenly stopped and looked at Art.

"It's you!" said the woman.

Art was there to support Sarah and hadn't been paying much attention to the pool game. Now he looked up and noticed that it was Jane, the attractive goth woman he had shared a smoke with a while back.

"Oh, hi. It's Jane, right?"

"Yes, that's right…" replied Jane, pausing before adding, "Art."

"Geez Dad, you really get around, don't you?" teased Sarah.

Jane's companion was a little shorter than her with ruffled, sandy hair and the beginnings of a shaggy beard. He sank an impressive combo shot and raised his arms in triumph.

"Take that, candy-ass!" he shouted and the two pool players laughed.

"I'm going back upstairs. You okay?" asked Art.

"Yeah, thanks. I'm good," replied Sarah.

"See ya," said Jane softly, preparing for her next shot as Art walked up the steps.

Art smiled and turned to see Jane's butt facing directly at him as she crouched to take her shot.

"How's Sarah?" Melissa asked when Art settled in next to her.

"She's good."

The makeshift band began playing "Little Red Rooster." BB Alight's voice was more Mick Jagger than Muddy Watters. The musicians in the band had obviously played together before. Art could tell what a good drummer Todd was.

In the poolroom, Jane's pool game had finished and her male friend left for the bathroom. She came over to Sarah and sat down next to her.

"How do you know Art?" Jane asked.

"He's my dad," Sarah replied with a smile.

"Oh! Lucky you," stated Jane.

"How do *you* know him?" asked Sarah.

"I don't really. We're just fellow blackstacks," Jane said then noticed Sarah's confused expression. "Smokers. We've shared a smoke together."

"Oh. Blackstacks, eh? I'll have to remember that one."

Jane's friend came back, but before he joined them he received a call on his cell and headed to the corner of the room, seeming agitated.

"Is he your boyfriend?" asked Sarah.

"Him…" Jane said, motioning to her friend, adding, "Umm, maybe, sometimes. He lives next door to me. We're just having fun, I think."

Sarah smiled, thinking Jane sounded a bit like Kelly.

"Do you have to be here with your old man? I mean, I know you're a youngster."

"I'm here to play in the Blues Jam."

"Oh yeah? That's cool," Jane said.

Sarah couldn't tell by how Jane said it whether she thought it really was cool, so she just smiled. They both looked over at Jane's friend who was getting more demonstrative on the phone.

"He's got some sort of shady business going on," said Jane.

Sarah wasn't sure what to say, although having spent so much time at Wilebski's, she didn't think it was unusual to hear about shady dealings.

They could hear the band playing "Dust My Broom." Sarah was glad to hear they were playing blues standards, ones that she had been practicing while preparing to play tonight. She could also hear that the drummer was very good. The bass player was also good. And of course BB Alight was a pro. The band sounded way better than she imagined it would. The two of them sat there listening.

Jane's friend finished his phone call and came over, obviously upset.

"Hey, babe, I've got to go," he said.

"Okay, Jerry, later," replied Jane. The young man grabbed his coat and left.

"I don't know. Maybe I should find somebody else," Jane said, staring at the pool table.

Sarah didn't know what to say. She hadn't even had a relationship with a boy yet.

After the song, the musicians switched up. Cullen was on stage, calling for another guitar and bass player from the signup sheet. He didn't call for another drummer though. Sarah was ready to play but, in truth, she didn't mind waiting a little longer. After some more tuning, the band started up again, playing "Born on the Bayou" with a woman singer. Sarah stood up so she could see the band. Zadie, the woman who had sold her the drum kit, was singing and playing a pink Gibson guitar that matched her bright pink hair.

"Good song," Jane said.

"Yeah," replied Sarah, adding, "I know the singer. Well, I've met her anyway. She sold me my drum kit."

"Oh, you're a drummer!" said Jane, as her eyes widened through her dark black makeup.

"Yep."

"Me too. Well sort of, I played drums in the school band," Jane said.

"Really? Me too!" replied Sarah.

"Cool beans," said Jane, as coolly as anyone could say such a thing. Sarah smiled, appreciating the odd expression.

They sat there listening to the next few songs, all blues standards. Then they played a song Sarah knew and liked,—it wasn't even blues, though the band played a bluesy version. It was Phoebe Bridgers' "Scott Street." Sarah always loved the way the drums came in on that song, and thought the blues version Zadie sang was awesome. From that moment on, Sarah would consider how songs that weren't blues could be done in a blues style.

When the song finished, Cullen again took to the stage. He called out for a couple of guitar players and a bass player, but not a drummer. Sarah sank into her bar stool. Jane noticed that her new acquaintance was disappointed.

"Wanna play?" Jane asked, nodding toward the pool table.

Sarah wasn't very good at pool, only playing at Wilebski's when she wanted a break from video games, which wasn't often. Jane stood up and smiled at her.

"Sure. Okay, sure. I'll play," Sarah said.

The two of them played through the latest group of musicians. Art walked over to check on Sarah, but when he saw her playing pool with Jane, he left the two of them alone. As he sat back down at the bar, Cullen walked by and leaned in.

"Sarah's up next," he said.

"Oh yeah? I thought we were going to have to wait until midnight," Melissa said.

"Well, you know, Todd never wants to sit down, but I told him we're switching next time," explained Cullen.

"How come he gets a say?" asked Melissa.

"He's a regular, so he does have a say. When Sarah's a regular, she'll have a say too," stated Cullen.

"Good, and I bet she won't be a dick about it," Melissa replied, showing her irritation at waiting all night to see Sarah play.

"I know, I know. Sorry guys," Cullen said.

Soon enough, it was time for another change. Cullen again took the mic and announced a new bass player, plus Sarah Zonnen as the new drummer. Sarah and Jane had finished their pool game and were now standing near the back of the dance floor.

"Whoa! You're up kid. Give 'em hell!" Jane yelled excitedly as she turned to Sarah.

"Thanks!" Sarah said, thinking it was the first time she had seen Jane less than the coolest of the cool. Then, with a nervous smile, she went to get her drumsticks she'd left with Art and Melissa. Cullen greeted her at the side of the stage.

"Hi Sarah. You ready?" he asked.

"As ready as I'll ever be."

"The guitarists play here, but I don't know the bass player at all," Cullen said.

"Neither do I," Sarah said with a smile.

"No, of course you don't. It'll be fine. Just play along and have fun," Cullen assured her.

As Sarah approached the drum kit, she smiled and nodded to Sarah Papenheim's name on the bass drum. She had dreamed of playing on this exact drum kit many times. Now she was near tears as she was about to do it. She moved over to take her seat on the throne. Todd was still close by; she felt his presence was menacing, but wasn't sure he meant it to be.

Just before she sat down, he leaned over and whispered in an odd monotone, "May luck be in your favor" and left. *What?* Sarah thought. She managed to smile back at him.

Sarah settled in and warmed up on the drum kit as the other musicians were preparing to play. It felt odd that they were all on their own but were going to be playing as a band shortly. She wasn't even sure what songs they would play. Soon enough, one of the guitar players who was a middle-aged, pudgy white guy with gray hair and a tweed *Peaky Blinders*-style cap stood facing Sarah and motioning the rest of the "band" to come toward him. The bass player was a nervous, short white man with shaggy sandy hair and a thick mustache. The other guitarist was a sturdy older black man with curly gray hair and a pencil-thin gray mustache.

"I'm Ed. To start, I'll sing," said the Peaky Blinder.

"I'm Louis," said a sturdy older guitarist in a businesslike tone.

"Jeff here. And I don't sing," the bassist said.

Sarah could tell he was even more nervous than her.

"I'm Sarah, and I don't sing either," she said, hoping she didn't sound as anxious as she felt.

Louis, with a very serious expression, looked directly at Sarah.

"You know kid, I don't play drums, but I can tell if you can," he said.

Sarah, not sure if he was joking, smiled along.

"Great, great. How about we play 'Boom, Boom?'" asked Ed.

"Okay," Sarah and Louis replied in unison. They all looked at Jeff. He had a puzzled look on his face.

"You know that one, son?" asked Louis.

"Umm, I think so," answered Jeff.

"Umm, I *don't* think so," Louis stated then asked, "What do you know?"

"I can play 'Little Red Rooster,'" replied Jeff.

"Alright, 'Little Red Rooster' it is. Take it away, Ed," said Louis, demonstrating he was the undisputed leader of this makeshift band.

The guitar players take their places on the stage. Sarah looked out at the large crowd on the dance floor. The booths surrounding the back and sides were full. She then looked over to the bar area to see Art and Melissa smiling back at her. She could see Jane in the back of the bar area standing by herself, of course looking cooler than everyone else.

"One, two, three," Ed counted down then started playing the intro to "Little Red Rooster." It sounded like he was playing the Rolling Stones version to Sarah. She started playing just as she had practiced playing along with Charlie Watts many times. Louis added the supporting guitar part. Ed's singing was much better than Sarah expected.

There was a problem though. Jeff's bass playing sounded off-key and was leaving notes hanging, and he wasn't paying any attention to either Sarah's drumming or the guitar players. Even so, Sarah was having her moment. She was enthralled playing drums on the Sarah Papenheim drum kit at Wilebski's. The crowd was having fun too. Later, Art told her how great it was for him and Melissa to watch her play. Sarah caught Jane smiling a cool, aloof, delighted smile at the back of the bar.

The song ended and some in the crowd whooped and hollered while others indifferently watched, drank, or continued their conversations. Sarah was surveying the crowd when she was interrupted by Ed, who had again come toward her and signaled the others to come in.

"You okay, son?" Ed asked, looking over to Jeff.

"What, me? Yeah, I'm okay," Jeff replied, startled by the question.

"It sounded like you were a little off on that one," Ed told him.

"Really?" questioned Jeff, apparently not hearing the song like the rest of the "band."

"Okay. Let's do another one," stated Ed. Having played many Blues Jams with shaky players, he was ready to keep going with the group they had.

"Wait a minute," Louis interjected before asking, "Jeff?"

"Yeah?"

"Can you play? Really, man, can you play?" Louis was serious.

This caught Jeff by surprise. He was trying, even if he suspected he might not have been ready to play with a band yet. Sarah felt bad for him although she, like the others, could tell he wasn't ready. At least she had experience with the school band, as well as her endless hours of practice. Still, she felt that they ought to try and make the best of it for tonight.

"Louis?" asked Sarah.

"Yeah, Tartan?" Louis said, referring to her sweatshirt as he slowly turned to face her.

Sarah, taken aback by his seeming dismissal of her, felt a sudden rush of emotion.

"Louis. Let's play. Jeff will be fine," she firmly stated.

Louis stared at her for what seemed like an eternity. Sarah stared right back.

"Okay, Tartan, we'll do it your way," he finally said. He looked at the others and announced, "'Got My Mojo Working.'" Then nodded toward Ed, "You sing."

Jeff looked even more nervous than before. Sarah could see he didn't know the song.

"Jeff!" she hollered at him. When he turned to her, she could see the fear in his eyes. "Follow me!" she ordered, pointing a drumstick at him.

Jeff nodded, like a wanna-be-bass-playing-bobblehead doll.

"One, two, three," counted Ed as he, Louis, and Sarah tore into the song.

Jeff tried his best to play along with Sarah and she conducted him as best she could, swaying her head in time for him to follow, frowning when he made mistakes, and nodding to let him know when he "got it."

Louis wore a dour expression for most of the song. But toward the end, he seemed pleasantly surprised their effort was much better than he expected. He glanced at Sarah to see her keeping Jeff playing along, and a grin spread across his face.

This "band" played a few more songs before they were switched out. Todd once again took over the drums. Sarah wanted to keep playing, but was also fine calling it a night. Art and Melissa congratulated her for performing so well. She knew the rush from playing would keep her up all night and indeed it did. She had never felt a rush like it.

Sarah continued to play at the Blues Jam over the next few weeks. She met the short, young bass player, Cliff Johnson and they played together, immediately forging an innate musical connection. Louis had warmed up to her, preferring her on drums for his sets over Todd. Sarah had thought Todd was sort of an odd duck when she first met him and this feeling continued. He was rarely friendly, and instead possessed an aura of being a superior musician compared to all other blues jammers. She soon learned there was a pecking order for the players, and Todd would make sure he always played with the better, more experienced musicians, especially on the rare nights BB Alight was there.

This left Sarah without ever playing with Alight or most of the other, better players. The exception was Cliff. She thought he was the best bass player, yet he was still happy to play with anyone. The first time he played with Sarah, he leaned over and to her surprise told her how impressed he was that first night she played, especially with how she helped Jeff out.

She learned Cliff was attending law school at Mitchell Hamline in Saint Paul. He told her his dream of becoming a professional musician. Sarah thought he was good enough. First though, he told her he was going to get his law degree. He had ambitions about helping people but also making some "real money" in his words, before embarking on a career in music. He had grown up in Eden Prairie and lived for a while in Minnetonka. During periods when they weren't playing, he would tell stories about his time on the lake and at Lord Fletcher's, a famous lakeside bar and restaurant. He often talked about how he knew Stevie Nicks and how she was a fantastic person.

Cliff had a quiet, cool way about him. He had a short afro and wore glasses with a slight tint. He was around 5'5" with a wrestler's build, meaning Sarah was slightly taller than him. On one of their first meetings, he casually asked if Sarah smoked pot. He knew she was in high school, but since he had started smoking in middle school, he knew lots of kids smoked dope. Sarah said she had tried it but didn't smoke regularly, leaving out her history with harder drugs. He was glad she didn't regularly smoke dope. Even though he still smoked and didn't think there was anything wrong with it, he wished he hadn't started so young.

Sarah quickly forged a close friendship with Cliff. She found him easy to talk to about (almost) anything. He became her best friend at Wilebski's and almost like the big brother she never had. They even began referring to each other as "Sis" and "Bro."

By mid-January, Sarah had become one of the regulars at the Tuesday night Blues Jams. Sometimes there were several other drummers, with Todd always there. Since he continued monopolizing the better musicians, it left Sarah to mix in with the others. The experience she was getting, along with the lingering high she would feel for the next few days, was worth the sometimes long stretches of waiting to play.

Art had grown comfortable with Sarah staying out late on Tuesdays to play drums in the bar. Most days he would drop her off and then come back when she texted him that she was ready to come home. Other days, he stayed and listened to the makeshift bands, enjoying the company of his friends working there, and some of the musicians he met. Sarah had introduced him to Cliff. Art recognized him as playing bass there before Sarah had even started. He bonded with Cliff and trusted him to look after Sarah. Although by this point, Sarah had proven quite adept at looking after herself.

On one Tuesday night, Sarah wasn't going to play. Instead, she was going to keep score for Coach Chatman and the Tartan girls' basketball team. They were playing Tina's East Valley High School. Tina was on the junior varsity team, and Sarah was excited to see her play. That year, with Sarah's newfound pastime of playing and practicing drums, she hadn't made it to any of Tina's games. Tina was now an even better 3-point shooter than she was back in the People to People days. Sarah was surprised she was playing JV. She thought if Tina was going to Tartan she would already be a star on their varsity team. Tina told her the East Valley team was loaded with great players who might play Division 1 basketball in college. Sarah knew the Tartan team was good but likely not the caliber of Tina's team. She was looking forward to seeing Tina and watching her play basketball, even though she was disappointed not to play at the Blues Jam that night.

On game day, Sarah stayed after school and practiced drumming. Coach Chatman stopped by to thank her in advance for keeping statistics. Sarah reached the gym just as the East Valley team was arriving.

"Sarah!" Tina shouted.

"Tina!" Sarah yelled. The two friends embraced.

"I've missed you!" said Tina.

"You too!" replied Sarah, adding, "I'm so glad I get to see you play."

"Yes, I can't believe we're playing you guys," said Tina.

"We have a pretty good team, but it sounds like your team is better."

"We'll see. I think we have a shot at winning state."

"Wow, that's great. Even so, I can't believe you're not on varsity," said Sarah.

"I know. Our team has a bunch of upper classmen. Sometimes, I feel lucky to have made the JV team."

"Tina!" a loud voice boomed from the other side of the gym.

"That's my coach. I better go," Tina said.

The friends hugged and Tina ran off to join her team.

Coach Chatman came over to help Sarah get set up to keep statistics for the game. She said the JV game likely wouldn't be close since East Valley's JV team was better than some of the varsity teams Tartan played. This proved to be accurate. Tina's team had three other guards who were very good, along with a power forward that was a great rebounder. Sarah enjoyed watching the game, especially seeing her friend play. Tina made five 3-pointers along with a few driving layups and pull-up jumpers to lead all scorers with 25 points. East Valley's JV won the game easily 65-32, even without Tina and the rest of the starters not playing much in the fourth quarter.

After the game, Coach Chatman again helped Sarah prepare to keep statistics for the varsity team. Tina came over with her East Valley sweatshirt.

"Great game, Tina!" Sarah yelled as Tina approached.

"Thanks Sarah!" she replied.

"Hello Ms. Wilson," Coach Chatman said, greeting Tina.

"Hi Coach," replied Tina, surprised Coach Chatman even knew who she was.

"Great shooting tonight," Coach Chatman said.

"Thanks," Tina said with a shy smile.

"Okay, Sarah, are you all set?" LaVonda asked, turning her attention to Sarah.

"Yeah. I think so," Sarah replied, then asked, "Is it okay if Tina helps me?"

"Sure, just as long as you pay attention to the game," answered LaVonda.

"We will!" Sarah promised.

Sarah was familiar with the routine, having kept statistics for a few games earlier in the season. Coach Chatman would review the statistics at halftime with her assistant coach, then decide on any adjustments they might make for the second half. Sarah took her role seriously and tried to keep accurate, detailed statistics.

"She's nice," Tina said.

"Yeah, I love her. She's been great to me even though I'm not playing basketball anymore," replied Sarah.

"Do you miss it?" asked Tina.

"Umm, not really…" answered Sarah, pausing, then adding, "Well, maybe, sometimes. Yeah, sometimes I do."

"You should play," said Tina.

"I don't think so. You know, I really like watching you play. You're such a great shooter."

The teams finished their warmups and came back to their benches for the introductions. After the visiting team was introduced, Tartan had a fancy introduction for their team. It was modeled after the Chicago Bulls introduction in the Michael Jordan era. Coach Chatman, being from Chicago, brought that with her when she was hired as coach. The lights would dim and then a song picked by one of the players would blast out as the public address announcer introduced the starters by shouting their names one by one. Regardless of how the team played, the introductions were always one of the highlights of the game.

"That was so cool," Tina said.

"Yeah," Sarah nodded. She loved the intros.

Coach Chatman was a defensive-minded coach and had taught her team the fundamentals of playing man-to-man defense.

She would have them recognize when a player was vulnerable to a trap. This could be in the corners or when a player crossed the half-court line since they would turn the ball over if they went back.

Tartan's defense was able to keep the game close in the first half, only trailing 30-25. LaVonda stopped over to look at the statistics. Two East Valley players, both seniors heading to D1 schools next year, had done most of the scoring. One was a guard who was better at driving to the basket and collecting fouls than 3-point shooting. The other was a forward/center who, when given a chance, could score close to the basket. LaVonda went back to talk to her assistant about ideas to slow these two down.

"You guys are good," Sarah said to Tina after LaVonda left, adding, "but I still think you could be playing varsity."

"Thanks Sarah. Hopefully I'll get a shot next year. Did I tell you I'm going to be playing with a good AAU team this year?"

"No. That's great! I hope I can watch you play."

"Yeah, I'm sure you can. We'll be traveling around the country but also playing lots of games around here," replied Tina.

"Hi Sarah!" greeted a familiar voice.

It was Tina's mom, Brix. Tina's parents were there for most of the JV game.

"Hi Mr. and Mrs. Wilson! Tina played great, didn't she?"

"Yes! We were glad to be able to make it. Traffic was awful," said Mark.

"I'm glad you two can spend some time together!" said Brix, who then looked at Tina adding, "Tina, we will see you at home. Bye Sarah."

"Bye, Mr. and Mrs. Wilson," said Sarah. Mark and Brix waved goodbye and left.

"It was really good to see them," Sarah said to Tina, as they both smiled.

"So, how are you doing?" asked Tina.

"I'm good, really good, actually," replied Sarah.

"Oh, that's great. You must be seeing someone."

"No, no, nothing like that," said Sarah. She could see Tina waiting for her to continue. "So, remember my dad bought me a drum kit?"

"Yeah. I remember. That's so great. So, you're practicing a lot?"

"I am…" Sarah paused, then continued, "I'm also playing at night…in a bar."

"Sarah! What? Where?" said a surprised Tina.

"It's in a place called Wilebski's, not far from where we live. I can even walk or cycle there when the weather's good enough."

"I can't believe it! I mean, that's great, I think. Are you in a band?"

Sarah laughed, thinking how odd this must sound to Tina.

"No, not really. So far, I just play on Tuesday nights when they have something called a Blues Jam."

"Blues! Of course!" said Tina.

"Yes, of course! Random musicians sign up and then play when their turn comes up."

"Are there any other kids? I mean, not kids, but teenagers like you."

"No, I'm the only one. Most are older but there are a few in their twenties."

"Does your dad know you're doing this?" Tina asked, looking serious.

"Yes! He's the one that got me to do it!" Sarah replied, shaking her head about how ridiculous it must sound.

"Wow!" Tina said, trying to imagine her friend playing the drums with a bunch of old bluesmen.

"You should come watch sometime," Sarah said.

"I'd love to. Tuesdays?"

"Yup. Pretty much every Tuesday…except this one!" Sarah said then laughed.

"Ha! Yeah, I'm glad you came to my game today."

The second half started. The two scorekeepers had to pay attention, leaving thoughts of meeting up in the local bar for later. Coach Chatman's strategy was able to limit the effectiveness of East Valley's two D1 players. She had her defense double-team them whenever either got the ball. This opened things up for the other players, but none of them were as good as those two. The game was close all the way to the finish, and Tartan was able to take the lead 58-57 with only ten seconds left. East Valley's D1 guard took the inbounds pass and tried to drive to the basket, even though she was hounded by two defenders and had multiple teammates open. She forced a shot that was missed badly leading to a Tartan celebration. Sarah was happy but tried not to show it, since Tina was disappointed her team lost.

"It was a good game. They could have used you," Sarah finally said.

"Yeah, it was a good game. Your coach is really good," said Tina.

Sarah smiled, closed the scorebook and the two of them stood up.

"Oh, I meant to ask, how's Kyle?"

"You always ask about Kyle! He's good. You know, he's got a girlfriend now."

"Oh," Sarah said, trying not to show her disappointment.

"Tell him I said hello."

"Will do. See you soon, I hope," said Tina.

The two friends hugged and Tina left to join her team for their bus ride back to East Valley High School.

Cliff texted while Sarah was awake in bed.

Did you hear?

What?

Huge brawl. Bar to shut down for days...maybe longer.

RU kidding?

Nope talk later.

Sarah wondered what happened. Maybe it was for the best that she missed playing at the Blues Jam tonight as she tried to imagine what it must have been like. She never feared for her safety at Wilebski's, mostly because she had grown up there with it being her father's favorite bar. There would be some rough-looking characters sometimes, though everyone she knew she thought of as normal. Even Todd was normal in his own arrogant, geeky way. She wondered what Tina and her parents would think of coming to watch her play in a place that had to be shut down for a few days because of a barroom brawl.

Art would sometimes have the radio on before going to work. Sarah seldom paid attention to it or the morning news. His station of choice was more juvenile comedy than news. But the morning after Cliff's text, one of the radio personalities who called himself

"Bolognese" asked the others if they had heard of the big fight at a bar in Saint Paul last night. Sarah had only been half-listening to the regular nonsense of the morning show but perked up on hearing about a fight. Art was cooking some eggs for breakfast and wasn't listening closely so missed the mention of a barroom brawl. The other morning DJs hadn't heard anything, so they quickly moved on to joking about how Bolognese would get upset when losing trivia games.

After school, Sarah did the dishes and changed clothes then walked through the snow to her Fox and Hounds practice room. When she got there, she texted Cliff to see if he could talk. Shortly afterward her phone rang.

"What happened last night?" asked Sarah.

"It was crazy. BB played so it was crowded. So, this guy, who it turns out was drunk off his ass, starts asking every woman in the place to dance," said Cliff, as Sarah imagined the scene.

"Apparently some of the women and their dates weren't crazy about the guy staggering around bothering them. So, one of these guys punches the dude in the gut," continued Cliff.

"Oh my God!" exclaimed Sarah.

"Yeah, well, the place erupted. For whatever reason, everyone wanted to fight. It wasn't a regular crowd—there were a bunch of college kids and out-of-towners. It was like some sort of movie set or something. Guys were hitting other guys with chairs and beer bottles. Some women were even fighting each other," described Cliff.

"On my God! That's crazy!"

"Yep, finally the cops came and busted it up," Cliff said.

"What did you do? Bro, you didn't get in a fight, did you?" asked Sarah.

"No, sis. I didn't fight. I was playing with BB and Todd when all hell broke loose. BB and I sort of stopped, but Todd just kept playing," answered Cliff.

"Of course, he did! I'm glad you didn't get hurt. Hopefully nobody did."

"One guy did for sure…" said Cliff, before asking, "You know Aamir, the bouncer? He saw a trainee cop he knew sucker-punch a guy then start kicking him in the face. He was even wearing some sort of steel-toe boots."

"Oh no!"

"Yeah, Aamir stopped him. They took the guy that was beat up away in the ambulance. I heard his face was a mess. Somebody thought it was the original drunken guy that riled everyone up. But it wasn't. I saw that guy milling around after the ambulance left."

"Jesus."

"Yeah, and the bar is in pretty bad shape. I'm not sure when they're going to reopen."

Sarah wasn't sure what else to say.

"I guess I have to hit the books on Tuesdays now," Cliff joked.

"Yuck! That doesn't sound like fun."

She then glanced over at her drum kit. "Hey?" asked Sarah.

"Yeah?" replied Cliff.

"Why don't you come over and practice at the Fox and Hounds with me?"

"Umm, you *really* don't want me to study, do you?"

"Ha! No, I guess not!"

"I'll think about it. Who knows, maybe Wilebski's will be open by next week."

"Yeah, sounds good, we'll see how it goes," Sarah agreed.

Wilebski's was still closed the next Tuesday. After school, before Sarah left for practice, Cliff texted and asked where to go. Sarah replied with a pin for the address and explained how to go to the door down to the right of the main entrance. She finished cleaning up and walked out into the freezing cold toward the Fox and Hounds. A typical Minnesota cold spell had settled over the Twin Cities. Temperatures of five to twenty-five below had lasted for several days with no immediate end in sight. It was cold, truly cold, but Minnesotans were accustomed to it. Sarah wore her heavy winter jacket with lined boots but no gloves or hat. She knew it wasn't very far and liked the way the freezing cold made her feel alive.

She had spare sweatshirts and sneakers in the practice room so she could change into more comfortable clothes when she got there. She grabbed her favorite Tartan Basketball sweatshirt, excited to have someone else to practice with, especially Cliff who was an accomplished bass player. She warmed up with blues shuffles, nervously awaiting Cliff's arrival.

After what seemed like an eternity but in reality was only about twenty minutes, there was a knock on the door. Sarah shot up to answer it and opened the door to find Cliff there bundled up with a tuque and ski gloves, holding his guitar case.

"You made it!" Sarah exclaimed, just as she noticed someone else was with Cliff. It was Zadie, the woman who sold her the drum kit and played at Wilebski's. She too was bundled up, wearing a dark-purple beret with her stylish Adidas by Stella McCartney winter coat Sarah had seen her wear at Wilebski's.

"Hey Sarah, I hope you don't mind if I brought some others," Cliff said.

"No, no, of course not. Hi Zadie," said Sarah.

"Hi Sarah. Cliff said it was okay if I came along," replied Zadie.

"Yes, it's fine. Great actually," Sarah said, trying to hide her surprise. Cliff had said "others" but Sarah didn't see anybody else as she started to shut the door.

"Hey Tartan!"

Sarah knew immediately who it was. Louis Boyd, the guitar player she had played with at her first Blues Jam. She looked out in the cold and saw Louis approaching. He was wearing his North Face trapper hat and a black leather jacket.

"Louis! It's great to see you!" Sarah said.

"You too, Tartan," replied Louis, before asking, "What kind of place you got here?"

"It's a practice room. I hope you like it," answered Sarah.

"We'll see. You know I'll speak the truth," Louis said.

"That I know," replied Sarah, knowing very well Louis was frank with his opinions.

"Is anyone else coming?" asked Sarah.

"Nope, this is it," replied Cliff.

"Okay," Sarah said shutting the door. She showed them the area. Since there were a few amps left over when it was a band rehearsal space, Cliff and the others didn't have to go back to get theirs.

"Alright, 'Little Red Rooster.' You sing, Cliff," Louis said after the newcomers warmed up.

Sarah hadn't heard Cliff sing before, but they played the blues classic, and she learned that Cliff sang like Howlin' Wolf. She was thrilled to hear him.

"Cliff, I can't believe you can sing like that!" she declared after the song.

"Pretty good, huh?" Louis added.

"Yeah, it was. Why don't you sing at the Blues Jam?" Sarah asked.

"There are always a lot of great singers there," replied Cliff.

"Sure, but there ain't no Howlin' Wolf there!" Sarah said.

"Ha, thanks, but I think you're exaggerating," Cliff said.

"Okay, that's enough. Zadie, let's play that one about the street," said Louis, putting an end to the banter.

"Umm, you mean 'Scott Street?'" asked Zadie.

"Yes, I think that's it," replied Louis.

"Okay. Sarah, do you know that one?" Zadie asked.

"Yes! I love that song and I love how you played it the one time," said Sarah.

"Thanks. I bluesified it, I guess you could say," Zadie stated. "Okay, ready?" Louis said, trying to keep the group focused. "Yep," Zadie said, then started the song.

Sarah loved Zadie's version as much as Phoebe Bridgers' original and had practiced it many times since she heard Zadie's take on it.

"Wow! You do know that song! Your drumming added a lot to my version!" said Zadie afterward.

"Thanks Zadie! I do love playing that one," declared Sarah. Louis sang the next few—a long, jamming version of "Sweet Home Chicago" followed by a rollicking version of Chum Fella's "Janitor Blues." After that one, they heard a knock at the inside door. Sarah opened it up to find Ron Salver.

"Oh, hi Ron. Hope you weren't knocking for too long," said Sarah.

"Hi Sarah. No, I was just listening. It sounds great!" he replied. "I was going to check on you to see if you wanted anything to eat."

"Umm, maybe," answered Sarah. Then she looked toward the others and asked the other musicians, "What do you think? Anybody hungry?"

"Sure you guys must be hungry. I'll go get some menus," Ron said, leaving before anyone could answer.

"Don't worry. He gives me the employee discount even though I don't work here," said Sarah to the group.

"That'll work," said Louis.

Ron returned with a few menus, and the four musicians surveyed them.

"Hey man, you should add more sports-bar food," stated Louis.

"I agree. The owner wants to keep the supper-club vibe to the place, but I keep telling him that it's dying," replied Ron.

"Got that right," Louis said, still looking at the menu.

"How about we just share some fries?" asked Cliff.

"Fine by me," replied Sarah.

"Me too," Zadie said.

"I need more than that. Can you make me a plain cheeseburger?" asked Louis.

"Sure. Okay, one cheeseburger and a basket of fries, coming up. Do you want anything to drink?" Ron asked. "I'll take a water," said Sarah.

"Okay, how about I bring a bucket of Budweisers or something?" Ron asked the others.

"Sounds good man," Louis answered. Cliff and Zadie look at each other and nod.

"I'll get the drinks," Ron said, before leaving.

The band played "Blue Bayou" with Zadie singing, finishing as Ron delivered the beers. Before he came back with the food, they played another Chum Fella classic, "My Baby's White Sox Lost Again," with Louis singing.

Cliff and Louis had played with Sarah several times at Blues Jams, but this was her first time with Zadie since Todd monopolized the better musicians. Louis found he enjoyed playing with Sarah ever since that first night they ended up together. If Zadie showed up, which wasn't often, she would play early and leave before the newbies like Sarah would get their chance.

Most of the Blues Jam musicians didn't practice together. BB Alight had gone through some of the regulars in the various bands he formed and inevitably disbanded. His current band, The Thrill, was rumored to be close to disbanding. Rumors spread that one reason BB was playing in more Blues Jams recently was to evaluate potential new bandmates.

To end the practice, Cliff sang the Howlin' Wolf classic, "Smokestack Lightning."

"Wow, Cliff, that was so good!" Sarah said.

"You got that right, Tartan," added Louis as Zadie nodded her agreement.

They gathered their things and bundled up to face the arctic air that would soon greet them.

"Thanks Sarah, that was fun!" Zadie said, getting ready for the blast of cold air.

"Sure thing. I'm glad you came. You too Louis," replied Sarah.

"I had fun. Thanks for hosting us in your private studio," Louis said.

Cliff stayed and talked with Sarah after the others left.

"That was really fun. If Wilebski's stays closed, you guys could come back next week," said Sarah.

"Yeah, it was fun. We'll see about next week, sis. I've got a big test coming up."

"Umm, okay. I never knew you were such a great singer. How did you learn to sing like Howlin' Wolf?"

"I don't know. I've always done it. My mom loved his music, so I've heard it my whole life," answered Cliff.

"Me too. My grandmother, and my mom, I'm told, loved him too," Sarah said. She hadn't talked to Cliff much about losing her mom, even though he knew she lived with her dad. "I told you my mom died, right?"

"Yes. I'm sorry," answered Cliff as he looked her directly in the eye.

"Thanks. I was only three, so I don't really remember her very well."

"That's too bad. Do you mind me asking how she died?" he asked.

Sarah looked down.

"That's okay," said Cliff, realizing he may have gone down too emotional a path for his young friend.

"No, it's okay…Mom was addicted to opioids," said Sarah, standing up and pacing across the room. Cliff watched in silence as his friend walked across the floor. "Dad didn't even know, nobody did. She kept it from everyone. She had a bad accident in high school and was in a lot of pain. That started her on them."

Although Cliff liked to smoke pot and drink, he hadn't experimented with many other drugs. He did have a cousin that became addicted to heroin but was able to beat it and was now fortunate to be living a drug-free life.

"Mom fell in love with the pleasure and powerful feeling of the high. She had a way of controlling it better than most addicts. I don't know how she did that," said Sarah, truly not knowing how her mom did it, as she wasn't able to.

"The feeling she got while high was the best she ever felt, or thought she ever could feel," Sarah said, now describing her own addiction. Cliff was listening closely. Later, he would wonder how Sarah knew to describe her mom's addiction so well when she had died so early in her life.

"Her death was an accident though. The heroin she used had been laced with fentanyl and it killed her." She stopped walking and looked at Cliff. "Dad found her. He was devastated. Still is, really."

Sarah paused, suddenly overwhelmed by the vision of her dad not only finding her mom dead, but also finding his daughter passed out, both from opioids. She bowed her head and asked a question more to herself than to Cliff.

"Can you imagine?"

"No. I'm sorry. That's tough," said Cliff shaking his head.

Neither said a word for a few moments.

"Well, I'm going to head home," Sarah finally said.

For a moment, she had thought of telling Cliff her own experience with opioid addiction. Kelly had been the only person other than Art and her rehab group she had talked to about it. Even though she hadn't known Cliff very long, the feeling of him being like an older brother had only strengthened.

"Yeah," Cliff said, interrupting Sarah's thoughts as he started gathering his things and bundling up. "Thanks for inviting me. Hope you didn't mind I brought the others."

"No, not at all. I mean, I was a little surprised, but it was fun. Lots of fun," replied Sarah, regaining her focus on the practice.

Wilebski's was still closed the following week. Cliff, Zadie, and Louis again joined Sarah for a practice session on Tuesday night. This time all three of them brought some songs for their new "band" to practice. Zadie had an original she had written called, "Selling Guitars." It was a bluesy tune inspired by her job working at the Guitar Center. Her other songs were a blues take on The Replacements' "Unsatisfied." She wanted Cliff to sing that one. Then she would sing a favorite of hers, "Wilder Days" by Morgan Wade, another song she bluesified. Sometimes, when singing this tune, Zadie would wander over toward Cliff as if she was singing it to him, causing Sarah to wonder if the two of them might be more than just acquaintances.

Louis brought a Blind Lemon Jefferson tune, "See That My Grave Is Kept Clean," and one he said was for Sarah, Sonny Boy Williamson's "Good Morning, Little School Girl." They all shared a laugh about that. He also had Robert Johnson's "Love in Vain," which Sarah fondly remembered playing as a youngster back in Traverse City.

Cliff only brought one, R.L. Burnside's, "It's Bad You Know" from his *Come On In* album, which was a mix of electronic production with Burnside's signature Delta blues. Cliff planned to have Zadie and Louis play the organ and harmonica parts with their guitars, giving the song a different sound than the record. However, at the next session, Zadie came in with a Turboharp electric harmonica. She had bought it for herself at her Guitar Center and quickly learned how to play it. With Zadie playing the Turboharp, the band was able to give "It's Bad You Know" a sound much closer to Burnside's recorded version. Zadie became so proficient with the harmonica that she used it on a few of the other songs too.

Sarah hadn't brought any songs but suggested Luther Allison's "It's Been a Long Time." The band would talk about each song before they played it, discussing who would sing and how certain parts were to be played. Other than playing in the school band, Sarah hadn't played in a blues or rock band yet. To her, this felt like she was part of a real band. They decided to work on Louis' songs first, then Zadie's, followed by Sarah's and finishing with Cliff's. They agreed that whoever brought the song was the "owner" of that song and had complete say about how it should be played. To begin, they would listen to the song so everyone would have a reference for how it could sound.

Louis's Blind Lemon Jefferson song was a version from Blind Lemon himself. It was performed Delta blues-style with only an acoustic guitar. Louis explained how he wanted to electrify it, as well as adding powerful drumming. He would do the vocals. They worked through the arrangements and played it over and over until they were satisfied.

Before beginning work on his last tune, Louis wanted to make it clear that he didn't mean any disrespect to Sarah for the "Little School Girl" song. He meant it in good humor and recognition of Sarah being in this practice band.

"It's okay, Louis! Tartan's onboard!" declared Sarah. They all laughed.

Louis played the original from Sonny Boy Williamson then Muddy Waters' version. He wanted them to play it more like the latter with a faster tempo and bolder sound. He told Sarah to play loud since, after all, she was the little schoolgirl. The four enjoyed practicing that one, happily thinking of their own little schoolgirl leading the way on drums.

They took a short break before starting on Zadie's songs. Sarah texted Ron to see if he could bring down a bucket of beers and some water along with four plain cheeseburgers and a basket of fries. Ron replied that he'd be down as soon as he could.

Zadie had the group start with "Unsatisfied." Cliff knew the song but loaded up the lyrics on his phone anyway. Zadie wanted him to sing in his best angst-riddled voice rather than his Howlin' Wolf voice. She and Louis would play their electric guitars with the lead in, rather than imitating the acoustic guitar on the original track. Zadie liked the way Sarah had played the drums boldly on the last number, so she directed her to do the same with this one. After a couple of starts and stops, the group played through the song and Zadie was satisfied with how it sounded.

They had already played "Wilder Days" several times in earlier sessions. After some practice, they got that one down. Zadie's original tune "Selling Guitars" started with a demo version she had recorded. It was just her and her electric guitar. She described how the song "walked" through a normal day with the twelve-bar progression then repeated, giving the impression of the same thing day after day, sort of *Groundhog Day*-style, with dreams of more interlaced through it. Near the turnaround, the song quickened only to end by slowing down and leaving with the singer back selling her guitars. Zadie stopped the band the first few times they tried to play it all the way through. Frustrated, she wondered if the song wasn't ready.

"Zadie?" Sarah asked. "How about I play a little shuffle until we get to the turnaround? Then I'll really rock it out and we keep going, the sound coming up rather than ramping it back down." Sarah shrugged her shoulders, smiled and added, "I mean, I don't know. Just a thought."

Zadie, still discouraged by how the song sounded, was silent for several moments, thinking it through in her head. The rest of the band waited, giving her the space she needed to continue. Suddenly, as if struck with inspiration, she turned and faced the band.

"Let's do this!" declared a suddenly confident Zadie, continuing, "Like Sarah said, at the place we add speed and sound, we will all turn it up. Then rather than turning it back down or keeping it loud, we'll just end—maybe a recorded version would fade out, but for now, we just stop."

The other three nodded, ready to give it a try. Zadie had them practice the end like she described, then they played it all the way through. Zadie liked it but had them play it again and liked it even better, so she had them do it one more time.

"I think there's something there, Stella," said Louis nonchalantly.

Zadie smiled. Sarah laughed. She hadn't heard Louis refer to Zadie as Stella before, but knew it was a reference to her designer jacket.

Ron came in with the food and beer. They were ready for a break anyway.

"Hey, what was that song you were playing?" Ron asked.

"It was a Zadie original, 'Selling Guitars,'" answered Sarah.

"Really? It sounded great!" declared Ron.

"Thanks Ron," Zadie said without looking up, still processing what she had heard.

After the break, next up was Sarah's choice of "It's Been a Long Time." She asked if Cliff would sing. He agreed but said she should sing it herself. Sarah laughed, shaking her head. She didn't consider herself a singer other than around her apartment. They were all familiar with this song, so it didn't take them long to get it sounding right.

Cliff's R.L. Burnside song was a mix of electronic and conventional instrumentation. In the sessions that followed, Zadie's electronic harp gave it a similar feel to the recording. Sarah's drumming drove the song. Cliff sang. Being able to handle this song gave the group of practice musicians a feeling that they might be able to sound like a real band.

Wilebski's finally reopened before the next Tuesday, but the group of four decided to skip that first Blues Jam and practice together again. This time Cliff had an app on his phone record their practice session. They decided to play the same songs from the week before in the same order, with two additions. Zadie added "Scott Street" to her songs and Sarah and Cliff added "Smokestack Lightning" with Cliff singing in his Howlin' Wolf voice. The two of them agreed to be co-owners of the song.

The rehearsal ran smoothly. Ron again brought down food, but this time he stayed to listen to what he called his favorite song, Zadie's "Selling Guitars." Cliff and Louis received several texts throughout the evening from Cullen and others at Wilebski's, asking where they were. After practice, Louis said they should play Wilebski's next week. Cliff agreed, but Zadie wasn't sure if she could make it. Sarah said she should be able to. The four of them would attempt to get together on stage at the same time, although the way it worked at the Blues Jam, it wasn't up to the musicians to decide who played. That was, of course, except for BB Alight who was allowed to pick his bandmates. The group all agreed that they would try not to play any of "their" songs with other musicians. They talked about when they could practice again, leaving it to be determined since there wasn't another day that worked for all four of them.

Sarah was in low spirits as she walked home. She found practicing with the others even more fun than playing at Wilebski's. The next few days, she would listen to the edited version of their practice session songs Cliff had recorded and shared. She loved hearing those versions, but knew if they had a chance to keep practicing, they could really get those songs grooving.

Over the next two years, Sarah would continue playing at the Blues Jam. The group of Cliff, Zadie, and Louis would meet every few weeks for a practice session. They were getting better, but still Sarah felt they weren't practicing enough to reach their potential. Everyone was busy with their own schedules which prevented them from getting together more often.

Sarah had grown from being a gangly teenager to a striking young woman. She was about to head into the summer before her senior year in high school. Many of her classmates had a plan for what they were going to do after high school. Tina knew she wanted to play basketball in college. She was getting lots of interest from Division 2 and 3 schools. Sarah wasn't sure she even wanted to go to college.

What she loved doing was playing the drums. She thought she was good enough to play in a band, although she had heard horror stories of failed bands from almost everyone that played at Wilebski's, especially Louis. And she still hadn't gotten to play with BB Alight whose band, The Thrill, as those familiar with him predicted, had indeed broken up. His new band was named Crossroads, which jokingly referred to him changing bands so often.

The drummer for Crossroads was still Todd Landry, the same guy who played in The Thrill, and always made sure he was at the Blues Jam when BB Alight played. Sarah felt it was unfair that she was always prevented from playing with BB. She blamed Todd some but mostly blamed Alight since he had a say who played with him. BB would often play early and leave before Sarah or any of the other drummers besides Todd had a chance. She wondered how he could he know who the best drummer was if he never heard them play.

As Sarah matured, her look became even more reminiscent of her mother. She was thin with an athletic build, and her hair was curly light red that might look blonde or sandy depending on the light. Her eyes had also taken on her mom's hazel color.

Art and Melissa had mostly broken off their fling after about a year. They remained close but decided the time wasn't right for a relationship. Sarah wondered, with her looking more like Kerstin every day, whether that might have freaked her dad out. The truth was Art and Melissa felt uncomfortable around the rest of their families. Only Sarah and Kelly were ever aware of Art and Melissa's relationship, both of whom hoped it might rekindle for the two of them again.

Sarah had found that another by-product of growing older and being attractive was the interest she received from boys at school and guys, sometimes even old men, at Wilebski's. She was quiet around most of them but would assert herself if she detected they were, as Kelly would say, creeps.

For a while she had a crush on a guitar player, John Gost, who would show up occasionally for the Blues Jam. The attraction wasn't his guitar playing since he wasn't very good, but rather his carefree personality and his looks. John was 6'2" with an athletic build and curly brown hair with bangs only hinting at his brown eyes hiding behind them. She learned quickly that she wasn't the only woman who was drawn to him. John would sometimes have his girlfriend with him, a beautiful woman who looked like she could have been a model. When his girlfriend wasn't with him, he would flirt with others, including Sarah.

At a Blues Jam, while Sarah was playing drums and John was there without his girlfriend, she imagined hooking up with him, the two of them making torrid love together. Her thoughts were interrupted when she saw from the stage that John was flirting with someone at the far end of the bar. When she finished her set, she slowly moved closer to them.

She stopped suddenly when she recognized who he was flirting with. It was Jane. Sarah always thought Jane was the best-looking and coolest woman she had ever seen, in her opinion much prettier than John's girlfriend. Tonight, she wore black leather pants with an orange flannel shirt over a spaghetti-strapped camisole, her long black hair lying on her shoulders. Sarah was wearing jeans and a loose-fitting t-shirt. Her heart sank as she thought, how could she complete with Jane? Dejected, she started walking back toward the stage.

"Sarah!" It was Jane yelling for her. "Get over here!"

Sarah turned and did her best to hide her disappointment with an exaggerated smile.

"Oh hi! I'll be right over," replied Sarah. First, she squeezed into the bar. Sunny saw her and before Sarah could even order had opened a Pepsi for her.

"Here you go," Sunny said, handing her drink to her.

"Thanks, Sunny," Sarah replied. Sarah would always pay if she was asked, but most of the time the bartenders, especially Sunny, would just give her a Pepsi for free. She took the bottle and turned back to where John and Jane were talking.

"Jammin' set," John said.

"Really?" replied Sarah.

"I thought so too," Jane said, adding, "I didn't hear all of it because of *someone* talking all the time." Jane smirked at John.

"Funny, you know, I talk…and I listen," said John as he leaned into Jane, implying that it wasn't just him doing the talking.

Sarah felt uncomfortable with the pair clearly flirting in front of her. She began planning to make a fast getaway.

"I gotta fly. Jerry said he has something to talk to me about," Jane said abruptly, making a face. "Bye, John. Bye Sarah," she said as she left, adding a wink directed at Sarah.

"See ya, Jane," John said as she disappeared out the door.

"Pepsi, eh?" John asked, quickly turning his attention to Sarah.

"Yep. That's about it," Sarah awkwardly replied.

"Must suck to still be in high school," stated John.

"Not really," Sarah replied, trying her best to look cool, adding, "Only one more year to go. So not too bad."

She slouched against a post, still trying to look as cool as possible. John had a beer on a nearby ledge. He picked it up and slowly drank from it, while his brown eyes found an opening through his bangs to look squarely into Sarah's hazel eyes. He lowered his beer and murmured, "Your eyes are heavenly."

She blushed as he kept his gaze fixed on her. At that moment, she felt even more attracted to John. He was certainly seductive. Sarah was flustered and aroused at the same time. She wasn't sure what to say to this man who she felt was inspecting her soul. Suddenly, John broke his gaze and finished the rest of his beer.

"Sarah."

"Yes, John?"

"It was delightful chatting with you. But I've got to go," John said, with Sarah fixated on his every word.

"Oh. Okay. Yes, good to talk," Sarah managed to say, trying to hide her disappointment.

John reached for Sarah's right hand and held it gently. "Another time," he said, then leaned over, kissed her hand, and added, "Peace."

What the… Sarah thought. No one had ever done anything like that with her. She didn't know whether to laugh or throw herself at him. She smiled broadly.

"Yes…" she managed.

John grinned, turned, and left.

John wasn't at the next Blues Jam. Then Sarah missed one when her "band" practiced on a Tuesday night. As the days went by, Sarah's crush became more intense before it started to wane. The more she thought about it, she realized John probably didn't want anything to do with her, at least romantically. She came to believe she would have to turn eighteen before a man like that would pursue her.

The kids at school didn't interest her. With her life at Wilebski's, she often thought of her high school classmates as children. She had always been intrigued by Tina's brother, Kyle, but as far as she knew, he never, not even once, expressed any interest in her. For now, she would concentrate on finishing her school year and look forward to the summer.

CHAPTER 19

GRAND OLD DAY

The summer began with hot, humid weather displacing the cool spring air by mid-May, earlier than usual but not completely unheard of in Minnesota.

Cliff had some news for the other musicians when he showed up for the semi-regular Tuesday night "band" practice. The four of them had gotten into a routine of ordering beer and food from Ron when they arrived. They'd have him deliver the beer right away and begin by tuning their instruments while having a drink.

Over time, Sarah had relaxed her attitude about drugs and alcohol. She came to believe she became addicted to opioids at a young age due to her care providers being unaware of the consequences of their best intentions. Now that she was older, she avoided most drugs; however, she allowed herself to have a beer or two during practice since none of the others objected. It was common for teenagers to drink, even being under the legal drinking age. All her bandmates admitted that they had done so, yet none of them were aware of Sarah's prior battle with opioid addiction.

Many high school parties she attended had young wannabe drinkers regularly puking in the bushes and sometimes even inside the homes of the host. Though she was aware of her dad's taste for whiskey, she only drank beer or White Claws. Aside from her fear of becoming dependent on alcohol, perhaps she was fortunate that she didn't enjoy the sensation of being drunk.

Pot was easily available at high school. The quality would range from surprisingly good to headache inducing awful. Sarah had smoked it a few times at parties. She wouldn't try anything other than pot, even though speed and cocaine were sometimes available, occasionally even mushrooms and other types of psychedelic drugs. She knew from counseling and experience it was especially dangerous for her to get involved with drugs. She felt lucky that the high she now craved came from drumming and performing.

"Okay, listen up," Cliff announced, ready to share his news. Sarah, Zadie, and Louis all stopped tinkering with their instruments and looked toward Cliff. When he felt their full attention, he continued.

"We have a gig."

"What? A gig? How?" Zadie questioned.

"Yeah, what ya cooking there, Cliff?" Louis asked.

"Okay, so this guy Steven I know runs a bar down on Grand Avenue in Saint Paul. He told me their opening band canceled for Grand Old Day," Cliff said, then asked, "You've heard of that, right?"

Grand Old Day was a yearly celebration kicking off summer in the Twin Cities on the first Sunday in June. Grand Avenue, that ran east to west in Saint Paul, would close to traffic while various bars would host bands in their parking lots and street vendors brandished their food and wares. There was even a parade in the morning, mostly for kids.

"Yeah, man, who hasn't?" answered Louis.

"It's Grand Old Day," chimes in Zadie.

"Is it? I thought it was Days?" asked Sarah.

"Nope, it's Day," assured Zadie.

"I'm pretty sure it's Days," insisted Sarah.

"What difference does it make?" interrupted an agitated Louis. Zadie and Sarah traded smiles, both thinking they could have kept up that bit for a while.

"Okay. Okay. Whatever," said Cliff, putting an end to the controversy, "So one of the bars, Billy's, needed a band for the noon-two PM time slot. Steven asked me if I knew of any. And I said I did…us."

"What? Really?" Sarah said, now trying to contain her excitement.

"Man, we're not a band," Louis stated.

"Sounds like we are now," said Zadie.

"Yes, we are now. If we want to be, that is," Cliff said.

"Grand Old Day is less than two weeks away," Louis said, adding, "Too soon, man. Too soon."

"I don't think so," Sarah said, speaking up. "We're ready. We've been practicing for, well, forever. Let's do it!"

Louis was looking down, shaking his head. Zadie looked over at Sarah and saw her excitement, and she smiled at the memory of how jacked she was before she played her first live show.

"I'm in!" Zadie said, nodding toward Sarah.

"Me too," Cliff said, adding, "Of course, you knew that since I already booked us."

"What? How could you do that? We don't even have a name," complained Louis.

"Yeah, not really. Steven said Billy's needed a name to book us. I couldn't think of anything, so I told him our name was Selling Guitars. You know, after Zadie's song."

"Really? Wow, kinda funny, but, of course, I like it," said Zadie with a laugh.

"I like it too!" Sarah said, turning to Louis. "Come on, let's do it!"

"Of course you do Tartan. You don't know nothin' bout nothin'," Louis said, then he looked toward Cliff and Zadie

"You two though; you all should know better," he declared.

Louis grabbed his beer and took a long drink. Finally, he looked at the others one at a time. He could see they were all very much onboard with the gig. He, like Zadie, could remember the excitement he had before his first time playing in a band. He also remembered the awful times, including when one of his lead singers quit halfway through the gig and others when bandmates showed up so drunk they could barely play. To Louis, playing in a band was serious business. Sure, this practice group was now making decent music, but to play a cohesive set in front of a live audience…that was different. The four of them had only played a handful of times together at the Blues Jam and even then just a few songs from their playlist.

"I can see you fools want to do this," Louis finally said. He paused before continuing, "Well, if I'm going to join you, we have to do it my way."

"What's your way?" asked Zadie.

"First, we need to name a band leader. Someone who will act as the leader of the band at shows or any public event. Next, we'll need a practice leader. This is who will run the practice sessions. Then we need a business manager and money handler."

Louis could see the group hadn't thought about any of this, and from their expressions he could tell they thought he was overdoing it. Even so, since he had some bad experiences in the past, he wanted to get things settled before starting.

"We need a band contract. It can be a simple one-page thing," Louis said, adding, "we could even write it out on a Fox and Hounds napkin if you want. But we all need to sign it."

Everyone was silent, considering what Louis had suggested.

"And if we can agree on all that, my way is that since it is only a couple weeks away, we need to practice every day before the gig. We have to get our setlist together, practice and then practice some more," stated Louis.

"Come on, Louis. It's just a damn opening act. There won't even be many people there," said Cliff.

"And practice every day?" asked Zadie. "I'm working some nights. I can't make every day."

"Then we'll have to practice before or after your work. I'm serious. I won't do this if we can't all agree," said Louis, making his conditions clear.

"Okay, before we promise anything, let's see how the days look," Cliff said as he picked up his phone and opened the calendar app. "I'm going to make a shared calendar with all of you. I'll call it Selling Guitars."

They went through the days they had before Grand Old Day (it was Day, not Days, landing on only one day in June) and scheduled at least a two-hour practice each day. Some were as early as 6:30 AM, and others not until ten at night. Doing this, the four were confronted with the reality of their commitment. Up to now, it had all been for fun. This, in contrast, felt like work. Nonetheless, every practice session was scheduled and they agreed to make it unless something unforeseen occurred.

The next order of band business was to assign the roles. Cliff spoke up first.

"I nominate Zadie as our band leader. She's one of our singers and has the balls to lead from the stage."

"Ha! Balls? Yeah, I got balls. Right!" said Zadie.

"You do! Well, maybe not balls exactly, but you've got the talent for it," stated Sarah.

"I agree, Sarah," Louis said, surprising everyone by agreeing that Zadie should be the band leader but also by calling Sarah by her name. She felt it was the first acknowledgment from Louis that he respected her and that maybe she did know a little something after all.

"Okay, Zadie's our leader!" Cliff declared, adding, "and now I think Louis should be the practice leader."

Although this seemed a good choice, it caught everyone off-guard in that they imagined Zadie would also be the practice leader. After all, she was the only one who had presented an original song for the group. Louis, though, had experience and a business-like approach to leading. He wasn't as dynamic for live shows as Zadie, but as a rehearsal leader, he fit.

Zadie spoke up. "I agree. Louis should be the practice leader."

"Me too," Sarah added.

"Louis, okay with you?" asked Cliff.

Louis seemed taken aback by his bandmates asking him to lead the practices. He thought for a moment, then said, "Alright, I'll do it. One thing though. A song owner still has the right to arrange their song, but as practice leader, if I feel something should be done differently, we have to do it my way."

So, if they had Louis be the practice leader, they would have to agree that he had final say over their other songs. Cliff and Sarah nodded in agreement. Zadie looked down. She wasn't sure she should give anyone, even Louis, that power. So far, she had only played one of her songs for the band, but she had several more that she thought they could play.

"Louis, I don't think I can do that for my original songs," Zadie said.

Louis considered this then nodded. "I understand. Works for me. All songs but your originals. I'll even add that if anyone comes up with original songs, they will have complete say over how we practice and perform those songs."

"Good deal. We have our show leader and practice leader," said Cliff.

"And you should be the business leader, since you already booked our first gig!" Sarah said to Cliff. They all laughed.

"Ha! Sure, okay," Cliff said. Then he looked at Sarah.

"That leaves you to be the money manager."

"Really? You want me to handle the money?" Sarah replied, laughing.

"It's all you, honey!" Zadie told her with a smile.

"Okay, sure, why not," Sarah said.

Cliff took Louis' suggestion of writing a simple agreement on a Fox and Hounds napkin. He wrote in the roles assigned with the practice leader exception rule and agreed to split all money evenly. Song writers would get any credit or royalties that came along. They all signed the napkin and Cliff, as business manager, kept it.

The practice session that night had a seriousness to it that prior ones lacked. As practice leader, Louis set the agenda for the rehearsal. First, any business matters would be discussed. Then an open discussion for whatever band members might want to talk about, followed by the practice schedule of songs to work on. He had them all agree to a tentative setlist for that Grand Old Day performance. They would start with Zadie singing, since she was the band leader. The first songs and their singers were:

"Wilder Days" – (Morgan Wade, Sadler Vaden) – Zadie

"Love in Vain" – (Robert Johnson) – Louis

"See That My Grave is Kept Clean" – (Sonny Boy Williamson) – Louis

"It's Been a Long Time" – (Luther Allison) – Cliff

"It's Bad You Know" – (RL Burnside) – Cliff

"Smokestack Lightning" – (Chester Burnett) – Cliff

The last song was a favorite of the band with Cliff singing in his best Howlin' Wolf voice. They felt they might be at about the one-hour mark, accounting for some slack time in-between songs. There wasn't a break scheduled for their set, although they planned to pause a little more after the songs in the first hour than in the second. People would be just arriving with the crowd building more nearing the end of their set due to popular local country/rock artist, Tim Sigler, following them at Billy's. This meant they would leave the stage with their largest crowd, even if very few would be there because of them.

The next songs would be for the last hour. If they needed to, they could repeat as many of the earlier ones to fill the time. The list included Willie Dixon's "Little Red Rooster" with Cliff singing, Chum Fella's "Janitor Blues" with Louis singing, and Robert Johnson's "Sweet Home Chicago" with Zadie singing. These were all songs they had played at Blues Jams, even if they hadn't been together. To end, they would play "Sweet Home Chicago" since he felt they could play that one all afternoon if they needed to much the same as the Blues Brothers did in their movie.

The final hour songs with their singers would be:

"Janitor Blues" – (Chum Fella) – Louis
"Little Red Rooster" – (Willie Dixon) – Cliff
"Scott Street" – (Marshall Vore, Phoebe Bridgers) – Zadie
"Unsatisfied" – (Paul Westerberg) – Cliff
"Good Morning, Little School Girl" (Sonny Boy Williamson) – Louis
"Selling Guitars" (Zadie Archers) – Zadie
"Sweet Home Chicago" – (Robert Johnson) – Zadie

Louis would have the band practice the first six songs one night then the final seven the next for several days. The Monday before the show they would run through the entire set from start to finish, recording the session. The next two days, they would go back to playing half the songs in a session, then finish with the full set the last three days. Everyone agreed to the schedule, and they went to work.

During a break in one of the practices, Cliff and Louis were discussing "Unsatisfied." Louis had concluded that it didn't fit in the set. Cliff disagreed, saying, "You could say that about any of the songs." Even though it was a Zadie song, she stayed out of it. She was softly singing a song she had just heard and fell in love with, "If I Ever Leave This World Alive" by Flogging Molly.

"What's that song?" Sarah asked, listening to Zadie practice.

"It's one I just started learning by Flogging Molly," answered Zadie, asking, "Do you know them?"

"No. But that's a cool song. I have no idea what it means but it's really beautifully heartbreaking," Sarah said.

"Yeah. I'm not sure either. My guess is that it means when a younger version of you changes, that earlier form of you dies, in a way. You know? I mean, I sometimes hear old people say they don't recognize who they were when they were younger. Or maybe it's about when you really die," said Zadie. She paused before continuing.

"It could be about a relationship that ended, you know, died. I don't really know," said Zadie, shrugging her shoulders. "Maybe songwriters don't even know what all their lyrics mean, it just sounds good to them."

"Ha! Whatever, cool song though," Sarah said laughing.

Two days later, Zadie played "If I Ever Leave This World Alive" for the band in a punk/blues style, and all agreed to add it to the setlist. Louis thought it was good to have another song anyway, so they wouldn't have to jam so long on others. Also, Cliff decided to sing "Unsatisfied" in his Howlin' Wolf voice to better fit in with the rest of the songs. Zadie loved it. Louis was unsatisfied but agreed to leave it in the setlist, though moved it after "Smokestack Lightning" followed by the newly added "If I Ever Leave This World Alive."

Practices were going well. The four worked together to perfect their setlist. Subtle changes in guitar licks or drum styles would be discussed for each song. While Louis was a natural lead guitarist, Zadie was an all-around guitarist. Along with Cliff's and Sarah's connection as bassist and drummer, Zadie's rhythm guitar laying down the melody was integral to the band's tight sound. She also amazed them all with her exceptional soloing interpretations.

Something else that had become clear over the hours of practice was that Zadie was by far the best singer. Cliff was unique with his Howlin' Wolf singing voice. Louis's voice unfortunately sounded like it had seen better days. He hadn't done much singing at Blues Jams, and since their arduous practice schedule began, his voice had only deteriorated. As good as his lead guitar playing was, his singing was out of sync with the band. Even so, the band remained committed to their agreed upon singing assignments.

That was, until the Tuesday practice the week of Grand Old Day.

Cliff had recorded their session from the day before. It was the first one where they played their setlist from beginning to end in one session. As everyone was tuning their instruments, chatting, and cracking open beers, Louis had an announcement.

"Hey, bandmates! I've got something for y'all."

The others stopped what they were doing and looked at Louis.

"After listening to last night's session, I've got a change," Louis stated. Since he was the practice leader, everyone nodded their agreement and waited for him to continue. "Zadie," he said looking at her, "you're going to sing my songs, except 'School Girl.' I got that one."

"Louis, what?" asked Cliff, adding, "You know, we only have a few days to go."

"I know. I know. I also know that I listened to that tape and my voice is awful."

"It's not awful. I like it," Sarah said, trying to reassure him.

"Sarah, thank you. But the way I sounded on that tape… man, it's not good," stated Louis.

"I agree with Sarah," Zadie said, adding, "I think you have a good, gravelly, you know, bluesy voice."

"I appreciate it. I really do," Louis said, pausing before adding, "but, I'm the practice leader. And I'm saying, tonight, Zadie is singing my songs, besides 'School Girl.'"

The other three looked at each other. Louis had been a fair leader. His experience had shone through, with his suggestions about arrangements and other advice. What he was now suggesting wasn't irrational. They all listened to the recording and could hear his voice struggling, but as Zadie said, an argument could be made that it did have a good, gravelly quality. At the same time, the recording only confirmed the brilliant singing voice of Zadie.

"I know you're the leader, but I think it should be up to Zadie whether she takes this on now or not," Cliff said, breaking the silence.

"Okay. Cliff, yes, that's right," replied Louis. He then looked to Zadie.

Zadie thought that if she took on those songs, she would be singing eight of their fourteen-song setlist. Still, the tapes had given her more confidence in her singing voice, and with the additional songs she felt she could explore her range. It also made sense that since she was the band leader on stage, that she should take the lead singing on most of the songs.

"I'll do it. You gotta help me with them, okay?" Zadie finally said.

"Sure. Yes, anything you need," replied Louis.

Cliff again recorded the next several sessions. They took longer than the previous ones as Zadie found her way singing the three other songs. After two sessions, the four band members agreed to keep it that way for the show. The setlist was finalized as:

"Wilder Days" – (Morgan Wade, Sadler Vanden) – Zadie
"Love in Vain" – (Sonny Boy Williamson) – Zadie
"See that My Grave is Kept Clean" – (Sonny Boy Williamson) – Zadie
"It's been a Long Time" – (Luther Allison) – Cliff
"It's Bad You Know" – (RL Burnside) – Cliff
"Smokestack Lightning" – (Chester Burnett) – Cliff (Howlin' Wolf voice)

"Unsatisfied" (Paul Westerberg) – Cliff (Howlin' Wolf voice)

"If I Ever Leave This World Alive" – (Flogging Molly) – Zadie

"Janitor Blues" – (Chum Fella) – Zadie

"Little Red Rooster" – (Willie Dixon) – Cliff (Howlin' Wolf voice)

"Scott Street" – (Marshall Vore, Phoebe Bridgers) – Zadie

"Good morning, Little School Girl" (Sonny Boy Williamson) – Louis

"Selling Guitars" (Zadie Archers) – Zadie

"Sweet Home Chicago" – (Robert Johnson) – Zadie

Following a 6:30 AM session, the four of them went to the local Spire Credit Union to open a business account for the band. Sarah would handle deposits and withdrawals. The Grand Old Day gig would only pay them $400, or a hundred bucks apiece. Louis suggested they put a tip jar at the front of the stage in case some "suckers," as he called them, wanted to give them anything. He warned that if they did find themselves playing more gigs, there would be some expenses such as travel and potentially food and lodging. For this gig, Cliff said his buddy Steven had promised them beer and food from Billy's since they were helping him out. Sarah didn't think she would drink beer at the show, especially since she knew her father and maybe others from her family would be there.

One person she hoped would be there was Kelly, who was continuing her nomadic lifestyle by working in an Australian soap opera. A break in production gave her the chance to come home, and though Kelly wasn't sure if she could make it on time for Sarah's Grand Old Day performance, she was going to try.

Art had been telling everyone he knew about Sarah's gig at Grand Old Day, the same street festival he attended years back before getting married. Even though it was held on Sunday afternoon and was over by 6 PM, it could dissolve into a huge drunk-fest. So much so, that some residents on Grand Avenue and many on the haughtier Summit Avenue (which ran parallel to the north) complained and even tried to shut it down. These efforts failed, even with the countless reports of attendees urinating on residents' properties.

Even though Art and Melissa were still on their self-imposed serious relationship hiatus, they decided they would attend Grand Old Day together. Ron from Fox and Hounds was going to attend. Tina was going to try to make it. She had an AAU tournament that weekend being played at Kennedy High School, not too far away in Minneapolis. It would depend on how her team did on Saturday whether she would be able to be there. It turned out her team won which meant she couldn't make it. Coach Chatman also missed it because of the AAU tournament.

It seemed all the regulars and workers at Wilebski's already knew about the gig. Many were planning to stop by before BB Alight and his Crossroads band's performance at 3 PM down the street at the Red Rabbit.

The penultimate practice session went smoothly, with only a few tweaks to the arrangements. They agreed that if, during the show, anyone wanted to take a break, they would take a short one after playing "Unsatisfied." For the final practice, a few people were enlisted to come watch, giving them experience of performing their set in front of a live audience, albeit a small one. Cliff recruited a couple of his law school classmates, while Louis brought his wife, Jada, and thirty-year old son, Denzel. Zadie showed up with her roommate, Janis, while Sarah brought Art and Ron, who wasn't working that weekend so this time he could watch the entire practice.

Ron supplied a few buckets of beer and sodas for the band and attendees. He would process food orders if anyone wanted something. Sarah planned to stick to Pepsi for this practice, since she hadn't told her dad she sometimes she was drinking beer. Before their practice began, Zadie thanked everyone for coming and introduced the band. She told them they would be performing the setlist for the next day's show. Then the band played. Without telling anyone, Cliff recorded the session. He didn't plan to share it with the others until sometime the following week. But he wanted to have it as something to build on, in case the band wanted to play more gigs.

The crowd had a great time. Ron, of course, whopped and hollered throughout the set, especially when they played his new favorite song, "Selling Guitars." Art loved watching Sarah perform. He could see her joy, as well as her enormous talent. Jada and Denzel enjoyed watching Louis, knowing how much this band had come to mean to him. Cliff's friends enjoyed the beers and seemed to like the music, although they looked to be more interested in eyeing Zadie and Sarah. The session came to an end after a long, jamming version of "Sweet Home Chicago."

The small crowd all stood and cheered, giving the performers positive vibes leading into the next day's show.

Grand Old Day arrived with a heavy rainstorm early in the morning. It finished by 9 AM and conveniently helped clean the street before the festival. After the rain, the staff at Billy's went about preparing the stage and setting up some amps and microphones.

Zadie borrowed a few smaller amps from the Guitar Center for the show. She also brought a microphone her grandparents had given her when she graduated from high school. The two of them, her dad's parents, were huge fans of her singing and encouraged her to continue with it after she sang in high school musicals. The microphone was a quality Sennheiser model, and Zadie had used it with The iIts, a band she put together while attending Hennepin Community College. They played a type of folk/punk mostly for their own enjoyment, never intending to last. Since then, she had kept the microphone safely stored in her apartment.

Sarah and Art had packed up her drum kit. This would be the first time she'd moved it since they set it up at the Fox and Hounds, and so they took extra care not to damage anything.

The four musicians had arranged to meet at 11 AM at Billy's. Cliff knew the people who lived in one of the old mansions on Summit Avenue just behind the alley. The stage, a flatbed for a tractor-trailer, was set up right in the alley facing toward Grand Avenue. The large parking lot had a slight decline toward the stage, which made it an ideal concert floor. Vendors were there setting up their stands all along Grand Avenue. To the side of Billy's, there was an area set aside for beer stands and then further down a row of porta-potties. There was an abundance of porta-potties on every block of Grand Avenue and within the various concert venues, in response to the anti-public urination locals.

Evan and Portia Leek were friends with Cliff. He called them hipsters, even though they were closer to retirement age than hitting clubs. The Leeks hosted an annual celebration for Grand Old Day. Their mansion was now a three-unit condo, and the Leeks had the upstairs unit. Their housemates, being part of the group that feared Grand Old Day rather than reveling in it, had all escaped elsewhere. This left the entire large parking area at the Leek house available for their family and friends to use.

Cliff had just bought an old '64 Chevy Nova he was planning to restore. He loved that it had a three-on-the-tree manual transmission. It was in good running condition aside from a gas gauge that didn't work. Cliff was very careful with everything in his life except cars. He loved owning an old car to restore, like this Nova. He had just sold an old maroon Ford LTD station wagon that was a wreck before he restored it. He drove the Nova to pick up Louis and his son Denzel, who was going to be their roadie and soundman for the gig. Art and Sarah picked up Zadie in Art's Nissan Maxima, a car that might soon be ready for Cliff to restore.

The access to the stage couldn't have been any better. A gate led from the Leeks' backyard to the alley with the back of the stage only a few feet away. The stage was a semi-truck flatbed that had been put in place the previous night. At Billy's, Steven was busy inside getting the bar ready. Even though the bar was going to be staffed, most people would be outside. After the festival ended at 6 PM, people who wanted to keep partying would flood the bars.

The Grand Old Day parade, mostly for families, was scheduled for 9 AM, but with the rain having stopped about then, it was delayed. That added to the congestion for the street vendors since they were just finishing setting up. It was forecasted to be warm with the sun clearing out the clouds by 1 PM.

The band set up everything early and did a sound check well before their show. They were ready. The bandmates didn't have any coordinated dress code. Cliff wore blue chino shorts with a gray Fleetwood Mac t-shirt and a white Mitchell Hamline Law School baseball cap. Louis had long black pants with a solid blue polo, dark gray sport coat and black flat cap. Zadie and Sarah had talked about what to wear. They decided to wear oversized t-shirts, Alison Wonderland-style. Zadie wore a white Led Zeppelin concert t-shirt while Sarah donned a black Tartan Basketball one, and both wore jean shorts. Zadie wore her pink platform boots with a pink beret to match, while Sarah wore her high-top black Converse. She recently had her hair cut to be just longer than shoulder length so she could thrash around while playing drums.

A sparse crowd had formed. The band gathered over by the Billy's kitchen entrance just next to the stage. All were drinking beer except Sarah with her Pepsi. Zadie motioned for the four of them to huddle around her. She was in charge as the band leader and was now ready to lead. She had them all put their arms over each other's shoulders then looked them in the eyes, one at a time. Louis was serious, and Zadie could see he was prepared. Cliff had his cool aura, signifying he was ready. Sarah was dripping with the enthusiasm of youth.

"I know we're ready. Louis, thank you for getting us here," Zadie said.

"Yay! Louis!" Sarah added as Cliff nodded his agreement.

"Look around…this is why we practiced all those hours!" Zadie continued confidently.

"Zadie! You're the boss!!" said an exuberant Sarah, everyone smiled.

"We are gonna have some fun today!" declared Zadie, and they all nodded their agreement.

"Okay! Let's fucking go!" yelled Zadie.

The four musicians broke their huddle and bounded to the stage. It was just before noon. The small crowd consisted mostly of friends and family. Art and Melissa were with Grandma Elizabeth, Karl, Stella and their kids, Jason and Anna. Jada was over with Denzel to help him with the sound board. Zadie's roommate Janis and a few other friends were in front of the stage. Then there was the Wilebski's contingent, Cullen, Sunny, Aamir, and Spring. Off to one side was Jane, but no sign of Jerry. At least for today, she had ditched her normal goth look for a flowery summer dress and big yellow beach hat. Cliff's law school friends Brett and Ogden had come with several others. The hipsters, Evan and Portia, were milling around with some of their friends and family.

Other than their acquaintances, no one else there knew of the band. Since they were a late addition, their name was only included on a few posters around Billy's, which featured Tim Sigler since he was the headline performer. Selling Guitars was added with permanent marker, listed as a "new-age blues band" opening the show. Cliff didn't know where that description came from.

"Hello everyone! We're Selling Guitars!"

Zadie greeted the crowd with her Sennheiser microphone. Then she turned to the band and immediately started playing the opening to "Wilder Days." As they had practiced, they played an elongated version of the song featuring guitar solos by both Zadie and Louis. Sarah found it interesting Zadie played her solo facing Cliff. When they finished after six minutes, the crowd had grown. Billy's was the band stage furthest to the west on Grand Avenue, and since the street was closed there were lots of people walking east who would stop into Billy's to listen to whomever was playing.

Sarah noticed Melissa and Grandma Elizabeth were over talking to the Wilebski's group. She thought Art had gone for more beers or off to the porta-potty since he wasn't over by Karl's family. Those listening could tell the band was well-rehearsed. This included a couple of attendees off to the side of the parking lot concert floor, BB Alight and his drummer, Todd Landry.

Zadie showed her vocal range with the next two songs, singing "Love in Vain" in alto followed by "See That My Grave is Kept Clean" in soprano. Zadie and Louis played beautifully while Cliff and Sarah were locked in, displaying their natural connection that was evident since first playing together at the Blues Jam.

"They're good," BB Alight said out loud, more to himself than anyone else.

Todd looked at BB whose head was bobbing in time to the music. "Yeah. I guess," Todd said. He had a pompous view of his own skills that made it hard for him to accept others' talent. He may have been worried that, after finally getting in a BB Alight band, his time might be short-lived. Of course, he, like everyone else knew BB was notorious for changing up his bands regularly.

"Thank you! Thank you!" Zadie said from the stage as they finished, adding, "That last one was from Sonny Boy Williamson. Give it up for Sonny Boy!"

The parking lot concert floor was now mostly filled in. Even though it was just 12:30 PM, beer sales were brisk. It was hard to know how many blues fans there were, but there definitely were fans of live music and beer.

"I'm going to turn it over to Cliff for the next three. Take it away, Cliff!" Zadie said, motioning to Cliff.

"Thank you! Let's hear it for Zadie!" he said. The crowd roared. Cliff nodded to his bandmates as they started playing "It's Been a Long Time." This song was the longest they played, and both Zadie and Louis again had guitar solos. Sarah killed her drum solo too, having imagined playing this tune in front of a crowd many times. They played for just over nine minutes on that one.

"It's Bad You Know" followed for seven minutes, the musicians mimicking the recorded electronic version, helped by Zadie quickly mastering the electric harp parts. Over time, the band had grown to love playing this unique song, which was now apparent in their performance.

Next up was Cliff's first Howlin' Wolf voice for "Smokestack Lightning." Real blues fans recognized this and yelled their approval. Others looked around, wondering what prompted this reaction.

"Unsatisfied" was played next, which now featured Cliff's Howlin' Wolf voice. Some in the crowd recognized the song and roared their satisfaction. When they finished, the band members were enjoying their first show together in front of a surprisingly large and enthusiastic crowd, and they decided not to take a break. Next up was the Flogging Molly song, "If I Ever Leave This World Alive" added late in the rehearsal sessions. Zadie's singing voice was magnificent with this melancholy song. It was a few minutes after 1 PM when they finished.

"How's everyone out there doing?" Zadie asked to loud cheers. "We're doing good too! Let's keep it going! Here's one of our favorites, Chum Fella's 'Janitor Blues.'"

Zadie played the familiar intro to Chum's classic, merging with Sarah's drums, followed by the rest of the band. Cliff was up next with another Howlin' Wolf-voiced song, "Little Red Rooster." The crowd now filled the entire parking lot. Beer stands were packed as well as the porta-potties, and the sun shone brightly on the supportive audience.

"Thank you!" Zadie yelled over the crowd noise, then announced, "The next one isn't really a blues song. So, we just bluesified it for you." Zadie began playing the intro to "Scott Street."

Since Sarah's drum part didn't start for a few stanzas, it gave her the chance to take in the crowd. She saw Jane standing with the Wilebski's group that now also included John Gost, her burgeoning crush, and his girlfriend, looking her supermodel best. She noticed BB and Todd now in the middle of the crowd. She couldn't miss Cliff's classmates up front, obviously enjoying the festivities. Then in the back she saw Art making his way toward the stage. Her heart skipped a beat when she saw Kelly was with him, wearing a two-piece summer outfit with a wallaby print. Kelly saw Sarah behind the drums then started jumping up and down, both arms high in the air. Sarah raised her drumsticks above her head smiling broadly, making her entrance into "Scott Street" even more joyous.

"Thank you! Thank you! You're so kind," acknowledged Zadie.

Next up was Louis singing his only song, the ode to Sarah, "Good Morning Little Schoolgirl." After the crowd quieted down, Zadie announced, "Now we have one from our fearless leader, Louis Boyd."

"Thank you, Zadie," said Louis in his deep voice.

"Y'all still doing good out there?" The crowd replied they were. Louis continued, "This next one is for our magnificent drummer, Miss Sarah Zonnen." Sarah stood up and waved as the crowd yelled in response. Louis and the band rolled into the song, the crowd rowdily responding to them in the sunshine.

Zadie had been nervous about debuting her original song, "Selling Guitars" to a real audience. She figured she would calm her nerves by trying to tell a joke in the introduction.

"Thank you! You guys are great," she said as the crowd quieted. "We're Selling Guitars. And this is a song I wrote called 'Selling Guitars.'" She paused as some of the crowd laughed. "Do you wonder which came first, the band name or the song?"

Sarah did a rimshot, and a surprised Zadie laughed, turned and bowed to Sarah. The portion of the crowd that was lubed up shouted "WOO-HOO." The more sober ones smiled tentatively, unsure if she was joking.

"So here it is, 'Selling Guitars' from Selling Guitars about, well, selling guitars."

Sarah played the song with enthusiasm supporting her friend the best she could. The crowd responded positively to the song, some even singing along to the refrain…

My alarm goes off, snooze, snooze

Another day, just another day, selling guitars.

When they finished the song, it was 1:50 PM. They had ten more minutes. That fit well with their plan for "Sweet Home Chicago." In the practice sessions, they had regularly jammed on this one, sometimes for over fifteen minutes.

Zadie thanked the crowd, introduced the members of the band, and thanked Billy's for the opportunity. Then they tore into the song, Zadie again displaying her vocal range. Halfway through the song, someone threw a triangle-shaped pirate hat on stage. Zadie smiled and tossed it back to Sarah who put it on.

The band finished to loud applause and gathered at the front of the stage arm-in-arm. Sarah flung the pirate hat back into the crowd before the Selling Guitars band bowed in unison. As they left the stage, Tim Sigler walked by and congratulated them on a great set. Next the four musicians ended the same way they began by huddling around Zadie.

"That was fantastic!" Zadie declared.

"Yes. Yes, it was," agreed Louis.

"Could not have been better!" yelled Cliff.

"Wow! What a rush! So fun!" Sarah shouted.

"I'm going to explore Grand Old Day. Thanks everyone, you were…well, you were grand!" Zadie said, as they all laughed and exchanged hugs.

Sarah introduced Zadie to Kelly. They immediately clicked. The three of them spent the afternoon going back and forth between Tim Sigler's and BB Alight's shows. In the waning hours of the festival, they joined Portia on the Leeks' deck that extended off their upstairs condo unit facing Grand Avenue and Billy's. They laughed and told stories of the Grand Old Day they had all enjoyed. Art and Melissa roamed Grand Avenue with Grandma Elizabeth, Karl and his family, on the gorgeous, sunny afternoon, for once not hiding their obvious affection toward each other. Sarah's only disappointment was Tina's basketball schedule didn't allow her to make it. She had hoped that if Tina did make it, she might have come with Kyle.

In the days that followed, Sarah spent as much time as she could with Kelly before she headed back to Australia in mid-June. That summer, Sarah worked at Taco Bell. The pay wasn't great, but she liked the flexible schedule. She got in the habit of practicing over at the Fox and Hounds in the morning, sometimes returning in the evening.

The four members of the band still tried to practice once a week. Louis was taking a trip over the Fourth of July to visit family in Chicago. This left the band as a three-piece for a few sessions. They began practicing new songs including three new Zadie originals, "Blue Sky Blues," "Gone Too Soon," and one celebrating their gig together, "Grand New Day."

Blues Jams continued every Tuesday night. They had returned to a hero's welcome after the Grand Old Day performance. Although Todd still monopolized drumming with BB Alight and other top performers, Sarah had gained the respect of everyone. To her surprise, this included BB Alight himself.

One time in mid-July when BB Alight was about to play, Todd made his way up to take over the drums from Sarah. BB blocked him and the two had a conversation on the side of the stage. Todd left angrily as BB turned and motioned for Sarah to stay. BB played three songs that night with Sarah drumming. Afterward, Sunny had a huge smile for her, along with a free Pepsi. Aamir came by to tell her how much he enjoyed her playing with BB. Before he left, BB stopped over to talk to Sarah as she was playing *Galaxian* at the back of the bar.

"Hi," BB said as he came up from behind Sarah. Startled, she turned around surprised to see it was "the" BB Alight.

"Oh, hi," she nervously replied.

"You're good. I've always thought so since I first saw you play here, what, it must be years ago now," stated BB.

"Thanks," Sarah replied, not realizing BB Alight had ever noticed her playing.

"You know, I've got a gig in a couple of weeks down in Iowa," BB said.

"Oh yeah?"

"Yeah, and I'd like to have you play drums and Cliff Johnson play bass."

"What? Really? But you have a band, right?" asked Sarah.

"I do. But they all can't make this date. Besides, I'd like to see how we'd sound as a three-piece. They want me, I mean us, to open the show, like you guys did at Grand Old Day. So, it would be a good chance to try some new things out."

"Wow. Just me and Cliff? Have you talked to him?"

"No. Not yet. I wanted to make sure you were on board first."

What! Sarah thought. BB Alight wanted her in his band before Cliff!

"Thank you, but..." Sarah said, pausing before adding, "But what about Zadie and Louis?"

"They're good, really good, but what I have in mind is a three-piece, blues-rock-country band with me singing a few original songs and covers. Besides, I think Zadie should lead her own band, not be in mine or anyone else's. Louis, maybe, but you know if it's just the three of us, the pay will be better with fewer musicians," replied BB.

"Okay. Umm, I don't know," said Sarah, wanting to do it but not wanting to cause problems with her friends. "Can I talk to them about it?"

"Sure. I mean, tell them to keep it quiet for now. I haven't told my band yet. It's not a big deal though, they shouldn't care. Let me get your number so you can let me know," BB said.

"Oh. Okay," replied Sarah, who gave him her cell number.

"It will be fun. I promise. Just a nice summer day in an Iowa cornfield playing music… See ya," BB said abruptly, turning and immediately leaving up the stairs and out of the bar.

CHAPTER 20

IOWA

"You sure you know the way?" asked Sarah.

"Yes, I'm sure. No problem. It's a straight shot. Easy-peasy," answered Cliff.

"No! You didn't just say that!" Sarah said, amazed at the geeky expression her cool friend just used. Cliff just slyly grinned.

The two were on their way to the Iowa outdoor concert that they agreed to play with BB Alight. It was BB's show. The three of them had rehearsed at the Fox and Hounds practice room several times. BB sang all the songs and was the unabashed practice and band leader.

These sessions were much different than those Louis led. BB was adamant about the sound he was looking for, but not about the precision of it. He was apt to improvise bits of songs without any notice. Sarah and Cliff learned to follow along with his tangents. When mistakes were made, BB would rarely stop to discuss what happened. He preferred to just keep going. This could lead to some ugly-sounding bits but after a few practices the three musicians learned to "hide" the stumbles.

BB was getting paid five grand and giving Sarah and Cliff $850 each and another $150 each for expenses. BB had left earlier on Friday, the night before the show. Cliff was driving Sarah there in his '64 Chevy Nova with the three-on-the-tree manual transmission and useless gas gauge.

It was past midnight before Sarah and Cliff left the Twin Cities. They would be staying at a house owned by an acquaintance of BB in Ames. It was usually rented out via Airbnb; however, it wasn't booked this weekend so the owner had arranged to put BB and his band up for the weekend for free, hoping they wouldn't destroy the place.

Sarah and Cliff were leaving later because of a Chum Fella show at The Cabooze. It was a small, famous bar in Minneapolis with a stage crammed into a corner close to the end of a long oval bar. Many local and national acts played there. Even the Rolling Stones had performed an impromptu show while in town for a sold-out concert at a nearby football stadium. The Cabooze was a small, sweaty club for both serious performers and up-and-coming bands.

That Friday night, Chum Fella was performing a Luther Allison tribute concert. BB had gotten a couple of tickets from one of his booking contacts. He gave them to Sarah after learning how she was a huge Luther Allison fan. He advised them not to get wasted and leave before midnight for the long three-and-a-half-hour drive to Ames. BB's performance was scheduled for 2 PM the next day, and he wanted them to be ready to leave the Ames house no later than 1 PM for the show.

Cliff stopped by the Fox and Hounds to pack up their equipment. Art was there. He echoed BB by telling them to take it easy at the Chum Fella show and drive safely. He was nervous about letting his teenage daughter go on a long weekend trip to Iowa and play at an outdoor concert; however, he trusted both Cliff and Sarah.

It was evident Cliff and Sarah's relationship was like that of siblings. Cliff knew Sarah had gotten a fake ID from someone at Wilebski's. It didn't bother him since he never knew her to drink much. Plus, as Sarah approached her senior year in high school, she not only looked like she could pass for being in her early twenties but acted like it too, having grown up in a bar.

The Cabooze was packed with a festive crowd. Having a popular performer like Chum Fella brought out some local celebrities, which for the Twin Cities included news anchors and athletes. Cliff was able to get a couple beers from the crowded bar. Then they made their way to the small opening at the far end of the club. Sarah was tempted to play the *Galaxian* game in the corner. Before she could, Chum Fella took the stage. He was in a discernable good mood, reveling in the small, packed, steamy bar compared to the larger venues he normally played. He started with "It's Been a Long Time" and continued making his way through Allison's catalog.

Finally, just past 10 PM after a rousing version of "Low, Down and Dirty," Chum announced he would take a short break before coming back to play a few of his own songs to end the show. The bar was jammed with people and becoming more crowded by the minute.

"We gotta stay," Sarah said as Chum left the stage.

"I'd like to. But, you know, we probably should go. It's going to be a long day tomorrow," stated Cliff.

"We'll be fine," said Sarah, her youthful enthusiasm evident. "Besides, you know BB. He'll be okay if we make a few mistakes," she added.

"Yeah, well, he was at practice anyway," Cliff replied.

"You know, it will take us an hour to get out of this place," Sarah said jokingly, since they were packed together like sardines.

Neither was drunk. They only had the one beer they were able to get when they arrived. Cliff was as hyped as Sarah was listening to Chum and his band.

"Okay, Sarah. Let's stay," agreed Cliff.

Chum came back out and tore through some of his hits ending with "Washing the Killing Floor" then coming back for an encore with "Janitor Blues."

The two friends drove down Highway 35 accompanied by Luther Allison's greatest hits. Cliff's old car didn't have Bluetooth, but he did have a cassette player installed. Luckily, he had collected numerous cassette tapes to play in his car. He even had a recorder at home that he used to record cassettes from streaming services. At the end of a song, Sarah turned down the volume.

"What's the deal with BB?" she asked.

"What do you mean?" Cliff answered her with a question.

"Well to begin with, what's up with his name? I mean is he BB because of BB King?"

"Ha! Maybe. Here's the story Todd told me," Cliff replied.

Sarah frowned, and Cliff noticed and laughed.

"Anyway, the story goes that his real name is William Robert Alight. And when he was little, kids called him Billy Bob, which he hated, so, he decided to go by BB."

"Funny! I'm not sure I can believe it though if you heard it from Todd. Maybe, I'll just ask BB," stated Sarah.

"Sure thing, yeah, go ahead and ask BB," Cliff laughed.

"What's up with Todd anyway? Why's he such a dick?" asked Sarah.

"I don't know. He's an odd duck, that's for sure. But, Sarah, even you have to admit he's a good drummer."

"Yeah, I guess," replied Sarah with a frown. "Why didn't BB just get Todd and his bass player to do this gig?" she asked.

"Who knows? Maybe he's at the *crossroads* with his band," joked Cliff.

A few miles passed with the faint sound of Luther Allison still playing.

"Do you think he wants us in his band?" Sarah asked, breaking the silence.

"It's possible. The guy switches bands so often, who knows."

"Do we have a band name tomorrow?"

"I think it's just as BB Alight. No band name," Cliff answered.

"Ha! Sounds about…Alight!" Sarah quipped.

"Hey, you know, if we, I mean Selling Guitars play any more gigs, I thought of a new band name for us," Cliff said.

"Oh yeah, what's that?" asked Sarah.

"Well, how about this…Two Foxes and Two Hounds!" Cliff proudly stated. Sarah burst out laughing.

Suddenly they could feel the car's power failing. It was pitch-black outside, nearly 3 AM Saturday morning. No other vehicles could be seen in either direction.

"What's happening?" Sarah asked as she sat up straight.

"I'm not sure," answered Cliff, although he had an idea. Thinking back on the day, he realized he didn't fill up his car with gas before picking up Sarah. This meant that they were running out of gas in the middle of the night somewhere in Iowa. He knew he had to be honest with Sarah.

"Sarah, we're running out of gas," said Cliff.

"What? Here? Now? Are you serious?"

"Yes. I'm afraid so. I forgot to fill up," admitted Cliff.

"Great," Sarah said slumping back in her seat. "Couldn't you tell that you were low?" she asked.

"No," Cliff replied, realizing Sarah didn't know about his gas gauge. "The gas gauge is broken. It doesn't work, so I try to keep it full," Cliff stated as they rolled to the side of the road. Luckily, they could see an exit sign within a walkable distance in front of them. He couldn't blame Sarah for being agitated. He wasn't sure what to do. They sat there for a few minutes, neither one of them saying anything.

"Shit. No signal," Sarah said after studying her cell phone.

"Me either," stated Cliff. There were no cars in sight. The night sky was intense, with stars providing the only hint of light.

"Let's go," Sarah said, opening her door. Cliff watched her then looked down the road. He could see nothing past where his headlights outlined. Without any better ideas, he grabbed his keys, opened his door, locked it, and walked away from the car, thinking he may never see it again.

The two walked in silence. Their enthusiasm had been sucked out of them with the last bit of gas. After a short walk, they saw the exit sign for 190th Street.

"Maybe there's a gas station or a house up there," Sarah finally said.

As they walked, she decided to start a conversation about something else.

"So how's the lawyer business going?"

"Okay. Except I'm not a lawyer yet. I have to finish one class and then pass the bar exam," replied Cliff.

"You should be good at that, spending so much time in bars," joked Sarah.

"Ha! I've never heard that before," Cliff said sarcastically.

"I'm sure you'll pass. You're the smartest guy I know."

"Thanks, though not smart enough to have a working gas gauge."

They started walking up the exit ramp to 190th Street. There didn't look like anything was in front of them. Certainly not a gas station.

"What do you know about this show we're playing tomorrow? I know it's outdoors but that's about it," Sarah said.

"You mean today," Cliff corrected her, since they were scheduled to start at 2 PM. It was now almost four in the morning. "Yeah, it's some outdoor concert on a farm. I think it's about thirty miles outside of Ames in the middle of nowhere. Kind of like an Iowa Woodstock."

"Bunch of farmers better be ready for some blues!" Sarah said laughing.

"I hope so," Cliff said, not even sure if they would make it.

Near the end of the exit, they could see 190th Street was an open road with nothing on it. They could see a farm about a half-mile or so down the road. It wasn't right on the road, having a long driveway leading up to a classic-looking Iowa farmhouse.

"Let's go," Sarah said starting toward the farm.

"I don't know," Cliff wavered, not moving.

"What's up? We need help."

"I'm just wondering what a good old boy Iowa farmer is going to think of a short black man and a pretty young white woman knocking on his door at four in the morning."

"Oh, come on Cliff. Really?"

"Really. You know I love you, sis. But you never know about random people," replied Cliff.

Sarah considered what Cliff was feeling. It was true she had been let down by some creeps, as Kelly would say, both at high school as well as so-called fans at Wilebski's. She would give anybody the benefit of the doubt until they proved her faith was misplaced. Like the middle-aged man who would watch her play video games. He didn't bother her until one day when he was drunk, he grabbed her butt. Sarah was shaken and yelled at him to get lost. She never saw that guy again.

At Wilebski's and her high school, there wasn't much overt racism. Cliff had a soft-spoken personality and seemed to get along with everyone. When she was with him, she always felt safe. She had only seen him angry a couple of times when someone in the audience at Wilebski's was unruly.

She couldn't know what it was like to be black in America though. Things she might take for granted like going to a farmhouse in the middle of the night in Iowa to get help might turn into a life-or-death situation for a black person. That night though, she wasn't sure if they had any other options, other than maybe just sitting at the exit and waiting for someone to pick them up. And hoping that someone was preferable to the farmer. They both stood there for a few minutes surrounded by nothingness except for that farmhouse in the distance.

"No choice, man, no choice. Let's go," Cliff stated then started to walk.

"Okay," said Sarah, adding something she wished would become true. "It'll be fine."

"I hope so," was all Cliff said.

Approaching the farmhouse, they wondered what fate was in store for them.

"Who's there?" a loud voice bellowed from the house. Cliff and Sarah stopped in their tracks just short of the wrap-around front porch, looking nervously at each other.

"Hello, our car ran out of gas over on 35," replied Cliff nervously.

"Hang on," said the voice. Now they could hear what sounded like an angry dog barking inside the house. "Butch, be quiet!" the voice yelled.

"Oh no, the dog's name is Butch!" Sarah whispered, grabbing Cliff's arm. He had a worried look on his face as the front door slowly opened.

A massive man appeared. Although he looked young, no older than thirty, he was heavy-set and stood 6'8" with bushy red hair and a beard. He was still fastening his overalls, having thrown them on in a hurry. The large man didn't have any reaction when he saw Cliff with Sarah clinging to him.

"I'm Billy. Welcome to my farm. Let's get you some gas," Billy said as he yawned.

"Thanks, we really appreciate it," said Cliff.

Billy walked over to the barn and disappeared inside. Butch started barking assertively again from inside the house. Cliff and Sarah anxiously waited for Billy, hoping Butch wouldn't come bursting through the door. They relaxed slightly as Billy emerged from the barn with a large gas can. He walked over to a brown Ford Escape that looked like it had seen better days, putting the gas can in the back.

"Settle down, Butch!" Billy yelled.

"Is everything okay out there?" a woman's voice said from inside the farmhouse.

"Yes dear," was Billy's only response. Then he turned to Cliff and Sarah and said, "Let's go."

The two stranded travelers walked over and got into Billy's Escape. Cliff rode shotgun while Sarah sat in the backseat.

"Which way is your car?" Billy asked as he drove up his long driveway toward 190th Street.

"We're just north of your exit on the southbound side," answered Cliff.

"Okay. We'll have to go up to C70 then come back this way," Billy stated. Sarah could see that Billy was still groggy after being woken up. Although he appeared to be a big, menacing man, he was soft-spoken and incredibly helpful.

"What brings you this way?" Billy asked as they neared the C70 exit.

"We're musicians. There's an outdoor concert just north of Ames we're playing at this afternoon," replied Cliff.

"This afternoon? You're not going to get much time to rest up," Billy said.

"No. That's for sure," agreed Cliff.

"How'd you happen to run out of gas?" Billy asked. "You know it could be dangerous out in the middle of the night all alone on the highway."

"Cliff's gas gauge doesn't work," Sarah said, answering the question Cliff ignored.

"Gas gauge doesn't work? Even this old thing I use to run around the farm has a gas gauge that works," Billy said, then took the C70 exit and turned around to head south back toward 190th Street.

"I made a mistake and didn't fill up before we left. Normally, I keep it full or close to it," admitted Cliff.

"How do you like it here?" Sarah asked, changing the subject.

"Oh. I like it. It's a lot of work though," replied Billy.

"Is it a family farm?" asked Sarah.

"No, although my brother runs it with me. We're not really farmers, but we are learning. I played football for the Cyclones, you know, Iowa State."

"Really, that's cool!" said Sarah.

"Yeah, it was fun. I even played pro for a couple of years."

"Where'd you play?" Sarah asked.

"I played in Chicago, for the Bears. That is, until my knee got wrecked. My heroic days on the field are in the past now," replied Billy. "Looks like that's you up there." Cliff's Chevy Nova was off to the side just in front of them, and Billy pulled in behind it.

He got out and began to pour the gas he brought into Cliff's Nova. "That should be plenty to get you to the truck stop off the next exit after mine. Can't miss it, Highway 20," stated Billy.

"Thank you very much for helping us," Cliff said, digging in his wallet and pulling out a fifty-dollar bill. "Please, take this for the gas and for your trouble."

"Nope. Glad to help. You better be on your way so you can rest up before your show."

"Are you sure?" Cliff asked as Billy shook his head.

"Thanks. Thanks again," Cliff said, putting away his money.

"Yes, thanks Billy! You've been so great to us. And sorry for bothering you in the middle of the night," Sarah said.

"You're welcome. I would have gotten up soon anyway. Now off with you."

Cliff and Sarah got back in the Nova and drove away. They made it to the exit for Highway 20 and filled up, the gas gauge still reading empty. Not much was said the rest of the way to Ames. It was now past 5 AM. They were exhausted when they finally got to lie down and fall asleep.

Someone banging on the door woke Sarah. Her cell phone, which she forgot to plug in to charge, showed it was just past noon. She lay there reflecting on the crazy night of watching Chum Fella, running out of gas, walking to Billy's farm, and finally making it to Ames, which seemed like only a few minutes ago.

"Okay, okay, I'm up!" she yelled.

"Good! We gotta get going!" It was BB at the door.

After showering and getting ready, Sarah sat down for some pancakes and bacon BB prepared. Soon Cliff joined her. BB was loading equipment in his van. He was planning to take everything with him. After they played, he was going to collect it and head back to the Twin Cities. Cliff and Sarah would drive separately in Cliff's Nova so they could stay at the show as long as they wanted.

It was going to be a hot, August day. Sarah was wearing a short-sleeve white cotton buttoned-down shirt with a Nike sports bra and jean shorts with her favorite black Converse. Cliff had a white tank top, showing off his guns as Sarah would say, with jean shorts and Nike tennis shoes along with his Mitchell Hamline baseball cap. BB was on brand wearing a BB Alight white t-shirt with beige cargo shorts and black Pumas. As Cliff walked into the kitchen, BB said, "See you there. Don't forget to lock the door."

Cliff and Sarah arrived at the outdoor concert venue a short time later. It was a large, open field with a stage set up not far from the farmhouse and barn. Cars were being parked just off Gretten Street. After parking, the two of them walked toward the stage, spotting BB's van behind it. People were just arriving, looking forward to a long day of music, sunshine, and merriment.

"This place is massive!" exclaimed Sarah.

"It is. And in the middle of Nowheresville, Iowa," said Cliff.

They had parked about a half-mile from where the stage was set up. In front of the stage was the huge open field. Some concertgoers were claiming their space by laying blankets and setting up folding chairs. The field was flat, leading from the stage with a slight hill on the way back. On the opposite side of the field from the parking lot there were the most porta-potties either of them had ever seen, arranged in a massive L-shape.

The BB Alight Band would play from 2 'til 4 PM. Following them was a local band from Iowa, Mike's Waterloo. As their name suggested, it was a band from Waterloo, Iowa that was well known across the state. There might be a few people showing up that had heard of BB Alight, but most would be there to see Mike's Waterloo and the other Iowa bands that followed.

BB's setlist was made up of blues standards like "Little Red Rooster," "Got My Mojo Working," and "Sweet Home Chicago." Also, rock and roll covers like "Satisfaction," "I Want to Hold Your Hand," and "Be My Lover" among others, followed by a mix of his original songs like "Down by The River" that were more country than blues. His style was to have the rhythm section, Cliff and Sarah, play solidly if unimpressively while his singing and guitar playing would shine. Being such a great experience for Cliff and Sarah, they had no problems going along with BB, especially considering their payday.

The soundman, Jim Weber, was with Mike's Waterloo. He was tall and thin, wearing a loose tank top, jeans, and flip-flops. Sarah joked privately to Cliff that Jim didn't have any guns to show off. BB walked with Jim out to the middle of the field where the soundboard was set up. When BB came back, he was shaking his head and frowning.

"I hope that guy knows what he's doing. Nice kid though."

"Oh no. What are you going to do?" asked Sarah.

"Nothing. No choice, man," replied BB.

"Are we going to sound like shit?" asked Cliff.

"Probably. Yeah. Well, maybe not, we'll see," BB said.

"There must be something we can do," pleaded Sarah.

"I told him how to run the board for us. I don't think he understood. What more can I do? Let's just hope for the best," said BB.

"Guess we'll just have to turn it up to eleven!" Cliff said emphatically.

As 2 PM approached, there wasn't a cloud in the sky. The temperature read 90 degrees. The field was filling with people; many had brought blankets, chairs, and even dogs. Beer and food tents were set up in the back and doing a brisk business, though some in the crowd had brought coolers with their own beverages. Tickets had been sold, but there weren't any gates. It appeared anyone who wanted could attend with or without tickets.

BB gathered Cliff and Sarah together. "Are you ready?" he asked.

"Yeah!" replied Sarah.

"Let's do it," Cliff stated.

"Okay. All the amps look good. Let's go," BB said.

Not quite the rousing pre-performance talk Zadie gave, but for this band it was all they needed. BB and Cliff put their guitars on, and Sarah mounted her drum throne. BB turned to them and said, "Follow me." And started playing "Satisfaction" the first song of their setlist, harvesting no interaction with the crowd.

Although BB was a pro, he didn't have the stage presence of Zadie, at least not at this performance. Maybe it was because he accepted that there weren't many people there to see them. He had the attitude that he was going to collect his money, play his songs, and then gladly leave the stage for the band following them. As was his process, he had already taken payment for the gig. Since he had been stiffed on a show years before, he always made sure that he was paid before performing. He hadn't given Cliff and Sarah their full cut yet, only the $150 each in expense money he gave them after their last rehearsal.

BB and his band were surprised the sound was good. Their fears about Jim, the Iowa sound guy, not knowing what he was doing were unfounded. Some in the crowd were enjoying their set. Most of them, though, were just milling around. The band was sweating in the Iowa heat. Sarah took her shirt off before she sweated through it. Cliff was drenched in his tank top, as was BB in his BB t-shirt.

As 4 PM approached, the band was enjoying themselves. BB started talking more with the audience in between songs. The festive crowd now filled in most of the area of the large field except the space in the back by the concession stands. Beachballs and frisbees filled the air. BB ended their set with "Sweet Home Chicago" the same as Selling Guitars did at Grand Old Day. Some in the crowd chanted for an encore. Mike from Mike's Waterloo was already standing next to the stage and shook his head no when BB looked at him. BB thanked the crowd and told them that Mike's Waterloo would be playing next, which drew a large ovation from the Iowans.

BB, Cliff, and Sarah broke down their equipment and packed it into BB's van. He was leaving to drive back to the Twin Cities. Cliff and Sarah were going to stay at the Ames house that night after hanging around the concert for a while longer then drive back on Sunday.

"That was fun. Thank you both for playing," BB said, readying to leave.

"Yeah, it was," Cliff said, then asking, "Hey, man, did you have our money?"

"I do. But it's a check so I'll get it to you next week," answered BB.

"A check? Don't you normally get cash?" asked Cliff.

"Yeah. But all they gave me was a check. I decided to play and take their word it was good."

"I hope so," said Cliff, slightly disappointed.

"Here. Take this," BB said, offering them both a fifty.

"Okay. Thanks. See you next week," replied Cliff.

"Yep. Thanks again," BB said.

BB drove his van slowly through the crowd making his way to the parking lot.

"I hope we get paid," Cliff said, watching BB's van disappear.

"Yeah. Even if we don't, it was still a blast!" Sarah replied.

"That's true," Cliff agreed.

"The crowd was nuts. Even if they weren't paying much attention to us," stated Sarah.

"Ha! Yeah, it was fun watching them. Right now, though, I need a beer," Cliff said, turning and walking toward a beer tent at the rear of the field. Sarah walked with him.

"You want one?" Cliff asked as he was ordering. Sarah nodded yes.

The humidity was increasing. Hot summer days in the Midwest could often come to a dramatic end with a severe storm. There had been a forecast promising rainstorms, but they weren't expected until Sunday at the earliest. This afternoon, there wasn't a cloud in the sky and with almost no wind, it felt even hotter than the mid-nineties temperature. Lots of men were shirtless, including Cliff. His sweat-soaked tank top was hanging out of his back pocket. Sarah had tied her buttoned-down shirt around her waist.

She wasn't alone in wearing a sports bra; plenty of women wore them, with others wearing bikini tops. Everyone was roasting.

Mike's Waterloo was playing mostly rock and country covers to the delight of the local crowd. Walking around was straightforward enough if you stepped over or around the occasional passed-out concertgoer. No one seemed to recognize Cliff or Sarah from the show. This made sense, since BB was the frontman dominating the performance, along with so many people not even paying attention to the stage. Cliff was one of the few black people in the large field. He projected a cool confidence, but Sarah could tell he was alert to any troubles.

After visiting one of the many porta-potties, they ate cheeseburgers from a vendor with a large charcoal grill. It was one of the most popular vendors with a constant long line, the smell of the beef searing on the grill drawing people in. Seeing the cook orchestrate the cheddar cheese square melt over the patty was pure artistry.

"Bro, my phone's almost dead. I forgot to plug it in last night. Ah, I mean this morning," said Sarah.

"Mine too. We'll have to remember to charge them tonight."

"So, it's just you and me in Ames tonight, right?" asked Sarah.

"Yeah. BB left right after the show," answered Cliff.

"Did he say why he needed to leave?"

"Not to me. Although, he did say something about not wanting to get stuck in the weather."

"It's hot for sure. But, hey it's summer. What'd he expect?" Sarah said.

They turned to see the stage in the distance. Mike's Waterloo just took a break. They had already played for almost two hours. They were going to play at least another hour before the headliner,

Tuckerized, took the stage just before sunset. It was a Marshall Tucker cover band named after one of their albums.

Facing the stage, the parking lot was to the left. It was the only area that had any trees, and it didn't have many. The porta-potties were to the right with the vendors behind them. The smell of the cheeseburgers was inviting even if they couldn't eat anymore. After a couple of beers, they had moved on to water bottles.

"Maybe we should go. It'll be dark in a couple of hours," said Sarah.

"Yeah. Maybe," Cliff said, considering Sarah's suggestion.

"Hey! Look over there!" Sarah said, now enthusiastically pointing in front of them about halfway to the stage.

"Do you see that?"

"It looks like a foosball table," said Cliff.

"It is! Let's play!" she said and took off jogging.

"Okay. Okay," Cliff said, following her.

They slowed down to a walk as they approached the table. There playing defense for one side was John Gost. He wasn't wearing a shirt, showing off his slim, athletic physique. Playing offense was a guy Sarah thought she'd seen at Wilebski's, wearing a blue Muddy Waters "I've Got My Mojo Working" t-shirt. They were both wearing sunglasses. A woman was standing behind John's end and talking to them both. She was slim with striking features, brilliant long red hair, and a yellow tank top.

BAM! John's partner slammed in a goal. They had won. A crowd was gathered around the table. John and his partner fist-bumped each other and the red-headed woman. It was fifty cents to play. There were three sets of coins already on the table. Sarah put her two quarters on the table.

"Hey sugar," John said. When Sarah looked at him, he did a finger gun in her direction.

"Hi John," replied Sarah with a smile.

"Oh, and hi to you too, Cliff," John said, nodding toward Cliff.

"John, looks like you're winning, eh?" said Cliff.

"Yeah. We're hot. In more than one way," replied John as he wiped away sweat.

"Hope you stay hot so we can play you," Sarah said.

"Babe, you know I'll stay hot," John said, grinning at Sarah.

"Hi, I'm Mia. This guy isn't very good at introductions," said John's tank-top friend.

"Hi Mia. I'm Sarah and this is my friend, Cliff."

"Hi, Sarah and Cliff," Mia said then pointed to John's foosball partner, adding, "and this is my boyfriend, Luca."

"Hi there," Luca said.

"Mia, could you do us a solid and grab some more beer?" asked John, flashing a tantalizing smile that was familiar to Sarah.

"Oh sure, why not?" Mia answered.

"I'll go with you," said Sarah.

"You want one?" she asked Cliff.

"Sure, I'll take one," he replied.

"Let's go," Mia said to Sarah starting toward a beer vendor.

Sarah joins her.

"You guys were good," John said to Cliff.

"You heard us?" Cliff asked, surprised.

"Oh, yeah, we were here early with a friend that lives down here. I saw it was Alight, but I didn't realize it was you and Sarah for a while."

"Glad you liked it, man," Cliff said.

Mia and Sarah walked together toward the beer tent. They were quiet most of the way. Sarah broke the silence with a question.

"How do you know John?"

"He went to college with Luca for a few years. John and Luca live in a house together in Saint Paul," replied Mia.

"Cool. Good you're all friends," Sarah said.

"Yeah. I've got a good job now but those guys still act like they're in college. Sometimes, like today, I can pretend I am one of them."

"Funny! I don't know John very well. I met him playing at the Blues Jam," Sarah said.

"That's what he said. He thinks you're a great drummer. But, if you know John, you know that's not all he thinks," said Mia.

Sarah laughed; pretty sure she knew what Mia meant.

They reached the beer tent and got five beers and turned to go back to the foosball game.

"Can you tell?" Mia asked.

"Tell what?" Sarah said, looking at her.

"That I'm… I mean, we're all, high as shit," Mia divulged.

"Ha!" Sarah said laughing, adding, "No, I can't tell. Of course, I don't know any of you very well."

"True. Well, John, who somehow can get just about any drug in the world, got some peyote. So, we're doing peyote for the first time."

"It's like mushrooms, right?"

"Yeah, that's what John told us."

"Well, I would have never thought you guys were high," Sarah said.

"Good, I'm glad. I'll say it's a pleasant enough high," stated Mia.

"It must be good for foosball playing!" Sarah joked.

"Ha! I think you're right. Those two are pretty good, but I don't think I've ever seen them play as well as they are today," Mia said.

They returned to hear another loud BAM! as one of Luca's shots rammed into the opponent's goal to win another game. John and Luca had beaten two teams so there was only one more set of quarters in front of Sarah's. A quick game dispatched that team. Sarah took the offensive end while Cliff manned defense. The two of them had played some foosball together at Wilebski's.

"Maybe we should play for something?" John asked suggestively before they started.

"Not this time," Sarah answered, momentarily shooting down his flirtation.

Sarah didn't have any fancy shots, but she could control the ball, sliding it back and forth and shooting quickly. Cliff was a solid, if unspectacular, defender. Both John and Luca played at a different level. John, who played goalie for a high school hockey team, had a knack for blocking shots, be it hockey or foosball. Luca had a variety of shots although his classic pull shot, when it was on, was nearly unstoppable.

Maybe it was overconfidence or fatigue for John and Luca, but Sarah and Cliff were able to take an early two-goal lead. The tide turned quickly though with Luca and John scoring all the remaining goals to win easily.

"Good game," said a disappointed Sarah congratulating her foes.

"Hey, you guys should stick around. We can party if we ever lose," said John.

"Maybe," Sarah hinted.

She and Cliff left to go to the porta-potties.

"Are you really interested in that guy?" asked Cliff.

"I don't know. I mean I don't think so. But, you know, he is… interesting."

"I guess that's one word for it. I'm not going to tell you what to do but be careful."

"Okay, Dad," Sarah said sarcastically.

Returning from the porta-potties, the sun had almost set. John and his friends were waiting at the foosball table. Their luck had finally run out, or maybe the effects of the peyote had worn off.

"There you are!" John exclaimed, seeing Sarah approach.

"Yes, it's me. You lost?" Sarah asked.

"Yeah, we were due. Besides I don't think I had any more sweat in me," John said laughing, then added, "We're gonna leave. You should come with us."

Sarah looked at Cliff who shrugged his shoulders. Then she looked back into John's glassy peyote-brown eyes sneaking through his bangs, giving her pause.

"Maybe next time," she said, realizing that she didn't want to start anything when he was doped up.

"See you back at Wilebski's," Sarah said, before turning to Cliff. "Bro, let's get a water."

"Okay. See you later," John said. Sarah hugged John, Mia, and Luca goodbye.

Cliff and Sarah roamed around after buying their water. Before heading to the car to leave, they stopped and listened to Tuckerized play "Can't You See." The night sky was magnificent. Both tilted their heads to look for the Big Dipper.

VROOM! VROOM! VROOM!

Suddenly there was a roar coming from the parking lot. Motorcycles, lots of them, streamed onto the field. Concertgoers were scrambling to their feet and yelling as the bikers slalomed around them. The bikers kept coming, one after the other. There had never been much sign of security, so there was no one there to stop them.

"What the fuck?" Sarah exclaimed.

"Let's go back here," Cliff said motioning to the vendor stands.

The two of them hurried away. A biker raced by them with a young woman on the handlebars. She looked scared. In a flash, bikers with women on their handlebars were circling around the field. Some of the women were naked from the waist up. What had been a fun afternoon and evening had suddenly turned terrifying.

Cliff and Sarah couldn't move as bikers circled around them. There was yelling and screaming all around. Without warning, two bikers raced at them then abruptly stopped next to them. One rider, a six-foot burly man with a graying, unkept beard and gamy scent grabbed Cliff in a tight bear hug. The other man, who was 6'5" with a short, what looked to be manicured black beard, stood close to Sarah.

"Leave him alone!" Sarah shouted at the man holding Cliff.

Cliff was being held so tightly he was struggling to breathe.

"Don't you worry, darling. He's fine," said the man now with his large hands on her shoulders. No other bikers were nearby, only these two large humans. People were scattering away. Yelling and screaming echoed around the field. Sarah wanted to yell, but she wondered who would hear it over the already deafening calls for help. Instead, she looked at this man's face, and his eyes covered by dark sunglasses.

"What do you want?" Sarah asked firmly, although she had an idea.

"Darling, you're going to be my bike ornament," the man plainly answered.

"Not a chance!" Sarah yelled.

The man just laughed. "Let's go," he said.

He then grabbed her by the waist and lifted her onto his bike. Sarah was terrified. The entire field had dissolved into a scene from a horror movie, with loud motorcycles circling the field many with women on their handlebars. The large man held Sarah firmly in place as he moved back to his seat and revved his engine.

"There's just one more thing," said the man in a menacing tone. Sarah was now just another woman screaming for help. Cliff couldn't move, still being held tightly by the gamy man.

KA-BOOM!

Sarah felt the grip of the man on her waist shrivel. She jumped and landed on her feet as the bike collapsed behind her. The man holding Cliff let go and ran away. Sarah turned around.

"BILLY!" Sarah screamed. It was the farmer who helped them early in the morning this same day.

"Sarah, Cliff, you two alright?" asked Billy.

"I am now!" Sarah said, wrapping herself halfway around Billy's barrel chest.

"Me too," said Cliff, adding, "How? What? Man, you saved us!"

"We can chat later. Let's get you out of here. Oh, and by the way, this is my brother Bob," Billy said nodding toward another large red-haired man.

Billy and Bob had Sarah and Cliff walk close to them as they made their way to the parking lot. Bikers were still riding around the field some with unfortunate women forced to become handle-bar ornaments.

"Where's your car?" asked Billy.

"Over there," said Cliff, pointing to his Nova parked close to the open field since they were early to the event.

"Okay. We're in the back. It won't be moving very fast, so we'll walk with you until we get to ours," Billy said.

With the bikers all in the field, it seemed like they were safer in the parking lot.

"I can't believe you're here! We're so lucky!" cried Sarah.

"Yeah, it's pure luck," agreed Billy, adding, "We finished work early and since you told me you were playing, I thought we'd catch your show."

"Plus, I'm a big fan of Marshall Tucker and Tuckerized," Bob added.

"Wow," was all Cliff could say.

As they approached Cliff's Nova, Sarah almost tripped over what was a biker passed out behind their car.

"I'll move him over there," said Billy, pointing to the side where the biker wouldn't be behind any other cars. He grabbed the biker by his boots and pulled him to a new resting spot. The unconscious man groaned as he was repositioned away from being almost run over.

"Let's get the hell out of here!" declared Sarah.

"Yeah, let's go!" Cliff agreed as he jumped in the driver's seat.

"Got enough gas? Sorry, couldn't resist," joked Billy.

Cliff drove carefully out to where Billy's car was, the same Ford Escape he had driven them in that morning.

"How can we ever thank you?" Sarah asked.

"Don't worry about it. I'm glad we were there. Some of those bikers are pretty dangerous," Billy said.

Approaching police sirens blared.

"Drive safe tomorrow. They say a bad storm is moving in," warned Billy.

"Yeah, we keep hearing that," Cliff said, adding, "We'll be careful."

Sarah and Cliff drove back to the Ames house in silence, replaying the happenings of the unusual day in their heads.

CHAPTER 21
JOURNEY HOME

It was past noon by the time both Cliff and Sarah awoke, finally securing the sleep they'd missed out on since leaving for Iowa. They showered then mixed up some pancakes. It had gotten cloudy outside, though it was still hot and humid. Sarah dressed in her favorite oversized Tartan basketball t-shirt with her jean shorts and Converse high-tops. Cliff wore a Mitchell Hamline maroon-colored t-shirt with his jean shorts and tennis shoes.

"Crap!" Sarah shouted.

"What?" asked Cliff.

"I forgot to charge my phone again and now it's dead," replied Sarah, frowning.

"Shit!" Cliff said, realizing he hadn't plugged in his phone either and it was dead too.

"If only that car of yours had a wireless charger or even a regular one," Sarah said sarcastically.

"Yeah, yeah. Finish up. Let's get out of here," answered Cliff.

Neither had much to pack since BB had taken their equipment back in his van. They threw their bags in the back seat. Sarah had grabbed a few Pepsis and bottled waters for the trip. Soon they were on Highway 35 driving north to the Twin Cities with a mixtape cassette of blues tunes playing softly.

"That was weird last night," said Sarah, stating the obvious.

"Sure was. I'm sorry I wasn't much help. It was awful watching that guy grab you like that."

"Yeah, I thought for sure I was going to be paraded around naked, like so many other poor women there," said Sarah quietly. After pausing, she continued. "The only difference was we were lucky."

"Yeah, I'm glad you convinced me to walk up to Billy's farm. You never know," Cliff said.

"It worked out, that's for sure," Sarah agreed as they sat in silence for a few miles.

"Okay, enough of that," she said, breaking the silence. "Tell me more about your lover."

"Who?" asked Cliff.

"You know, Stevie Nicks. Tell me more about you and Stevie," insisted Sarah.

"Ha! She's not my lover. But you already know that."

"No. No, I don't. I want to hear more about you and Stevie."

"I connect with her is all. I've met her a few times and we hit it off. That's it. That's all you need to know," replied Cliff. Sarah looked at Cliff who maintained his poker face.

"Okay. Sure. So, if she's not your woman, who is?" she asked.

"Well, Sarah, if you must know, I don't have a woman at the moment."

"You should date Zadie. You guys would be great together," suggested Sarah.

"What? Did she tell you?" Cliff asked, looking surprised.

"Tell me? You dog! You *are* dating her!"

"No, no," said Cliff, now realizing Sarah didn't know about his brief fling with Zadie.

"So what? Come on, tell me!"

"Alright. We were seeing each other for a while. We had fun. Then she broke it off."

"I wondered about you two, especially the way she always flirts with you when singing 'Wilder Days,'" Sarah said.

"Ha! I told her somebody was going to figure it out about us if she kept doing that!"

"Why did she break it off? Was it another man?"

"No. I don't think so. I'm not sure why. You know Zadie is kinda a free spirit and also sort of a loner. We're still close. It's all good."

Sarah looked at her friend who was exuding cool as always. If he didn't feel so much like a brother to her, she could see herself involved with him romantically.

The sky was yellowish, even though it was early afternoon.

There weren't many cars on the road and only a few semi-trucks.

"Zadie's like the most talented musician I know. And singer! My God, she's an amazing singer!" said Sarah.

"I agree! And she's a great performer. I've thought for a while she's like some sort of combination of Phoebe Bridgers and Samantha Fish," stated Cliff.

"Umm, I hadn't thought of her like that. You might be on to something, or just on something," joked Sarah. "But, of course, she's herself, the one and only Zadie Archers."

"You're right about that. She's a star!" Cliff agreed.

"I can't believe you dumped her!" joked Sarah.

"Jesus!" said an exasperated Cliff.

"You know, we should become a real band! Zadie's band. We'll play anything she wants," Sarah said.

"That would be fun. But you'll have to do it without me."

"No way! You're the bass player and that's final," objected Sarah.

"Sorry, sis. I'm buried in student loan debt. I got to go to work. Real work. For real money," explained Cliff.

"We'd make money in Zadie's band. I'm sure of it," said Sarah.

"Who knows, maybe you're right. You know, I've got some requests for us to play more gigs. Even one from Wilebski's."

"Wilebski's? Really? Why haven't you told us?"

"I was going to this week after our Iowa gig. These gigs aren't for sure yet and none of them are for much money. Just requests to see if we'd be interested."

"Awesome!" Sarah exclaimed, not concerned about the money, only the prospect of playing more gigs.

"Like I said, I might not keep playing. I could stay on as the band manager if you want me to, but I have to start working for real."

"Oh, come on bro. You even came up with that new name for us. What was it again?"

"Ha! Two Foxes and Two Hounds. I knew you'd like it since you're one of the foxes!"

"Yeah, and you're one of the hounds!" said Sarah as they shared a laugh.

Regardless of the new band name, Sarah could tell her friend was conflicted. She knew he did want to keep playing in their band, but the reality of making a living was weighing on him. The two friends sat silently, reflecting on their band's future for several miles.

They passed the exit for the Flying J Travel Center where they had filled up the previous day after stopping for help at Billy's farm.

"Should we stop?" Sarah quipped.

"Funny! I think we're good this time."

"How can you tell?" Sarah said, still laughing.

"Okay. I need to fix the gas gauge."

"Or just get a car built within the last decade!"

"We were lucky to run into Billy. Have you ever seen horror movies? You know, the ones where a couple runs out of gas in the middle of the night and are hacked up at the house they stop at?" Cliff said, changing the subject from his beloved Nova.

"Oh yeah. I've seen some of those. I was really trying not to think about that while we walked up to Billy's farmhouse."

"Me too. But after hearing Butch, man, it got me thinking—that could have been it for us."

"Our time wasn't up," Sarah responded.

"Nope. Not yet," agreed Cliff.

"You know my mom died, right?" asked Sarah.

"Yeah, you told me. Very sad. Opioid addiction is a powerful thing."

"Yeah, it sure is," Sarah said knowingly. She looked at Cliff who glanced toward her. At this moment, she wanted to tell her friend her truth. Not knowing how to start, she decided to just say it.

"I told you about my mom, but I didn't tell you about me."

"What? What do you mean?"

"Only Dad and my Aunt Kelly know."

"What do they know?" asked Cliff with a concerned expression.

"Well, here it goes...I'm an opioid addict," Sarah said in a tone that Cliff could tell she wasn't joking.

"What? Seriously? How?"

"It was when I was younger. After I was injured playing basketball."

"Really?" said Cliff, pausing before adding, "I'm sorry. Are you still addicted?"

"No. I stopped taking the pills. It was tough though. Really tough. I'll always want it. Always."

"I feel like an idiot getting you beers," Cliff said.

"Oh. Don't. It was my choice. So far, alcohol doesn't do much for me anyway."

"Jesus, Sarah."

"Come on, Cliff. Don't get all weird on me now."

"What kind of injury was it?"

"My knee, playing basketball. It was fun and I made some great friends, even if I don't play now. I'll never forget them or my coaches," said Sarah, proudly adding, "I was damn good too!"

"I bet you were. I played some but since I was short, I ended up wrestling," Cliff said.

"I didn't know you wrestled."

"I was okay. But I always liked basketball better. At practice, when we had a break, I would shoot baskets. I got to be a good shooter. We should play horse sometime."

"You're on! I'll kick your ass!" Sarah said excitedly.

"Jeez, it must have been a bad injury that they gave you opioids."

"I guess. I didn't really know. My dad and Melissa were conflicted when the doctors asked them," said Sarah, pausing before adding, "because of Mom."

"I'm sure. Thank you for trusting me enough to tell me. You let me know if there's ever anything I can do. Promise?"

"I promise, bro. Mom didn't mean to die. You know? She just needed those drugs. I need them too. I could have died just like her."

"I can't say I understand exactly, even though I've been close to a lot of death. My mom died of cancer a few years ago. Before that, my dad died in a boat accident."

"I'm sorry, Cliff."

"Thanks Sarah. My grandpa told me once 'Live your own life, because you will die your own death,'" Cliff said, adding, "He died about a week later."

"I'm sorry to hear that. I think about death sometimes. You know, I often visit Mom's grave. I'll sit and talk to her. In a way, after my experience with drugs, I know exactly how it happened. I could have been right there beside her, with my own simple gravestone."

Cliff didn't say anything as he processed his friend's admission.

"I'll sit next to her and talk to her about my life…and hers. I know she wishes she was here with me. But she's not. And it wasn't her fault. She didn't want to die."

Cliff nodded, understanding Sarah's pain.

The sky turned from yellow to gray, and several more miles passed.

"Was that your Aunt Kelly at Grand Old Day?" Cliff asked, starting a new conversation.

"Yep. That was Kelly. She's more like a sister than an aunt."

"Maybe you'll introduce me next time," Cliff suggested.

"Yeah, sure thing," Sarah said, winking at Cliff.

"I've never seen her around. What does she do?"

"She's an actress!" Sarah said with pride, adding, "She travels all over the place. Wherever she needs to be for work. Right now, she's in Australia working on a soap opera."

"Good for her. Hopefully she'll get a gig closer to you."

"Yeah. I really miss her even though we Facetime a lot. She told me she has an audition for some big HBO show that's coming up. She couldn't tell me much about it. The only thing she said was something about dragons. I'm not sure what that means, but I hope she gets it."

"Dragons? Jeez, I hope it works out for her but that sounds ridiculous."

"Ha! I thought the same thing!" agreed Sarah.

"What's up with your dad and Melissa? Isn't she your aunt?" asked Cliff.

"Ha! Yeah, she is. She's Mom's sister."

"Those two look like they could be a couple."

"For sure. I think they want to be, but are sensitive about how Mom would've felt about it."

"Complicated, eh?" asked Cliff.

"Very. I think they're getting over it. I hope so anyway. They're happiest when they're together," said Sarah.

"Your dad's an EMT or something, right?" asked Cliff.

"Sort of. He drives for a company called Kare Kabs. Not really an EMT, more like an Uber service for the elderly. He loves it though. He really likes helping people. The pay isn't great, is the only thing."

"Loving your job is worth something. Maybe not enough to pay the rent though," Cliff said.

"Melissa's got a great job. She loves it but is sometimes embarrassed about how much she makes, especially compared to Dad."

After sitting a while in silence, they approached the Minnesota border.

"I can't believe you're going to leave the band," said Sarah, frowning toward Cliff.

"Yeah. Maybe. As soon as I pass the Bar Exam, I'm a lawyer. And lawyers can make some *real* money."

"Oh, good for you! Just kidding. I'm happy for you. You'll do great."

"Thanks, sis."

"So, you'll be the next Louis. Just playing at the Blues Jam from now on," Sarah said.

"Yep. Me and Louis, the Blues Jam duo."

"Who's going to be our bass player?" asked Sarah.

"I'm sure there's somebody out there. Maybe not at the Blues Jam, but somewhere," replied Cliff, knowing he was always the best bass player at the Blues Jam.

"What if BB asks you to play in his band? Would you do it?" Sarah asked.

"No!" Cliff answered quickly, adding, "I'd play for Zadie before I'd play with BB. I mean, I like the guy, but you know, it was different working with him. He's very self-absorbed. Plus, he goes through bands so often, he'd dump me soon enough."

"I know what you mean. But I'd still play with him—that is, if Zadie doesn't want me in her band."

"She wants you!" Cliff said emphatically.

"How do you know? Is it because your lover told you?" asked Sarah.

"Jesus, Sarah," Cliff said as they both laughed. "Seriously. You're the best drummer I know. And you're only going to get better."

"Thanks, bro. But do you really think I'm better than Todd?"

"Yes. No doubt. You're a natural. Besides that, everyone, and I mean *everyone*, including BB would rather play with you on drums." Sarah shared a warm smile with Cliff.

"So, tell me something Sarah."

"Yeah, what?" Sarah replied.

"You wouldn't seriously hook up with that dude, John Gost, would you?"

"Ha, ha! Jealous, are you?" asked Sarah with a chuckle.

"It's not that," said Cliff in a serious tone, adding, "I care for you. And I don't think you should get involved with that guy. I mean, I can't count the number of women I've seen him with, and that's including his alleged girlfriend."

"Yeah, I know the guy's a ladies' man. But there's something about that guy. And you know it's flattering that he's interested in me."

"Maybe. But I'm concerned about you getting mixed up with him. Really."

"I don't know," replied Sarah, now with a serious tone. "I probably won't. Besides he knows I'm not even eighteen yet."

"You will be soon, right?"

"Yeah, pretty soon. Then I can screw all the guys I want!" said Sarah laughing, adding, "Just kidding, bro."

"Ha! You know you don't need to tell me but...are you a virgin?"

"Woah! You really going there?" asked Sarah, staring at Cliff.

"Hey, I said you didn't need to tell me. We can talk about something else if you want."

"No. Let's talk about it. Besides, Kelly and Tina are the only ones I ever talk to about sex and stuff like that. It would be good to talk to a man."

"Okay. Well, I am a man."

"You're more than just a man to me," said Sarah, and they shared a smile. "The answer is yes. I'm still a virgin. Although there have been a few opportunities... I almost screwed a guy at a party a couple of weeks ago but stopped because he didn't have a condom. He still wanted to do it, of course. And to be honest, so did I. I heard later he told everyone we did anyway, so I guess we might as well have."

"Are you in love with him?" asked Cliff.

"Eww, no!" Sarah scoffed. "I barely know him. We were having fun hanging out, so we went to an empty bedroom and started fooling around. We got naked and I wanted to keep going. But I stopped. And he stopped. He told me he wasn't going to keep going if I didn't want to. We cuddled together for a while. That was it. I haven't spoken to him since."

"Sex is great, but you should never feel like you *have* to do it. I'm glad to hear the guy stopped when you wanted to."

"Yeah. I'm glad too. You know, to be honest, I am looking forward to a wild sexual relationship. You know? The kind you see on TV or read about. There is a guy I do really like, and I think I could fall in love with, but I don't think he's at all interested in me."

"Ugh! I hope you don't mean the John Gost character!"

"God no! I don't mean him," replied Sarah.

"Good!" said Cliff, adding, "It'll happen. I'm sure of it. I bet men will come after you in droves—maybe even some women too."

"How was your first time? Was it with Stevie?" asked Sarah.

"I was just a kid, younger than you—" started Cliff, but was interrupted by Sarah.

"Sure, I'm like an old maid!" Sarah frowned.

"No, no, that's not what I meant."

"I know, just kidding. Keep going," said Sarah.

"Okay, anyway, I was in high school and a young woman a couple of grades ahead of me seduced me on a camping trip."

"Your friends must have thought you were hot stuff after that."

"I guess so. Looking back, I wish it could have happened differently. I mean, it wasn't something I had planned to do with her. She came to my tent and, well, it's not like I objected, but I didn't know nothin' about nothin', you know."

"I still don't," Sarah laughed.

"You will, don't worry. I've had some great sex even though I haven't had that many lovers."

"I know, just Zadie and Stevie!" Sarah joked.

"Ha! Very funny. Anyway, don't worry about it. You know, some people wait until they're married to have sex."

"I know. My Aunt Cindy had a talk with me where she told me I should do that. Maybe. Who knows. Maybe that's what it will take for me."

"Maybe!" said Cliff, as they shared another laugh.

The weather conditions worsened outside, and the sky had turned an ominous shade of gray.

"What are you going to do when you graduate?" asked Cliff.

"I don't know. I'd love, I mean *love* to play in a band with Zadie," answered Sarah.

"I'll tell her that. I'll tell her she should start a band with you and Louis and whatever bass player she wants. I mean, I could do it part-time, but if you get busy playing gigs and touring, someone else will need to take over."

"We'll make you play with us! Seriously though, it would be great if you told her that. I'll tell her too."

"What would you do if she isn't ready to start a band?" Cliff asked.

"Well, both Uncle Karl and Melissa have told me and Dad that they would help pay for college," answered Sarah.

"That's a good deal. Do you think they'd want to pay some of my student loans?"

"Ha! Maybe! I'll tell them they need to so you can play bass in our band."

"Oh, they'll pay up for sure if you tell them that!" quipped Cliff. "If you went to college, what would you study?"

"I don't know for sure—music, I hope. And maybe something to do with fighting or at least, gaining a better understanding of… opioid addiction."

"Makes sense," said Cliff seriously.

"Yeah. We'll see," stated Sarah.

The clouds continued to get darker as the wind howled outside the car. They passed a bridge overpass with cars parked underneath.

"Did you see that?" asked Sarah.

"Yeah, odd they were parked there. It's not even raining."

"I know, but the sky sure looks weird."

"We'll stop and park under the next one, how about that?"

"Sounds good."

Howlin' Wolf was singing "Smokestack Lightning" on the cassette player just loud enough to be heard. The two friends looked at each other and smiled, secure in their lasting connection.

CRACK! A loud thunderclap sounded, and they both jumped. Heavy rain immediately followed, drowning out Howlin' Wolf. The wind roared, with debris outside the car performing a hostile dance around them. The sky was so dark they could barely make out the overpass just ahead.

Art and Melissa were sitting at the dining room table. They were quiet as they nervously waited to hear from Sarah. BB King's Bluesville station was softly playing their Sunday acoustic set.

They had spent the night before in downtown Saint Paul watching the Saints play baseball at CHS Field. It was a beautiful summer evening in the city. Afterward, they enjoyed a nightcap at the Fox and Hounds before spending the night at Maple Manor. An impassioned night of love-making followed. While holding each other, they had a long conversation where they confessed their love for each other.

Kerstin's memory would always be there. Now, though, the two of them had grown close. They completed each other in a way they had always known but had, until now, avoided. Plans were made to find a place to live together after Sarah graduated high school.

The two talked about marriage, but they agreed to live together for a while first before taking that step. They fell asleep cherishing each other and their future together.

The next morning, their contentedness was under threat as they watched scenes on social media showing the chaos from the Iowa cornfield. Neither Sarah nor Cliff was answering their phones or replying to texts.

Weather reports of a severe late-summer storm blowing through the northern Iowa border also shook them.

Their joyous night now seemed faraway.

An acoustic cover of "Smokestack Lightin'" by Chum Fella played on Bluesville.

Just then, Art's phone rang. It wasn't a number he recognized. Art and Melissa shared an uneasy look then held each other's hands as he answered the phone.

On the other end, an excited Sarah exclaimed, "Hi Dad!"

ACKNOWLEDGMENTS

I'd like to thank my wife, Trish Rice. Trish has always been supportive of me and encouraged me to write this book. It was very difficult and without her timely pep talks I might not have completed it.

I have loved the blues ever since I was young, long before I even knew what it was. I'm not a musician, just a fan, and I marvel at the ability of those who can play this wonderful music.

So, my book would have blues music at its core. The idea of a young woman drummer came to me via Sarah Papenheim who was senselessly murdered in the Netherlands. This novel is not her story but my way of honoring her, and all people who love the blues, particularly young people.

Having lived in Saint Paul, Minnesota most of my life, I decided the highs and lows of my characters would be experienced in this fine city.

The secondary location is the Netherlands. Sarah Papenheim losing her life in this magnificent-beguiling country I've visited several times was tragic.

Sudden death and its effect on loved ones is a subject I wanted to explore. It can be particularly devastating the younger someone is when they leave this world.

My father, Arthur Rice, and my mother, Faye Rice, supported me and my siblings in many ways. As youngsters, they encouraged us to read and express ourselves. Later, as I struggled to find my place in the world, they continued to believe in me. I will never be able to thank them enough.

My brother, Ted Rice, and my sister, Penny Nolte, also encouraged me to write. Were it not for their enjoyment of my short stories, I may never have pursued this dream. I am very grateful to them.

My children, Keith Rice and Darcey Mickelson, supported my writing too. They had known me as their father who wrote code as a computer programmer but not as a writer of fiction. Even so, they enjoyed my stories and urged me to write more.

Other beta readers who have been extremely important to me are James Nolte, Barb Birchem, Kara Rice, Jared Mickelson, and Seth Rice. Thanks to all of them for taking the time to read this book. It benefited greatly from their thoughtful feedback.

I learned that my grandfather, Karl Rice, had done some writing. I thought of him sitting there behind a typewriter, and this encouraged me to do the same—although I was happy to be able to use my computer instead! Thanks, Grandpa.

Thanks to Dominic Wakeford for his copy-editing work. The book has benefited significantly from his efforts, and I can't thank him enough.

Thanks to Veronica Scott for her cover design. I appreciate her insights and professionalism.

I would like to thank all the fantastic blues musicians who have given me so much enjoyment over the years. I could never thank them all, but I want to specifically acknowledge Howlin' Wolf and Luther Allision.

Lastly, I want to thank local blues clubs like The Blues Saloon (formally Wilebski's Blues Saloon), and Shaw's Bar and Grill. These clubs are keeping the blues alive. Check them out!

ABOUT THE AUTHOR

Stephen Rice was born and raised in Henderson, New York, about an hour south of the Canadian border. He moved to Saint Paul, Minnesota to attend Hamline University. After college, he worked various jobs including driving and basketball coaching. He decided to go back to school at Brown Institute in Minneapolis to learn computer programming. There he met and fell in love with his wife, Trish. They raised two children, Keith and Darcey, in Eagan, Minnesota, before returning to Saint Paul.

Stephen works as a software consultant and computer programmer, designing and writing code for software systems.

Printed in the USA
CPSIA information can be obtained
at www.ICGtesting.com
LVHW091204230624
783763LV00001B/1

9 781962 987370